Then I
FOUND
You

BOOKS BY RACHEL BRANTON

Lily's House Series
House Without Lies
Tell Me No Lies
Hearts Never Lie
Your Eyes Don't Lie
Broken Lies
No Secrets or Lies
Cowboys Can't Lie

Noble Hearts
Royal Quest
Royal Dance

Finding Home Series
Take Me Home
All That I Love
Then I Found You

Other
How Far

Picture Books
I Don't Want To Eat Bugs
I Don't Want to Have Hot Toes

UNDER THE NAME TEYLA BRANTON

Unbounded Series
The Change
The Cure
The Escape
The Reckoning
The Takeover

Unbounded Novellas
Ava's Revenge
Mortal Brother
Lethal Engagement
Set Ablaze

Other
Times Nine

Imprints Series
First Touch (prequel)
Touch of Rain
On The Hunt
Upstaged
Under Fire
Blinded
Street Smart
Hidden Intent

Colony Six Series
Insight (prequel)
Sketches
Visions
Travels

Then I FOUND You

RACHEL BRANTON

WHITE STAR PRESS

This is a work of fiction, and the views expressed herein are the sole responsibility of the author. Likewise, certain characters, places, and incidents are the product of the author's imagination, and any resemblance to actual persons, living or dead, or actual events or locales, is entirely coincidental.

Then I Found You (Finding Home Book 3)

Published by White Star Press
P.O. Box 353
American Fork, Utah 84003

Copyright © 2017 by Nunes Entertainment, LLC
Cover design copyright © 2017 by White Star Press

Originally published by the author as *Eyes of a Stranger* under another pen name.

Printed in the United States of America
ISBN: 978-1-939203-87-8
Year of first printing: 2017

To my husband and seven children,
for their continuing love and support.

Note from the author

This novel is centered around a fictional event involving the Hawthorne Bridge in Oregon. Fictional meaning, of course, that it didn't happen, except in my very fertile and sometimes scary imagination. I researched numerous overwater bridges for this book, and I hope you enjoy!

*T*he first day of her new life was hotter and more humid than Tawnia McKnight had believed possible. The sweltering heat blasted inside her green Pontiac Grand Prix as she peered through the open window at Portland in the distance, the city rising high above the traffic. One of the ten Willamette River bridges was in sight, and she was as impressed as the first time she had visited the city with Bret, even though he wasn't around to point out the unique structural features.

Thoughts of Bret came naturally since they had come here together last year—five months after the funeral in Nevada. She'd felt the pull of the city on her then and knew it was only a matter of time until she had to answer its call. The same thing had happened when she'd moved from Kansas to Colorado and from there to Utah and on to Nevada. Ten years and five different states. Her parents, who had particularly hated this last move to Oregon, alternately blamed her restlessness on a desire to annoy them and a fear of commitment.

She knew her decision to move again wasn't a fear of commitment. She would have committed with Bret.

Maybe.

There had come a time when she had not seen Bret's resemblance to Christian every time she looked into his face, but Bret could not seem to forget that she had been the last one to see his brother alive. The one who cradled him at the base of the tree as they waited for the ambulance.

Annoying her parents was not high on her list, either. They had been good to her over the years, if smothering and strict. She knew they wanted the best for her. As an only child, and adopted at that, she had felt a lot of pressure to succeed. So she had. She had landed that coveted art director position at an advertising firm in Nevada, and now she would be a creative director here in Portland. A nice career move.

Yet she still couldn't say why she'd felt so compelled to move to Portland or how long she might stay. What magic did the city hold?

Or secrets.

Why had her mother cried when she'd mentioned Portland?

Giving one last frustrated thump to the buttons on her broken air conditioner, Tawnia laid her MapQuest directions on the passenger seat and edged back into the thick traffic. Just her luck to be arriving at what appeared to be the busiest time of the afternoon. After driving a good part of the past two days in the July heat, with the wind and her shoulder-length hair beating at her face, she was feeling more than a little irritated. According to her new landlady's instructions, she had to find the Hawthorne Bridge. Then she would be in a perfect position to stop by her new job before heading to her rented bungalow.

"Where are you?" she muttered aloud. There was a bridge

ahead, but it didn't look like the one she'd seen on the Internet. About the right length but not the right shape.

A car behind her honked. "All right, already. I'm going."

She was on the bridge now, and there wasn't any choice. She thought she caught a glimpse of the right bridge in the distance, but it was impossible to be sure. A glare came off the water, punishing her tired eyes.

At least it's green here, she thought. Nevada had its own austere beauty, of course, but it wasn't the green Kansas where she'd grown up. Portland seemed more lush than both of them.

She turned left off the bridge and looked for a place to pull over and study the map. "Come on, people," she fumed. "I'm going the wrong way. I think."

At last she spied a place to pull out of traffic. "There we are." As she rolled to a stop, there was a deafening burst of sound, almost like an explosion. Her car began shaking and a horrendous, grating noise filled the air. Metal grinding against metal, a long, drawn-out sound.

"Not now," she moaned. Up until this trip her Pontiac had always been reliable, but first the air conditioning had gone and now this. Maybe she'd been wrong about Portland being the place for her. How could it be right if getting there was so hard? It wouldn't be the first time she'd been mistaken. Nevada had ended up being awful.

Yet would she have given up knowing Christian and Bret?

The grinding noise was louder now, but the car was stopped, so it wasn't coming from the car at all. And a good thing, because the battery on her cell phone was completely run down. Around her, other drivers were slowing, puzzlement on their faces, but almost immediately the cacophony faded. In its place a huge plume of smoke rose into the air several streets behind her and to the right. With the absence of the grating noise, the simple rumble of the traffic seemed muted.

"What on earth?" She craned her neck to get a better view, but there were too many buildings in the way to get an idea of what might have happened.

With a loud screech, a car on the highway came to an abrupt stop in the road near where Tawnia was parked, narrowly missing being hit by the person behind him. Too many drivers gawking. Horns blared impatiently, and slowly the traffic moved on.

Sounded like a building collapsing, Tawnia thought. She'd seen a real building purposely demolished on television once. The newscaster reported that dust had radiated for miles.

The dust from this event was quickly dispersing, though the cloud was still noticeable over the city. Fortunately, traffic was picking up as though nothing had happened.

Forcing her mind back to the problem at hand, Tawnia studied her MapQuest directions, comparing them with her car map. Somehow she'd actually managed to pass the Hawthorne District, so she was closer to her new bungalow north of Burnside instead of her future place of employment.

It's just as well, she thought. She was arriving in the city later than she'd hoped, and if she didn't find the rental house soon, her new landlady might wonder if she'd changed her mind. Besides, she was sweat-soaked and exhausted from her drive, and she didn't want to run into any future coworkers looking like this. She wasn't due in to work until Monday, anyway, so she had two and a half days to find her bearings. After a good shower and a call to an auto repair shop, of course.

With a long sigh, she pulled into traffic just as the wail of an ambulance siren cut through the air. She glanced in the rearview mirror where the plume of dust had become a silty sheen poised above the buildings.

Someone must have gotten too close, she thought. *Probably caused a pile-up. I hope everyone is okay.*

Shakily, she drove to her rented bungalow, making only three more wrong turns in the process. She was directionally impaired, or so Bret had joked. Her father said she became lost on purpose on a subconscious level, a helpless act that was actually a bid for power over the male species.

Right, Dad.

Glad he wasn't around to see her now, she raked her fingers through her lank hair, wishing she had an elastic band handy. The medium brown color was dull with dirt from the beating it had taken from the air coming through the open window. She looked decidedly worn. Worse, the contact in her left eye felt gritty. *Oh, well.*

Slipping from the Pontiac, she started up the walk, comparing once more the number on the bungalow to the paper in her hands. This was it. But where was the landlady? She'd said something about doing yard work that morning. If she wasn't still around, Tawnia would have to drive to another address to get the keys.

What a day.

The bungalow was one in a row of close-set houses, similar in size, with sloping roofs and front porches running across the narrow fronts. Hers had a tiny, immaculate yard, with a line of bushes growing up against the red brick porch. Potted plants lined the porch wall, and a lounge chair and a rocking chair took up most of the available porch space. The front of the house was white siding, framed by more of the red brick, giving it a quaint appearance. A gable jutted from the middle of the roof, but it covered a disguised attic vent instead of a real window. A tiny strip of grass separated the houses.

"Cozy," she murmured, pleased with her choice. If the inside was half this neat, she would love living here. Even the street exuded a sense of peace. Maybe she'd finally discover what she was searching for. She took the three steps in two leaps and rang the doorbell.

No answer. Instinctively her hand went to the knob to test it—after all, she'd paid her deposit and first month's rent. As her hand brushed the metal, the knob turned and the door flung open.

A robust woman with a flushed face, an anxious smile, and short, tightly curled, dishwater hair stood in the doorway, impressive in her purple muu-muu. She wore bright, matching eyeshadow and a thick layer of face makeup. Her mascara was apparently bought in bulk.

"I thought I heard someone coming up the walk," she said.

"Are you Mrs. Gerbert?"

"That's me. And you must be Tawnia." Her gaze ran quickly over Tawnia's cropped jeans and fitted T-shirt. "You're much younger than I imagined. You said thirty-two, right? But never mind all that. Thank heaven you're here!" With a sigh, the woman pulled her into a rather exuberant embrace.

Tawnia tried not to stiffen, though the last thing she wanted was a hug from Mrs. Gerbert or any other stranger. Her family had never been demonstrative, and she had to work hard not to put people off with her craving for space. But even for friendly people this display seemed over the top. What had she gotten herself into? Mrs. Gerbert had sounded normal enough on the phone.

Mrs. Gerbert pulled away, dabbing at the sudden tears under her eyes. "Oh, I've embarrassed you, haven't I? I'm sorry. It's just that I've been so worried since I heard the news about the collapse. After all, I told you to come by way of the Hawthorne Bridge, and when you were late . . . Oh, I'd never have forgiven myself if something had happened to you!"

Tawnia stared at her. "What are you talking about?"

"Oh, my! You mean you haven't heard?" Mrs. Gerbert's hand went to her heart.

"No."

"Come on in," the woman grabbed her arm with strong fingers, tugging Tawnia through the door and into the living room of the bungalow. "It's on TV right now. I was straightening the house and watching the news. You know, waiting for you, and then it happened. Oh, I can't believe it! They're still pulling bodies from the water. They have all kinds of boats out looking for people. So many cars simply sank! And the people on the walkways fell with no protection from the debris." She closed her eyes as though to shut out the horror her words conveyed.

Tawnia dragged her gaze from Mrs. Gerbert's tortured expression and stared at the images on the television. One moment there was the Hawthorne Bridge, the bridge she had seen on the Internet, and in the next camera shot most of the bridge was missing. Some distance away from the damage, a large boat floated sideways, the top completely shorn off. The dark surface of the water was covered with debris, including a bicycle helmet, a coat, and a plastic bag. People were in the water too, some waving their arms, others swimming. A woman was floating on her back with a baby on her stomach. Tawnia couldn't tell if the child was moving and was relieved to see a boat approaching her.

A man appeared on the screen, a grave expression on his face. "As you see, rescue efforts continue, and more and more people are being plucked out of the water. Still no word on just how this happened, but for some reason either the lift did not go up or the boat you see here was not in the correct position to pass under it. Whatever the case, this boat hit the bridge, setting off this terrible devastation. Five of the six spans have collapsed, including the span with the vertical lift. For some time after the initial collapse, part of the lift with the cabin and controls remained attached on the one side, but it eventually sheared off and fell into the water. We've confirmed that the bridge operator was able to climb to safety before that happened, but we've had unconfirmed reports of more than a dozen fatalities already—and there are sure to be others trapped in their cars under the water. This is a sad, sad day for Portland, and it's hard to know what to say."

He shook his head and brought a hand briefly to his left eye as he struggled to keep his emotion in check. "Police are saying—as I've stated several times already—that people should not go down to the waterfront unless they are uniquely qualified to help. The rescue personnel need space, and the crowd down there is threatening to hinder rescue efforts. So stay home, please. We'll do our best to keep you informed. We hear police have located a security video of the crash, and we hope to have access to that soon. Meanwhile, we're going to our reporter live at the scene. Julie, what can you tell us?"

A woman with short blond hair appeared on the screen. "Well, Daniel, it's an unreal scene we have before us. People swimming to shore; others going out and trying to save them. People walking around with dazed expressions. Many are wounded. Surprisingly, there has been little screaming and shouting here, just a determination to do everything possible to save as many as we can. Divers are here now, and hopefully they will be able to help those who may be stuck underneath the water." She shook her head. "But it doesn't look promising. That bridge is very heavy, and so are the cars. I fear this is going to be far more serious than any of us imagine."

"Have you managed to talk to any of the victims?"

"Yes, we have a couple right here. Tom and Angie Stewart. They were the first ones out of the water and have stayed to help others." She turned to a middle-aged couple beside her. "What can you tell us about the accident?"

"It happened without any warning," the woman said. She had a blanket around her shoulders, and mascara ran down her face. "One moment we were driving, and the next, we were falling toward the water. The car ahead of us—it was crushed by the bridge. I know there was a child in the car. I—" She started crying, and her husband put a comforting arm around her.

"I opened the door and we got out," he continued. "Started swimming. A man came by in a boat and helped us."

Tawnia felt a numbness spread through her heart. She had to get down to the waterfront! Now. She was halfway to the door when Mrs. Gerbert's voice brought her back to her senses.

"Thank heaven you weren't on the bridge."

Tawnia turned. What had she been thinking? Hadn't the man on television told people to stay home? It wasn't as though anyone she knew had been on that bridge.

"I think I turned off too late. I went over another bridge—I never could follow directions very well. But I heard the sound. I saw the dust."

Mrs. Gerbert's round face wrinkled with concern. "I'm so sorry. What a terrible welcome for you. But what's important is that you're safe." She glanced back toward the television. "My daughter is a real estate agent. Goes across that bridge four or more times a day. She's also safe, thank heaven. I couldn't call her—the cell phone lines all seem to be busy—but I know she had homes to show up north today. It's a terrible, terrible tragedy. But thankfully, those we know are all right."

Tawnia nodded as her eyes fixed once more on the television. By whatever fates were in control, she had taken another route and was safe. Why then did she feel as if someone close to her had died?

"Tawnia!" shouted Christian from the tree. "Come on up!"

"Be careful!"

"There's a squirrel up here. He's jumping from limb to limb. I have to get a picture of this."

"It's really high." Tawnia started to climb the tree. Her parents had never approved of tree climbing, but she had the right build for it, and physical activities always came to her easily. "I'm coming." A tremor of fear went through her heart as a small branch plunged past her, nearly hitting her cheek.

"Sorry!" Christian shouted. "I needed a place to put my camera. Didn't mean to let that fall."

"I'm okay."

"Good, because I'm hoping for a kiss at the end of this date!"

She smiled. Maybe he'd get one. He seemed to be a nice guy, not the player some of her coworkers claimed he was.

Silence came from above as he snapped pictures. She was halfway up the tree now and having second thoughts. It was so high. Certainly not something she would ordinarily do in her right mind. But Christian's exuberance and vitality had a way of rubbing off on people. When she'd been moved to his group at work, she immediately recognized how opposite they were. Yet he brought out who she wanted to be. Or maybe who she would have been in another life, raised by different parents.

Maybe if she'd been raised by her birth mother.

Or if she'd had a sibling, and her parents hadn't been so careful with her.

Not that the person she was wasn't enough. It was. She was proud of everything she'd accomplished.

There was a brief shout of surprise, and then something else was falling toward her. Something large. Too far away to be a danger to her. Her heart started pounding, recognizing the situation before her mind could fully comprehend.

"Christian!" she screamed.

In panic, she half-climbed, half-slid down the tree, tears wetting her cheeks, unmindful of the bark and bits of tree that dug into her skin. "Christian!" she called over and over. "Are you okay? Talk to me!"

She fell the last several feet, and the breath whooshed out of her. She crawled to where her friend was lying on his back.

"Christian?" His eyes were closed, but he was breathing.

She reached for her cell phone but remembered she'd left it home. His phone was in his back pocket, and she carefully slid her hand under him to get it so as not to move him more than necessary.

No service.

She knelt by his inert body. "I'll be right back. I'm going to get help."

He gave a weak moan, his eyes fluttering once.

"You hang on!" With a cry, she leapt to her feet and ran down the path. It was a mile before she found anyone—a group of hikers who had a working phone. They called for help while she ran back to Christian. She held his hand as they waited for the rescue workers. But Christian died later that day during surgery at the hospital.

The first time she'd met Bret, she'd had to tell him how his brother died.

Tawnia remembered how she'd felt then.

It was how she felt now.

Bret Winn wondered what Tawnia was doing at that moment. She'd probably already arrived in Portland by now, perhaps even days ago. Would she visit the restaurant he'd taken her to last year? Or dance in the club where he'd begun to think they might be falling in love?

Not that it was any of his business. Not anymore. But he wished her a good life.

Opening the drawer of his desk, he brought out the strip of pictures he and Tawnia had taken in a booth together one day at the mall. They were sticking out their tongues at the camera, rolling their eyes, and pulling each other's hair. He smiled. The memories were good. It surprised him how good.

Sighing, he shut the photos back inside, focusing again on his work.

"Come quick!" His coworker John Thompkins came into Bret's office at a run. "You have to see this."

Bret reluctantly tore his eyes away from the calculations on his computer screen. "Now? I'm busy." He didn't try to keep the annoyance from his voice. Bret didn't enjoy the pranks or humorous Internet sites that seemed to be the base of John's existence.

"The Hawthorne Bridge in Portland has just collapsed," John blurted. "Or most of it. People are in the water. A dozen dead already."

Bret sprinted down the hall to the breakroom, where half a dozen engineers were gathered around the wide-screen television. They stared in horrified fascination as the camera showed the rescue efforts.

The Hawthorne Bridge demolished! The oldest vertical lift bridge in operation in the United States had been his favorite of all the overwater bridges he'd seen in Portland. That it was gone in what appeared to be a matter of seconds, according to witnesses, was impossible to believe. The nightmare of every engineer who had ever designed a bridge.

"There'll be an inquiry," someone commented. "Wonder if they'll call here." Bret didn't take his eyes from the screen to see who spoke, but he could feel eyes on him. He'd been on the committee of independent engineers who reviewed the tragic bridge disaster in Minneapolis some time back, volunteering for the job when no one else had wanted it and even becoming spokesman for the group. The experience had been both horrifying and educational.

"You've been to see that bridge, haven't you?" John asked Bret.

Bret nodded. He'd seen every overwater bridge of importance in the United States and many out of the country. Overwater bridges were a particular hobby for him, which was ironic because he worked in Nevada where most bridges were nowhere near water. But working here did have advantages. Nevada had one of the best reputations for safe bridge operation.

Bret watched with the others for thirty minutes before a thought came to him: *Tawnia is in Portland.* Had she been near the bridge?

Worry ate at his insides. No, she couldn't have been. This time of day, when many would be on their way home from work, she would likely still be at the office. Like him, she was serious about her job, and because hers was a new one, she'd be even more inclined to work overtime.

Unless her job hadn't started yet. He tried to remember the details of their last conversation, but all he remembered was the sinking feeling and the realization that this was goodbye for good.

He had to know. He reached for his phone and dialed, but her voice mail picked up immediately.

There, she must be on the phone. Safe.

Unless the phone was in the water.

Bret was beginning to feel a little idiotic. Tawnia was out of his life, and he shouldn't be worrying about her. The likelihood that she'd been on the bridge when it collapsed was almost nil.

"Bret, can I see you for a moment?"

Bret tore his gaze away from the television to see his boss, James Griffin, motioning to him. "What's up?" Bret asked as he reached Griffin's side.

"You know a man named Clyde Hanks?"

"Sounds familiar." Bret shrugged. "Can't place it, though."

"He's the manager of the Bridge Section at Multnomah County."

Which meant, of course, that Clyde Hanks was the man responsible for the maintenance—and therefore the collapse—of the Hawthorne Bridge.

Bret nodded. "That's right. I met him last year. Nice guy." He and Tawnia had shared a lively conversation with Hanks about overwater bridges and the collapse in Minneapolis. Yet despite Hanks's knowledge on the fascinating topic, Tawnia had captured most of Bret's attention that day.

I miss her, he thought.

The realization didn't change the facts of their relationship, but it did make the situation more sorrowful. Somewhere out there, Tawnia was living her life without him. The way it had to be.

"I just got off the phone with Hanks," Griffin was saying, bringing Bret's thoughts back to the present. "Come into my office. We need to talk."

CHAPTER 2

$\mathcal{A}$utumn Rain tried to breathe, but when she opened her mouth, water rushed in. She was cold. Oh, so cold. Blackness surrounded her. So tempting to give herself up to it. Yet something wouldn't let her give in. She became aware of light above the murky black and forced her body to move in that direction.

Pain sliced through her right arm, piercing her mind with more awareness. Fear replaced her desire to sleep. She remembered only a loud boom and then metal grinding against metal. The shock and disbelief as the back of her car was crushed. The horrid plunging sensation as they fell into the water.

Winter!

But Winter wasn't anywhere. She couldn't see him or the car. How had she gotten out? She remembered something about her safety belt and then hitting her head against the door.

Her lungs were burning. She had to take a breath, but if she did, it would all be over. She wouldn't see Winter again, and he was all the family she had. Clenching her lips tightly, she swam with her left arm, the other hugged uselessly to her chest.

A little more. Soon. The light was almost here. She broke through the water, gasping and gulping in air that felt like both fire and life. Coughing sent waves of pain through her arm. She floated a moment on her back, her eyes darting, taking in the chaos of the river. Boats of all sizes were scattered over the water, now dark with silt and debris. People called for help. She heard the sound of a siren, and a helicopter flew overhead.

She drifted, feeling so numb the cold water no longer caused her any discomfort. Even her arm, motionless now, didn't hurt. Her eyes were so heavy.

Winter.

The thought made her lift her head and tread water, searching the boats and the distant shore. Nothing she saw made sense in the orderly world she had known. There was a huge empty place where the bridge had once been. At the edge of the water a mound of rubble and cars were piled atop one another like a scene from an earthquake. Had there been an earthquake?

Beyond the rubble and dust she could see an undamaged part of the road that continued on the east side of the river beyond the bridge. The section wound under the I-5 freeway that passed along the water's bank, whole and complete as though nothing had happened.

"Please help me!" came a cry. "My baby!"

Autumn awkwardly swam toward the woman who was scrabbling about in the water frantically.

"My child. I can't find her!" The woman stared at Autumn pleadingly, but there was nothing she could do.

"Here!" called a voice.

A black-haired man in a small canoe held a limp girl in his arms.

The woman shook her head.

The man laid the girl down in the boat. "Come on! We'll find her."

"She must be in her car seat!" the woman took a breath and dived under the water. She didn't come up again.

Tears mixed with the water on Autumn's face. She gazed up at the man in the boat, sobs shaking her chest. He nodded and dived into the water. Autumn waited by the boat, too weak to pull herself in with one arm. Where was the man? The woman? Did she really expect to find her car and free her child?

Mothers had done such things before.

Surreal. None of this could be happening.

The man broke the surface, the woman in his arms, unconscious but still breathing. He hefted her into the boat with a thud. "You next," he told Autumn, treading water next to her.

"I can't find Winter—my dad." She had always called him by his first name, and she had to remember to add in the relationship so everyone would understand how important he was to her.

The man shook his head. "Someone will find him. Get in the boat, or I'll put you there."

Under normal circumstances, Autumn would never have allowed anyone to force her to do anything she didn't want to do, but she realized quickly that her drowning wouldn't do Winter any good. She grabbed the boat with her good arm.

When the man saw she was injured, he pushed her in from behind, and then swung up himself, using the weight of the unconscious woman and child to balance his assent. "Let's get you three to shore. I can't hold any more."

Autumn scarcely paid attention to the journey. Her eyes

were still locked onto the river, searching every person, every piece of debris. *Winter!* Her father had to be around somewhere. Yet no one looked familiar. Did she look familiar? With her short, red-highlighted brown hair plastered to her head and her T-shirt and jeans dripping, her father might have a hard time recognizing her. And it could be the same for him. So many of the people in the boats or on the shore were covered with blankets, becoming unrecognizable lumps. Winter could be anywhere. She clung to that hope.

On the east bank, she was helped from the boat by a group of women. "Come on," said one, placing a comforting hand on Autumn's back. "We've set up a triage section over this way." She motioned to Autumn's bare feet. "Careful of the rocks."

"I can't leave! My dad." Autumn started back to where the water lapped the shore.

"He may be there already," the woman offered.

Blindly, Autumn let herself be led across the rocky ground, her left arm supporting her right against her chest. The sun blazed down overhead through the haze of debris in the air, but she felt cold. Carefully, so as not to hurt her arm, she pulled her shirt away from her body. Warm air rushed to her stomach.

Great. Now she felt nauseated.

Her eyes scanned everyone they passed, but Winter wasn't among them. She shouldn't have let him come with her today. Though she adored spending time with him, he would have been better off in his herb store than trailing through yard sales with her. They hadn't even found anything of real value, except an antique ceramic pot. Certainly nothing worth his life.

In the triage center, marked off with yellow caution tape, people were lying on the ground, covered with blankets. The more severely wounded were being carried to the arriving ambulances for transfer to area hospitals. A man in a police uniform was taking down names on a clipboard, and Autumn veered toward him.

"First let someone bandage your shoulder," the woman said.

Autumn looked at her right shoulder in surprise. Her shirt was ripped, and blood oozed from a large gash. The wound didn't hurt at all, not like the lower part of her arm near the elbow that burned with fire every time she moved. "I don't care about that," she said. "I have to know about my dad." She pushed by the woman and hurried to the man with the clipboard.

"Please. I need to find my father."

"What's your name?"

"Autumn Rain."

"Autumn Rain?" he asked, in the surprised voice people always used when they first heard it.

"Yes," she gritted. "My dad's name is Winter."

"Winter Rain?"

"Is he on the list?"

"No. I'm sorry."

"You didn't even look."

"I would remember a name like that."

He had a point. No one had ever forgotten her father's name. Or her mother's. Or her own, for that matter. Winter, Summer, and Autumn. The only thing missing was a sister named Spring.

"Look, I'll write your name down, and if he comes through, I'll be sure and tell him you're safe."

Autumn was no longer listening. Her eyes had gone to the blanket-covered mounds some distance away from the injured. The mounds were bodies, she was sure. More than a dozen. She started toward them.

"No, miss. You can't go over there," called the man with the clipboard.

Autumn didn't stop. Two officers were blocking the way to the bodies, but she dodged past them and kept walking. The one with brown hair grabbed her right arm, and she gasped loudly from the pain in her elbow. Tears sprang to her eyes, spilling onto her cheeks.

He grimaced at the gash in her shoulder. "Sorry about that. Look, you can't go over there."

"Yes, I can." She lifted her chin, jaw clenched. The officer was a foot taller than she was and had at least eighty pounds on her, but she had a purpose. "My father might be under one of those blankets, and I'm going to see if he is. Now, are you going to help me, or do I have to talk to those reporters over there?"

He glanced at the reporters talking to several policemen outside the triage center. "I want to help you. I do. But we've identified half of the victims. I have the list of names here. All the unidentified ones are women." He paused and then added, "Men usually carry wallets in their pockets."

But the women's purses were lost. Like hers.

"No, they brought in a man a minute ago," the other officer corrected. He glanced in Autumn's direction but not directly into her eyes.

"My father didn't believe in identification," she said. "He didn't even have a driver's license. Cars pollute the universe." Yet he had ridden in hers today.

"I'm taking her over," the man said to the other policeman. "Where did they put him?"

"On the end, there."

Autumn went with the officer to the blanket-draped figure. Her heart was pounding, and she had goose bumps from her scalp to her shins. The mound was about the right size to be her father. She was crying again, her stomach roiling with the effort to contain her emotion.

"Are you okay?" the officer asked, kneeling by the corpse. His hand was on the blanket.

She bit her bottom lip hard and nodded.

He pulled back the blanket. There lay a man with dark hair and olive skin, beautiful features. Probably in his forties. Not her father. Her knees weakened with relief, and the officer rose quickly to offer support.

"Not him," she croaked through suddenly parched lips.

"I'm glad." He covered the body.

"I need to see the others," she whispered. "What if they made a mistake?"

"We didn't. The ID was taken from their pockets."

"Please."

He sighed. "How about you tell me what your father looks like, and I'll go look. If anyone is remotely like him, I'll take you there. Okay?"

"Okay." He was being kind, much kinder than she'd expected. "He has long hair. Gray, almost white, and a beard—a short beard." He'd cut it for her. "He was wearing Levi's. Faded. Hole in one knee. A multicolored shirt. Or a shirt with an animal on it. I can't remember which one he had on today. But something bright."

"I get the idea. Any markings or unusual features?" Involuntarily, the officer looked at her right eye and then her left. He'd noticed the difference, but Winter didn't share her oddness.

"A tattoo on his right arm. A heart with my mother's name—Summer."

"That should be enough. Why don't you get your shoulder looked at? I'll meet you over there."

Autumn walked several steps toward the triage center, her bare feet scraping against the weeds and debris. Finally, too tired to go on, she slumped to the ground, legs folded and crossed in front of her. Now that she was alone with nothing to do, the emotions crashed in on her. Sobbing, she let her head hang, chin to her chest. She would have loved to hide her face with her good hand, but she didn't dare take the support from her right elbow.

She thought of the unidentified body. That poor, beautiful man. Did he have a family? Did he have a wife or daughter looking for him? And what of the child still trapped in her car seat?

How could this happen?

Autumn was freezing, her chest shaking as much with cold as with sobs. Why was she so cold?

"There you are."

Autumn looked up quickly, hoping to see Winter, but it was only the woman who had led her to the triage area. What kind of shape was she in not to tell Winter's voice from a female stranger's?

"I brought you a blanket and some bandages. It'll only take a minute." She knelt beside Autumn, draping the blanket over her undamaged shoulder and arranging it around her back and over her lap. "Now I'm going to clean your shoulder. Might sting a little."

It did, terribly, but Autumn didn't cry out.

"Good. Let's get it dry too. It's kind of deep. I think you should get stitches if you want to prevent an ugly scar."

A scar was the least of Autumn's worries. "I have to find my father."

"They're doing everything they can. Look, is there anyone I can call for you?"

Autumn thought a moment, because surely there was someone. She had friends, of course, and so did Winter, but what she needed now was family. She shook her head. "I'm fine. I'll get a ride home later. I have my phone." But she didn't. It was in her purse somewhere in the river. "I mean, I'll borrow a phone."

"Is there anywhere else that hurts?"

"No." If the woman knew about the pain near her elbow, she might force Autumn to go to the hospital, and she wasn't leaving here. Not without Winter.

"I'll come back to check on you soon." The woman pulled the blanket over Autumn's bandaged shoulder.

Autumn tried not to wince. "Thank you." She was feeling warmer now.

She let her eyes wander over the scene, which resembled something from a disaster movie. Workers were serious and purposefully occupied. Victims appeared dazed. Ambulances were leaving at a steady rate.

How had it happened? It was so unfair! Just when she had felt something wonderful was going to happen. How could she have been so utterly wrong?

The brown-haired officer was returning, and by the smile on his face, she could tell he hadn't found her father. "There's still hope, then," she murmured.

"Would you like me to find someone to drive you home?"

She shook her head. "I'm not going yet. I have to wait and see."

"I'll get you something to sit on."

"That's okay. I like to sit on the ground."

The officer hesitated, but a stumbling, gray-haired man in

an immaculate suit was approaching them, angling toward the blanket-covered mounds, his face full of agony.

"I have to go," the officer told Autumn. "Let me know if you need anything."

I need Winter.

But she didn't say the words aloud. The young officer had plenty to deal with as he led the newcomer to his deceased wife. "She didn't answer her phone," the husband sobbed. "When I heard about the bridge, I knew she had to be here. It was on her way home."

Autumn was glad when they moved out of earshot.

She waited. Someone brought her a drink and a sandwich. A woman she hadn't seen before wrote down more detailed information and then tried to get her to leave in one of the ambulances. Autumn refused. Fewer people were being brought into triage now, but she clung to hope.

Hours passed. As darkness fell, the authorities announced the unlikelihood of more survivors. Divers were still bringing up the occasional casualty, but at least eleven people reported missing were still unaccounted for.

Autumn skirted the triage area and walked down to the river's edge, determined to trace the bank as far down as she could. Maybe Winter had been swept downriver and managed to climb out on the bank. A few officers looked at her but seeing the blanket and her expression, none challenged her presence.

"Miss!"

She turned and saw the man who had pulled her from the river. His face was worn and tired. He was probably about her father's age, judging from the heavy sprinkling of white in his black hair. She hadn't noticed that before.

"Why haven't you been taken to the hospital?" he asked.

"I'm not hurt. I don't need to go."

"Then they'll release you there."

"I can't go yet."

"You can't stay here."

She looked away. "Leave me alone. I gave them my information."

"Come on. I'll drive you."

"I can't." There were tears in her voice now, and she hated the weakness.

"Why?"

"They haven't found my father."

"You don't know that for sure." His brow creased, and sorrow showed in his brown eyes. "The best thing to do is go home and wait."

Home. Where she lived with Winter, who wasn't going to be there.

"No."

"Then do you have another place to go? A friend's?" When she didn't respond, he said in obvious frustration, "Look, you have to go somewhere. Now tell me where, or I'll have to report you."

For the first time she noticed an insignia on his T-shirt. He was with the fire department. What were they doing here? Apparently every organization had been mobilized.

The immensity of the disaster hit her. "Okay," she whispered. "I'll go."

"I'll drive you. Let me tell someone I'm leaving."

He jogged away, and she was tempted to continue her search along the river. But her arm throbbed and her knees felt weak. She was too exhausted to walk another step . . . or even to cry. Sinking to the short weeds on the bank, she sat with her legs folded and tried to meditate. She sent her thoughts, her soul, out into the air.

Winter, where are you? He'd taught her the universe was all connected and if she listened hard enough, she could find what she needed.

Nothing.

She sat motionless, no longer noticing the pain in her arm.

And then she felt it. Someone was out there. Someone who was connected to her.

He's alive!

He had to be. She hadn't felt that connection with Summer since her death when Autumn was only eleven. That meant Winter was out there somewhere.

Unless it was some other relative. Not her birth mother, though, however much she might wish for that. Winter and Summer had told her that the girl who'd given birth to her had died.

"Miss? Are you okay?"

She opened her eyes to see the fireman. She nodded, too weak with hope to speak.

"It's a little bit of a walk. Come on." He reached for her, but she ignored his hand, not wanting to release her right arm.

"I can carry you if your feet hurt too much," he added.

She knew he thought she'd lost her shoes in the river, but she hadn't worn any—she almost never did—and the rocks and weeds and trash did little damage to the toughened soles of her feet.

"Do you have a name?" he asked as they climbed the bank. "I'm Orion Harris."

"You must have had parents as weird as mine. I'm Autumn Rain." The way was easier going once they were on the walkway near the river front.

The man smiled, and doing so instantly changed him. Ten

years peeled away. He had a deep dimple on his cheek. "Your name suits you."

"I do look rather rained on," she tried to make her voice light, but it trembled despite her effort.

His smile was gone, and his face looked sad and old again. "You need to get home and rest. That water is really cold. You've been through a lot."

Emergency vehicles were parked all around the fountain on Salmon Street. Orion led her to a sleek black Jeep with a boat trailer attached. She recognized the boat he'd used earlier, and an impossible lump grew in her throat.

The baby in the car seat. Where was the mother now?

He moved aside pop cans and a couple of fast food bags so she could sit down. As he waited for her to enter the vehicle, she met his gaze and saw that he had become aware of her eyes. He didn't ask about them, though, and she was glad.

"Sorry I don't have the top on," he said, shutting her door. "You're probably chilly with all that water."

"I'm fine." She was cold, but the night was warm, so it was probably shock.

He started the engine. "Where to?"

"A place called Autumn's Antiques."

"A store? You want to go to a store?"

"My store. It's really close."

After she gave him directions, she found herself dozing in the seat, despite the discomfort of the cool wind against her shivering body. The movement of the car lulled her.

"Are you sure this is it?" he asked some time later.

She jerked awake to see he'd stopped outside her tiny antiques store, scrunched in between the Herb Shoppe owned by Winter and a music store that specialized in jazz.

"Yes. I have a room in back." Orion was looking at her doubtfully, so she felt compelled to add, "I have an apartment, too, but I'd rather be close to the river."

In case they find him. She said this last to herself silently.

"You shouldn't be alone."

"I'll call a friend."

He watched disapprovingly as she slid from the Jeep. "How are you going to get in?"

Despair fell swiftly upon her once more, though she'd thought she'd vanquished it for the time being. Her purse and the keys were somewhere under the water. Perhaps with her father's corpse.

It was all she could do not to collapse in a sobbing heap on the sidewalk. She should have gone to the hospital. She should have let them take care of her or call a friend. But who? She couldn't think of anyone she wanted to call at the moment.

I don't even have friends, she thought with a gloom that felt right in the face of her tragedy.

She was an orphan. Again.

"I don't have my keys." She would have to ask Orion to take her home, after all, and wake up her neighbor who had an extra set of keys.

But there was a movement inside her store, though it was way past closing time. Dare she hope it was Winter?

"Autumn!" Jake's bulk tumbled through the glass door, his black skin almost fading into the dark night. If it weren't for his dreadlocks and those ridiculous white pants he was wearing, she might not have recognized him.

Relief flooded her. "Oh, Jake!" Tears started down her cheeks again.

His eyes took in her bedraggled state. "You were on the bridge, weren't you?"

She nodded wordlessly.

"Winter?"

She lifted her shoulders in a slight shrug, teeth biting down on her bottom lip to stop the sobs.

"Oh, no." His arms went around her tightly, causing a searing pain through her arm. "I'm so sorry, Autumn."

She gasped. "Let go. My arm!"

"Are you hurt?" He released her gently.

"Just a few bruises, and I twisted my arm. I'm fine, though."

Jake hesitated. "About Winter. Where did they take him?"

She knew he expected her to name a hospital or a funeral home. "I don't know. They could still find him. Jake, I felt something there by the river. Maybe he's alive."

Jake's brown eyes had filled with tears. "Come on, let's get you inside. Looks like you need to clean up a bit." He looked past her at the black Jeep where Orion still waited. "Thanks for bringing her. I'll take care of her from here."

Orion nodded. "I'll stop by another day to see how she is."

You don't need to, Autumn wanted to say, but the sadness on his face prevented her. Besides, she owed him her life. "Thanks, Orion. For getting me out of the—" She couldn't finish. "Well, thanks."

He nodded and with a last contemplative look at Jake, he drove away.

Jake opened his mouth to say something, and Autumn knew him well enough to know it would have been about Orion. Jake was always teasing her about finding a man, and this would top his list of Ideas Never to Use to Find a Date. But even Jake knew this wasn't a time to joke.

He swallowed hard. "I've been so worried since you and Winter didn't show up. I've been busy all day, for a change. Seems everyone wanted herbs. I even sold a few of your antiques."

As he spoke, Jake held the door open and put his hand on her back, gently pushing her inside. "Anyway, I heard about the bridge, and after a few hours I called your phone. Then I closed up and went to your apartment. When you weren't there, I knew something was wrong. I came back here to see if you'd left a message."

"It just collapsed," Autumn whispered. Automatically, her eyes scanned the items in her store. Sure enough, the big vase by the register was gone, and one of the grandfather clocks. On any other day, those sales would have meant a lot to her.

The double doors she and Winter had installed between the Herb Shoppe and Autumn's Antiques were open, as they always were, especially when they left Jake on double duty. Sharing one full-time employee was better than two part-timers, and Jake, with his chin-length dreadlocks that curled into Medusa-like snakes and his penchant for exercise and healthy eating, had been perfect for the job. He liked the herbs better than the antiques, though he was better at selling antiques to the ladies than she was. He was muscular, charming, and his teeth were beautiful to behold. Women would buy just to see his smile turned in their direction. Jake was smart at many things, though his dislike of reading and formal learning had caused him to drop out of college. She worried that someday he'd leave, but so far he'd seemed content with the meager salary they could afford to pay him.

Jake led her to the narrow back room that ran nearly the entire width of the antiques shop. There was a long worktable where she prepared and ticketed items, a basket of papers that shared a corner with a stack of books, an old stove, a mini refrigerator, and an easy chair that she sometimes napped in when business was slow. She was often out early or up late finding antiques, sometimes driving hours for a private viewing, and when she wasn't working she was at one of the area clubs dancing, so she liked to catch up on sleep whenever possible. A door at the end of the narrow room led to a bathroom, and she headed there now.

"I'll make you some tea," Jake said, reaching for a pot to set on the stove. That was one thing about being next door to an herb store owned by your father. You never ran out of herbal tea.

In the bathroom, she let her borrowed blanket drop to the ground and used the toilet quickly. Her arm was still useless but feeling better than earlier. With her left hand, she splashed water on her face and then stared in the mirror. Her red highlights hid the real color of her close-cropped hair, which was a medium brown, now sticking every which way as though she hadn't washed or combed it for a week. Her eyes were only just beginning to wrinkle above the prominent cheek bones. The slight dimple in her chin was very noticeable in this light. Her skin was tan, and her body thin and taut. Her small breasts were unfettered by support—Summer had been a firm believer that brassieres had caused her cancer, and Autumn thought she might be right.

Her features could belong to any woman. All but the eyes. The left was blue and the right hazel, or a lighter greenish brown, as some people described it. The condition was known as heterochromia and was caused by a bit of extra pigmentation. Nothing serious. In her case it hadn't been caused by disease or head trauma but rather a genetic fluke, probably inherited, though Autumn would never know for sure.

The difference in her eyes, like her name, had garnered comments during her early years for those attentive enough to notice. However, the average person on the street never remarked, and a lady in her apartment building had known her five years before she finally noticed.

So much we don't see in the people around us. Winter had said that to her often. He was right. What had she missed in the people she was with each day?

Tears filled her mismatched eyes. "Winter," she whispered.

Her mascara was all over her face, and the water had done nothing to help. Maybe that's what Orion had noticed earlier, not the mismatched color of her eyes. The black was even imbedded in the new scar under her left eye.

"Are you okay in there?" Jake tapped on the door.

"Yeah. I'm coming."

With her good hand, Autumn rubbed a bit of lotion on her face and wiped it with tissue before splashing more warm water on her skin. She was shaking now, feeling cold, though her shirt and jeans were long dry. Somewhere in the back room she had a sweatshirt that should remedy the shaking.

Jake had the sweatshirt ready, along with the hot tea. "Here. Let me help you put this on."

"Careful of my arm."

"You should get that looked at."

"It's just a little twist. I'll be fine tomorrow."

"Well, you just sit in this chair and don't worry about anything."

Gratefully, Autumn did as he requested. Soon she was drifting off to sleep, her unfinished tea on top of the mini refrigerator next to her chair.

CHAPTER

3

On Monday morning, two and a half days after the collapse of the Hawthorne Bridge, Bret was on a plane to Portland, Oregon. Clyde Hanks, the Bridge Section manager at Multnomah County, had extended a plea for him to examine the Hawthorne Bridge—or what remained of it. Bret knew he was a logical choice, since he'd been prominently involved in the Minneapolis inquiry. That he'd already met Hanks was a plus.

Bret had jumped at the chance, his fascination with over-water bridges too strong to deny. In fact, if it hadn't been for his family in Nevada, he might have changed jobs years ago to somehow include them in his work. He was glad his boss had agreed to let him go, particularly as it was a busy time for the firm. Of course, any publicity for the company was a good thing and meant more business down the road.

As part of Bret's invitation, he'd been given all the information available regarding the bridge collapse, including a list of the dead and missing. He'd been relieved to see Tawnia's name was not listed. He'd called her repeatedly on Friday and Saturday, only to keep getting her voice mail, so he was glad to have the information. He hadn't left a message and had stopped calling her after that. Since she hadn't returned his calls, he suspected her phone had probably been turned off and his attempts hadn't registered. He was happy she wouldn't know he'd called so many times. Perhaps he'd try later in the week and ask her to dinner. Friends did that when they were in town, so it would be a natural thing to do. At least that's what he kept telling himself.

At the airport he was met by a Multnomah employee and taken immediately to the county offices to meet with Hanks. "Come in, come in," Hanks said, extending his hand. "It's good to see you again. Thanks for coming."

"I'm glad to be here." Bret shook the man's hand. Hanks was exactly as he remembered, a managing, suit-wearing type with an average build and looks, his stomach going flabby from lack of exercise. The only thing unique about him was the thickness of his dark hair that waved slightly on top.

"Have a seat." Hanks poured a mug of dirty brown liquid from the hot pitcher on his desk, offering it to Bret, who shook his head. "No thanks."

Hanks settled in his own chair with the drink. "Down to business, I guess. You may not know this, but Multnomah controls and maintains six of the ten Willamette River bridges as well as twenty other bridges in the county, so we are taking this collapse very seriously."

Bret did know this information. He knew a lot about all their bridges. What he hadn't known before, he'd researched since Friday. He also knew Hanks hadn't been involved in the actual maintenance of the bridges himself but had orchestrated the work of others.

"From what I understand," Bret began, never one to prolong niceties, "you presume the boat hitting the bridge on the right side just under the lift was the primary cause of the collapse."

"Well, there is some doubt about what actually happened, and of course our surveillance recordings went down with the control cabin. The bridge operator says everything was lifting just fine but that the captain was too far to the right. The man barely escaped with his life, so I tend to believe him. However, the boat captain claims the lift seemed to be stopped or coming back down, and that was what they hit." He took a gulp of his coffee.

"You said there was a video from a security camera?"

"Yeah, but the angle isn't good. It's a hard call."

Bret leaned back in his chair, noting the discomfort despite the black leather upholstery. "Whether the boat hit the lift or the side, neither should reflect on your bridge maintenance. I'm still not sure why you want me here. There hasn't been a formal request for an inquiry, has there?"

Hanks set down his mug. "It's only a matter of time. But for right now, you're here mainly because of public opinion. Believe me, we're doing everything we can to get to the bottom of this, but with forty-one people injured, twenty-three dead, and eight still missing, people are clamoring for answers. Nevada has the best reputation for safe bridges, and the company you work for is the foremost in the entire West. We feel bringing in an outside firm early shows our commitment to finding the truth and making sure such a tragedy never happens again. That you personally have been involved in past inquiries for bridge failures makes your presence even more valuable to us." He reached for his mug but only fingered it, setting it back down without taking a sip.

Bret sensed there was something more. What was the man

hiding? "Nevada bridges are generally not over water, and the dry air lowers maintenance significantly. That's part of why my company has such a solid reputation."

"Yes, but the average person won't know that. They'll see only that we've brought in the best."

"What aren't you telling me?"

Hanks met his gaze and sighed. "Even if the boat hit the bridge to the side of the lift, or if the lift didn't go up all the way, it shouldn't have caused so many sections to collapse. Five out of six spans are gone. We can't explain it. This bridge was completely renovated less than eight years ago, and we are rigorous with regular maintenance."

"You've ruled out terrorism?"

"We've ruled out nothing except an earthquake." Hanks shook his head. "But the governor of Oregon did cross over the bridge directly before the explosion. He was still near enough to feel the ground shaking under his car. At this point the police think it's a coincidence, though they're looking into it, of course, and they've advised the governor to be alert for threats. Meanwhile, we certainly aren't going to tell the public anything related to the governor until we have solid evidence of tampering."

"Does the governor commonly get threats?"

Hanks shrugged. "I really don't know. A lot of people think he's too liberal and complain that he's not fulfilling his campaign promises, but they tend to say that about every politician. Bottom line: we may never understand exactly what happened—and that won't sit well with the public."

"So having me here reassures them that every precaution is being taken to prevent recurrence," Bret guessed.

"And that the rebuilt bridge will be of the safest and highest quality. We would, of course, like a complete check of all our

Portland bridges while you're here. That will also go a long way to alleviating the public's worry."

"Of course." Bret shut the notebook on his lap. He hadn't taken any notes because Hanks had given him a folder with all the updated reports with his temporary ID badge. "I'd like to see the video first, and then go to the bridge to examine the structure."

"You can examine the part that still remains and the wreckage we're gathering on both sides. After three days, we're still bringing up an incredible amount of rubble. And bodies." Hanks gave a long sigh.

"What about the Navy Seals? That worked in Minneapolis. They have the right sonar equipment."

"Call's already out. They should be here tomorrow. The sooner we find all the missing people, the better. That way the families can go on."

Go on. That's what you did after someone you loved died. Even when that someone you loved was your only brother. Bret's stomach clenched as his thoughts drifted to Christian. They had been as different as brothers could be—Christian was popular and charming, careless and irresponsible. Their sister, Liana, had even taken care of his finances. As long as he had a nice car and a job to bring in money to pay for the things he loved and to take out women on lavish dates, Christian was happy. Or had been happy.

By contrast, Bret had driven a secondhand car, had put money aside for retirement, and worked so hard he barely had a social life. He had occasionally dated sweet-faced girls who had never interested him more than his work—until the model Britanni, who was gorgeous, high-maintenance, and more like Christian than Bret cared to admit. Fortunately, he'd seen the light in time and broken things off with her; in fact, it had taken his brother's death to remind him of what was important. And he'd met Tawnia, of course. Too bad the only woman he wanted was the one woman he could never have.

Hanks stood and came around his desk, hand extended. Bret rose to meet him.

"Thanks, Bret," Hanks said, vigorously pumping his hand. "I'm glad you're here. I'll look forward to your suggestions once you go over the reports. If you do find anything out of the ordinary, I want to hear it. They should have the video footage set up, and then I'll have someone from the regular maintenance crew drive you out to the site. Meanwhile, I'm drafting a press release. The sooner we give people confidence, the better. Your name is spelled with one T, right?"

"One T on the first and two Ns on the last." Bret let himself be ushered out.

He knew Clyde Hanks didn't really expect anything of him, but he was good at what he did, and if there was something suspicious to find, he'd find it. Thoroughness was the answer. Complete absorption by the job. Another thing he was good at.

"Janey," Hanks told the young office secretary, "take Mr. Winn down to see the video coverage. It should be set up in the employee lounge."

She stood, pushing her long, straight blond hair behind her ear. "This way, Mr. Winn."

He sat before the television as the smiling young woman handed him the remote. "The collapse has been recorded three times in a row," she informed him, "but you may want to see it more times. I'll be at my desk down the hall if you need anything."

Bret watched the collapse in fascination. Hanks was right about the angle. Too awkward to tell exactly where the boat hit the bridge. The bridge was low enough that just about any kind of river traffic would require the lift to rise, and in the recording, the lift had risen but not fast enough. It even looked like it might have come back down a little. Could the boat have cleared? Bret didn't think so, but it was so close that he wouldn't give testimony of the fact. Maybe the bridge itself could tell him more.

He watched the DVD three more times to be sure.

Tawnia's here somewhere. The thought came seemingly from nowhere, but she was never far from his mind. If he was honest, he'd admit that he was here as much for the chance of seeing her as for his fascination with overwater bridges.

Christian and Tawnia. He couldn't think of one without thoughts of the other coming soon after. So much to regret.

Most of all he regretted not being with his brother that last day, but he'd been too worried about Britanni's admiration of Christian. Stupid. In the end, Bret discovered he didn't even like Britanni. Maybe as the younger brother, he'd only been trying to impress Christian.

So Tawnia had been alone with Christian when he fell. Why she would have chosen to go out with his brother was a mystery to him. They were nothing alike. Tawnia, well, she was more like Bret.

What if Christian had lived? What if he'd brought Tawnia home to meet the family? Would Bret have watched from the side while they had fallen in love? Or would Christian have lost interest as he usually did, leaving the way clear for Bret?

He would never know. Since their first meeting, Tawnia had filled his every waking thought and more than a few in his sleep. The void left by his brother's death would have been easy to fill with Tawnia. Except for the guilt.

He was good at guilt.

Sighing, Bret turned off the DVD player and the television.

Today was Monday, and the bridge had collapsed on Friday. Nearly three whole days had passed. Three days during which evidence could have been lost or accidentally destroyed.

Or purposely destroyed. The thought made his stomach clench.

"See anything new?" The voice came from behind.

Bret turned to see a stocky man with red hair and a freckled, ruddy complexion. Probably part Irish. "It's a difficult angle."

The newcomer nodded sympathetically. "Yeah. That's the breaks. Sometimes it's for you, and sometimes against you. Anyway, welcome to Portland, Mr. Winn. I'm Robert Glen, the one who's driving you to the bridge."

"Nice to meet you." Bret shook his hand. "Please, call me Bret."

"Sure thing. Right this way, now."

Bret sized up his companion as they walked down the maze of hallways. Robert Glen had a friendly, common sort of face, one that held no guile. He'd be painfully honest, Bret thought, and uncomfortable in groups of people. Unlike the suits in the office, he was in work overalls, obviously his clothes of choice as he wore them well. Robert seemed exactly like the type of person Bret would hire over maintenance for his bridges, if the decision was his to make. Robert would do a conscientious job, but he wouldn't be obsessive about his work like Bret. Bret's career was his life, but now he found himself wondering if he'd chosen the wrong love.

Robert Glen wouldn't have volunteered to fly to Nevada to see one of our bridges if it collapsed, Bret thought. He'd want to be home with his wife and three, no, four kids.

"Look, I'll need to change." Bret told him in the silence of the maintenance truck.

"Yeah, I wondered how you were going to inspect anything in that suit."

"Could you stop at my hotel? I came directly from the airport, but I had my luggage shuttled there."

Thirty minutes later, Bret was dressed in jeans, a T-shirt, and work boots. He also had his toolbox, a calculator, and a pen.

Robert took in his appearance from the hotel lobby where he'd waited. "Now you look like you mean business."

"I'm anxious to get to work."

"We should stop and get lunch, though. It's a tad early, but it'll save us time in the end."

"Good idea." Bret really wasn't hungry, but that was true a lot these days. Mostly he ate while he worked or at his mother's on Sundays. He tried to go there more often now. With Christian gone and Liana in Wyoming helping her sister-in-law on her farm while her husband recovered from a heart attack, Bret was all his parents had left.

"You married?" he asked Robert over a hamburger and fries. Not his food of choice, but Robert seemed to be enjoying himself.

"Naw. Almost. I was engaged once."

The answer surprised Bret. So he'd been wrong about Robert's supposed wife and children. "Me too. What happened?"

"She threw me over for another guy who made more money. You?"

"She cared only about fast cars and expensive clothes and restaurants. She was a model."

Robert nodded. "Women! That's the breaks. Right now I'm living with my sister, Noreen. Not too bad. She cleans and makes meals, and I don't have to pay her for it." He stuffed in the last of his hamburger. "You ready?"

"Sure." Bret left half his fries but took his chocolate shake, which in his view was the best feature of hamburger restaurants.

"We'll drive to the intact side first, so you can see where it broke off."

As they came close to the Hawthorne Bridge, Bret's mind struggled to comprehend the sight. After the first span, the bridge simply quit, not jagged as one might guess, but cleanly sliced where the lift had once been. He'd seen bridges in progress before, but there was something sinful about this devastation. They were lucky that so far only twenty-three people were accounted for as dead, he realized. It could have been much, much worse. The fact that the bridge lift had been up had saved all those waiting on the west side, but at that time of day there would have been heavy traffic coming from the Hawthorne district. Four spans of waiting cars, all dumped into the river.

Eight people were still missing. He could see the search and rescue boats on the rivers. Divers were coming and going. Not the Navy Seals—until tomorrow, Hanks had said. They'd find the last victims then.

Mounds of rubble were being stacked, examined, and then carted away, covering sections of the once-beautiful waterfront park on his side of the river. Workers scurried over the massive piles, cordoned off with yellow caution ribbon, while people gathered to watch. There was a hushed reverence, or was it fear?

"More of the wreckage is actually being processed on the other side," Robert said quietly. "Not as much room as here, but some of the last span actually fell onto the bank. Everything sort of shifted that way, so it's easier to get to. Plus, it doesn't ruin the park." He gave a mirthless chuckle.

"We can drive onto the remaining span?"

"Yeah, nearly to the break. It's safe, or should be. Can't say for sure now, can we? Have to show ID to get on. I'm assuming you'll want to check out this side first. Then I'll drive us back around to the other side. They're gathering the pieces there. We've examined what we've found so far for evidence, but they're bringing up more every hour."

The entire bridge area was cordoned off, and Robert showed his ID to get them through. He drove onto the bridge as far as they were allowed to go and jumped out of the truck. Bret followed him, lugging his toolbox.

The gap from this vantage point was even more unbelievable, and Bret struggled to take it all in. The entire bridge wasn't completely gone as most of the television footage had implied. Some of the trusses still rose from the water, twisted and dark, like the crooked fingers of an evil creature emerging to take revenge.

Robert peered through binoculars for a few minutes before handing them to Bret. "Looks like they found someone." Sure enough, a couple of divers were lifting a corpse onto a boat.

Only seven missing now. Twenty-four dead.

Bret's stomach churned, and he wished he'd forgone the greasy burger. Maybe it was time to rethink his diet. Christian had always asserted that you got exactly what you paid for.

Robert looked at the hand Bret had pressed against his stomach. "It does it to me, too," he said. "It's almost too much to believe."

Bret forced himself to give back the binoculars and open his toolbox.

Robert stayed with Bret as he examined the bridge, going down the sides of the structure in a portable lift to check the lengths of steel. The equipment showed stress, but nothing that would signal a collapse of this magnitude. Nothing that would affect the normal operation of the bridge. Of course he hadn't yet checked it all, as he intended to over the next few days, but from this first look, he had to agree with Hanks that the collapse should not have occurred. Then again, this was the part of the bridge that hadn't collapsed, so he would expect such readings here.

His stomach was hungry again before he was ready to cross the river. "You could save the debris until tomorrow," Robert suggested. "It's already quittin' time."

"I'd rather start today," Bret said. "You could just drop me off and get me in with the right people."

Robert grinned. "And miss the overtime? Not on your life. We maintenance engineers don't get paid as much as you guys in design. I'm happy for you to stay as long as you'd like."

"Let's go, then."

It took nearly twenty minutes to cross the river on another bridge and make their way to the opposite end of the collapsed one. The sun was still hot overhead, but the air had picked up a welcome breeze while they'd been in the truck.

"This way." Robert needlessly motioned to an enormous pile of metal and concrete on the edge of the bank. Several cranes were hard at work positioning the pieces. The enormous scope of the cleanup was mind-numbing.

"There's more junk on that barge as well," Robert said. "Helps to take it out of the area." The barge floated on the river near the bank, more concrete and metal . . . and cars. Cars that had been flattened, cars with dents and scratches, cars that looked untouched. Bret wanted to examine everything.

"These all the cars you found?"

"So far. You think one was carrying a bomb?"

"Well, I'm not a demolitions expert, but I'd say no after watching that recording. More likely it was done under the water—I mean, if it was a terrorist attack."

"You see a lot of that in Nevada?" There was a slight mockery in Robert's voice to match the bright smile.

Bret laughed. "Hardly. I did some work for the army early in my career, and I saw a few things overseas. I was glad to get out. They did help pay for my education, though." He'd been grateful for the experience forced on him by missing out on a college scholarship, but he hadn't wanted to stay in the military any longer than necessary.

"I know what you mean. I was in the Marines for a while myself."

This side of the river was also cordoned off, and the place was crawling with even more workers, who moved in a strangely graceful dance as they went about their work.

"Come on," Robert said. "I'll take you to meet some of the guys on the barge. See what they've found. You might as well start with the new stuff, since they haven't found anything interesting in the other junk we've pulled up."

On the barge, two Multnomah County employees were examining new pieces of salvage. "This is Kurt Funn," Roberts said, pointing to a young man with brown hair and tanned skin, "and this here is David Cho, but we just call him Cho." Cho was of Asian descent, with a compact body and ageless face. Both men looked at Bret with respect, but he felt an underlying tension and understood that they didn't like the fact that he'd been called in to look over their shoulders.

"I guess you know why he's here," Robert added.

"I'm here for public opinion," Bret said quickly. "I won't be doing anything that you aren't already doing. But I love bridges, and yours here in Portland are some of the greatest. I jumped at the chance to see them. There are so many more challenges with overwater bridges, don't you agree? It's amazing they stand as long as they do."

"Humidity does a lot of damage," Cho agreed, relaxing slightly. "Come on, we'll show you what came up today. We might have found one of the reasons why so much of the bridge went down. But if so it won't be at all good for public opinion."

They took him to a large piece of mangled truss. Large patches of rust were eating into the metal.

"This didn't happen over the last few days," Bret said.

"Exactly." Cho ran a gloved finger along the rust.

Robert shook his head. "Regular maintenance would have discovered damage of this kind. I'd stake my reputation on it."

"Is there any more?" Bret asked.

"Not yet," said Cho. "We're still looking."

"It's possible this piece was from the original bridge," Bret suggested. "Maybe it fell while they were building it, and they never found it."

Relief filled the men's faces. "That could be it," Cho said.

Robert nodded. "Better than thinking our guys messed up."

"It still wouldn't be why the bridge fell." Bret fingered the metal, scraping off a bit of rust with his nail. "At least not that much of it. Like Robert said, large sections of this would have been too big to miss."

"The boat must have hit it just right," Cho said.

Bret wanted to tell him he was making hasty assumptions, but he didn't want to destroy the fragile relationship he was building with these men, so he simply nodded. "I guess we should test this to see exactly where it came from. Anything else to see?"

"Naw. Everything that came in today is in this section or on the bank. Nothing new." Kurt looked at his watch. "Cho and I are knocking off. Been here too long as it is. Hot as Hades today, anyway, even here by the water. Besides, my wife's waiting dinner."

"You guys go ahead," Robert said. "We'll stay for a bit."

The men were right. There was nothing else in the piles of rubble that could shed any light on the cause of the collapse. Clyde Hanks had said it was possible no one would ever understand what had really happened, but Bret also knew they would have to put a name on it, anyway. Their best guess, and he wasn't about to proffer one without more research. He'd have to examine, inch by inch, the remaining section of the bridge, including going under the water to get at the base. Something had happened to make this bridge fall, and he was determined to exhaust every method of examination available to him before giving in to guessing.

Bret stood and stretched his back, looking around the area, wiping the sweat from his brow. He was seeing nothing but tangled bits of metal now, and his eyes refused to focus further. There were fewer men working, but it was obvious an evening shift would continue the salvage effort until dark.

"That the boat?" he asked Robert as they left the barge. He meant the one that had hit the bridge.

"That's it."

The ruined boat floated some distance down the river, moored to the bank. Though the timing couldn't be pinpointed to before or after the collapse, the boat had certainly hit the bridge, as shown by the missing top that had been completely sheared off.

"I'd like to go aboard."

"They checked it out already. There's nothing there."

"I'm sure. But call me curious."

"You want to go today? Because I'd have to find someone to open it up."

"Any day is fine." Bret made a note to do it at first opportunity—without Robert. He was a nice guy, but Bret didn't need him looking over his shoulder.

"You done for today, then?" Robert asked, arching a thick reddish brow.

"I think so."

"I'll drive you home."

Bret didn't reply. He had spied the girl standing by the bank, staring out into the darkening water. Something about her demeanor drew his attention. Unlike the workers, she was unmoving, standing with her arms folded over her chest. Even in the heat, she wore jeans and a gray sweatshirt, though her feet were bare. "Who's that?"

Robert shrugged. "A woman who was on the bridge at the time of the accident. She comes here every day looking for her father. They tried at first to keep her out, but she kept finding a way through. Finally, they decided to let her in."

"Then her father's still one of the missing." One of the remaining seven who were in a watery grave.

Bret started walking in her direction. It would be good to get a victim's perspective of the collapse. And if she really had been hanging around since Friday, she might have seen something out of the ordinary, something that might be important. Bret's mouth twitched at the thought. What was he thinking? Portland wasn't exactly a primary target for terrorism, and if anyone seriously suspected such a thing, the Feds would have taken over. Still, his sense of duty required him to thoroughly examine all the options.

"Where're you going?" Robert took a step after him.

Bret stopped and held up a finger. "Just give me a minute, okay?"

Robert looked between him and the girl. "She'll be all right. Some guy always comes for her." When he saw Bret's interest, he continued. "Tall black guy, with hair like snakes. Gives me the creeps, that hair." He faked a shiver. "Must be her boyfriend. And according to Cho, there's another guy that comes and keeps an eye on her. A fireman. One of the first emergency workers on the scene when the bridge fell. He doesn't talk to her; he just checks up on her from a distance. It's kind of weird, if you ask me."

The fireman might be someone of interest as well. Bret would have to ask her about him. "I'll only be a minute."

Robert shrugged, his wide, freckled face hiding any impatience he might feel. "I'll wait for you in the truck. You want me to take your box?"

Bret had completely forgotten about his tools and equipment, some of it very expensive—and heavy. "Yeah, thanks."

He turned back to the girl. She was facing the river, which gave him a side view. She was slightly shorter than average and thin, too thin for his taste, and her brown hair was dyed red on top, cropped short in back but longer around the crown and on the sides by her cheeks. As he approached, he saw that her hair was ratty and lank, as though she hadn't combed it for days.

Since Friday.

Her eyes fixed on the water, and her tanned face seemed carved from stone. Did she really expect her father to suddenly emerge, dripping and alive? There was something inordinately sad about that.

He tried to approach silently, but she heard him coming.

With a deliberate motion, she turned her whole body toward him, her eyes meeting his. There was surprise there; she had obviously expected someone else.

Her surprise was nothing compared to his own. He knew her! Her hair was different and she was thinner than before, but he would know those eyes anywhere. One blue and one hazel.

Her presence floored him. How could she be here on the bank of the river? He had known she was in the city, of course, but she hadn't been on the list of victims. He'd triple-checked just to be sure, yet she'd been caught in the disaster after all.

He quickened his pace. "I had no idea you were on the bridge when it collapsed! Why didn't you call me? I know we didn't part on the best of terms, but you should have known I would help." He felt angry, though he had no right to expect anything of her.

She blinked once, twice, her neck tilted back so she could look into his face. Her upturned nose looked almost sharp in the still-bright light of the summer evening. But her eyes were exactly the same as he remembered. He loved those eyes. Large and oval, set slightly too far apart for perfect beauty.

She opened her mouth, and when she spoke, her voice was rough from disuse. "I'm sorry. Do I know you?"

CHAPTER 4

*T*awnia surveyed her office at Partridge Advertising with satisfaction. Large and spacious, with her own window, it was everything she'd been hoping for. Not an executive suite, not yet, but much better than the small shared office in Nevada, and the space signaled a promising future. She was on her way.

The day had been grueling. There had been a meeting this morning to get through with the executives and the creative directors who managed the other two design teams, complete with all the political garbage and jockeying for position. She'd been introduced to many of the firm's employees, including the team she would be managing—a copywriter, an art director, and a graphic designer. She'd also met a score of production artists and programmers who would be working on every team's finished designs.

At present, there were half a dozen important accounts assigned to her team, three currently in production and three in the design stage. She had to familiarize herself with each aspect of every account or risk depending too much on her art director. In her new position as creative director, she would be doing less actual artwork, but she would be directly responsible for brainstorming ideas and designing all the accounts with input from her team.

Normally, she was great at new situations and could hold her own against any competition, but today she'd felt distracted. There was a tragic undercurrent flooding the office, intensified because some of the employees had been directly affected by the collapse of the Hawthorne Bridge. One woman had a sister who'd lost a husband, and another said her next-door neighbor was still in the hospital with serious injuries sustained from the collapse. Everyone had stories to share, even if it was only about a brother's friend's sister's cousin.

Except Tawnia. She listened with horrified fascination to each story as though it were her own, putting them all with the footage from the security video the major networks had been playing repeatedly since it was released by officials. Tawnia had an active imagination, but her brain kicked into overdrive as she considered the possibilities.

What would it have been like to have been on the bridge? To have plunged into the cool water? Had there been time to register what was happening? Some part of her felt connected to the event, as though she, too, should have a story to share.

Shaking off these disconcerting thoughts, Tawnia fumbled through the thickest files on her desk, planning to take a few home to cram in overnight. She hadn't slept well the past few days anyway, and these might actually help.

A knock came at her office door. "Come in," she called, standing in case it was anyone from upper management. Standing made her feel in control.

Dustin Bronson, one of the other creative directors, poked in his head. "Hey, how's it going?" Dustin had been assigned to show her around that morning, and he'd been more than helpful. He had ultrashort hair, spiked slightly on top in a way that was far too young for him. She thought he did this to hide the fact that his dark blond hair was thinning. Still, by any standard he was a handsome man.

She smiled, glad to see him. "I'm about ready to head home. It's been an interesting day." She picked up another file.

"Terrible, more likely." His lean body followed his head inside the room. "I still remember my first day as a creative director. I'd already worked here for five years as a copywriter, but I was terrified someone would find out I wasn't qualified to be in charge." They laughed.

"You showed them."

Dustin eyed the files in her arms with a quirk of his eyebrow. "That'll wait until tomorrow, you know. Unless you're trying to beat everyone out on getting the account with our newest client."

"And which client is that?" Tawnia hoped she hadn't been distracted during that part of the management meeting but asking now was better than waiting until she really looked stupid. Besides, Dustin didn't seem the type to be overstressed with perfection.

"You haven't heard?"

"Heard what?" If she knew him better, she'd tell him to stop gloating long enough to spit it out. Maybe in a day or two their relationship would be at that level. He was interesting enough that she wouldn't mind getting to know him better.

"Multnomah County."

"That means nothing to me. I'm new here, remember?"

"They're in charge of the Hawthorne Bridge—and quite a few other bridges in the area."

"Ah. The bridge collapse."

"Yep. They want us to help them create a sense of security. People are in a panic and want someone to tell them that all the other bridges in the city aren't going to fall down. Others are looking for someone to blame, and they perceive Multnomah County as having deep pockets. Four lawsuits have already been filed."

"You've got to be kidding."

"About the lawsuits? Or the client?"

"The client. The lawsuits are inevitable."

"Well, they've got insurance, and I assume most will settle. But in my opinion nothing can really be done to satisfy public opinion until they determine the cause, which by all reports, they seem to be having trouble doing. According to the memo, they've called in outside experts to help."

"Good idea. Makes them seem serious about finding the truth." She bent over and with her free hand opened the bottom desk drawer, where she had stored her narrow black purse, which matched the red and black power suit she had chosen to wear this first day.

"Exactly the angle they want us to play up at this point." He placed both hands on her desk and leaned over. "So, are you going to try to get the account? They'll be assigning it to a team tomorrow morning."

She straightened and met his eyes. "Me? I just got here, remember? For the time being, I'll take what they give me."

"Where's your initiative?"

Tawnia didn't know her team members or their projects well enough to know if they could handle another account.

Then again, something that high profile would be good for her career, and she was confident she could do most of the work herself if the others were overloaded. She hadn't been in advertising ten years for nothing, and it wasn't as if she had an active social life to get in the way.

"It'd have to be done quickly," she said. "They need to start reassuring people right away. Radio, television, interviews with experts, logos. A catchy blurb. A fresh design for their image, with a little bit of community togetherness thrown in to discourage lawsuits."

Dustin grinned. "I like the sound of that. The more ads you sell them on, the more money for our company. And the better for them, too, of course. In the long run a good ad campaign will save them money in lawsuits alone."

Tawnia's mind was going fast. She'd like to talk to the engineers herself, get a feel for what the county actually did to maintain their bridges, but that wasn't likely to happen. She'd meet with their director and be permitted to use only what information he'd give her, information that was likely one-sided. But she'd grown accustomed to that. Advertising was all about touting your strengths, not owning up to weaknesses.

Too bad she couldn't give Bret a call and ask for his point of view about the whole thing. Likely he'd give her some specific information she could use in the ad campaign. And why couldn't she call him? She had his number in her cell. He wouldn't mind. He loved bridges, especially bridges that spanned the water. She'd learned that much on their little road trip to Portland.

"You've never been to Portland?" Bret asked.

It was five months after Christian's funeral, and they were watching television at her place—a travel show that visited Oregon.

"Not yet. Looks beautiful."

"I've been three times. I love the place. They have the most incredible overwater bridges. I also know a nice little seafood restaurant that makes the best crab cakes I've ever tasted."

"Sounds heavenly."

"Why don't we drive up, then? We'll make a weekend of it."

And they had. Tawnia had enjoyed herself thoroughly, especially since Christian hadn't come up once in the conversation. They'd driven over every one of the ten Willamette bridges in the city—several times—ate crab cakes until they nearly burst, and then danced until the wee hours of the morning, barely putting in a few hours of sleep before driving back to Nevada.

They laughed and talked as though they would be together forever.

As if. He hadn't even kissed her, except once on the dance floor.

"Tawnia?"

She blinked, looking at Dustin but not really seeing him. Her hand was already reaching inside her purse for her phone. Her fingers tightened over it, but she didn't set down her files. Calling Bret about the bridge would be an excuse. Just an excuse. She didn't need him, and he certainly didn't need her. Wasn't that part of why she left Nevada?

She slowly replaced the phone. "Just thinking."

"Atta girl. You want to get a drink? We could brainstorm a bit."

She shook her head. What she really wanted was to be alone. "Raincheck?" she asked. "It really has been a long day."

"Then a drink is just the way to relax. Better yet, you need food. I know a little place nearby that serves the best home-made meat pies, even if they do label them organic. If you don't think they're the best you've ever had, I'll buy you dinner every night for a week. I promise, you'll love them."

Her stomach growled at the thought, and suddenly going to her empty bungalow to eat a boring TV dinner didn't seem so appetizing. "You buying?"

He gave her a crooked grin. "Of course. But I'll get my payback. I'm going to pick that brilliant brain of yours."

"Who said I was brilliant?"

"Our boss. He told everyone before you came. We were all jealous."

Tawnia blushed at the compliment. "Fine. Pick my brain then. Just so long as you don't pick my teeth. Now that would be gross."

"Brilliant and witty."

"Yeah, right. You forgot beautiful."

"I didn't forget. I was trying not to be too forward." He indicated the door. "Shall we go?"

"We shall. As long as we agree we each get to keep our own ideas." She placed her files and purse in her briefcase and snapped it shut.

"Sure." He grinned. "Whatever."

Her office led into a large outer room, where the others on her team had their desks partially separated by room dividers to provide a degree of privacy. In the corner near the door to her office sat a long table where they would plan their strategies. Two of her team members were there now—Canda Woodworth, the copywriter, and Sean Coombs, the graphic designer. Both were staring at a laptop on the table, but Sean jumped up as she exited her office.

"Tawnia—hi. Leaving?" He was in his mid-twenties, with the awkward, gangly body of a teenager and mournful brown eyes that seemed to follow her wherever she went. There was a touch of worship in the gaze that was flattering to Tawnia's ego, but already she was fervently hoping his crush wouldn't become an annoyance.

Canda pulled Sean back down into his seat. "See, that's spelled wrong. Didn't you take any English classes?" Canda had short platinum blond hair and a complexion so smooth it brought to mind a porcelain doll. Her figure was decidedly round, but she was so striking and dressed so well that Tawnia found herself envious of her figure. There was a woman who knew when she looked good and didn't need a scale to tell her she was beautiful. "How'd you get this job if you can't spell?" Canda added in disgust.

"Because I'm good," Sean shot back. Spoken with all the confidence of youth.

Canda rolled her eyes. "Whatever. Change it." She leaned back in her chair, bringing a foot to the edge of the table— black high heels that for a second drew every eye. "The copy wasn't this way when we gave it to you."

"I got distracted." Sean began typing furiously, a faint red tinging his face.

Canda cast a sympathetic glance at Tawnia. "Yeah, I bet."

"Well, I'll see you two tomorrow," Tawnia said into the awkward silence. After her management meeting in the morning, she'd scheduled a meeting for the next day so her team members could give a rundown on their progress.

Canda stood. "I'm going home, too."

"What about this?" Sean protested.

"Your problem. You can show us tomorrow at the meeting." Canda blew him a kiss, smiled at Tawnia, and headed to her cubicle in the far corner.

Tawnia returned the smile, shaking her head and exchanging

an amused glance with Dustin. She felt a surge of gratitude for her new job. *I can do this. I like these people.* In a few weeks, she knew they'd become like family.

Family. Her mother and father. They'd likely be flying to Portland soon to check out her new accommodations—and to tell her what a mistake she was making, moving even farther away from home. She heaved an internal sigh.

Dustin's little restaurant, Smokey's, was located one block over and half a block down. To save themselves the trouble of parking two cars, they walked. The streets were filled with traffic, though the sidewalks had few pedestrians. The air was still very warm, though the main heat of the day had passed. The buildings, the architecture, the street lights—everything was unfamiliar to her, and yet somehow Tawnia felt a sense of belonging.

"You're very quiet," Dustin said.

"Just taking it all in. It's nice here."

"Bit busy."

"Not like Las Vegas."

He chuckled. "Is anything like Vegas? Ah, here we are." Smokey's sat on a street opposite a slew of smaller stores—shoes, music, antiques, herbs, dresses, children's wear, a bicycle shop. Soon she would investigate every one.

Smokey's was nothing like she had imagined. Not a dark bar with a few greasy tables but a light airy place with many spotless tables and a long snack bar along the wall opposite the kitchen area. The place smelled heavenly.

"Mmm," Tawnia said. "I like it already."

"Wait until you taste the food."

They had come during a lull, so a young waitress immediately came to take their order. "Did you do something to your hair?" the girl asked Tawnia. "I like it."

"It's always been this way." Tawnia smoothed down a length of her straight hair.

"Wasn't it red on top, and short?" The waitress looked at her more closely and shook her head, causing her blond ponytail to swing slightly. "I'm sorry. I'm probably confusing you with someone else."

"I'm new in town," Tawnia told her. "But if your pies are anything like my friend here says they are, you'll be seeing a lot of me."

"Great! Keep in mind that we're the only organic restaurant in the area. All of our menu choices, with the exception of a few desserts, are made of completely organic ingredients. Even our desserts are made with as many organic ingredients as possible. Much better for you." With a smile, the girl left.

"You must have one of those faces," Dustin said.

"I guess."

Their pies were brought in less than five minutes, which told Tawnia the restaurant was preparing for a rush of customers. Even now the tables were beginning to fill up with a mixture of colorful clothes and corporate suits.

"This really is good." Tawnia ate with unabashed enthusiasm. In fact, she'd like to order another to take home, but maybe she shouldn't reveal her voracious appetite to Dustin just yet.

"So, you're going for the bridge account, I can tell." He smiled at her.

"What makes you say that?"

"Your eyes. You look like you're thinking. Plus, I'm not used to being ignored. So what's the plan? Soldiers dropping out of an airplane carrying signs that say 'Our bridges are so safe I dare to parachute down to one?'"

She chuckled. "A little too subtle for me."

"Ha ha. That's right, though. Can't hit people over the head with it. Subtlety really is what's needed at this point. There's what, like twenty-three dead?"

Her smile died. "Twenty-four. Canda heard it on the radio after lunch. They found another body."

Dustin shook his head, his brow creased. "Still hard to believe. There has to be something more to this whole mess."

"You mean than just a boat hitting the bridge?"

"Engineers plan for things like human error. There are redundancies. In my view, it doesn't make sense."

Tawnia nodded. "I know an engineer, and he's like that. Careful."

"Boyfriend?"

She made her face expressionless, forcing a nonchalance she didn't feel. "The brother of a guy I used to work with in Nevada. Both really nice guys." Was her voice too casual?

Dustin smiled. "I was thinking if we had an interview with an engineer, a face the public could trust, that might be just the thing for this account."

Tawnia thought of Bret. He would be the perfect subject for an interview, though it would be out of the question since he wasn't employed by Multnomah County. Besides, he would be too serious. People would believe him, but he wouldn't catch their imagination. No. They needed someone real, someone closer to the heart of the people than an engineer.

"I think a victim would make a better face for television and radio. If you could find someone who actually was on the bridge and whose life changed because of it, and yet they still put their trust in the county . . . Now that would be something to grab the imagination." She stopped eating and stared into the space above Dustin's left ear.

"The person would have to be just right, of course," she added, "and the wording perfect. You wouldn't want it to seem manipulated. And you'd back that up with some connection to the new logo and everything else we'd create. Not sure what."

Maybe a color the victim was wearing? Or would it be enough to have the new logo appear after the spot? Yes. Probably. Unless she could come up with something better.

She went on, "The county should support a few local events as well. Maybe sponsor a little public television. Then we publicize those acts in the media. That's free advertising we shouldn't pass up."

"Great ideas."

The waitress appeared at the table. "Did you guys want dessert?"

"None for me, thanks," Dustin replied at the same time Tawnia said, "I'll have a piece of chocolate cake, please."

She grinned at him and shrugged. She wasn't going to make excuses for herself. He was the one with the spare tire beginning around his waist, though the dress shirt hid it well. The piece of cake was large and covered in hot fudge and whipped cream. She ate the whole thing, not offering him any.

It's just too soon to be sharing food, she reasoned to herself, *and if he'd wanted some, he would have ordered a slice and kept me company.*

Besides, it was good.

While she finished her cake, he kept up a steady stream of conversation about the bridge account, asking her opinion on every angle. Finally, she set down her fork. "That was good. I wish I could say it wasn't, so you'd have to buy dinner all week, but alas, my parents taught me not to lie."

"I think I can honestly say that I've never seen a woman eat so much."

She shrugged. "I was hungry." She was always hungry, but she didn't need to mention that and, fortunately, she didn't need to battle the weight issue yet, though at thirty-two, she suspected that day was just around the corner. Until then, she would enjoy her metabolism and her size six pants.

"Is something wrong with your eye?"

She must have been blinking her left eye again. "It's just my contact. It's bothering me." She'd have to throw it away and get another one.

"Contact?" He peered closer, but she averted her face. She didn't want to talk about it. Being new at a company was hard enough without all her differences being discovered from the beginning.

He had already paid the waitress, but now he pulled out money for a tip. Tawnia was pleased to note he was generous. She'd been a waitress in college and knew all about the sore feet and low wages.

They walked back to the office, where they collected their cars from the underground parking lot. "Thanks," Tawnia told him. "It was fun."

"I'm glad. See you tomorrow."

She nodded and climbed inside her Pontiac. The air-conditioning still wasn't fixed, so she rolled down the windows. Twenty minutes later she was at her bungalow. She'd take out her single contact, put on her pajamas, and go over her files until she was too tired to think. That should put an end to the sleeplessness she'd experienced since arriving in Portland, caused by the fact that every time she closed her eyes, she saw the collapse of the bridge and the newscaster interviewing the victims.

Seven still missing.

Her phone rang as she was preparing a snack to keep her company on the front porch. "Hi, Dad," she said.

"You get your car air-conditioning fixed?"

"Not yet. I have an appointment tomorrow. I'm dropping it off at lunch and should have it by the end of the day." She still hadn't figured out how she'd get home from work if they had to keep it longer than promised.

"Your mother wants to know if you wore the red suit?"

"Yes, I did."

"Did you act confident?"

She rolled her eyes at the statement. "Yes, Dad." She was always confident—they'd raised her to be a high achiever. Confidence wasn't her problem, except in her relationship with them. But she'd learned to be a good actress in front of her parents, or reap the inevitable lecture.

Her mother got on the phone next. "You're wearing your contact, aren't you?"

"Yes."

"Good, because it might not be wise to stand out in that sort of way right in the beginning."

Not for the first time Tawnia thought it must bother her mother no end that her only child was less than perfect. As a teen she'd even wondered if her parents would have given her back to the adoption agency if her eye color had been fully developed at birth.

"I just got home, and I'm really tired. I still have a stack of files to read tonight."

Her mother didn't appear to hear. "It looks like we'll have a tornado tonight. It reminded me of you. You always loved tornados."

Tawnia had always longed for them to take her away to

experience adventure, like Dorothy in *The Wizard of Oz*. Once, back in Kansas when a tornado was expected, she'd purposely left a hose unattached to the outside faucet. Instead of dancing by the house, held by the connection, it had been dragged up and away, a flying snake disappearing toward a new adventure. She could almost imagine following it. But she would never tell her mother about that desire. Her parents had done a fine job raising her, and she knew she should be grateful. Many adopted children didn't have it half so good. If she'd stayed with her birth mother, who knew where she'd be now?

Yet why was she so restless? What adventure had she hoped to find? Five states in ten years, and she still didn't know. It didn't have anything to do with being adopted. At least she didn't think so.

In her last two years of high school, she'd gone through a secret phase of searching for her birth parents, as did many other children with closed adoptions. She had no success. Her parents were characteristically silent on the matter, and she hadn't probed for fear of hurting them. Almost no one who knew their family was even aware that she wasn't their biological child. The phase had passed by the time she started college.

She turned her mind back to the conversation. "If it looks bad, you'd better get down to the basement."

"We will. Just to be safe. Don't forget to charge your phone tonight. I was so worried about you this weekend."

"I will. I bought a new charger." The old one had disappeared somewhere during her journey—probably left at the hotel where she'd stayed Thursday night. When her phone was off, incoming calls wouldn't register, but the voice mail worked, and thankfully only her parents had left messages while the phone had been out of commission, so she hadn't missed anything vital.

"That's good, honey. Take care. We'll call you in a few days."
I know. "Thanks, Mom."

Tawnia blew out a sigh and hung up. Going to the front porch, she sat on the rocking chair, glad that the cushions were clean and comfortable. Her files sat on her lap, but she didn't open them. Instead, she stared over the tiny lawn at the house across the street. Why was she in Portland? Would she finally discover what she was apparently searching for, or would next year find her moving again?

She might have stayed in Nevada if things had worked out with Bret. But she couldn't think about that now. Opening the top file, she went to work.

CHAPTER

5

*A*utumn stared blankly at the man, trying to place him. Had he been a customer at her shop? Or perhaps he'd been an acquaintance of her father's.

"Of course you know me!" He spoke as though it was very important that she did.

Had she suffered a head trauma in the accident? No. She remembered everyone else in her life. Or at least she thought she did.

"I'm sorry. I really don't think I know you." Turning her face from him, she gazed out over the water again. The connected feeling was still there, and while it lived, so did her hope for her father.

"Tawnia." He grabbed her arm.

She gasped and pulled back. Tears flooded her eyes at the sudden pain.

He dropped his hands to his side. "Did I hurt you?"

She blinked away the tears, struggling not to show how much she was hurting. "I twisted my arm, that's all. But honestly,

I don't know you, and I just want to be left alone." She waited a few seconds to add in a soft voice, "Please."

"You don't remember Nevada?"

Autumn had been to Nevada several times on business, as well as many other western states, but she hadn't known this man. Or . . . she gazed deeply into his eyes. Could he be related to her somehow? Could he be part of the connected feeling she'd been experiencing? Maybe he was a half-brother or a cousin she'd never met. The problem with being adopted was that you never knew.

He reached out to her again, stopping short of actually touching her. "You don't remember Nevada. What about my brother? What about Christian?"

She shook her head slowly. "I don't know you or your brother. I've lived here in Portland all my life." There was an annoying itch on the side of her face, but she didn't dare let go of her arm to scratch it.

The man shook his head, eyeing her intently. "Okay, yes, there are some differences, I guess. But you look so much like her. Even the eyes."

That got her attention. She had never met another person with eyes like hers, though she had read about others having them, including a few celebrities. "Well, I'm really sorry. I'm not who you think I am."

He sighed. "I can tell, now that we're talking, but it was a shock at first. Really, you could be twins with a woman I know. I mean, if your hair was the same and if you weren't so skinny—uh, if you weighed a bit more."

Her lips twitched at his awkwardness. "They say everyone in the world has a doppelganger."

"So they do. I never believed it before." He smiled, and for the first time she noticed how handsome he was, though in a rather reserved sort of way. He had a nice build, narrow hips, and blond hair. His eyes were his best feature, and she admitted that she felt something as those eyes ran over her face and then fell to her dirty jeans and sweatshirt. What did he think of her? She found herself wondering what the woman who looked like her had been to him. Had they been in love? Who was she and why weren't they together now?

"My name is Autumn Rain," she offered.

"Autumn Rain. Beautiful."

"Most people think it's weird. My mother's name was Summer, and my father—" She broke off and for a moment she couldn't continue. "My father's name is Winter."

"He's still missing."

It wasn't a question, but she answered it anyway. "Yes." She dropped her gaze to the ground. Her bare toes peeked out of the hems of her jeans, dirty almost beyond recognition.

"I'm sorry. And your mother?"

"Summer died when I was eleven. Breast cancer."

"Summer and Winter," he mused. "What unique names. Must have been interesting people."

"Yes." Autumn had enjoyed being raised by so-called flower children, able to eat whatever she wanted regardless of nutritional value, allowed to roam wherever she chose, and given rein to wear whatever caught her fancy. She was the envy of her friends for all of this but most especially because she called her parents by their first names.

Now Autumn regretted calling them by name because those weren't big enough or important enough to label the loss in her life. *Mom* would have been enough. *Dad* would have been. Pain rolled through her at the memories.

Winter, I should have called you Daddy.

Bret was quiet a long time, for which she was grateful. It

was a comfortable silence, one she had not expected to share with a complete stranger. "My older brother died last year in a climbing accident," he said at last. "Some days I still forget and think about calling him up to play racquetball or ask if he wants to watch the big game. It's weird."

"Not so weird as you think. I talk to Summer all the time." She smiled at him. "So who are you, anyway?"

"Oh, I didn't—I—" His fumbling reminded her of the little boys who came in her dad's shop to buy his sugarless health food candies.

He recovered, pulling out a badge that was clipped to the pocket of his jeans. "I'm Bret Winn, an independent engineer called in by Multnomah County to investigate the bridge collapse. I'm from Nevada." He seemed to be watching her reaction carefully, as though he didn't quite trust that she wasn't the woman he had originally mistaken her for.

"Nice to meet you. I'd offer you my arm, but—" She lifted her undamaged shoulder in a half shrug.

"You really should get that looked at."

"I know." She sighed. "But I keep thinking that's when they'll find him." Tears pricked the backs of her eyes, and she looked away again so he wouldn't see.

"I don't think they'll be bringing up much more tonight. Most of the men have left, including the divers. And I have it on good authority that the Navy Seals will be here tomorrow. They have sonar equipment that should help. If you get the arm fixed tonight, you can be here tomorrow. Ready . . . for whatever."

For whatever. Autumn knew he thought her father was dead. He was probably right.

Suddenly, she was exhausted. It had been a long, hot,

wearying day standing in the sun. She wanted nothing more than to go back to her store and lie down in her easy chair. She hadn't been able to face going home to the apartment yet. Jake should be here any minute to get her, shouldn't he? She had no concept of time anymore. All the hours that made up the past few days were a blur.

"I can take you to the hospital." Bret gestured to her arm.

"You know what? I think I would like that." Her arm was in fact feeling worse since her ibuprofen was wearing off—and his manhandling of it hadn't helped. "But could you take me to the after-hours clinic at my doctor's office instead?"

"Sure, that'll be less expensive for you anyway."

As they walked up the bank, Autumn spied Orion Harris coming toward them, his long arms swinging at his side. "Autumn," he called.

He'd shown up here every night since they'd met, though he hadn't talked to her. Instead of feeling uneasy that he was watching her from a distance, she'd felt reassured by his presence.

"Hi, Orion."

"How are you?" he asked, glancing at Bret with a mixture of curiosity and distrust.

"I'm okay."

"Your arm?"

"Fine." She'd decided he felt a sense of duty toward her—probably since he'd saved her life.

"What's going on?" Orion looked from Autumn to Bret. "Who are you?"

"I'm an independent engineer brought in by the county. From Nevada. Bret Winn." Bret proffered his hand to Orion, and they shook.

"Orion Harris. I'm a fireman."

Bret nodded. "If you're the guy I think you are, you were one of the first on the scene after the bridge collapsed."

"That's me. I was driving nearby—on this side."

"I'd like to talk to you sometime, if I could. About what happened. But right now, I'm taking Autumn to the doctor."

Orion's gaze met Autumn's. "You haven't gotten that arm looked at yet?"

"I'm going now. With, uh—what did you say your name was?" She'd known it seconds ago, and it wasn't like her to be so forgetful, but that was the least of her worries at the moment.

"Bret Winn."

"You can't go with him," Orion protested. "You don't know him."

No one had ever told her such a thing since she was five when Summer had told her it probably wasn't a good idea to go to Kansas with the biker who had come into the Herb Shoppe for vitality vitamins. She'd only wanted to find Dorothy from the Wizard of Oz.

"He's got a badge," she said, attempting to make a joke of Orion's challenge.

"Anyone can get a badge."

Autumn sighed. "I didn't know you, either, and I let you take me home the other day."

"That's different."

"Because you saved my life?" The truth was that she almost wished he hadn't pulled her from the water. The tears were coming again.

"No." Orion's reply was more a growl than anything, and once Autumn would have thought it romantic, even though he was so much older than she was. She had revised her first impression of his being her father's age, but he was still at least in his mid-forties.

"Look, I've made up my mind. I'm going to the doctor with Bret." *So get over it.* Even last week she might have said the words aloud, but she couldn't today. So easily they could be thrown back in her face.

Winter was gone. Get over it.

Orion nodded. "Fine. I'll let you know if they find anything here."

For a moment Autumn was torn. Maybe she should stay.

"Do you have her number?" Bret asked.

Autumn frowned. "My phone's lost." She looked out to the river where her phone and her purse lay somewhere beneath the shadowy water. And Winter? Was he nearby as well?

The men fell silent, understanding what she didn't say aloud.

"Take my number down," Bret said into the awkwardness. "I'd like yours, too, if you don't mind."

Autumn stood numbly watching the murky water flowing in the river while the men exchanged texts to capture each other's phone numbers. Satisfied, Orion nodded at her and continued down the bank.

"Can I use your phone?" she asked Bret. "I should call my friend Jake so he doesn't come to pick me up."

Bret handed her his phone. Looking at her arm, he asked, "Want me to dial?"

Autumn didn't want him to but she had little choice. She wasn't up to working a strange phone with her left hand. Besides, she must have forgotten to eat again because his face was moving around at an impossible angle.

"Please." She gave him the number, and he dialed before passing the phone to her.

"Jake? It's Autumn. Look, don't come down to the river for me. I have a ride. No, I'm okay. I promise. Don't worry so much. I'm actually going to see about my arm. Thanks. See you tomorrow. No. I won't be at the store. If it gets too busy, just close down my side. Okay. Bye."

She handed back Bret's phone.

"Are you all right?" he asked. A line of worry gathered between his eyebrows.

"I'm a little hungry."

"So am I. We could stop and get a burger."

"There's a place called Smokey's. They have a great whole wheat bagel sandwich." She would kill for one of those right now. Smokey's was the only place she like to eat out at these days. At least they tried to use organic ingredients. They fell short with their fantastic desserts, which she still ate anyway, but the main dishes were healthy.

"Okay, we'll stop at this Smokey's place first. But I hope you're okay riding in a truck. I came with a guy from the county."

"I love trucks." As an irresponsible teenager, she had adored riding in the back, standing up as she held onto the cab window. Not something she'd do these days. She'd learned only too well what it meant to be mortal.

If she'd owned a truck instead of a little car, would her father be with her now? She shut her eyes against the pain in her chest. Or was it her arm? Her whole body seemed to ache.

They had arrived at the truck, and Bret was talking to a wide-faced, freckled man with red hair. She didn't understand what they were saying, though she was close enough to hear the conversation.

Her mind wandered back to Orion. Why did he keep coming to the river? Was it for her, or was he looking for something? It didn't make sense that he was interested in her—beyond a hero type of thing. He hadn't even seen her with her hair combed or any makeup on. Idly, she wondered what it would be like to kiss him.

Whoa. She was really out of it. She felt flushed and hot, though the sun hung lower in the sky now, and there was a nice breeze gusting up from the river.

"Come on. You get in first. Robert says he knows where Smokey's is. Then he'll drop us off at the clinic. We'll catch a taxi home. Or I'll call the hotel and see if they've arranged my rental car."

Autumn was relieved that she was no longer in charge. She nodded, but her head seemed to waver more than it should. This was exactly how she'd felt after accidentally swallowing one of Summer's pain pills when she was eleven. Everything was out of kilter.

Bret stepped back so she could climb inside the truck, helping her as best he could without touching her arm. "There you go."

The other man, Robert, looked at her with open curiosity, and Autumn found herself hoping she didn't smell. After a dip in the river and three days of not showering, it couldn't be good. Her mind refused to follow the thought and the idea was lost, except for the lingering feeling that she didn't like Robert's face. He wouldn't have been a person she would have gone with on her own. But Bret, he was like Winter. Well, in a twisted sort of way. Or Winter was twisted. Or something.

She gave up trying to think and let herself sink into the numbness that was spreading over her body. *Sleepy*, she thought. Why was she so sleepy all the time? It seemed she could only stay awake if she was at the riverbank.

Autumn noticed the truck had come to a stop and Bret had

opened the door. She scooted over, not wanting to be left alone with Robert.

"Why don't I just get you—what was it? A bagel sandwich?" Bret asked.

"That's okay. I'll go in with you."

"You're not wearing shoes."

"So?"

Bret nodded. "Okay, then. Anything for you, Robert?"

"Nah, I'm good. Noreen'll have dinner waiting."

Every table was full, but most of the customers were already eating. A young waitress with a blond ponytail came their way. Autumn recognized her from her weekly trips to the restaurant, though she'd probably only been served by her once or twice.

"I've got a table in the back," the girl said. "Nearly clear. If you'll wait a moment."

"It's take-out," Autumn said.

The waitress stared. "Weren't you just in here? A meat pie, right? And chocolate cake?" She shook her head. "No, that must have been someone else. Your hair is red. Sorry."

"That's okay. But that meat pie does sound good. I'll have one of those."

The waitress pointed to a counter near the door. "Takeout's ordered over there. Have a good day." With another curious glance at Autumn, she was gone.

That's right. Takeout wasn't ordered from the waitresses. Autumn shook her head to try to clear it.

"I'll have a meat pie," she told the lady at the take-out counter. "And an orange squeeze. No, raspberry lemonade. And fries—large. And a donut. No, chocolate cake. Well, maybe I'll have the whole wheat bagel sandwich after all. Large, with extra peppers and mustard. No mayo. Wait. That meat pie does sound good." The problem was, she was so hungry that every-thing sounded good. "Maybe I'll have both." She rested her hurt arm on the countertop and felt for her money. It wasn't there. She was sure she'd taken a couple of twenties from the till. Of all the stupid times to have lost money.

Bret watched her closely, an unreadable expression on his face. "Don't worry about it. I've got it." To the woman, he added, "Bring us two meat pies and a bagel sandwich with mustard and extra peppers. And all the rest of what she said."

"Lemonade," supplied Autumn, "and chocolate cake."

"Might as well throw in a donut." Bret smiled at her, and she smiled back.

He was like Winter, insisting on buying her everything she was hungry for. At that thought, the pain in her heart hurt so much that it far outweighed the torture of her arm.

She gobbled the sandwich in the truck as Robert followed her directions to the after-hours clinic. Before they arrived, the chocolate cake and the donut had disappeared, too, and she'd begun breaking off the crust on the meat pie. She hadn't thought about the complication of getting the filling to her mouth with only her awkward left hand.

"I have never seen anyone eat so much," Bret commented. Then his face went still. "Except Tawnia."

"Tawnia?"

"The woman I thought was you."

Autumn met his gaze. He was looking at her face as though not sure what to make of her. Did he still think she might be this Tawnia? Ludicrous. Still, if she looked enough like her, maybe she was related. Questions bubbled up inside her, threatening to break free in a flood of words.

"Here we are," Robert announced.

Autumn decided her questions could wait. Likely it had been years since Bret had seen the woman who resembled her. His memory might be faulty. Her mismatched eyes and her build might be enough for him to see a resemblance, but it wasn't worth getting her hopes up. Sustaining hope of finding another relative was too much effort to maintain in her current state. Besides, all she really wanted was Winter.

"What about your tools?" Robert asked as they got out.

Bret deliberated a moment. Autumn could see he was loath to leave his equipment and wondered how much it had cost. Some of the items in her store cost so much that she would have gladly lugged them across the entire North American continent, even on foot, rather than give them up. She had no idea what sort of tools an engineer would have. "Would you mind taking them back to the office? Locking them up? I'll come in early to get them."

"Sure. No problem. I'll see you tomorrow. Good luck, ma'am." Robert lifted a hand and drove away.

"Thank you," Autumn said. He'd turned out to be a nice guy, and she felt bad for judging him. Winter and Summer had taught her better.

Autumn was feeling better since gobbling the food. She wasn't dizzy anymore, though she still felt hot in her sweatshirt. They went to the desk where a white-haired receptionist greeted them impersonally. "Name?"

"Autumn Rain."

"You can sign in here. What's the problem?"

"I hurt my arm." Autumn laughed somewhat hollowly. "It's probably nothing. Just a sprain."

"Do you have insurance?"

"Yes."

"Can I see your card?"

Another thing that was lost to the river. Autumn felt suddenly light-headed. "My information should be on file."

"I'll still need your card," the woman said sweetly, as though that piece of plastic would give her permission to move. "To make sure there haven't been changes."

"I don't have it with me. It's lost." Autumn exchanged a telling look with Bret, whose mouth tightened—probably with pity. "This is my regular doctor's office," she added hurriedly. "I'm sure I'm in the computer. The information is up to date."

The woman pursed her lips and took the sign-in sheet, typing on the keyboard, her face rigidly staring at the computer screen.

Color rose in Bret's face. "Look, I'm willing to sign a paper saying I'll pay for this, if necessary. Just get us in as quickly as possible."

"I found her information," the woman said icily, "but I do need to take the co-pay now. That'll be thirty dollars."

Bret whipped out his wallet and shoved some bills in her direction. "How long will the wait be?"

"Thirty to forty minutes."

Autumn's arm was throbbing now, and she wondered if she should ask for ibuprofen. Why hadn't she thought to carry some in her pocket?

"Come on." Bret guided her to a chair.

Across from them, a blond man in his fifties nodded at them and then covered his mouth with his hand to cough, looking away from them apologetically. A haggard woman in the corner cradling a young child stood as her name was called.

Autumn folded her feet under her and adjusted her arm carefully over her stomach before opening her Smokey's bag.

The delicious smell of the pie was calling to her. With deliberation, she pulled the pie carton from the bag, barely managing to hook her pinky finger around the plastic-wrapped fork seconds before the bag fell to the ground. Balancing the pie in her lap, she ripped open the plastic around the fork with her teeth, proud of herself. She scooped up a taste of pie—only to have it fall down the front of her sweatshirt.

Oops, she thought.

Not that it really mattered. The sweatshirt already sported bits of the granola Jake had made her eat for breakfast that morning. Or had it been yesterday morning? And there was mustard from her sandwich, frosting from the cake, and who knew what else. Her jeans were worse. Autumn usually didn't care if her clothes were matching, or in style, or even if she wore them for a week, but she did like her clothes to at least look and smell clean.

She lifted her gaze to see Bret watching her. "You need help?" he asked.

"No. I like wearing my food."

He laughed and reached down for the bag, pulling out a napkin, which he held out to her. She wiped the gravy from her chest as he took the pie from her lap and balanced it on a stack of magazines he laid on the armrest. "There, that should be easier to reach."

A heavyset woman with dark hair rushed through the doors of the clinic. "I just called," she said to the receptionist.

"Your card?"

The woman pulled out her wallet.

"Very good. Sit down for a minute, and we'll get you right back."

Fat chance, Autumn thought as the woman sat opposite them, a hand pressed against her heart.

Yet less than five minutes passed and the woman was ushered back to the examination rooms.

Two more groups of people came in, and the tiny room became even more compressed. Autumn's arm throbbed incessantly as she tried to concentrate on the meat pie. It was good, though the flavor was somewhat lost on her.

Fifteen minutes later, the coughing man had been ushered inside, though most of his germs had probably been left behind, and now the receptionist was calling back one of the others who had come in after them. Autumn's meat pie was long gone.

"This is ridiculous," Bret muttered under his breath

Autumn thought so too. "Let's just go. My arm's fine."

"You need to get it X-rayed."

"It's fine."

"You always say you're fine." He stopped abruptly.

She shook her head. "I'm not your friend."

"I know." He blew out a frustrated breath. "That just slipped out. Sorry."

Another thirty minutes dragged by.

At last, Bret crossed to the reception desk. Hands on the counter, he leaned over close to the receptionist. "How much longer is it going to be? We've been here an hour already. I know it might not seem serious to you, but my friend was on the Hawthorne Bridge when it collapsed. That's why she doesn't have her card—it's at the bottom of the river. And she hasn't seen a doctor since they pulled her out of the water because she's been down there every day waiting to see if they find her father. He's still missing."

Instant pity replaced the woman's cold stare. "I was about to call you." She herself took them to an examination room.

"Could I get some ibuprofen?" Autumn asked. She was

embarrassed that Bret had to practically force their way in, but a part of her was angry too. Through the open door, she saw one of the people who'd come in after her saying goodbye to a dark-haired man in a white coat. "Is that the doctor?"

"The P.A.," replied the receptionist.

"Physician's assistant?" Bret stared at her through narrowed eyes. "Isn't there a doctor?"

"Not tonight. Just the P.A. and the nurse practitioner."

"I see." He looked about as pleased as Autumn felt.

"I'll get that ibuprofen for you now."

The receptionist returned almost immediately with the pain reliever, staring at Autumn with undisguised interest. Autumn looked pointedly away. She didn't want to answer questions.

Another half hour crept by.

"That lady came in thirty minutes after we did!" Bret said, staring out into the hallway as yet another woman said goodbye to the dark-haired P.A.

Autumn was beginning to feel claustrophobic. She had never done well in tight spaces. "I think we should leave." She stood and walked to the door, only to find her exit barred by a petite black woman with the most perfect facial features Autumn had ever seen—large eyes, prominent cheek bones, heart-shaped face, and the most lovely brown complexion. Her hair was braided tightly against her head in elaborate pencil-width braids.

"Hi," she said in a matter-of-fact voice. Her eyes wandered briefly to Autumn's bare feet and back to her face. "I'm sorry to keep you waiting. I'm the nurse practitioner. What happened to your arm?"

"I fell," Autumn lied, not caring to explain. "It's probably nothing. The swelling has gone way down."

The nurse felt the arm gently, studying her face for signs of pain. Autumn didn't disappoint her. "We'll definitely need an X-ray."

Bret gave her an I-could-have-told-you-that look, and Autumn couldn't help but smile. He was like an impatient child.

"Will I need to take off my sweatshirt?" she asked.

"Do you have a shirt on under it?"

Autumn nodded.

"Probably a good idea then—especially if we need to cast it."

"Should I leave?" Bret asked.

"No." Autumn started pulling down the sleeve of the sweatshirt over her hand. It took both her and the nurse practitioner a good minute to get off the sweatshirt, and Autumn was blinking back tears by the time they finished.

The nurse practitioner took in the torn sleeve where the triage bandage had covered her cuts since the day of the bridge collapse. "Same fall?" she asked.

Autumn nodded dumbly. "I was bleeding. Someone put on a bandage."

"I'll want to look at that."

Autumn clenched her jaw as the woman removed the bandage, clicking over the size of the cut. "This should have been stitched. It's too late now, so you'll have a noticeable scar, though it does seem to be healing fairly well."

All this preoccupation with scars, thought Autumn. What about the ones they can't see?

"You should have come in before," Bret told her.

She felt a surge of anger at this stranger who acted like he knew her. "I guess my father wasn't around to make me."

"I'm sorry."

She lifted her left shoulder. "It's okay. I just don't care about a scar."

A new bandage and fifteen minutes later they were waiting

outside the X-ray room. But thirty more minutes passed as they sat there, and Autumn found herself starting to fall asleep. The pain reliever had deadened the pain, and she couldn't feel the cut because her shoulder was numb.

Finally, the door to X-ray opened, and the woman who'd been grabbing her chest in the waiting room emerged with the P.A. "We want you to go over to the hospital for more monitoring," he said. "Whatever it was seems to be gone, but better safe than sorry where the heart is concerned."

Her heart. So that was why she'd been rushed inside so quickly.

X-rays took another fifteen minutes. Autumn gasped as the female technician moved her arm to get all the right angles, having to repeat one of them for lack of a good picture. Autumn was beginning to wish she hadn't agreed to any of this, though the technician, who reminded Autumn of her middle-aged kindergarten teacher, was as gentle as possible.

The nurse practitioner studied the X-rays and then called in the P.A. for backup. Autumn strained to hear what they were saying, but she managed to grasp only a few words: *crushed* and *fractured*.

"Looks like you broke it," Bret said from his chair in the examining room.

Autumn groaned. They were supposed to send her home with a patronizing pat on the back. This was her right arm they were talking about. How was she supposed to run a store? Not that she had been doing much in the past few days. If it hadn't been for Jake, she wouldn't have made a dime.

The medical personnel worked more quickly after that, though Autumn's confidence in them wasn't very high when they pulled out a medical book to decide how they should splint her arm.

"You've got to be kidding," Bret whispered. "Tell me again why didn't we go to the hospital?"

"This is cheaper," she said.

"Hey, you know what," the X-ray technician said to the P.A. "I'll do the splint. I did a million of these at my last job."

The nurse practitioner readily agreed, and Autumn was soon wearing a splint that went from her wrist to halfway past her elbow. The technician hadn't needed to consult the book.

"Did you see them looking it up?" Bret asked the technician.

The technician pushed her frizzy, shoulder-length hair behind her ear, and Autumn couldn't help wondering if the yellow-orange color was natural or a dye job gone bad. "Yeah, I saw them. A little scary, huh? That's why I said I'd do it. Now you need to wear this for the next seven days. Eight, tops. After that you have to take it off and begin moving it a little. Otherwise you may lose mobility in your elbow. You should use the sling as much as you need after the splint is off, but throw away the splint so you won't be tempted to use it. They'll give you some medication to take for the pain. You should come back in a week for an X-ray to make sure it's healing properly."

Over my dead body, Autumn thought. This experience had already met her yearly quota of time at the doctor's. But she smiled and nodded.

"It won't be fully healed for at least six weeks," the technician warned. "Don't lift anything heavy until then. Nothing."

There went any rearranging at the store. Not that she cared. It all meant nothing without Winter.

Outside the clinic, dusk had fallen. Nearly three hours had passed since they'd gone inside. "I've arranged a car with my hotel," Bret told her. "It's supposed to be here now. Ah, there it is."

In minutes they were ready to go. "Where do you live?" Bret asked.

"I'm going back to my store."

"Where's that?"

"Across from Smokey's. It's an antiques shop."

"You sleep there?"

"I have."

"What about a shower?"

"Are you saying I stink?" She made her voice light.

His mouth curved into a smile. "Not exactly, but I couldn't help noticing that you are wearing a lot of food."

"I haven't changed since the bridge."

"Yeah, I figured." All amusement was gone from his voice.

"Look, I don't have a car anymore. It'll be easier if I stay close, so I'm going to my store. Once we get there, I'll pay you back for the clinic."

"I don't want the money. But I would like to know what happened on the bridge. From your point of view, that is."

Probably the reason he'd stuck with her so long. That and the fact that she looked like someone he knew. All at once her weariness felt crushing. "No."

"No?"

"Not tonight. Tomorrow I'll be at the river. We can talk then."

"The divers may not find him."

"I hope they don't."

"You think he's still alive? Perhaps wandering around Portland with memory loss?"

She looked away. His words stung because that was exactly what she hoped. Why else did she feel a connection? It wouldn't be there if he was dead.

Or would it?

She was too tired to think about it anymore. "Turn here," she said, as they reached her street. He had almost retraced their path exactly. She bet he was a good engineer. Maybe he would find out the reason for the collapse, though it didn't really matter to her. If Winter was dead, who cared how it happened?

He walked her to the door of the store, picking up her newly copied key when she dropped it onto the sidewalk. "Thank you," she whispered. The store was dark and held none of the vibrance that had filled it when her father was there.

"Are you sure you don't—" he started.

"Good night." She firmly shut the door in his face.

CHAPTER

6

*T*awnia was stunned. She had sat up half the night making plans for the bridge campaign, enlarging upon what she had told Dustin, only to have him present much of her plan to the executives as if it were his own. She felt betrayed, though in hindsight he had said he was going to pick her brain.

She should have known better than to trust a man she didn't know. In fact, she was beginning to wonder if there were any men she could trust. Her father had worked more than he was home, she'd caught her first real boyfriend kissing her best friend in high school, Christian had died before they really knew each other, and Bret . . . well, she didn't want to think about Bret. The bottom line was that she didn't have a great track record with men. But stealing her ideas—Dustin was the lowest scumbag of all.

"Well, those are some great ideas," said Joseph Sumpter, the CEO of Partridge Advertising. "Tawnia? You're up next. What do you have for us? Anything to top getting a victim to speak in the county's behalf?"

She was tempted to expose Dustin's deceit, but she suspected no one would believe the new girl on the block. "Well," she stalled, "his ideas are very good." She looked at him pointedly, hoping he'd feel the venom in her words. Because of that jerk, she'd have no choice but to claim she didn't have anything better to offer.

Unless . . . She took a deep breath and plunged on. "I think there are many great ways to go after this account, and I would certainly use the voice of the victims in the campaign, but what if we had a well-known person—someone famous in these parts, someone people trust, to be the spokesperson for all the new ads. That would go a long way to make people feel safe again. If we added in victim compensation, counseling, and outside inspections of the bridges, I think everything will go back to normal in as little time possible."

Sumpter rubbed his shaved chin thoughtfully. "Very good ideas. But it would likely be too expensive. First paying the celebrity, and then all the people that will pop out of the woodwork wanting reimbursement for their pain and suffering."

"I can just imagine it," Dustin said. His voice became high and trembling like that of an old lady. "My brother's cousin's daughter died in that collapse, and she was very special to me, though I only saw her once when she was baptized at the church."

Everyone laughed, except Tawnia, whose face flushed. "There would be an initial cost," she said in a rush, "but we'd expand with new logos and advertisements that in the long run would bring a lot of visitors to Portland. It would be good for everyone, and there's nothing like prosperity to help people forget a tragedy."

Everyone was silent as Sumpter considered, and Tawnia dared to hope. Finally he shook his head. "Though I actually agree with you, I don't think the county would go for it. Too much initial cost when they are focused solely on protecting their good name. I think as we get into the campaign, we should encourage something like Tawnia is suggesting, but for now, Dustin, you're going to run with this. But good job, everyone, especially on such short notice. Dustin, you'll meet with county officials today and pitch your plan. Tawnia, you can pitch to the other new account on Friday." That meant the small computer company with limited funds who wanted to make a few signs and radio ads. Not much excitement or leeway with funds, but she'd give it her best.

As everyone congratulated Dustin, Tawnia schooled her face to show no emotion. After life with her parents, she was good at that. The very ability had made Bret uneasy, but how else could she protect herself? Maybe if she had reacted when he'd called it quits between them something might have been different.

She walked slowly from the meeting to her own office, carefully placing one navy blue heel in front of the other. She'd worn this suit dress today because, according to her mother, navy screamed business and demanded that she be taken seriously. It usually worked.

Someone tugged on her sleeve, and she turned—to look into the face of scumbag number one.

"Good one in there," Dustin said. "I thought for a moment you had me."

She let the annoyance into her voice. "You're despicable."

"You know what they say: 'All's fair in love and war.'"

"Well, we certainly know which this isn't."

"Oh, come on. One doesn't rule out the other." He raised his eyebrows in what she supposed he considered an attractive manner, but she had seen him for what he was. "I told you I was going to pick your brain—you really didn't think I was going to pass up any good ideas, did you?"

"My ideas were supposed to be mine, and a little credit might have been nice."

"You're kidding, right? Besides, you don't want this campaign. You're still getting settled in. You haven't been here long enough to have your finger on the pulse of what makes this city tick. I'm doing you a favor."

She rotated sharply on her heel. "If you excuse me, I need to find a bathroom. I think I'm going to be sick. All this kindness turns my stomach."

"So does that mean we're not going to Smokey's tonight?" he called after her. "I'll buy."

She didn't bother to reply.

Tawnia met her team at the table in their offices to go over their projects, all in different stages of production. Among the most important were a shoe account, a T-shirt account, a motivational speaker who was self-publishing a third book, and a cereal, which Sean vowed he had tried and hated.

"It's hard to come up with something good to say about that junk," he said with a disgusted face.

Kacey Murphy, the art director for their team, rolled her eyes. "Well, guess you should be grateful you aren't the art director or the copywriter. Just design what we tell you. We didn't taste the cereal."

"I did," Canda said, "and I liked it."

Sean looked at her aghast. "You've got to be kidding."

Canda smiled. "Must be a woman thing. It's been proven that men don't have good taste, and besides, women are the ones buying the cereal."

"So let's see what you've got," Tawnia inserted, forestalling whatever Sean had been about to retort.

Kacey opened a folder. "Here's their rough design—completely unappealing, of course—but it gave me an idea of what they want."

"At least their design matches the taste," Sean mumbled. "Sorry," he added when he saw Tawnia look at him reproachfully.

"So I thought," Kacey continued, "if we change the background color, spiff up the image with a cute kid, nix that ugly logo, and put something like this . . ." She pulled out another piece of paper sporting a detailed swirl with the name of the company inside.

"Nice," Canda said.

"It's too girly," Sean protested.

Kacey put her hands on her hips. "And what's wrong with that?"

Tawnia understood what he was saying. The design was fluid and beautiful, but it would be better used for advertising a feminine hygiene product, which was kind of amusing, given Kacey's appearance. With her stocky figure and close-cropped dark hair, she wasn't the picture of femininity like the curvaceous, flowing-haired Canda. Even Kacey's clothing—a black suit—was reminiscent of a man.

Tawnia knew it was time to take control of her team. "It's a great design, Kacey, though I'm not sure it's right for a cereal. I want to see two other designs. And another from you, Sean, since you seem to know so much about it."

He groaned. "It's going to be hard when it tastes so gross."

"You aren't paid to taste their stuff, just market it. I want preliminary drawings by tomorrow morning. Nothing as fancy or detailed as Kacey has here until we decide on one. But not too masculine, either, because Canda's right when she said women are buying the cereal. Canda, what have you got for copy?"

"Nothing solid yet."

"By the end of the day I want to see a rough draft. We're meeting with them in two days."

"Any suggestions?" Canda looked around at them.

Sean grinned. "Eat this cereal, and death won't seem so bad."

"Something about helping you wake up in the morning," Kacey said. "Energy. People like that."

"It would wake me up, that's for sure." Sean pulled down a foot from the spare chair. "And that gives me an idea for a design." He started tapping on his laptop.

"Wait, did you fix the T-shirt design?" Canda asked. "I think Tawnia and Kacey have a meeting with them today."

"What was wrong with it?" Kacey demanded with a touch of panic.

"He spelled *imagine* wrong, if you can imagine it."

Tawnia smiled at the pun. The logo for the T-shirts was *Imagine It and Soar.*

"Let's see it," Kacey said.

Sean showed everyone the revised designs, and Tawnia was impressed. "Good work, you guys," she said. "That design is excellent."

Kacey smiled. "Wait till you see the commercial. They have that in production now. I'll bring it to you before our meeting with them."

Tawnia was grateful for her support. Kacey would be vital until Tawnia made her own connections with their clients. "The book guy wants to see his new dust jacket and hear the radio ads as well," Tawnia said. "I've scheduled to meet with him tomorrow."

"Be careful with that guy," Sean warned. "He'll have you going for our CEO's job."

Tawnia laughed. "Not a chance. I like it right here. I think we'll make a good team. But about what Canda said—that women buy most of the cereal. That's true with books as well, even if they're targeted toward men. So is there anything we can add to the book jacket that will catch a woman's eye as well? I mean, I know he's talking about getting rich, but . . ."

"A nice house." Canda leaned over Sean and clicked on the cover file. "Right now we have only those dollar bills against the white, but there's not a woman alive who wouldn't stop and look at a really nice house twice. Maybe something with a turret. It could go in the background."

"I like it." Tawnia looked around and saw that everyone was in agreement.

"Sean and I will fiddle with it a bit," Kacey said.

"Good. Meanwhile, we've been assigned a new account, which I'm pitching on Friday. A small computer firm who wants a new logo and radio ads. Low budget stuff, really, but I expect our best work on this." Even if the computer account didn't turn out to be a big one, Tawnia never discounted the chance that a large company might be impressed enough with her work to ask for her particularly. She had made a vow to treat every account as though it was worth millions.

"I've put copies of their request and their current marketing attempts in your boxes." Tawnia continued. "I was hoping to convince our computer client to do a direct marketing coupon as well, but we'll see. By tomorrow two of our current accounts should be wrapped up, and we'll hit this new one hard then or by Thursday morning at the very latest. Thank you, everyone."

Tawnia arose before adding, "Could I see you a minute in my office, Canda?"

Canda came to her feet, moving languidly like a contented cat. Today she was wearing white pants topped with a fitted pink short-sleeved jacket over a white shirt. Tawnia herself usually avoided white because she always managed to spill on it, but Canda obviously didn't have such fears.

"I made a few suggestions for the blurb on the dust jacket of the book," Tawnia said as she walked with Canda. "I'd like to see what you think."

Canda arched a brow. "This author's very particular about his blurbs. Sometimes I have to give in to him. Quite a change from most people, who let me do what I want."

Tawnia handed her a marked copy. "I think moving this sentence to the end concludes everything with a better focus. And that makes the old last sentence redundant."

"Finally, someone who can spell *redundant*," Canda said with a sigh. "I like it. And I think he will too. He's a good writer for the most part. Too bad he's married." She sighed, but she didn't look unhappy. Tawnia felt the statement might be more of a warning for her to stay away for her own good. Well, she had no intention of pursuing any of her clients, so Canda didn't need to worry.

Canda walked toward the door, proof in hand, but she turned around before she had gone halfway. "I heard what happened this morning."

"Oh?"

"You went to eat with Dustin last night, and suddenly he has ideas for a new account." Canda snorted delicately. "No one who knows him believes that. Those were your ideas, weren't they?"

Apparently around here gossip traveled faster than light.

"Why'd you want that project anyway?" Canda asked. "We're already booked with nearly as much as we can handle."

"I know. I was going to do a lot of it myself."

"Well, I wish I'd known. I would have told you to avoid Dustin. He always does this."

"Steals ideas?"

She nodded. "He doesn't have a creative bone in his body, though somehow he's convinced upper management that he does. Usually he steals ideas from the graphic artists or from some of the co-eds at the local college where he teaches a class once a week. Everyone ends up really hating him. Too bad he's so cute. Most of the younger set here is hung up on him. And his female students worship him."

"Not you?"

She smiled. "Not anymore. I did go out with him, but he's not smart enough to hold my attention."

"Good for you."

She walked the rest of the way to the door, swaying becomingly in her high heels. "We'll get him next time. I'd pit our team's ideas against his team's anytime."

"Thanks." Tawnia felt slightly better. At least she wasn't Dustin's only dupe, and she wouldn't be facing him without backup.

That was when the phone rang. She looked at the caller ID as Canda left, expecting her parents, but it was Bret. A tremor of . . . something rolled through her. Fear? Eagerness? Need? She didn't care to examine her feelings close enough to know.

What did he want?

Well, she couldn't talk with him now. She was already a mess from the incident with Dustin, and she had a ton of work to get through before her meetings today. If he left a message, she'd call him back. She focused on her computer screen for all of ten seconds.

"Oh, who am I kidding?" She grabbed the phone. "Hello?" But he'd already hung up, and there was no message.

She dialed his number quickly, but his voice mail picked up. He was probably on the phone.

This was working up to be one lousy day. Good thing she'd stopped this morning to buy donuts. She'd bought a dozen for her staff meeting and had forgotten to take them from her drawer.

Hooking a finger inside a chocolate iced donut, she opened a file and went to work.

CHAPTER

7

*T*uesday morning Bret's engineering tools were missing. Robert had placed them under lock and key, but they were gone all the same.

"Probably got mixed up with the company tools," Robert said. "I'll put out the word. Meanwhile, you can borrow the company's. What do you need?"

"I want to measure the stress the metal sustained, and I'll need to add in the weight and wind factor of everything." Bret tried not to be worried about his equipment. He'd spent years paying for some of it because he liked having the best at his fingertips.

Robert began jotting down a list of equipment. "I've got the necessary tools for any new testing you want. We have the top of the line. Better than anything the size you could carry in that toolbox, big as it was. And I printed readouts of all the regular testing we've done."

"I would like to look at those tests." Bret rubbed his jaw.

"It still doesn't make sense that the bridge would collapse like that, even if that boat—" He broke off. The boat. He'd completely forgotten about it after finding Autumn.

Autumn. How weird that she looked so much like Tawnia. Or was his mind just filling in the blanks? It had been months since he'd seen Tawnia. Months that felt like years.

Wouldn't she want to know he was in town? Even casual acquaintances often called each other in similar situations. Taking out his phone, he pushed the quick dial shortcut he still had for her number. Within seconds it was ringing.

"Hi. You've reached Tawnia. Sorry I can't answer. Leave a message."

He hung up. Even her voice sounded like Autumn's, except it also contained the perky cheeriness that was all Tawnia. Then again Autumn hadn't much to be cheery about.

Tawnia's voice had made a lump of something settle in the pit of his stomach. What? Remorse? Well, the ball was in her court. The phone had actually rung this time, before going to the message, so she'd probably see him on her caller ID and would return the call. If she wanted to. Meanwhile, he wanted to talk to that fireman. His number was here somewhere.

"This is Orion," came a voice.

"Bret Winn calling. We met yesterday. I took Tawn— Autumn to the doctor."

"How is she?"

"Broken arm."

"I knew it."

"Don't blame yourself. She's pretty stubborn."

"Sometimes women don't act as if they have a lot of sense."

"Yeah, well, she's been through a shock," Bret said. "No word on her father?"

"None."

"I didn't think so. I probably would have heard here. I'm down at the county going over some reports before heading to the river." Bret hesitated before adding, "Look, you were there from the beginning. Did you actually see the collapse?"

"No. I was driving by, like I told you before. Saw the debris in the air and hurried over."

"You had a boat with you?"

"A canoe. Just happened to be on my trailer. I'd had it out the day before, and I was taking it back to where I store it."

"That was fortunate."

Orion's voice became sharp and angry. "Are you insinuating something?"

Bret hadn't been, but why was the man so defensive? "Not at all. Autumn says you saved a lot of people, including her."

"Not enough."

"You did what you could. No one could have predicted the tragedy."

"The county could have. If they'd maintained their bridges, none of this would have happened. It's all their fault." The fireman's voice rang with certainty.

"Why do you say that?"

"The bridge collapsed, didn't it? It shouldn't have done that. And it's not the first time they've had problems. There have been suicides off the bridge, failures in the lifting mechanism, and I'm sure a lot more the public doesn't know about."

"I read about the lifting failures, but that didn't do more than cause temporary traffic jams. As for the suicides—"

"Look, you asked me what I thought. I told you. But I'd rather you not use my name on any reports. I'm employed by the city, and all government is connected."

"I'm only trying to get a feel for what happened. I won't be using any names. But did you notice anything strange when you arrived on the scene?"

"You mean other than dozens of people in the water and most of the bridge being gone?"

Bret ignored the sarcasm. "Naturally, there would have been that, but I meant any strange people around. Anyone not helping. Or people leaving the scene."

"If there was anything like that, I didn't notice. I was focused on getting those people out." Orion's voice was gravelly now, filled with emotion. Bret decided not to push. Not yet. He didn't really have anything to go on—except a general feeling that something at the bridge wasn't adding up.

"Well, if you think of anything, let me know."

"Are they calling in the Feds?"

"Local authorities are working with the FBI to rule out terrorism. But that doesn't seem likely. So far no one has taken responsibility for the act."

"Then it was the boat. It's the county's fault, just as I said. And I hope they pay." On that rather bitter note, Orion hung up.

Bret sighed and started going through his stack of reports.

Bret's entire body was sore. He'd spent the day checking and rechecking each piece of information at his fingertips. The old reports, the new tests—everything. He'd examined more of the standing part of the bridge and looked at the girders from water level. He used the county's equipment to test stress levels of the metal debris. At one point he'd even helped pull concrete and metal pieces from the river. Nothing pointed to foul play. Sure, there had been stress fractures, but they hadn't enlarged over the years and shouldn't have contributed to anything of this magnitude. His final evaluation would have to be that the county had fulfilled its duty to the residents of Portland. He had found nothing to refute that claim.

He still had several more days until he had to give an official opinion. Those days might shed more light on the collapse, as more debris was salvaged from the water, but he didn't think they would. This was simply one of those tragic freak accidents that would be remembered for decades to come.

Being at the bridge site all day meant he'd also been there when the Navy Seals found two more bodies. Only five missing now, one of them Autumn's father. More cars were being pulled from the muddied waters. None of them was Autumn's.

When he arrived at the river bank, she was there again, wearing the same jeans and gray sweatshirt as before. She stood, a small tragic figure looking out over the water. A black man with dreadlocks came to stand beside her in the early evening, the thick, snake-like strands of his hair looking oddly out of place among the hard hats worn by all the other men. Bret couldn't hear what they were saying, but it looked like an argument. The man kept motioning with his hand, and she would shake her head. Finally he left her there.

Bret admired her determination. She was a lot like Tawnia in that. No wonder the two were confused in his mind.

Beyond where Autumn stood he could see the boat with its top sheared off. He wanted to look at it but not with the shadow that had been following him all day.

"Robert," he called to the shorter man. Robert's freckled face had burned in the sun, despite his hat, making his normally ruddy complexion even more red. He looked hot and uncomfortable.

"Yeah?"

"I think it's time we knocked off. It's been a rough day."

Robert nodded. "You want to get a beer?"

Bret shook his head. "I need to talk to that girl again."

"I see." Robert gave him a knowing smile.

"Just want to make sure she's okay."

"A guy with a hero complex."

"She reminds me of someone I know."

"Your sister?"

"No. My sister's tough as nails. This girl isn't." But even as he said it, he remembered a time when his sister, Liana, hadn't been tough. When they had cried together after Christian died. He'd promised then to be the big brother she needed, and he had been, except that she was married now and expecting a baby. She didn't need him as much these days.

"So, you coming out again tomorrow?" Robert asked.

"Yeah. I don't expect to find much more, but you know the drill. I've got to go through the motions. There are large sections still under the water."

"Hey, I don't mind. They're paying me overtime for anything extra I do while you're here, and I can tell you, they don't give us overtime often." With his hand, Robert indicated the others around them. "These guys are doing shift work and getting paid crap. The county could care less as long as the job gets done."

"The county doesn't pay well?"

"What government job does? I mean, unless you're near the top. That's where the bucks are." He shrugged. "I've been meaning to leave for a private firm, and this cements it. I don't like being blamed for something that ain't my fault. This bridge was safe. I'd stake my life on it. But look at it now."

This was interesting. "Someone blamed you?"

"No, but I'm the manager over the engineers. I'm the guy who double-checks their work. If they go down, who do you think the scapegoat will be?"

"I don't think you have anything to worry about. All the readings look good. You guys did your job."

"I'm glad you think so." Robert offered his hand. "Well, seeing as you have your car, I'll go back to the office and do a once-over again for your tools before I check out. I'm sure they're around somewhere. And you go ahead and romance your lady friend over there."

Before Bret could protest, Robert turned and strode up the bank, heading to where they had left their vehicles.

Shaking his head, Bret walked in Autumn's direction. Men were leaving in small groups now, but there were more coming to take their places, as though having the Navy Seals there had encouraged a greater show of manpower. Not that it would do the victims any good. Dead was dead, as Christian would have said. What did it matter how long they were under the water? That would be just like his brother, not a thought for those remaining. The dead were fine, but the survivors' pain went on.

Autumn heard him as he approached, and she turned, her cautious expression becoming a smile. "Hi," she said softly.

At that moment she looked too much like Tawnia on the night he'd first kissed her at the door to her apartment. She hadn't invited him in, but that was okay because that kiss had told him everything he needed to know. Neither of them had wanted it to end.

She was speaking, but he was so engrossed in his thoughts of Tawnia that he didn't understand the words. "Excuse me?"

"I asked if you found anything." Autumn lifted the brow over her hazel eye—the right eye. "Are you okay?"

"I'm fine. It's just—" No use in bringing up Tawnia again. Autumn couldn't help her appearance.

"I know I'm a mess." Autumn looked at her clothes. "But my arm feels a lot better, thanks to you." She turned back to the water. "I thought they'd find him today."

"I'm sorry."

"You don't have to be. Whatever happens, Winter wouldn't want me to be unhappy."

Bret smiled. "How did he get a name like that? Did his parents really call him Winter?"

"He was born Douglas Rayne, spelled R-A-Y-N-E, but his friends called him Winter because he went white so early. I never saw him with any color in his hair. He says it happened when he was serving in the army overseas. He saw action in, well, I'd say Budapest, but that's probably wrong. Geography isn't my strong point. When he met Summer—that's my mother, and it's her real name, believe it or not—the nickname stuck even more. He finally went and had his whole name legally changed before they got married."

"Well, it makes sense then. I guess."

"They were special people." She lifted her chin defensively. "Weird, I'll admit, but special."

"If I'd called my parents by their first names, I would have gotten a spanking." He hoped the words would make her smile.

She looked at him steadily, her face expressionless. "I wish I'd called them Mom and Dad." Her eyes dropped as she added, "Now that they're gone."

Silence, deep and uncomfortable, fell between them. Bret didn't know what to do. Christian would have had this woman laughing inside a few seconds, while he seemed only to bring out the worst in her.

"Look, I'm sorry, okay? I didn't mean to . . . I don't know.

It's hard to know what to . . . I just came to see if you're all right. The arm and everything."

Her smile was back now. "You sound about two years old, you know? Like your mom caught you with your hand in the cookie jar."

He laughed. "That's pretty much how I feel. I'm glad your arm's feeling better. Let me know if you need anything."

"You leaving?"

Was that regret he saw in her face? "No, I'm about to go take a peek inside that boat."

She looked over her shoulder. "That's the one that hit the bridge." The words came stiffly. For the first time he noticed the sheen of sweat on her forehead under the unruly top mass of red-dyed hair. By contrast, the brown part underneath hung limply, shiny against her neck. Had she even combed it today? She certainly hadn't washed it.

"Yeah. I think the FBI and the other authorities have been through it already, but I'm curious. The captain and the crew claim they were heading right under the lift. They say there's no way they would have hit it if the bridge operator had done his job, but some think they actually hit the side, not the lift itself, which would indicate they're lying."

"What do you think?"

He shook his head. "It's impossible to tell from the video angle, however much they fiddle with it. And I don't like to guess."

"Sometimes life is guessing." She tilted her head as she spoke, looking so much like Tawnia it was uncanny. But Tawnia was from Kansas and Autumn from Oregon. They had no connection.

"Yeah." He nodded at her and started for the boat.

To his surprise, she came along. When he lifted a brow at her, she shrugged. "I'm curious, too. Do you mind?"

"No." He slowed his pace to match hers. She was moving carefully, as though every step jarred her arm, and he wondered if she was in pain.

The boat was roped off and watched by the young guard currently in charge of keeping sightseers out of the entire area. He came toward them as they arrived at the boat. He was just a boy, really, with light brown hair and average features, someone no one would look at twice in a crowd. When he saw Bret's ID badge, he let him onto the deck. "You'll need this key for what remains of the crew quarters," he said, tossing it to him. "Unless you want to climb in through the top."

Bret looked up where the top part of the boat should have been. Not an easy climb for someone with a broken arm. "Thanks."

"Just see that you lock up and get it back to me before you leave the site."

"Sure."

"They'll be taking off the cargo tomorrow or the next day," the guard added. "It's been cleared. What are you looking for, anyway?"

"I don't know." Bret started up the ramp that led onto the ship. "Anything that stands out."

"They found a bottle of gin inside the part that was cut off," the guard volunteered. "That's about it. The captain was supposedly on the bridge when it hit, but they found him on the deck, safe. He must have jumped. There were people in the crew quarters below the bridge, and they had their ceiling torn right off. Must have been weird, one minute having a ceiling and the next, nothing."

"The captain was drinking?" Bret had read the report, but there hadn't been anything about alcohol.

"He swears not. But he doesn't remember anything. He said he was at the wheel, and the next thing he knows, someone's shaking him awake."

"Odd."

"Well, he hit his head pretty badly. They were lucky there were no injuries."

"There were plenty of injuries," Autumn retorted.

The young man nodded at her, his cheeks going red. He seemed even younger than before. "Sorry about your loss, ma'am." He obviously knew Autumn by sight and, like all the other workers, afforded her a cautious respect. Bret noticed that his gaze didn't exactly meet Autumn's. It was a sight he himself had grown accustomed to after his brother died. People didn't know how to treat you after a tragedy—which made perfect sense, because even after more than a year, Bret still didn't know how to act when meeting someone who had known Christian.

Autumn nodded at the guard's apology and turned away.

"Did you hear anything else?" Bret asked.

The guard shook his head. "Only that the captain swears he was dead center. He says the bridge operator did something wrong."

"The bridge operator was interviewed thoroughly. He claimed the captain was coming on too fast, but that it would have been fine if he hadn't hit the side."

"The side definitely hit something. That's for sure."

"I don't see any damage." Bret studied the boat.

"It's on the other side."

"But it hit the right side of the bridge, not the left."

"The boat's turned around. You can see it if you walk to

the other side. What we can't say is if the damage happened before or after the first impact." The guard took a few steps back. "Well, I'll leave you now. I've got to do the rounds. You wouldn't believe how many people come to gawk. They really get in the way."

"Thanks again."

The boat's deck was full of huge plastic transport containers. A few of the containers were open, exposing cardboard boxes that were in turn filled with cargo, but most of the containers were shut tight. Bret sighed at the impossibility of finding anything here.

"Like looking for a needle in a haystack," he murmured.

"It doesn't look this big from the shore," Autumn commented.

"Let's walk to the other side of the deck. I want to see the damage there."

Sure enough, the metal on the far side was deeply scraped and dented. Several sections of metal were missing. What remained of the crew quarters was caved in on this side, and some other structure—a stack of some sort?—had been ripped off and thrown into the rest of the boat. But had the boat hit the side of the bridge and then bounced into the lift, sheering off the top? Or had it happened in the reverse? Or more nearly simultaneously, as the video coverage hinted?

Bret shook his head. A waste of time, this. Robert was right. The fact remained that even allowing for the extra weight of the missing part of the boat, the math and the measurements of the equipment didn't lie: the boat couldn't have caused such extensive damage unless the bridge was otherwise damaged. And Robert's records would have shown that.

Unless Robert had forged them.

Bret had a hard time thinking such a thing. Yes, Robert

was worried about shouldering the blame—he'd admitted that already—but even if maintenance records could be forged, the current readings couldn't be manipulated, and they supported Robert's records. Besides, Robert seemed sincere.

Yet something didn't add up.

They walked past the containers and went below, where they were greeted with more of the same. Bret wondered if authorities would have to go through all the cargo. Probably not, since the cargo seemed to be incidental to the accident. Still, what if the cargo was somehow illegal? What if the accident had been sabotage of some sort to take something quickly off the boat when chaos ensued?

Then it would likely be gone already. Bret shook himself. He wasn't the type to envision what-ifs. He only wanted the facts.

Fact: the Hawthorne Bridge had collapsed.

Fact: the boat couldn't have caused the collapse alone.

Fact: the bridge had stress fractures and needed some repairs but shouldn't have collapsed on its own.

Fact: Robert had somehow misplaced his tools, but Bret had used the county's better ones for his tests. The test verified that the bridge shouldn't have collapsed.

So what was he missing? There must be a piece of evidence yet to be found.

"Let's go see the crew quarters," Autumn said.

Bret let them in with the key, though there were several broken windows and he wondered why anyone bothered with a key at all. "What a mess." Garbage, pieces of metal, and a scattering of bedding and personal belongings. Apparently, everyone had been in a hurry to leave. Understandable, given the events. Overhead the sun was sinking into the west, and its light shown on the few cirrus clouds above, turning them into bright pink and orange streaks in the sky.

Autumn shivered. "It's just not right, seeing sky from in here."

"I know what you mean." He started looking in the lockers, slowly going over everything. The police had already been here and the FBI. What did he think he could find?

Autumn sat on one of the intact lower sleeping berths. On the floor near her feet was a brightly colored wooden chest about the size of a six-pack cooler. She picked it up with her good hand and looked inside.

"There was a child on board," she said. "Look, crayons, clay, and a coloring book."

With her left hand she clumsily unwrapped a corner of the huge piece of red clay, tore off a chunk, and began kneading it. "I used to love clay."

Bret slowly finished his search, hoping to find a scrap of paper with a clue. Or perhaps diving gear with remains of materials that signaled some sort of sabotage to the bridge. When he opened the next locker, he was surprised to see a pair of fins belonging to a diving suit. But what did that say anyway? He was on a boat. It was only natural that some member of the crew was interested in diving, though what use fins would be on a commercial boat, he wasn't sure. The captain wasn't likely to stop and let the crew have fun diving when he was on a deadline. What about the rest of the suit? Perhaps the authorities had confiscated it to run tests, just in case. He'd have to remember to ask if they'd found anything.

Autumn was rolling the red clay into a snake on her pant leg. She didn't look well. Her eyes had taken on a glazed look, and every so often, she gave a small shudder as though she was cold.

He sat on the bed next to her. "Autumn?"

"Hmm?"

"You okay?"

"I was thinking about Summer. We used to make all sorts of things out of clay. Pots and stuff. Sometimes we sold them at the store. Like for a dollar or something. I felt rich."

It took him a moment to understand that she was talking about her mother and not the season. He reached out and touched the hand that held the clay. It was like touching a rock on a hot day. She had a fever, and what was he supposed to do now?

"Let's get you home."

"I can't go home. He needs me."

"You have to rest."

"I can feel him, or something. I can't sleep. I need . . ." Her face crumpled, and she whispered, "Oh, Winter. Daddy." Tears leaked from her eyes, yet she wasn't exactly crying.

Bret hesitantly put his arms around her. "It'll be okay," he whispered. "Not tomorrow or next week, or even months from now, but it does get better."

The words calmed her, though she didn't reply.

He released her and stood, gently urging her to her feet. "I'll drive you home."

"We should have had Spring. Then I wouldn't be alone." She slumped back down on the thin mattress.

She wasn't making any sense, but then people with fevers often didn't. He wondered if he should take her back to the clinic or to her store. But who would watch her? He had a job to do, and he certainly couldn't get her cleaned up. She needed another woman. Too bad she seemed to have cut herself off from all her friends.

He considered the options. None of them would do Autumn any good, and that meant he needed to find another alternative. But what? Well, maybe he needed to do what he was doing with the bridge—start with the facts: Autumn wouldn't go home, and she needed help, preferably a woman's.

Of course, the biggest fact of all had been staring him in the face, but he had overlooked the possible meaning until now. "Are you adopted?" he asked.

She opened only one eye, the blue one on the left, as though it was too much effort to respond.

"Well?"

"It only meant they loved me more." Her voice was low and sleepy.

He had to call Tawnia. She hadn't expressed interest in finding her birth family, but maybe she would feel differently after meeting Autumn. Their similarity might be a family connection, however distant. At the very least she could help with getting Autumn clean and dressed in something other than the dirty jeans and sweatshirt. It wasn't just an excuse to call her. It wasn't.

He took out his phone, hoping she would answer.

*H*ands full of plastic grocery sacks and her purse in her mouth, Tawnia struggled to open her front door. Inside, she dropped her purse on the chair in her tiny living room, kicking the door shut with her foot. She was starving and angry.

The day had gone from bad to worse. First her car repair had taken an hour longer than promised, and then she'd spent another hour trying to find her way home from the grocery store. She'd printed out the directions from her computer at work, and it seemed simple enough to get there. But the directions had dead-ended into street construction, and she was positive the detour signs had been placed by a madman whose only goal was to make her life miserable. When she finally found the right street, after stopping to ask directions three times, she'd missed her turn not once but twice and had to circle around through the construction again.

Staggering into the kitchen, she plopped the sacks onto the small round table. There were deep red marks on her wrists where the sacks had dug into her flesh. She slumped into a chair, pulling out a half-eaten bag of chips from one of the sacks. Baked, because she knew she'd eat the whole bag, and while she didn't have to worry about her weight now, her mother insisted there would come a time when she would. Her mother had gained twenty pounds when she hit fifty. Being slim was one thing they'd always had in common, despite their lack of shared genes, and Tawnia thought her mother mourned the loss of their being alike more than the actual weight gain.

Tawnia sighed as she thought about her mother. She was all about appearances and the proper way to go about life. Some things you simply didn't discuss in any company—like adoption. They had not told even Tawnia about her origin, leaving the discovery to an accident when she was five.

"I don't know where she gets the talent for drawing," her mother said, coming into her bedroom, *"but she is very good."*

Six-year-old Tawnia was sitting on the floor of her parents' walk-in closet because it had shelves just the right size to make her Barbies a three-story house. She hadn't expected to be bothered here since her mother had been in the kitchen and her father hadn't yet come home from work.

"Maybe her birth mother was an artist," her father replied. *"You know how irresponsible those kinds of people are."*

"Well, environment has a lot to do with raising a child too," her mother said with a sniff. *"That means us. We'll teach her to work and to succeed. She's a good little girl. And so beautiful. I couldn't have hoped for more if I'd had her myself."*

"Even her eyes?"

"That can't be helped. Really, Sherman, we must look at the good side of things."

"I am, and you are right. She's a special girl."

Tawnia sat frozen, wondering at what she had heard. Birth mother? What did that mean? And what was wrong with her eyes? She stood and walked to the doorway of the closet. Her parents were kissing right there in front of her, and they never did that.

Her mother looked over and saw her. She drew away from her husband. "Tawnia, what are you doing here? I thought you went to your room to play."

Tawnia tried to point to her Barbies to explain, but the words wouldn't come. "What's a birth mother?" she said instead.

They had explained what adoption was, and for a week Tawnia had been scared that something terrible was going to happen. That maybe her birth mother would come to snatch her away. But the week passed, and nothing unusual occurred, so she put it in the back of her mind.

She was eight before she realized what they had meant about her eyes, and by age ten she'd been fitted for a contact lens to hide the defect.

These chips were doing nothing for her hunger. She'd have to put in the frozen pizza she'd bought. A nice one with thick green peppers and mushrooms and sausage. Hopefully the precooked crust wasn't too awful.

She'd changed into black stretch pants and a T-shirt and barely sat down to eat the pizza when her phone began ringing. Her parents probably.

Or maybe it was Bret.

Tripping over the legs of her chair, she scrambled to her feet to reach her purse in the living room. *Please don't hang up.* Her hand closed over the phone. She checked the caller ID. It *was* Bret!

"Hello?" She tried not to sound out of breath.

"Tawnia."

"Hi. Who's this?" She faked nonchalance.

"Bret."

"Oh, hi, Bret. How's Nevada?"

"It was fine when I left."

"Left?"

"Yeah. I'm in Portland. That's part of why I'm calling. I, uh, got called in to do an independent review of the collapse of the Hawthorne Bridge."

"You did?" She should have known. He loved overwater bridges and had been quite chummy with some of the county officials they'd met last year during their visit.

"Yeah. Odd, huh? The county called when it happened and invited me to come."

He loved bridges, that was true, but could he have also come partly because of her? No, she shouldn't assume anything. It had to be only because of the bridge. That was his passion. "The company I work for is doing publicity on the bridge," she told him. "Not my team, but a group from my company." If she'd won the account, she could have interviewed Bret extensively. It might have taken days. Longer, if she stretched it out.

Stop, she told herself. There was a reason she'd left Nevada, and Bret figured into that. No use clinging to a relationship that was going nowhere.

"I heard something about a marketing firm. Didn't know it was yours."

"Interesting stuff. So why did the bridge collapse?"

"To tell the truth, I haven't a clue. It shouldn't have. Nothing adds up."

"The public won't buy that."

"I know. I'll have to go with the best theory in the end. I haven't visited the other bridges yet, but I'll do that this week. They want to be sure the rest are safe."

"That would go a long way toward helping the county

recover. I hear they've already got lawsuits brought against them. You'll probably be called as a witness."

Bret sighed. "Probably."

"So." She walked back into the kitchen and sat down at the table. Was he going to ask her out? Or did he call to talk? She nibbled on the edge of her pizza.

"Look, Tawnia, I have a little problem, and I need help."

The air rushed from her chest. He needed help. Of course. A man in a strange city has a problem, and he calls the one person he knows for help. He wasn't calling to say that he'd made the biggest mistake of his life. Or to admit that he couldn't live without her.

"What's wrong?" she asked, keeping all expression from her voice.

"Honestly, I wouldn't have called you if I hadn't thought you'd want to know. I would have taken her to the clinic, or something, except for her . . . well, you have to see for yourself."

"What are you talking about? I don't understand."

"It's this woman. She was on the bridge when it fell. Her father's one of the missing people, and she goes there every day in the hope that they'll find him. I took her to a clinic last night and found she'd actually broken her arm in the fall. For three days she'd gone around with that arm. It's really sad. And now she's got a fever, and I don't know what to do. She's dirty. Needs a bath. I don't think she's combed her hair since the collapse."

"Doesn't she have friends?" Tawnia didn't want to feel pity for this woman who was apparently important enough to Bret that he would call and ask for her help.

"I've seen a guy who works in her father's store and a fireman who pulled her from the river. If there's anyone else, I don't know about them. I only know her because I'm snooping around to find clues about what really happened."

His words made Tawnia shiver. "What do you mean? Is there something about the bridge you're not telling me?"

"No. Or at least I don't think so. I'm trying to find out."

"You should take the woman to a doctor."

"I would but, really, Tawnia, I think you should come. There's something I want to show you."

"About her?"

"Yes."

"Can't you just tell me?"

"I'd rather you see for yourself."

This was getting stranger by the moment.

"So are you going to help me here?" he asked. "We're at a shop she owns right now, and she won't tell me where she lives. The only other thing I can do is take her back to my hotel. It might not get her clean, but I can't leave her here alone."

Oh, so that's how it was. Tawnia knew the type. No doubt the woman was a bleached, overly made up tramp in risqué clothing who would pretend to be helpless until she got her hooks into Bret, and then he'd pay in a hundred ways. As miffed as she was at him this minute, she couldn't let that happen. He was such an innocent in the ways of the world. "Where are you?"

"At a place called Autumn's Antiques. Got something to write on? I'll give you the address. It's next to an herb shop and across from a restaurant called Smokey's. Maybe you know it."

"Smokey's? I've been there." Her stomach growled at the thought of those delicious meat pies. For all his conniving, Dustin had at least given her that.

"Can you find your way here?" Bret's voice showed his doubt.

"I work near there."

"Good, because I'm sort of tied up here. I don't know what I'd do if you got lost and I had to come find you."

There was a hint of laughter in his voice, and Tawnia steeled herself against it. So what if he remembered how hopeless she was at finding addresses? It didn't mean anything.

"I'll be there in twenty minutes, twenty-five tops." That was allowing for a few wrong turns, but he didn't need to know that.

"Thanks. I really appreciate it. And I'm really looking forward to seeing you."

She froze. Had he actually said that? Or had it been her wishful thinking? Well, it didn't matter because she wasn't going to dwell on it. "I'll see you in a bit." She hung up.

Taking a huge bite of pizza, she clumped around the kitchen, placing dishes in the sink and making sure the oven was off. "I can't believe this," she complained through sausage and peppers. "Three months since we've spoken, and now he suddenly calls me to help with this woman. Would he have even called me if he hadn't met this tramp? He's just a stupid, stupid man. I hate men!"

She stood over the garbage can with the rest of her pizza but then took another huge bite and another. No use in letting a man ruin perfectly good sausage and cheese. The crust wasn't that bad, either. She'd have to remember the brand name.

Gathering her purse, she was nearly out to her car when she noticed what she was wearing. Her mother's voice ran through her head. "No, dear, that's not what to wear when you want to impress a man." In this case she was probably right, and the last thing Tawnia wanted was to look like a frump when she saw Bret. Three more minutes were lost as she changed to chocolate cords and a white shirt topped with a thin, multicolored sweater. This was more attractive, at least, though it made her look about twenty.

She left the bungalow, running a brush through her hair

to freshen her look. A bit of lipstick once she arrived would be the final touch.

Like I even care what he thinks.

But she did care, and that was the part she couldn't figure out. They had decided it wouldn't work between them.

No, he had decided.

But she had agreed.

It was that simple. She'd moved on, as she had at other times with other men in her life. When something wasn't working, it didn't pay to hold on, to get in too deeply that others became involved. Others, like children. Better to call it quits before more complication entered the equation.

All the streets looked different at night, but just when she had begun to suspect that she was lost she spied Smokey's, the sign illuminating the street. From the look of the place, the restaurant was completely crowded. Maybe after she helped Bret with this woman, they could swing by for something to eat. Bret was a man who didn't mind that she could out eat him.

Smiling, she drove down the street until she found an open spot to park. Good thing it was a Tuesday and not a weekend, or she would probably have been out of luck.

She looked into the mirror, checking her hair and applying lipstick. She was ready. It was then she noticed she was wearing the navy pumps she'd worn to work and they didn't match her brown outfit.

Well, it was dark. Besides, what did anyone expect being called out on an emergency like this? She was lucky she had shoes on at all. Good thing her mother wasn't here.

She had to walk half a block to get back to the antiques shop. All the other shops nearby were closed, but there was a faint light on inside Autumn's Antiques. As she approached, the glass door swung open.

"Tawnia!" Bret looked good. Instead of his usual dress pants and shirt, he wore jeans, work boots, and a blue T-shirt that made his eyes bluer and his hair blonder. She didn't have time to take in more before he whisked her into a hug. Not a careful hug between acquaintances but one that showed he was glad to see her. She tried not to let the emotion become important because she understood his motives were mixed at best and completely selfish at worst, though she had never considered him selfish before. But wasn't that what it was called when you were too wrapped up in your own pain to care about how much you hurt others?

"Bret," she murmured as he set her back to look at her. His eyes ran over every part of her face as though starved for the sight. The intensity frightened her because she had the distinct sensation he wasn't really seeing *her.*

"I was right," he said.

"What?"

"Come on. You'll see." He pulled her inside the store, his hand locked onto hers.

"Bret, what's going on?" She was beginning to feel frightened, though Bret had never before given her any reason to fear for her safety. Had he become someone entirely different over the past three months?

"Her name's Autumn. I met her yesterday. She's the one who's sick. Only there's more than that, and I think it has something to do with you." They were at the back of the store now, and she could see the light coming from an open door leading to some kind of back room. The rest of the store was dim and filled with old furniture and knickknacks. She felt as if she were in some kind of museum in the middle of the night.

He'd stopped and was staring at her again, outlined as she

was by the light from the back room. "You're wearing your contact."

"I just got home from work. Sort of." She felt it was an excuse, though her choices were absolutely none of his business. So what if she hadn't been wearing the contact on the day they'd first met? Christian had that effect on people. You wanted to be unusual around him. You wanted to stand out—even if you'd spent your life trying to be ordinary. Normal.

Bret's hand reached out and slid along the curve of her cheek, but he said nothing, and she didn't know what to say, either. She'd thought they had said it all, and yet the connection she felt here was almost tangible. How long they stood like that, she couldn't say. She didn't care if it was forever.

Bret gave his head a sharp jerk. "Autumn's in there. And this is her store, if I didn't tell you before." He waved a hand at the shadowy objects that seemed more menacing by the minute. "She was born in Portland, or so she believes." His hand was on her back, burning fire into her skin as they went through the narrow door together.

Immediately Tawnia saw the woman lying on her side on an easy chair, her face away from the door. The foot rest was open, but she had her feet pulled up to the seat and tucked under the blanket that was covering her. She was thin, that much Tawnia could see despite the blanket. She had short brown hair, dyed red on top, and her face was flushed. The illness didn't seem to be an act; the woman shivered with fever.

Tawnia walked around to the other side, her hand out to touch the woman's forehead, a silly gesture because she really had no idea what a fever felt like. In the next instant, she froze as she saw the woman's face. The upturned nose, the angle of the cheekbones, the chin—everything was familiar. Sharper than she was accustomed to seeing, but familiar. Too familiar. A warmth crashed over Tawnia, a feeling that had to be some kind of shock.

"Autumn, I brought a friend to help you." Bret touched the woman's shoulder.

Her eyes opened, and Tawnia received another shock. Her muscles were still frozen in place, but she heard a gasp escape her lips. Those were *her* eyes.

The mismatched eyes blinked, but they didn't appear to see Tawnia. They fluttered closed. Slowly, Tawnia leaned closer, grabbing the top edge of the chair for support.

"She's adopted," Bret said. "Just like you. At first I thought she *was* you. That you'd changed your hair, lost too much weight, but she didn't know me, and after talking to her, I realized there are a lot of differences in speech and stuff. But there's a lot alike, too. A couple of times I almost forgot she wasn't you."

"How old is she?" Tawnia's voice came out a whisper. Her world had tilted into something unexplainable.

"I don't know. This is only the second time I've seen her. We spent several hours getting her arm set last night. We talked then, but age never came up. Do you think you and she could be related?"

Tawnia wanted to say no, but how could she? She knew nothing of her birth parents or how many other children, cousins, or siblings they might have. "I don't know. It's possible, but I've heard of unrelated people looking like each other."

"This close?" He sounded doubtful. "You could be twins."

"We need to get her into a bed somewhere."

"Where?"

"My house."

Bret met her gaze. "Are you sure?"

"Well, I'm trusting you that she's not an axe murderer."

A smile tugged at his lips. "I don't think so. But she's pretty messed up. Her mother died a long time ago, and now her father's missing. He was on the bridge with her." His voice lowered. "And you know what that means."

"Autumn?" Tawnia gently shook the woman's shoulder until the eyes opened again. "I'm Tawnia, and I'm going to help you. Will you come with me?"

Autumn sighed and shut her eyes.

"You're just going to have to carry her to my car," Tawnia told Bret.

"Are you sure we shouldn't take her to the hospital?"

"It's just a fever. She'll probably be a lot better in the morning. My mother always says that you can have a fever for three days before it's really serious. At least if you're not throwing up or having other symptoms."

As an afterthought, she added, "Does she have other symptoms?"

"I'm just tired."

They both looked at Autumn, who had opened her eyes again and was struggling to sit up. "You don't have any pain?" Bret asked.

"Just my arm." She patted her right arm that was hidden under the sweatshirt.

"You don't have any dizziness or sensitivity to light?" Tawnia asked, which was one of the questions her mother asked every time she had the flu, though even if Autumn said yes, she wouldn't know what to do except take her to the doctor.

Autumn shook her head slowly. "No. I'm just really tired. I have a few more pills left from those the clinic gave me. I feel weird when I take them, but it kills the pain."

"Where are they?" Bret began looking around.

"Bathroom. On the sink."

He found the pills, filled up a glass of water, and handed one to her. "I think you should go with Tawnia. She lives nearby. You can clean up at her house."

"I have to be at the river tomorrow."

"I work near here," Tawnia said. "I'll bring you back."

"Okay." Autumn let her eyes shut.

Bret had to pull her up from the chair. "Come on, then." To Tawnia, he added, "I'll follow you to make sure you get her settled."

Tawnia was glad. She was having second thoughts about taking this woman in, even for one night. There could be dozens of unseen repercussions.

Why does she look so much like me?

"You could be twins," Bret had said.

Twins. That was impossible, and yet as Tawnia stared at Autumn, she felt something move within her. Tears gathered in her eyes.

"Are you okay?" Bret asked, struggling to balance Autumn on her feet.

Tawnia nodded. "Do you see anything she might need?"

"I don't know. This is the first time I've been here."

Tawnia scanned the small room, looking for a purse, but found nothing. "Let's go, then." She led the way to her car, with Bret half-carrying Autumn, though the night air seemed to bring her back to life somewhat.

"Why does she look like me?" Autumn said in a loud whisper. "It's like looking into a mirror, only in reverse. Is she the woman you told me about?" She tripped and let out a short laugh. "I don't know where my feet are. Do I still have feet? That would be so funny if I didn't have feet."

She had feet, Tawnia noticed, but they were bare. There hadn't been any shoes in the back room at the store.

Bret steered Autumn away from a street lamp. "The medicine must be working."

"I do feel funny." Autumn hiccupped and then giggled.

Tawnia opened the back door to her car, helping Bret push Autumn inside. Tawnia locked the door just in case.

With Bret following in his car, Tawnia carefully retraced her path to the bungalow. Now would not be the time to get lost, with Bret tailing her and Autumn lying in the back seat, giggling quietly to herself. Wait, it was quiet now. Maybe she'd fallen asleep.

In front of the bungalow, they helped Autumn from the car. Tawnia scooped up the blanket before it could hit the ground, pulling it over Autumn's shoulders. One of her neighbors was sitting on his porch, watching them with undisguised interest and making Tawnia wish the street lights weren't so bright. She gave him a friendly wave, hoping he wouldn't think it odd of her to bring a drunk-looking woman and a man to her house after nine o'clock.

As she helped Autumn into the house, she caught a whiff of something sour. Definitely a bath was a good idea. She'd wash all of Autumn's clothes and the blanket too.

"Cozy place," Bret commented.

"It's not big, but it was a good price, and I was tired of apartments. I can have flowers here."

"I saw them."

"Those are the landlady's. She comes to water them every day, though I told her I'd do it. I think she comes to chat with the neighbors. She lives with her daughter now, but I think she misses it here."

Bret nodded.

Stop babbling, Tawnia told herself.

Bret waited in the living room while Tawnia helped Autumn down the hall toward the bathroom. She was no longer giggling but seemed morose and withdrawn. Fever still flushed her face.

"They said she shouldn't unwrap that cast for three days," Bret called after them. "But after that she can take it off to shower. In a week she's supposed to take it off permanently."

"Then I just walk around with a broken arm," Autumn muttered darkly.

"It'll probably be healed enough by then." Tawnia started filling the bath with warm water, adding in a large amount of bubble bath. Then she helped Autumn undress and step into the water, pulling the curtain most of the way for a modicum of privacy. The shirt Autumn had been wearing under the big sweatshirt smelled awful and the shoulder was ripped. But the bandage on her shoulder looked clean and fresh.

"I'll help you with your hair," Tawnia offered. Kneeling by the bathtub, she leaned over and washed Autumn's hair gently, silently, rinsing it with bath water she scooped up in her hands. With a wet rag, she rubbed dirt from the fingers on Autumn's broken arm, propped on the edge of the bath. She felt a strange sort of contentment in the motions of helping this stranger who seemed to be someone she knew.

"Thank you," Autumn whispered. Her eyes were shut, but her fingers closed over Tawnia's.

"You'd do the same for me," Tawnia said, somehow knowing it was true.

"He was wrong about your eyes. They aren't like mine."

Tawnia went to the sink and found her contact supplies. In seconds, she removed the contact, feeling Autumn's eyes on her. Then she sat by the bath and opened her eyes for Autumn to see.

Autumn's mouth fell open slightly. "So that's why he was so freaked out."

Freaked out. That was putting her own feelings mildly, though Tawnia had been raised never to use such words.

"I feel all fuzzy," Autumn murmured. "This is all a dream, isn't it? I'm going to wake up in my store, and Winter will still be missing."

"Winter?" Was she hallucinating?

"My father." Tears dripped down Autumn's face, disappearing into the bubbles.

"I'm sorry." Tawnia didn't know what to say. "I think we've soaked off most of the dirt. Let's get you out of here. Can you stand? You can put on my robe while I dry your hair with this towel. Then I'll find you something else to put on."

She helped Autumn out of the tub and into her thick, red terry-cloth robe that her mother had bought her last Christmas. She wrapped a towel around Autumn's hair.

Autumn moved slowly. "I think I need to lie down."

"Come on." Tawnia took her to her own bed and put the covers over her, robe and all. She walked to the door and turned out the light. "Call me if you need me."

"Can you stay awhile?"

"Sure." Tawnia went to sit on the edge of the bed. Autumn's left hand reached for hers. From the light spilling in from the hallway, Tawnia could see the tears on her cheeks.

"It's gone," Autumn whispered. "The feeling. I thought it was Winter, but it wasn't. It was you all along. It was you. You came."

Tawnia didn't understand a thing Autumn was saying, but

somehow it made sense. She had come to Portland for a reason. Maybe tonight she had discovered that reason. How or why didn't matter.

"It's going to be okay." Tawnia's own tears slid down her face.

She held Autumn's hand until the regular breathing told her she was asleep. That was when she remembered Bret. She found him lying on the couch in her living room, one arm sprawled out toward the floor, his mouth slightly open. She had the urge to lie down next to him and curl that arm around her cold body.

Sighing, she picked up the remote and silenced the small television. Bret started, coming to a seated position, one hand over his mouth to stifle a yawn.

"You need me?" he asked.

"No. She's asleep. I think the medicine is doing something to her."

"Doesn't help that she probably hasn't eaten."

Tawnia sat down next to him. "I didn't think of that. I'll make sure she gets a good breakfast tomorrow."

"And then what?"

"I don't know. I can't stay home. It's my first week on the job."

"Neither can I." He sighed before adding hopefully, "Maybe she'll be better."

"Maybe. But she can't stay down at the river like that. She has to go back to her life."

"Has to?" His brow furrowed. "Why? What if she doesn't want to?"

"Are we talking about her or you?"

He glared at her without speaking as long seconds ticked by.

Then he let out another sigh and allowed his face to relax. "I guess I deserved that."

He deserved more, but she wasn't going to pursue the matter. Their story was in the past. She was more interested in Autumn and the warmth that had filled her heart from the moment she'd seen her face. "When they find her father, she'll be able to deal with it better." She spoke with sureness, though she didn't really know Autumn. Or did she?

"The likeness," he began.

"Tell me everything about her."

"I don't know anything besides her name and the names of her parents—Winter and Summer Rain. Only Winter had another name. Can't remember what at the moment. Oh, and the last name was spelled differently. You'll have to ask her in the morning."

"I will." Excitement and anticipation rose inside her. "I think she's the reason I came here."

Bret arched a brow. "What?"

"Five different states in ten years. I kept moving." She couldn't say what she was really feeling, that perhaps she'd been searching for Autumn, because that was too personal and too strange for someone like her who was raised to always do the proper thing.

"If you didn't find her, you might have moved again."

She shook her head. "No." Then feeling suddenly doubtful, she added, "Maybe. But I'm going to follow this through. All my life I've wondered where I came from. It's time I learned."

"And if there's no connection?"

"You've seen her face. You brought us together. How can you doubt?"

"I don't know. Stranger things have happened." He stood,

stretching his arms in the air. "I'd better get going. I need to be at work early tomorrow."

She walked him to the door, realizing that she had nothing more to say to him. He'd rejected her once, and she wasn't about to pave the way for another shot.

At the door, he turned and looked at her. "This didn't work out the way I'd planned. I called you this morning. Thought maybe we could go out for dinner or something. Sorry it got messed up."

Tawnia decided to give him the benefit of the doubt—for now. "You did the right thing asking me to help." Of course Autumn still might be a drug addict or a lazy woman who leeched off others, but her heart told her something different. Tawnia hadn't been much good at following her heart, and the few times she'd tried, it hadn't worked out, but in Autumn she saw something worth the risk.

Bret looked as though he wanted to say something more. His eyes dropped to her lips, a sure sign in the past that he was going to kiss her. He was endearingly clumsy that way. She steeled herself, not knowing how she should react. She didn't need him in her life. She didn't want the problems. It wasn't as though they were still dating now. He'd made certain of that.

"Look, it's just not working," he said, shaking his head. "I can't . . ." He didn't finish, and she was stung into a reply.

"You mean you can't get past that I went out with your brother, or that I was the last one to see him alive?"

"It's just that I wonder if he'd lived, what would have happened?"

"What does it matter? I was Christian's friend. We worked together. I admired him—everyone did. He was talented and funny, and he had a way of making a woman feel beautiful." Not

like you, she'd wanted to add but didn't because that wouldn't be true. She would only have said it to hurt him. "But he died. We'll never know any more than that."

"I see him every time I look at you."

She knew that wasn't true. When he kissed her, he had no vision of his brother. This was an excuse. An excuse not to be happy without Christian, and a year was more than enough time to have waited. "Then I guess there's nothing more to say." She'd turned and left his apartment on foot, angry that he couldn't have chosen a more convenient place to break the news.

She called a taxi. The closest she came to looking back was sending him an e-mail telling him of her impending move. He'd called her then, and they'd chatted casually, which left a sour feeling when they hung up. To herself she admitted she'd been fishing for something more. Not that it had mattered then.

Or now.

Something in her expression must have registered in his brain, because abruptly he nodded and stepped backward. Or perhaps he realized what he was doing and came to his senses. "I'll call tomorrow. See how you two are doing. If you need anything, give me a call."

"I will." She watched him go, irritation at him flaring in her chest. At least irritation was better than longing. That much she had already learned.

awnia examined the fever strip in her hand, the one
her mother had packed in her emergency kit when
she had first left Kansas. It read 100. Too high to
be normal, but not so high as to elicit immediate worry. Then
again, since it was on the forehead and not internal, you had
to add a degree. Or was it two? She couldn't remember. Either
way it wasn't horribly high, and Autumn wasn't exhibiting any
other signs.

In fact, she was sleeping peacefully, still snuggled in
Tawnia's bed wearing her red robe. She appeared young and
vulnerable in her sleep, and Tawnia wondered if she looked the
same when sleeping. For though it was morning and plenty of
light spilled in from the window, the face on her pillow was still
hers. A slightly undernourished version perhaps, but hers all the
same. The upturned nose covered by a scattering of persistent
freckles, the high cheek bones, the shape of her cheek, and the
dimple in her chin. And don't forget the wide-set, mismatched
eyes. Those were the most notable of their similarities. Only

the fresh scar near Autumn's left eye and her short, red-dyed hair was different, though the under color, a medium brown, was the same as Tawnia's.

The resemblance in their faces might be explained away, but heterochromia was rare, and to have both the looks and the eyes . . . well, she wasn't a geneticist, but that couldn't happen often. Or maybe ever.

Even with a sibling?

Tawnia's heart thudded in her chest, almost too slowly. She could feel the pounding in her ears. Thud-thud, thud-thud.

What had bothered her most in her teen years about being adopted wasn't that her mother had given her up—she figured there were extenuating circumstances of some sort, be it a drug addiction or a teen pregnancy—but that somewhere out there she might have relatives, close ones that were living without her, never knowing she existed. Going along their merry lives loving each other. A grandmother, a brother, an aunt, a cousin. But she didn't even know if these mythical people existed, and they would never know about her. Neither felt the loss of the other. It just wasn't right.

Or was it? Didn't the new family make up for everything? The new family that wouldn't have been complete without the adopted child? Yes, it made up for an awful lot. It made up for everything else.

Tawnia guessed it was simply not knowing that bothered her. She liked everything in its place. She was like her mother in that—her adoptive mother.

Autumn had been adopted, too. What could that mean? Could she be a little cousin, born shortly after her own self? Yet to look so much like Tawnia. Surely even half siblings wouldn't resemble each other so much. It was ludicrous. Wasn't it?

Well, she wasn't going to learn anything staring at Autumn

all morning. If she didn't leave soon, she'd be late to work. She'd leave a note for when her guest awoke, telling her to help herself to anything in the kitchen.

What if she helped herself to more than just food? Tawnia decided to take her most valuable papers and belongings and leave them in her car trunk. That was who she was. Careful. Most everything could be replaced, except her identity and her jewelry.

A shiver ran through her. This woman could easily steal her identity. The thought made her question for the hundredth time if she was doing the right thing by letting Autumn stay at the bungalow. But what else could she do? Kick her out with a fever, dressed in nothing but that red robe? She felt a small comfort in knowing that at least Bret knew about the two of them. He should be able to tell them apart.

Sighing, Tawnia went to the minuscule closet and found a pair of jeans and a T-shirt. To this pile, she added underwear but no bra since Autumn hadn't been wearing one. These clothes seemed about Autumn's style, and at least she'd have something clean to wear when she awoke. In fact, if she threw Autumn's clothes in the washer right now, they'd be finished tonight and Autumn wouldn't have to borrow anything more. Tawnia wasn't good at sharing her clothes. Her mother had never smiled on borrowing, and since she didn't have a sister . . .

A sister.

Longing swift and deep sprang from somewhere inside her. It had been a long time since she'd dwelt upon her youthful desire for a sister. No, not a desire. A need. A deep, soul-shattering need.

Yet how could she feel such a deep longing for something she'd never known? Unless she actually had a sister somewhere. One she didn't remember.

No. The idea was too preposterous. Just her imagination going wild again.

Automatically checking the pockets of Autumn's jeans before throwing them in the washer, she found a few crumpled bills—twenties—a set of keys, and nothing more. Not a shred of ID. Of course not. If Autumn's story, and Bret's, was true, her ID was at the bottom of the Willamette River. Slamming the washer shut, Tawnia hurried around the bungalow, throwing papers and valuables into a plastic crate.

She was hurrying down her sidewalk with the crate when her landlady, Mrs. Gerbert made an appearance. Today the rotund figure was wearing all red, from the flattering wide-legged dress pants to the shirt that hung halfway to her knees. As on the first day they'd met, she wore a copious amount of eye shadow and gobs of mascara. Her cheeks and lips were painted red to match her outfit. Even her pointy flat shoes were red.

"Hi," Tawnia called. "Sorry, I can't talk now. I'm going to be late to work."

"No worries. Just came to water the flowers." She was peering over Tawnia's shoulder at the house.

"You must get up early." Then Tawnia realized her new neighbors had probably reported her late night activities to Mrs. Gerbert. She hoped they'd at least seen Bret leave. She'd signed a contract stating that aside from the occasional visitor, she'd be living alone. "I do have a girl who stayed the night with me," she hurried to say. "She wasn't feeling well, so I brought her here to look after her. In fact, she's still got a fever. I'm wondering if maybe I should take her to the doctor."

Mrs. Gerbert appeared relieved, and now that she could rest assured her house was not being used as a den of iniquity, she seemed eager to help. Or did she want to make sure Tawnia was telling the truth? "You go along, dear. I'll see to your friend.

I raised two children. I know all about fevers. They're mostly just the body's way of helping you heal. As long as it's not too hot or doesn't go on too long, fevers aren't usually dangerous."

"Thank you. I really appreciate it." At least Autumn wouldn't be able to walk off with much under the eye of this careful lady. "I was worried about leaving her alone."

"Well, go along now. You really don't want to be late your first week."

Tawnia balanced the crate on her hip and dug into her purse. "Look, here's my phone you can give to her. I'll call in a bit to see how she is." There was no phone at the bungalow; she hadn't seen a reason to install a land line as long as she had a mobile phone. If Autumn took off with it, she could always buy a new one.

With this unpleasant thought, she hurried to her car. She'd better not get lost, or she would most certainly be late. She hated not having enough time. When you were directionally challenged, you always made sure to leave plenty of time for mistakes, a buffer for wrong turns or road construction.

Worse than having no buffer, her stomach was terribly, achingly empty.

Autumn awoke to the glorious smell of something cooking. She couldn't tell what, but the smell was enough to rip her from the fevered dream in which she had been with her parents at the fair. That she was only eight or so and holding both their hands didn't bother her at all. She gladly would have stayed forever.

The food forced her back to a reality she wished she could avoid.

She wasn't at the store or at her apartment, but she wasn't

sure exactly where she'd ended up. She remembered being with Bret. Was this his place? But no, she was wearing a woman's red robe—not her own—and she seemed to remember a woman. A woman with her face.

No, that had been part of the dream. Yet she was in the dream bed, wearing the dream woman's clothing. How much was real?

She should feel hot with the robe and blanket, but she was comfortable. Her arm wasn't even aching that much, though the medicine had worn off.

Just as well, she thought. Hydrocodone was dangerous. First it made her giggle like an idiot and think about kissing Bret, and then it made her so depressed she wanted to throw herself off what remained of the Hawthorne Bridge. It made her ask a total stranger not to leave her alone and to hold her hand until she fell asleep.

Or had that part been the dream? Obviously, she shouldn't use the medication, except perhaps right before bedtime. That was when her arm hurt the worst anyway.

She stretched her legs languorously, looking at her surroundings. There was a dresser, a plain, straight-backed chair, and flowery curtains that matched the bedspread. Pictures in mismatched frames covered much of the space on every wall, some looking very ancient, though absolutely clean. It was a tiny room but seemed larger because it was uncluttered. Autumn felt a rush of longing for the apartment she shared with Winter, packed with memorabilia from their lives and the many antiques she couldn't bear to sell.

The aroma wafting in from the kitchen made her stomach growl. When was the last time she'd eaten? Memory eluded her.

Movement outside the door, and a heavyset woman dressed in red entered, looking flushed under the short, dark blond, tightly curled hair. Certainly not the face from her dreams. "Oh, thank heaven," the woman exclaimed. "You're finally awake. Feeling better? I hope so. You've nearly slept the day away."

"I have?" Autumn tried to rise on one hand. The light coming from the window was slanted too low to be morning. Just how late was it?

"Don't look alarmed, dear. It's okay to sleep when you're ill."

"My father. I should be at the river." She started to throw back the covers, but the woman clicked her tongue and drew them back over her.

"Not in your condition, young lady. I don't know who your father is, but he wouldn't want that."

"But—"

"No buts. For now, you need to eat."

Autumn's stomach *was* going crazy.

"I'll bring you a bowl of stew. Stew is just the thing for a fever."

Autumn had to take her word for that. She could never remember if she was supposed to starve a fever and feed a cold, or feed a fever and starve a cold, so she always fed everything. Her stomach liked it that way.

Before the woman completely disappeared, Autumn called out. "Wait. Did you hear if they found anyone else? From the Willamette, I mean. The bridge." The words felt like sawdust in her throat.

The woman returned to the room, her gaze resting gently on Autumn, who sat on the bed, her knees pulled to her chest. "The news said the Navy Seals found another body this morning."

"Who?"

"They didn't say. Except it's a woman. Poor thing."

Autumn sighed with relief. Until she realized that meant Winter was still under the water somewhere, trapped, with all sorts of river life swimming by or even crawling on his face. She let her head drop to her knees, not meaning to cry, but unable to help herself.

A hand landed on her head, stroking it comfortingly, just as her mother had done many years ago when she was sad or sick. Autumn took a deep, slow breath.

"What is it?"

"My father and I were on the bridge," Autumn said, her face still buried in the blanket over her knees. "He's one of the five that's still missing—or four, I mean, now that they found the woman."

"Oh, no." Other sounds of sympathy followed. "I didn't know. I'm so sorry, dear. I don't know quite what to say. It was a horrible, horrible accident."

Autumn nodded. Her tears had dried as suddenly as they'd started, and now she was feeling numb again. And hungry.

The hand left her head. "You'll feel better after you eat. My stew is pretty good, if I do say so myself. My husband said it was the best he ever tasted, but I never did know if he said it just to please me."

She didn't seem to expect an answer, and Autumn was relieved when she left the room. She put the pillows behind her and settled back, wondering how she would make it to the river. She could call Jake. Or maybe Bret. Or even Orion. She had other friends, of course, but they seemed so removed from everything that had happened to her. She didn't want to explain to anyone else why she needed to be there.

The woman came into the room, carrying a bed tray with a large, steaming bowl of chunky stew. *Beef,* Autumn guessed.

Baking powder biscuits sat on a small plate, and she was disappointed to see only two. She loved baking powder biscuits and could eat a half dozen at a single sitting, even if they were made of white flour. The woman placed the tray on her lap before sitting in the chair. The smell of the food was so wonderful that Autumn actually felt dizzy with anticipation. She didn't care that the meat probably contained hormones and that the vegetables weren't organically grown.

"I'm Mrs. Gerbert, by the way," the woman said. "You don't need help, do you? I can feed you, if you want."

Autumn wondered how long it had been since this woman had felt needed. "Thanks, I can manage."

Poorly, as it turned out, since her right arm was immobilized in the splint, but the robe could certainly be washed. The chunks of meat, potatoes, carrots, and onions were so good that Autumn nearly forgot Mrs. Gerbert in her eager attack on the food.

"Tawnia didn't tell me you were her sister," Mrs. Gerbert said suddenly. "But I can clearly tell the family resemblance. You are definitely sisters. Twins, I'll bet."

Autumn choked on a piece of meat. So last night hadn't been a dream.

"Sorry, dear. Is it too hot?" Mrs. Gerbert jumped up from the chair and hovered by the bed.

"No, I'm fine. It's just I don't remember much of what happened last night." And should she admit that she didn't have a sister, much less a twin?

"Well, that's natural when you're sick, but it's good you have a sister to take care of you. Do you live in the area?"

"Yes. I own an antiques shop in the Hawthorne district." How weird to say the words when she felt so far removed from them, almost as though that life belonged to another person altogether. Her store had been so important to her, but suddenly she'd realized how meaningless it was. All the traveling, the objects, the research. None of it really mattered without Winter.

I should be at the bottom of that river, not him. Not gentle Winter, who didn't even use a car for fear of what it would do to the environment.

She was crying again, but she quickly shoveled in several spoonfuls of stew to hide that fact. It was hot enough to burn her mouth, and soon she was blinking with that discomfort instead of the other pain.

"Go slowly. There's more. I'm making a cake too. German chocolate. Do you like German chocolate?"

Autumn nodded vigorously, her mouth too full to speak. This stew was the most wonderful thing she'd ever eaten. Of course, her perceptions after enduring the past week weren't completely trustworthy.

"Anyway, your sister has already called once. She left her phone and the number to reach her if you want to call. I'll go get it." Mrs. Gerbert left the room.

Autumn didn't want it. What would she say to this woman she didn't know?

Yet the connection she'd felt was still in her mind or heart or wherever it was. To this woman who looked like her, not to Winter. It didn't make sense. Nothing did—especially why this woman had her face. No wonder Bret had been so confused.

A piece of sky blue stationery on the floor by the chair caught her eye. Gingerly, she dropped her spoon and set the tray aside, swinging her feet over the edge of the bed. Her head spun at the movement, but she bent down for the paper anyway, shivering by the time she returned to the covers. *Stupid fever,* she thought.

I've left clothes for you on the dresser, if you need them. Help yourself to any food you find. I'll be home around six or so with dinner. I hope you're still here. We need to talk. We're both adopted, you know. Could there be a connection?

I'll take you to the river later if you want. And I'll call immediately if I hear any news about your father.

Tawnia McKnight

There was something more after the name, but it was crossed out. Perhaps something Tawnia had decided was too personal? Or maybe it had warned Autumn not to make off with the china—if she had any.

She re-read the note. Nothing personal, though there was at least curiosity. *That makes two of us.* Autumn was adopted, that much was true, but Winter and Summer had known her birth mother. They'd told stories about her and had even given Autumn a picture of her. Wouldn't they have told her more if there had been anything to tell?

CHAPTER 10

*T*awnia was late to work. Fortunately, there wasn't a managers' meeting and because she was late, she literally ran into a Mr. Lantis in the lobby who was from a billboard company. After making sure her laptop hadn't damaged his leg, she began answering his questions about Partridge Advertising. Before she knew it, she'd invited him up to her office, and they were brainstorming ideas for the fifty-five billboards he owned throughout the city. He'd recently fired his graphic designer and was looking for someone to do his designs as well as his marketing so he could focus on other business interests. He was impressed with her ideas and promised the company the account on the spot. She'd have to go through the right channels, of course, but she knew from experience the account was as good as hers.

Eat your heart out, Dustin, she thought with satisfaction. Sometimes nice guys don't finish last.

During her lunch break, Tawnia did an Internet search on Autumn Rain. For fifty bucks, she could find out everything there was to know publicly. She typed in her credit card number, feeling slightly dishonest, though she was only protecting herself. This woman was sleeping in her bed.

Autumn Rain. No criminal arrests or bankruptcies. She wasn't on a sex offender list and she didn't have any claims against her, except several mortgages. The value of her apartment and store were shown, along with the addresses and names of neighbors. Listed relatives were Winter Rain, Douglas Rayne, Summer Evans, and Summer Rain. There was no record of an adoption.

How strange, she thought. Autumn's birthday was the same year as Tawnia's and only one day later.

Tawnia printed out the report for later study. Autumn was exactly her age, except for the one day difference. It was uncannily close, and Tawnia didn't believe in coincidences.

What am I doing? She groaned and bit into the sandwich she'd ordered from a delivery service. It was filling but not very tasty. And it did nothing to touch her cravings.

Any of her cravings. She craved to talk to Autumn. She craved to be with Bret.

No, I don't!

Sighing, she picked up the folder on the motivational speaker whose book they were working on. He'd be here in ten minutes, and she needed to make sure everything was in order. After he left, she'd call Autumn again and see if she was finally awake.

Tawnia's meetings lasted until quitting time. She'd called Autumn once more, but no one had picked up. What could that mean? Had Mrs. Gerbert taken her to the hospital after all? Or had Autumn left the bungalow?

Well, there was nothing she could do about it now except go home. First, she'd run over to Smokey's and grab some meat pies. That would do for dinner.

Yet after Smokey's she didn't go home. She found herself driving through the Hawthorne District, finally parking and asking directions until she was approaching the east bank near where the bridge had collapsed. Was Bret still working there, or would he be on the other side—or perhaps off examining some other bridge in Portland? He was probably enjoying himself, despite the tragedy that had brought him here.

Putting on her sunglasses, she walked down to where yellow tape marked off the area where crews were still removing debris from the edge and from the river. There were several other sightseers ahead of her, and they were being turned away by the impossibly young-looking guard. Maybe she could ask him about Bret.

As she approached, he smiled at her broadly. "I wondered where you were today. Hey, you did something with your hair."

Tawnia was wearing it pinned back because there hadn't been time to style it that morning, but he couldn't possibly know that. She'd never seen him before. Still, she smiled politely. "I'm trying to find a friend. Name's Bret Winn. He's an engineer called in by the county."

"You mean the guy you were with yesterday? He was here earlier, but he left a few hours ago. They pulled up some debris on the other side of the river that he wanted to look at. But your other friend is here. The fireman. I don't know his name."

Tawnia didn't either, though, she remembered Bret saying something about a fireman. Encouraged by the guard's help-fulness, she asked, "Did the Navy Seals find any more people?"

"Two more today."

She swallowed hard. She heard about the one woman

this morning, but not about the second victim. Could it be Autumn's father? "Who were they?"

"I don't know the names, but both were women. They found one this morning and one around three o'clock." His expression was sympathetic. "Not your father. I'm sorry."

My father? Tawnia thought. Then she understood. This boy thinks I'm Autumn. The realization shocked her even more than seeing Autumn for herself.

"They should find him soon," the guard added. "And the other two. You can go on down, if you want."

She knew she shouldn't, but obviously everyone here had given Autumn deference because of her father, and she was curious enough not to want to pass up this opportunity. "Thank you," she murmured.

"You're looking good," the guard added as she passed. He colored a deep red. "I mean, I'm glad to see you're feeling better."

He'd noticed the change of clothes, probably, and the ten extra pounds she wore would make her look healthier. Tawnia knew a compliment when she heard it, but when did young boys become guards? Had she aged that much?

"Thank you. I am feeling better," she said.

He nodded, and she could feel his eyes on her as she walked down the bank. She was glad she'd chosen wide-heeled shoes with her maroon suit today so it was easy to navigate the ground. She thought of Autumn's bare feet. Had she come here without shoes?

Around her men worked with large cranes and vehicles and tools on massive mounds of debris, each intent on his job, but she noticed the wave of eyes that drifted briefly her way. In the few faces she could make out she clearly saw pity. How did Autumn stand that? Maybe she hadn't noticed.

From the television coverage, she could see they'd made

good progress here, but even so there was a lot more to clean up. Huge blocks of concrete and steel lay stacked awaiting disposal. A barge full of debris floated near the river.

She was within twenty feet of the water when a man broke away from some others and came toward her. "Autumn."

Uh-oh. She watched him saunter toward her. Was this the fireman? If he was close to Autumn, he would guess right away that she was an imposter. She folded her arms loosely across her stomach in a defensive gesture, smiling slightly. Maybe if she stayed quiet, she wouldn't get kicked out.

He was a tall, strong-looking man, older than she was, probably in his mid-forties. His black hair was sprinkled with bits of white, and his serious brown eyes appeared to see more than she wanted to show. He was undeniably handsome and definitely within the age bracket of men she dated, though why her mind was able to note all of this while worrying about being discovered, she couldn't say.

"I just got word," he said. "They're bringing someone else up. It's a man."

Shock must have registered on her face under the sunglasses because his arm went around her. "I'm sorry. But I'll stay here with you. I know his description, so I'll look first."

Tawnia's throat was dry. She shouldn't be here. She needed to get to Autumn, see how she was, and possibly bring her back. "I should go."

"What?" He looked at her as if she were crazy. "You've been waiting for this. At least I thought . . . Or maybe you're still hoping he's alive."

Tawnia didn't reply.

He put his hands on both of her shoulders. "Not finding him isn't going to bring him back. Don't you know that? Autumn, you can't let them beat you. You have to go on."

Let them beat her? What was he talking about?

"I'm fine," she whispered.

"No, you're not. You're in denial. When my daughter died, I couldn't believe it. Not even when they showed me her body. My baby was gone. But you have to go on. That's the way you win."

He was leaning toward her face, so close she could smell his aftershave. Her stomach fluttered. He was really good looking. Were he and Autumn as close as his words implied?

"I know we barely know each other," the man went on, "and I know it's too soon, but I—" His lips brushed Tawnia's cheek lightly. "I care about you."

She reeled from the closeness. She hadn't been kissed by a man since Bret, and she hadn't expected to feel so attracted to one whose name she didn't even know. A sound escaped her throat, part moan, part sigh.

"Did I hurt your arm?" he asked, looking down at her folded arms.

"It's okay." More than okay, since Autumn was the one with a broken arm. If he glimpsed under her jacket sleeve, he'd see there was no splint. She'd better put the brakes on this conversation right now. Stepping away, she turned her face to the river, where some distance away a stretcher was being taken from a boat.

A man came jogging toward them. "Orion, we're ready for you." He appraised Tawnia with a frank stare, and this time she was the one who blushed. Maybe she should get a job for the county. She might get more dates that way.

At least she knew the fireman's name. Orion. Leave it to Autumn to have a friend with an unusual name. Tawnia watched Orion trot to the group. He was a beautiful man—strong, mysterious, and good-looking.

Orion was gone a long time, and Tawnia began to worry. If he asked her to identify the body, she'd have to confess. She didn't know what Winter looked like, and she didn't exactly want to see a dead body today. Or ever, now that she thought about it.

He came back to her more slowly, as though dreading telling her the news, but he smiled as he arrived, which made her feel oddly excited. "Not him," he announced. "Too young. No beard." The smile vanished. "Not a pretty sight, though, after so long in the water. I think you should know about that. To be prepared."

Nearly a week of water and river creatures. No, she didn't expect the sight would be agreeable.

They watched as the men brought the victim up to a waiting ambulance, the body covered from view.

After a few seconds of silence, she asked. "Orion, how did your daughter die?" Too late, she wondered if Autumn already knew the details of his daughter's death.

His eyes seemed to dig into hers, though he couldn't possibly see through her sunglasses. "She jumped off the bridge." His eyes lifted to the remains of the Hawthorne bridge in the distance, leaving her in no doubt about which bridge he meant. "Three years ago."

"Why?"

"I don't know for sure, but she had just broken up with her boyfriend. His parents shipped him off to some fancy college back east, and he quit calling. She was never very strong emotionally since her mother died a few years before that—complications of surgery."

"I'm so sorry."

He didn't move or speak for the space of several heartbeats and then, "This bridge has cost us both a lot. I would give anything to make it so none of this had ever happened. I want you to know that."

"Of course you would. I feel the same."

He nodded. "Well, I guess I'd better get going. I'm actually working tonight. Once a week we take turns on the night shift at the fire station. Are you staying here?"

"For a while longer."

"Is Jake coming to get you?"

"No, I drove."

He smiled again, and she wished he would do that more often. Her stomach felt all funny when he smiled. "That's it," he said. "Don't let them win."

"Who's them?"

"Everyone."

Tawnia wished he didn't have to go. "Will I see you again?"

"If you want to."

"What about what you want?"

"I pulled a lot of people from the water, but I don't come to the river to see them every day. Only you."

The reference clicked. This was the man who'd rescued Autumn after the bridge collapse. "I'm glad." She was glad, and she hoped Autumn was, too.

"Did I give you my number?" he asked.

Tawnia had no idea. "I don't have my phone with me."

"That's right." He looked out at the river, as though pondering the whereabouts of her phone. "You'll have to get a new one."

"I did." She gave him the number, making a note to change her message to something more generic. Of course, she couldn't keep up this pretense for long. She'd have to tell at least Autumn about it. For all she knew, Autumn might be in love with this guy.

Or she might be gunning for Bret. Tawnia pushed the thought to a dark corner of her mind.

Orion took two steps away, looking younger and more vital than when she'd first seen him, as though his load had been lifted. She knew the feeling, having experienced it herself after Christian's death. It was good to talk about those you had loved and lost.

He paused and turned. "Oh, and I'm glad your arm's feeling better. If that nosy new friend of yours hadn't told me it was broken, I would never have guessed."

Tawnia looked down at her right arm, still folded on top of her left, more by luck than by design. *If only you knew.* "See you later," she called.

"Goodbye."

Just her luck. She'd met a cute, available man, who actually seemed to like her, and he thought she was someone else. *I should have told him the truth.*

Yet a part of her relished how much fun it was pretending to be someone else. She'd always imagined having a twin sister to change places with.

But I don't have a twin, she reminded herself.

This was too bizarre. Time to get home and begin finding out exactly what was going on.

When Tawnia drove up to her bungalow, she imagined many scenarios as to what she might find—her clothes missing and Autumn vanished, Autumn sleeping in bed, or Mrs. Gerbert calling *America's Most Wanted.* But finding Autumn lying on the lounge chair on her porch, wrapped in a blanket and talking with Mrs. Gerbert, wasn't one of them. Her face was still flushed, her eyes bright with fever, but she appeared a lot better. She was eating a huge piece of cake in a cereal bowl, her movements awkward with her left hand.

"Ah, there you are, dear." Mrs. Gerbert came heavily to her feet and met her at the stairs.

"Have you been here all day?" Tawnia asked. Babysitting wasn't in her contract, and she wondered if Mrs. Gerbert would call her on it.

"Goodness, no. I did a lot of errands, and I visited the neighbors."

"She's mostly been here all day," Autumn contradicted.

Tawnia watched her bring a forkful of cake to her mouth. "I see."

"I took the liberty of making your sister a stew," Mrs. Gerbert said. "There's a bit left over, if you like. I guess I didn't make as much as I thought."

Autumn laughed. "I just ate a lot. It's really good, too."

Tawnia was starving, and only now did she realize that she'd been so caught up with her thoughts about Orion that she'd left the Smokey's bag in the car. She'd have to go back and get it—along with the crate of her belongings. But that could wait for a few minutes at least. She didn't want to offend Mrs. Gerbert by rejecting her stew.

She sat down on the rocking chair Mrs. Gerbert had vacated. "We're not sisters. We only met yesterday."

Mrs. Gerbert's eyebrows rose, her face going from one of them to the next and back again. "I find that hard to believe."

"We're both adopted," Tawnia said, more to see her reaction than anything.

"Well, that explains it then. You're related somehow. Still, if Autumn here gained a bit of weight—you really are quite skinny, dear—and if you colored and styled your hair the same way, you'd be hard to tell apart. Well, except Autumn has those different colored eyes. Such a lovely effect." She shook her head, dismissing the subject. "I'd better get home. My baby girl will be there soon. And my grandson. You let me know if you need any help. And Autumn, I'll write down my recipe for you and bring it by another day."

"Thank you for everything," Autumn said.

They watched Mrs. Gerbert leave in silence, a heavy silence that made Tawnia feel at a loss. Where did they go from here?

"I'm sorry I was so late," Tawnia said. "I went to the river."

Autumn was about to take her last bite of cake, but she let the fork drop to the bowl. "Did they . . . ?" She left the sentence hanging, snuggling deeper into the blanket, despite the heat of the summer evening.

"They found three victims total today, two women earlier and a man while I was there—not your father." This last Tawnia hurried to say because she could see how much Autumn needed to know.

Autumn sighed. "Only two still missing then." She looked so sad that Tawnia felt like crying herself. Better to change the subject.

"I saw a friend of yours at the river. A fireman."

"Orion?" Autumn smiled. "He's still hanging out there?"

"Looking for you, I'd say. He must like you."

"He just feels responsible since he saved my life."

"He's really attractive."

"Attractive?" Autumn laughed. "He's old. I mean older than us. I never thought of him that way." But her face colored.

"Never?" pressed Tawnia.

"Okay, once. I thought about what it might be like if he kissed me. But it was only for a second, and I wasn't feeling well that day. He's really not my type. He seems too, well, old. And I don't mean age-wise, because I'm the first one who wouldn't care about something superficial like that."

"I think he looks older because he's sad. His daughter committed suicide, you know. Three years ago. Jumped off the Hawthorne Bridge after she broke up with her boyfriend. And he lost his wife a few years before that."

"I didn't know." Autumn was quiet for a few seconds. "So you really like him?"

Tawnia leaned back in the rocking chair, her elbows on the armrest. "Have you ever seen him smile?"

"That was when I thought about kissing him. But don't worry about me. If you like him, I say go for it." Autumn picked up her fork again, shoved in the last bit of cake, and set the bowl on the porch.

Silence again. "He thought I was you," Tawnia said quietly.

Autumn's eyes widened. "You let him think you were me?"

"Hey, that was how I got down near the river in the first place. Everyone knows you there."

"They didn't notice you look different?"

"Do I?" There, Tawnia had done it. She'd brought up the issue they'd been dancing around since she'd arrived home.

Autumn's eyes were on her face. Though the rocking chair and the lounge were close, they both sat up and leaned closer. Autumn's hand touched Tawnia's cheek, a fluttery touch. "I don't know how this happened," she whispered, "but I don't believe it was an accident." She drew back and sank into her blanket once more. "If my parents were here, we could ask them."

"I did some research today."

"And?"

"You were born a day after I was. I couldn't even find a record of your adoption."

Autumn snorted. "Tell me about it. When I turned eighteen, I had to go through all sorts of trouble to prove I existed. We finally told the government that Summer had me at home. We didn't know what else to do. Apparently, the doctor who found me for them didn't exactly follow the rules."

"You were kidnapped?" Tawnia felt a thundering in her chest. If there had been something suspicious about Autumn's adoption, maybe hers wasn't what she had always thought.

"Oh, no! My parents knew my birth mother. She lived with them for a few months before I was born. It was she who chose them. Later, she died having me." She gave Tawnia a sad smile. "That's why I know we couldn't be twins like Mrs. Gerbert wants to believe. My parents wouldn't have lied to me about something like that. My birth mother was very young, but I suppose she could have had a baby before me, but if you and I are the same age, that pretty much rules that out."

"I see." Tawnia's hopes fell. She'd been hoping . . . hoping what? "As a child I always wanted a sister." She didn't realize she'd spoken the words aloud until Autumn responded.

"So did I."

They looked out over the tiny expanse of grass. Several neighbors were out working on their yards, pausing every now and then to surreptitiously study them.

"What now?" Tawnia asked.

"We still could be related. I think we should do a little research. For all we know, we come from the same family line. I knew some cousins once that looked a lot alike. If they hadn't been ten years apart, they might have been even more similar."

Tawnia began to feel better. "The doctor who placed you might know something."

"He might. We could try to find him. I don't remember his name anymore, but I have a box somewhere with all the information. What about your parents? Maybe they have some papers."

"I can ask, but I didn't even know I was adopted until I heard them talking about it one day. And we never really talked about it after that. Practically none of their friends ever knew."

"They kept it a secret?"

"Not exactly. It just wasn't mentioned. We didn't talk about anything that wasn't normal."

"Are they why you wear a contact?" Autumn peered at her to verify its presence.

"I guess so. They didn't like people staring."

"I love the stares. It's fun being unusual. In fact, I hate it when people don't notice. That means they don't really see me."

Tawnia had never thought of it that way. "I guess I wanted to stand out for my talents, not because there was something wrong with my eyes."

"There's nothing wrong with your eyes! Or mine. And there's nothing wrong with standing out because of your looks or your talents. Because in the end, neither of those are anything without hard work."

Something they could agree on.

The conversation moved on, covering their childhoods, Tawnia's graduation from college, and her career in the art field. Then they were on to Autumn's one semester in college, where she flunked out of everything but her antiques and history classes. "I hated been cooped up and doing all those papers," she said. "I already knew what I wanted to do. I could add and spell well enough to run my store, so I took the plunge and went into business. Winter paid the first six months of my mortgage, but since then I've been solvent."

"That's amazing. I would have been too afraid to do something like that." Tawnia admired Autumn's confidence. She herself made it a habit to never risk more than she could afford to lose.

"Sometimes risks are worth it."

The sun was low in the western sky now, and Tawnia's stomach had started complaining. "I just remembered. I have some meat pies in the car."

"From Smokey's?" Autumn looked happy. "Bring them on."

Tawnia ran down to the car and back again with the food. "They're actually still warm. Not hot, but enough that I don't think we'll need to zap them in the microwave."

"Good, because I don't use microwaves."

"You don't?"

Autumn shook her head. "I don't want radiation in my food."

"Most everything I eat comes from a microwave," Tawnia confessed.

"Believe me, it's not healthy."

"Okay."

That was weird, but Tawnia thought perhaps it was no weirder than a woman with perfect eyesight wearing a contact every day. "You look like you're feeling better," she said as they ate. In fact, Autumn looked pretty, even beautiful. *Do I really look like her?* she wondered.

"I think my fever's almost gone." She hesitated a moment before adding, "You know, this is really strange, but I feel I've known you for a long time."

Tawnia nodded and looked away so Autumn wouldn't see the tears gathering in her eyes. She'd felt the same thing, but saying so seemed to risk a commitment she wasn't ready for. She didn't make close friends easily. "So what are you going to do now?"

"Go home."

That was a good sign. "You sure you're up to it?"

Autumn shook her head. "No, but I've been thinking about it all day. I have to face the apartment sometime, and I have to go back to work. Jake—he's the guy who works part time for both Winter and me—he's been running the stores. He's had his fifteen-year-old sister in there some of the time. But they can't buy new inventory or tell customers the background of my pieces. I think I can go back now."

"What about your father? I mean, I know you've been going to the river." Tawnia didn't add that doing so was strange because she had the feeling she might do the same thing had the situation been reversed. Well, if her father had been more like Winter, instead of the remote man who'd seemed to sit down and talk with her only when she'd done something wrong.

Autumn sighed, blinking back tears. "I don't need to go to the river anymore. I thought I felt him there, but it wasn't him at all. I think he's gone. Besides, everyone's right that my being there won't help him."

"I'll go with you, if you want. To your apartment. You shouldn't be alone. Even if we're not sisters . . ." The fact that they couldn't possibly be sisters was so disappointing after all their similarities that Tawnia didn't care to complete the sentence.

"Even if we're not sisters," Autumn repeated, reaching out to rest her hand on Tawnia's, "we can still be friends. I'm glad Bret introduced us. I really am."

Tawnia smiled. "Me too."

Bret squatted down by the remains of the huge metal girders the cranes had just brought up from the river. He'd seen this kind of damage before, and it wasn't caused by stress fractures, however severe. He ran his fingers over the twisted metal, still cool from the river. Some sections were sheared off.

He stood and waved his hand to Robert, who was examining another pile of rubble. Robert jogged over. "Find something?"

"Look at this."

Robert stared without comprehension. "What am I seeing? It looks like all the others."

"No, this is completely different. I saw damage like this at least half a dozen times in the army. This bridge didn't fall because of a boat hitting it. This damage was made by explosives. Really powerful explosives."

Robert's eyes widened. "Are you sure?"

"Absolutely. We'd better call the FBI. They'll want to see this. And we'll need to talk with the men who brought this up. There's got to be more evidence down there. I think we might just get lucky."

As Robert hurried away, Bret sat back on his heels, thinking hard. He had known the collapse hadn't seemed right, and today he'd finally found the missing link. Only the sheer size of the disaster had prevented him from pinpointing it earlier. The debris farther from the charges showed nothing, but this damage had occurred closer to the blast and couldn't be masked.

Yet Robert hadn't recognized the sign of explosive damage, and that meant Bret's presence in Portland hadn't been in vain.

Of course, the existence of the explosives brought to light even more problems and quite possibly threatened the entire city.

Who had set the charges and why?

*A*utumn was enjoying herself, and even the thought that she would have to go back to her apartment tonight didn't destroy her euphoria.

The more she got to know Tawnia, the more she liked this woman who was so different from and yet so similar to herself. They shared a love of fiction, had a talent for getting lost, held the same political views, and adored eating more than just about anything else—though Autumn preferred organic. It didn't matter that Autumn hated shoes and college classes and microwaves and could barely draw a stick figure, or that Tawnia had no use for herbs, wouldn't know an antique if she tripped over it, and that she was far too careful with her emotions.

While Autumn had never experienced problems chatting with strangers before, the connection she felt with Tawnia was different. They simply fit. Autumn felt indebted to Bret for connecting her with Tawnia.

She was especially amazed that Tawnia had offered to go back to her apartment with her. Autumn had been afraid to be there alone, but at the same time she hadn't wanted Jake or any of her other friends with her. They were too much a part of the old life with Winter. But Tawnia seemed to belong to who Autumn was now. She opened her mouth to accept Tawnia's offer but Tawnia's words interrupted her thoughts.

"Speak of the devil."

Autumn looked up to see Bret pulling to the curb. He sauntered up the walk, looking tired but also somewhat jubilant.

"We were just talking about you," Autumn said.

"So that's why my ears are burning." His face flushed as he said it.

Autumn laughed at his discomfort. "Silly boy. Don't worry, we were only saying how grateful we are that you introduced us."

"Oh." Now he seemed deflated. Men were so transparent.

"What's up?" Tawnia asked. "You look like something's happened."

Autumn swallowed hard. So Tawnia had noticed his demeanor, too. Dread leapt to life inside her. "Have they found another victim?" Her father, she meant, since there were only two people still missing.

Bret shook his head. He'd reached the porch stairs and took them in one leap. "No. Not that. But there is news, except that it's still ultra secret, so you can't tell a soul. But just now we found damage on the rubble from the river—damage that could only have been caused by some kind of explosive device. We're still looking for more clues, but I'm fairly certain the bridge collapse was not an accident. It was sabotage."

"A bomb." Tawnia shook her head. "That's crazy."

"An explosive device," Bret corrected. "Or rather, multiple devices, given the extent of the collapse."

Autumn rolled her eyes. "If it blows up, it's a bomb. So who did it?"

"That we don't know. We've shown the evidence to the Feds and we'll be working with them to determine exactly what was used. That will help us catch whoever did it. Hopefully by tomorrow they'll have more to go on. They're pulling an all-nighter as we speak, but I needed a break."

"I can't believe someone would do something so terrible." Tawnia stared out over the small yard, her face solemn.

Autumn shivered. "After 9/11, I believe anything."

"Do you need another blanket?" Tawnia asked.

"No. I'm fine." Autumn pulled the blanket she had up around her neck.

"It's possible the explosions had a political purpose." Scooting one of the flowerpots aside, Bret sat on the small cement wall surrounding the porch. "They've kept it out of the media, but the governor crossed the bridge on the way to some public appearance shortly before the collapse. He might have been a target."

"There are easier ways to knock people off," Autumn said dryly.

Tawnia nodded. "And if they planned something so elaborate, why would they miss?"

"Might be a complete coincidence," Bret conceded. "You have to admit, though, it'd make some statement. Blow up the bridge to kill the governor."

Autumn snorted. "Yeah. It'd say, Look at me. I'm a crazy nutcase. Lock me up."

Bret shrugged and leaned over as though to dig a finger into Tawnia's half-eaten meat pie. "Can I have the rest of this? I'm starved."

"No!" Tawnia slapped his hand. "But my landlady made some stew. You can have the rest of it. Go on inside."

"Great." Bret was inside the house before Autumn finished laughing.

"If you want to talk handsome," Autumn said, winking at Tawnia.

Tawnia looked at her blankly. "I don't. Not if it's about him."

"Are you sure? I thought you and Bret had a thing."

"*Had* being the key word." Tawnia looked upset. Autumn knew because her own face wore that same expression when she was out of sorts.

Time to change the subject. "Well, I guess I should get home." Autumn threw off the blanket and swung her legs to the ground.

Tawnia had an odd look on her face now, one Autumn didn't recognize. Not a shred of emotion showed through. "So," Tawnia said, her voice casual, "do you want me to come with you? You never said. If you'd prefer, I can ask Bret to drive you there instead."

"I'd like you to come. Hey, why don't we have a sleepover?"

Tawnia grinned. "Okay, then. Come inside while I get some things." She held open the screen door for Autumn. "You'll have to tell me how to get there."

Autumn laughed. "I hope I can find my way from here." Her step was a little shaky, so she slid her fingers along the door to steady herself.

"Not you too!" Bret groaned, coming from the kitchen with a bowl full of stew. "Tawnia gets lost going to the grocery store."

"I do not!" Tawnia retorted. "Well, not if it's a grocery store I've been to before."

"Don't mind him," Autumn told her. "I get lost a lot, but I see more that way. I can't tell you how many times I've stumbled onto treasures I would have missed had I been on the right road."

Tawnia smirked at Bret. "See? It's good to be directionally challenged."

"Hmhahoin," he said.

"Directionally challenged—I love it!" Autumn settled on the couch, feeling dizzy. "And don't talk with your mouth full, Bret. It's not polite."

He looked ready to protest, but Mrs. Gerbert's stew was too compelling. "Whatever." He took another huge bite and sat down on a chair in the corner.

"Once when I was in Kansas," Autumn said, pulling her legs under her, "I got lost during a tornado. Seeing all those hoses dancing in the air, still attached to the houses, was hilarious until I realized I was in danger of being blown off the road. But none of the road names were familiar, so eventually, I stopped and knocked on some door. No one answered, but the door was open so I went in. Found the family huddled downstairs in their basement. They told me to come right in and help myself to a cup of brew they had steaming on a camp stove. It was pretty funny."

Bret shook his head. "Doesn't sound fun. You could have been hurt."

"By the family?"

He rolled his eyes. "No, the tornado."

"Aw, it was only a little one. My rental car didn't even blow away. The best thing was that in the basement, I found a bunch of antiques belonging to the old grandma of the family who'd died at about a hundred years old. I gave the family a good price for them, and we all went happily along our way."

Tawnia started laughing. "I can just see it. You wheeling and dealing as the tornado sweeps over the house."

"Actually, it was after dinner. The tornado was long gone."

"You ate dinner there?"

"Sure. After the tornado. They invited me. Friendly people there in Kansas. Lots of fields too."

"I know. I'm from Kansas, remember?"

"Oh, that's right. Why'd you leave, anyway?"

"Because my parents were there." Dead silence filled the room, and Tawnia's face lost all color. "It's a joke, you guys."

But her tone was so serious that Autumn wondered about the people who had raised her.

"Actually, I left because I felt like it," Tawnia went on quickly. "I wanted to see what else there was in the world."

"Where'd you go?" Autumn asked. "Nevada?"

"Colorado. Stayed for a few years, then went to Utah, and from there I ended up in Nevada. And now Oregon. Five states in ten years. Just call me a nomad."

Autumn felt a little chill. Tawnia had named the states she'd most frequently visited over the same ten-year period in her hunt for antiques. In fact, with the addition of California and Washington, Oregon's immediate neighbors, those had been the only states she'd visited. What an odd coincidence.

Or was she looking for fire where there wasn't even a hint of smoke? They both lived in the West—well, Kansas was the Midwest—but it was entirely logical that they would visit the same states. Winter might find some sort of deeper meaning in the coincidence, but that didn't mean one existed. Still, it was a little disconcerting to think that she and Tawnia might mirror each other in ways that went beyond physical similarities.

"What about you, Bret?" Autumn asked.

"I've pretty much stayed in Nevada, but I lived in California as a child. I've been to Arizona, as well, and overseas in the army. And then here, of course. Oh, and my family and I took a trip to New York once."

New York. An odd sort of relief washed over Autumn. A little over a year ago in April, she and Winter had flown to New York City to visit an aunt of his who had been ill. They had caught a few Broadway hits while they were there. It was the first and only time she remembered Winter flying on a plane. New York was far away from the states where Tawnia had lived, and because Autumn had been to New York, that proved there was no odd, subliminal pattern in her trips.

"I almost went to New York," Tawnia said into the silence. "Last year in the spring. I got to thinking that I really should go because all my friends have been. But I . . ." Her face drained of its color, becoming paler than when she'd talked about her parents. She stopped speaking and stared helplessly at Bret, all poise deserting her. His spoon was frozen in the air.

"What happened?" Autumn asked. Whatever it had been, it concerned both Bret and Tawnia somehow. That Tawnia's planned trip was so near the time of Autumn's own New York adventure put things back into the supernatural realm again, but she would think about that later.

"Something came up, that's all." Tawnia walked stiffly toward the short hall leading to the bedroom. "I'll just be a minute for my things. And I bet your clothes are washed now." She glanced at the jeans and T-shirt Autumn wore.

"I think your landlady put them in the dryer, so I can change into them and give you these clothes back now."

"Don't bother. I can get them tomorrow." With a last glance at Bret, Tawnia disappeared from view.

"What was that all about?" Autumn asked.

"What?" Bret shoved another spoon of stew into his mouth.

"What happened last year?"

Bret chewed and swallowed, contemplating her silently for

what seemed like long moments. "My brother died. Tawnia was with him when it happened. That's kind of how we met."

There was more to the story, but Bret stood and headed for the kitchen, his strides long and purposeful. "I think I've had enough of this stew, though it really is excellent. So what do you ladies plan on doing this evening?"

Though she was bursting with curiosity, Autumn let him change the subject. Maybe Tawnia would tell her more later. "I'm going home," she called after him. "To my apartment."

"You really have an apartment?" Bret came back wearing his normal smile. "I was beginning to believe you lived in that tiny back room at your store."

"It's not tiny."

"Somehow that doesn't make me excited to see your apartment."

"Good, because you're not invited. This is a girls' sleepover."

"Man, I always wanted to attend one of those." He sat beside her on the couch. "Girls get all the fun."

"Sorry, can't help you there." The bantering was fun. She hadn't figured him for the type. He seemed so, well, serious. But then, they had met under serious circumstances. This last thought sobered her, and she felt the sadness of the past days come rushing back.

"Even if you could help me," he said, "I have a previous engagement."

"Oh?"

"Yeah, Clyde Hanks, the guy in charge of Multnomah's bridges. Basically, the guy who's responsible for my being here. He's meeting with the FBI right now, but he wants to see me as soon as they finish."

"Shouldn't you be there?"

"Nah, right now they're pretty crazy, trying to find what terror organization might be responsible. I'll just keep doing my job, and when the noise dies down, I'll tell them what I know."

"Won't you be leaving soon? I mean, now that they know it wasn't an accident?"

"Maybe. I haven't checked out all the bridges yet, but that might not be a priority with this new information. Still, the FBI will need engineers to consult with, and they may want to use some of us who are already familiar with the project."

"What's weird is that no one is claiming responsibility for the bombs." Autumn still found the whole idea hard to believe. Some jerk with an axe to grind had set multiple bombs to send a message, and because of that Winter was dead. She'd almost died. The baby in the car seat had drowned. No, better not to think about her, or the mother. So much wasted life. Why? Autumn pulled her knees to her chest.

"If someone's claiming responsibility, the FBI's not telling the rest of us. For all I know, they've had information all along they haven't shared. But we didn't even know the cause of the collapse until we found the debris tonight. I think you're right that people who do this sort of thing aren't satisfied unless they take some kind of credit, so I expect we'll hear something soon."

"I'm ready!" Tawnia came down the hall with a small suitcase, and only then did Autumn realize how close Bret was sitting. Close enough to look romantic. Guiltily, she pulled away as far as her position allowed, though she had nothing to hide.

Bret smiled up at Tawnia before glancing back again at Autumn. "I can't get over how alike you two are."

That gave Autumn an idea. If he thought they looked alike now, how much more would they look alike if, as Mrs. Gerbert had suggested, their hair was the same and Tawnia wasn't wearing her contact? It might be fun to find out. She'd have to think about that further.

Bret stood and sauntered to the door. "Well, ladies, thanks for dinner. Have fun tonight. Call if you need me."

"You're leaving?" Tawnia took a step in his direction. She still wore the maroon suit she'd worn to work, and now her sure movements held no trace of insecurity.

Autumn admired how stunning and in control she seemed. Autumn herself had never worn a suit in her life. Well, at least not a classic one that was all one color, though she'd once owned a knitted neon yellow one that she'd been very proud to wear until she snagged and broke a thread on an antique table. Half the jacket unraveled before she noticed.

"Have to meet with the county guys. We'll probably be working on this all night."

Tawnia walked with him to the door. "Don't work too hard."

Bret said something Autumn couldn't hear, and Tawnia shrugged in response. "I want to." She shut the door behind him.

"He's really cute."

Tawnia chuckled. "Whatever. You ready?"

"You're really not interested in him anymore?"

"No."

Was there a slight hesitation? Autumn couldn't tell, nor did the inscrutable expression on Tawnia's face give her any hint.

"I'm just going to check the back door and turn out the lights. Would you like some sandals?"

"No. I don't wear shoes." Autumn wondered if it was time to explain her lifelong hatred of footwear. As a child Summer had even let her go to school without shoes until the principal threatened to call child services. Every year until sixth grade she managed to slip under the man's radar until about October. At the first frost, everyone suddenly started paying attention to her feet. After Summer's death, Autumn didn't have the heart to put up a fight and had worn the hated shoes. Later, as an adult, she'd had problems with her back—probably from lifting items in the store—and learned that it was better when she didn't wear any kind of heel. Since then, she'd pretty much given up wearing shoes again, except for important business or outside in the dead of winter.

Tawnia was staring at her. "I know, it's weird," Autumn said. Usually, she refused to make excuses, but somehow she cared what Tawnia thought. "Just think of it as going with the name."

Tawnia laughed. "What about work?"

"What about it?"

"Do you wear shoes there?"

Autumn grinned. "Nope. I have an in with the boss."

They managed to find their way to Autumn's apartment building with only one wrong turn, which really wasn't their fault, because the road had been blocked with yet more construction. All too soon, they pulled into the parking space where Autumn normally left her car.

"Wait." Autumn's hand went out to Tawnia's to stop her from exiting the car. "My neighbors." She pointed to a couple emerging from a car near the building. "I'm not ready to see them."

She knew Jake had been to her apartment to water her plants, and he would have talked to her neighbors—he talked to everyone. They would all know about her father and ask questions. Some had already been down to the store to check on her when she had been at the river. While she appreciated their concern, facing them tonight wasn't high on her list of priorities.

"Let's wait until they go inside. Do you mind?"

"Not at all." Tawnia settled against the seat, dropping her hands to her lap in a graceful motion.

The couple was barely out of sight when a teenage boy came by the car, a boy Autumn often shot baskets with in the hoop that was poised over the parking lot. Finally, the way was clear.

"I'll go first," Tawnia offered as they walked to the building. "What floor is it?"

"Lobby floor. To the left."

Tawnia peered through the glass window in the outside door. "Coast is clear."

Autumn felt for her spare set of keys and awkwardly opened the door with her left hand. This broken arm stuff was really annoying. Of course, that was the least of her worries. She went up the three steps inside the lobby and used another key to open her apartment.

As she stepped inside, she began shaking and heat enveloped her, as though her fever had returned. Images of the water, the terror of the fall from the bridge, the woman screaming for her baby, the man crying over the still figure of his wife.

"Autumn? Are you all right?"

"I'm fine."

"Baloney." Tawnia put an arm around her and urged her the rest of the way into the apartment.

Autumn's senses took in the stale air, with pronounced traces of the herbal tinctures Winter had been experimenting with last week. She could detect the fragrances of chamomile, peppermint, and the vodka that made up the base of the tincture. There were other scents as well but so diluted and mixed she couldn't identify them.

The apartment was small—a living room, a kitchen, two bedrooms, and a bathroom. They had turned a large storage closet into a computer nook because they had a huge back room at the Herb Shoppe for long-term storage.

"Sit down here." Tawnia's hand guided Autumn to the couch. A worn crocheted afghan, one Summer had made, lay on the cushion, and Tawnia pulled it over Autumn's shoulders.

With relief Autumn pulled her shaking legs under her. She could smell Winter. At any moment he could walk out of his bedroom. Closing her eyes, Autumn laid her head back on the couch. A tear trickled from her left eye. The blue one.

"This is a lovely room," Tawnia said. "Are these couches antiques? I love the woodwork on them. You must have redone the fabric, though." She ran her hand over the patterned flowers. "It's perfect Victorian. I bet you did it yourself, didn't you?"

At Autumn's weak nod, she went on. "That's what I call art. You have a creative talent that's as good as drawing." She trailed her finger lightly over a bowl and some figurines on the coffee table. "This stuff is fabulous. They're antiques, too, aren't they?" She was silent for a few brief seconds and then gave an appreciative gasp. "Oh, look at that ogre statue! That's unique. I've never seen anything like it before. Looks like he's guarding the TV."

The sound of Tawnia's voice washed over Autumn in soothing waves. She commented on the textured walls that Autumn and Winter had worked so hard on to get just right. For a whole five minutes she gushed about the antique chandelier above the coffee table—really too low for the room—that Autumn hadn't been able to part with at the antiques store.

Gradually, Autumn's breathing slowed and her panic abated. *I can do this,* Autumn thought.

"If you've made things this nice in such a small space, I can't imagine what you could do to my parents' mausoleum."

Autumn knew Tawnia must feel rather crowded after the stark orderliness at the bungalow, but she was nice to keep Autumn distracted. "Your parents are rich?"

Tawnia sighed. "I don't really know. My father's an economist for a big company. But I don't know who works harder, my father to earn the money or my mother to spend it."

Autumn laughed. "It must have been nice growing up."

Tawnia's face took on the inscrutable expression that Autumn couldn't decipher. "They didn't deny me anything I needed. I was fortunate."

It sounded cold to Autumn. She thought of Summer and Winter and how much they had loved each other and her. They had lacked many comforts in the early years but never companionship and love. Autumn could have no sooner have left Winter behind and moved to another state than she could have cut out half her heart. He was her best friend.

And he was gone.

Yet wasn't there still some slight chance of his survival? It was dangerous to hold to that hope, but Autumn had never worried much about danger.

"Thank you for coming here with me," Autumn said. "It's harder than I expected."

Tawnia smiled. "You're welcome. But now I think it's time to get you to bed. You've just spent two days with a fever, and you need to rest."

Autumn was about to protest that she had been resting all day when a crushing exhaustion descended upon her before she could voice the words. "Good idea. The couch opens to a bed. The sheets are in the bathroom closet. Here, let me—"

"No. You get to bed. Which room's yours?"

Autumn pointed to the second door.

"Go ahead, then. I'll come check on you in a bit."

Nodding, Autumn started to walk past Winter's room. The door was ajar. She hesitated, desperately wanting to feel him close. "On second thought," she said, "you take my room. I think I'll sleep in here."

Tawnia studied her closely and then nodded. "Okay, but remember I'm here if you need me."

Autumn walked inside Winter's room. Everything was exactly as she remembered it. Except he was missing. And he might never be found. What would she do then? No body to lay to rest, no grave to cry over. It would be as though he'd gone on a trip and never come back. Would it be better to think of him drinking a mai tai on a beach somewhere? But, no, instead she would think of him under the water with who-knew-what kind of river creatures. Winter might actually have preferred disappearing like that—it fit his flower-child nature—but she didn't feel the same. There was comfort in saying goodbye at a funeral.

She still remembered the funeral they'd had for Summer as if it were yesterday. A home burial, they'd called it.

Winter made the coffin himself, and all their friends came to decorate the wood with paints, leaving their messages of love for Summer. Autumn drew a humongous heart on the top with the words Summer and Autumn inside the unsteady curves. She made it purple, Summer's favorite color, and no one had stopped her, even though hearts weren't really supposed to be purple.

After the decorating was complete, all the friends lifted Summer's still form and placed her inside.

"She really looks peaceful," said Willow, Summer's best friend. Murmurs of agreement filled the room.

Autumn looked closer at Summer's face and saw that it was true. All the pain of the cancer was gone from her face, making Summer look so young, like Autumn's sister instead of her mother.

"She must be in a happy place." This from Lennon, another friend of her mother's. His face was wet with tears. Autumn liked him more than all her mother's friends because he always brought her pressed flowers. He had wanted to marry Summer before Winter came along and captured her heart, but that never seemed to bother anyone, as far as Autumn could see.

Seeing Summer's peace made Autumn feel just the tiniest bit better. The pain around the lump that was her heart seemed to ease.

They talked around the coffin nearly all night, way past the time when Autumn normally fell asleep. Eventually they all slept, mostly where they happened to be at the moment. Autumn awoke on the couch early in the morning before anyone else stirred. Her father was snoring gently next to her. There were people on the floor with blankets, and several sprawled on the other couch. Stealthy as a cat, she crossed to the coffin.

To her relief, Summer was still there, looking as peaceful as the night before. Autumn stroked her cheek. "Goodbye, Summer." Then more quietly, so even she couldn't hear the word, she added, "Mommy." Then more loudly, "I wish you'd take me with you."

A hand covered hers. Autumn looked up to see Winter smiling gently down at her. "She can't take either of us, Autumn. Not yet. You and I will keep each other company—and we'll be happy. That's what she would want. She didn't want to leave us, but sometimes we don't have a choice. Trust me, okay? Everything is going to be all right. I promise you."

He hugged her tightly, and her tears were soaked up in the

fabric of his shirt. That was when she remembered he always told the truth, and she felt peace.

By the bed the smell of Winter was stronger, and she could almost hear his voice as it had been in the weeks and months following Summer's death, when she had crawled into his bed at night, trembling with longing for her mother.

"There, there, baby. You're shaking like a leaf. Come here. I'm here. There's nothing to fear. It'll be okay." He'd called her Leafy for a time after that, teasing her gently during the day until the night terrors faded to nothingness and she was able to sleep through the night in her own bed.

She slipped between his covers, burying her nose in his pillow. She imagined his bearded face pressed there. "Winter," she said and then more softly, she added, "Daddy." She was a child again, smoothing her mother's still cheek. She sent her thoughts up and outward, but there was nothing. No connection to him. He had gone to a place where she could not follow. She was alone in the world.

But no, there was Tawnia and the undeniable connection that didn't relate solely to their physical similarity. Tawnia, who hadn't wanted her to face the apartment alone.

With that comforting thought, Autumn closed her eyes and slept.

CHAPTER

12

After leaving the women, Bret drove to the Multnomah County offices for his meeting with Clyde Hanks, but his mind was far from the bridge disaster. He was thinking instead of Tawnia and Autumn. When he'd been sitting on the couch with Autumn, he'd known she was Autumn, and yet the way her nose twitched every so often as she spoke, and the way one arch of her top lip rose slightly higher than the other as she smiled—that was all Tawnia. Their movements were also alike, fluid and purposeful. And their eyes. It was uncanny, to say the least, and it made him feel as if he knew Autumn as well as he knew Tawnia, which was far from the truth. The way Autumn looked at him made him feel as if she could see his very thoughts.

He hoped not, because they were confused. Was he attracted to both women, or did he feel something for Autumn because of her resemblance to Tawnia? There was a chance it could be something new, something that wasn't mixed up with the memory of Christian. Would it be wrong to hope for that?

Hanks looked haggard when Bret entered his office, as though he hadn't slept well since the bridge collapse. Probably he hadn't.

"Thanks for coming." Hanks indicated a chair in front of the desk, and Bret settled into it.

"Anything new?"

Hanks sighed as he sank into the chair behind the desk. "They don't have proof, but the FBI seems to be pointing the finger, at least in part, at the bridge operator. He's saying the boat hit the side of the bridge and that there was no error on his part, but the captain and crew swear otherwise. They say the lift wasn't up in time, or that it stopped and started back down, or some such nonsense. Some think the bridge operator may be somehow involved with the explosives and was trying to make it look like an accident."

"You've got to be kidding."

"They say everything was timed just so. Had to be, in order to make it look like the boat caused the collapse instead of the explosives."

Bret thought a moment. "Maybe they're right. If everything is pointing that way."

Hanks shook his head. "Absolutely not. I know the bridge operator, and if he says he wasn't aware of any plot, then I believe him. They have the wrong guy."

"How can you be sure?"

Hanks hesitated, raking a hand uncharacteristically through his hair, upsetting the natural flow of the thick waves. There was something more here, something Bret didn't understand.

"Look." Hanks leaned over, lowering his voice, "The truth is that the bridge operator is my son. I gave him the job last year when he dropped out of college." He gave a snort of disgust. "Twenty-three and still no degree in sight. But this job didn't require more than a few weeks of training, and he's actually done a great job."

"Then you have nothing to worry about. The FBI will figure it out. Until they do, everyone is guilty. They have to think that way. Taking a lie detector test might help things along."

"You don't understand." Hanks stood and paced to the door and back, his hands clasped in front as though walking up an aisle in a church. Ready to make penance.

Feeling uneasy, Bret came to his own feet. "I'd like to help, if I can. What exactly don't I understand?"

Hanks came to a stop, his eyes flat and staring. "It's just that my son wasn't in the control cabin when the boat came through. He was supposed to be, but he left with a . . . a woman. She came looking for someone who used to work at the lift. She was in tears—quite upset. My son was in the cabin alone that day. There weren't any boats in sight, and since they can't let unauthorized personnel into the control room, he saw nothing wrong with stepping out for a few minutes to talk to the girl. He carried his radio, so he'd be notified if a boat needed something. Besides, the boats know they can't get through without approval. If a boat came, it could wait."

"So how long was he gone from the cabin?"

"Ten minutes. Fifteen, tops. Or so he says."

Bret arched a brow. "Or so he says?"

"He swears it was only ten minutes, but you know how difficult it is to judge these things. He got her to stop crying, but she stayed and talked a while. He walked her down the bridge to the park. He swears the river was clear. But she was very flirtatious and a bit physical, if you know what I mean."

Bret could imagine the mystery woman kissing the young bridge operator to distract him. "Aren't there an average of six lifts a day? Why would he go so far from the cabin?" It was irresponsible to a huge degree.

Hanks shook his head. "That kid has never had any sense when it comes to women. He finally did extricate himself when he noticed someone had started the lift, but he got back only in time for the whole thing to come collapsing down."

Bret swallowed hard. At least the lift had been up. That was the only thing that prevented even more deaths, though with the backup of traffic on the east side, the effect had still been horrendous.

"My son was almost knocked over the edge of the bridge and had to climb to safety. That's why people believe that he was in the cabin when it fell."

"Someone had to start the lift."

"Well, whoever it was must have run to safety seconds before my son got there. Maybe he hid in one of the waiting cars."

"And your son didn't think any of this was important to tell the police?" Bret demanded. How could he not? And how could Hanks not have come forward once he knew the truth?

"He's still just a kid."

"Then maybe he shouldn't have been operating the lift."

Hanks glared at him, and Bret realized he'd overstepped his bounds. He was the employee, and though his job wasn't at risk, word would get back to Nevada. Still, he couldn't believe Hanks was covering for his son.

He held Hanks' gaze. "He has to report this. You know he does. Think about it."

The anger subsided from Hanks' eyes. As the anger left, so did whatever had been holding his shoulders in place, and they slumped with the weight of his duty. "You're right. He should have come forward, but he didn't, and coming forward this late . . . he risks not only his job but mine as well."

"Not necessarily. When did you learn about it?"

"Last night. I swear I didn't know it before."

Bret felt the weight of unwanted power. All at once, Hanks was no longer the confident manager but rather a simple man looking to him for an answer. For absolution. For an easy way out. Bret could give him none of that.

"I think you ought to tell the FBI. Now. Before they discover it themselves."

"Maybe they won't."

What little remained of Bret's respect for the man vanished. "Maybe you ought to worry more about finding who did this instead of what people are going to think about you and your son."

Turning his back on Hanks, he strode to the door. He knew Hanks's type. He was the kind who covered for his son the time he accidentally broke the neighbor's window or vouched for him the night the school was vandalized, though the boy's ball was missing and he'd seen cans of spray paint under his son's bed. He was the kind who used his city position to get his son's speeding ticket dropped, a man who gave his son a key job when he wasn't the top applicant. He'd made it easy for his son to be unmindful of consequences because he'd never had to suffer any.

"Wait!" Hanks scuttled after him, defying his middle-age bulk. "I'll tell them—I will! I just want a little time. I want to find out about this woman. I thought maybe you'd help. You know all the players. Someone has to be hiding something. My biggest fear is that this is an inside job."

Bret hesitated. The guy was asking not telling, and despite his disgust, Bret was curious. "You have a name for the girl?"

"Sheree. Thin, blondish hair, good-looking. Alec drew a picture. He's good at drawing."

Alec, the boy's name. Alec Hanks. "He draws?"

Hanks hurried back to his desk and grabbed a thick sketch pad. "Quite well. He draws when he's not busy with the lift. Here, this is it. Pretty little thing, but you can tell by the eyes that she's up to no good."

Eyes. The reference startled him, as he'd so recently been thinking about Autumn and Tawnia's shared oddity, and he was relieved to see the girl in the pencil sketch didn't resemble them in the least. The hair first drew his attention, so thick and long and wild—the epitome of every young man's dream. The hair framed a small face with closely set eyes that wore too much mascara. At first glance, Bret would have called her beautiful, but upon closer examination, he saw her face was really quite ordinary, even homely. It was her hair that made her stand out. Otherwise, she was short, with high, small breasts and a straight waist that would tend to thickness later in life. The fitted T-shirt she wore left little to the imagination; the kind of shirt that only the very young could wear well.

Hanks was right, the close-set calculating eyes told the story, yet Alec had been duped. Strange that he could draw the feeling of the eyes so accurately without understanding what it meant.

Bret tapped the sketchbook. "Could I borrow this? I'll make copies tonight and give it back to you in the morning."

"You can use our copier." Hanks led the way from his office. "It's out here, at the reception desk."

Bret waited for the machine to spit out five copies of the drawing.

"I really appreciate this," Hanks said.

"I don't know that I can help. I'll pass the picture around tomorrow. But I still think you should go to the police."

"I will."

Bret wasn't sure if he believed him, and he made a mental note to keep an eye on the situation. The last thing he needed was to be implicated in a cover-up.

"There's nothing more we can do tonight," Bret said as they walked to the door. He hesitated. "I was going to be checking another of your bridges tomorrow, but in light of what's happened, I'd rather be on hand for whatever else they find."

"The other bridges don't matter now. We aren't at fault, and we don't have to prove anything anymore. The explosives say this was terrorism, not engineer fault."

Bret shook his head. "But why here? I mean, terrorism should be in New York or Washington, D.C., or at a major airport. Why here in Portland?"

"Portland has so many river bridges. Do you know what that means for travel? Once word of this gets out, panic will start. People will be afraid to go to work or shopping. Parents won't want to send their children to school. Our entire city could come to a complete standstill. Thousands will be affected, and that will catch the nation's attention fast."

Bret thought Hanks might be overestimating the impact, but he wasn't in a position to hypothesize. "Well, now that we know what we're up against, I'd like to do some tests to see exactly what kind of explosives might have been used and how much. That'll give us an idea of who did it and how."

"I gave the FBI your name. They want to consult with engineers. And if you're on site, you can ask about the girl."

"Ask the FBI?"

"No, everyone else." Hank shoved out a hand and pumped

Bret's vigorously. "Thanks again. I owe you one." Before Bret could protest, he'd turned around and was gone.

Minutes later, Bret looked at the drawing in his hands, lit by the weak interior light inside his rental car. This mysterious Sheree could be anywhere by now. If she was a participant in the bridge attack, she might never be found. Then again, maybe there was no girl. For all he knew, Alec Hanks was making everything up to cover the fact that he'd made a serious error in judgment with the lift.

Bret put the car into gear and flipped on the radio, stifling a yawn at the late hour. As he drove near the Willamette River, he saw floodlights and numerous vehicles. Apparently the FBI was still at it. He felt an urge to go to them and give them Alec's drawing, but then what? What if Alec was lying? Better to do a little checking as he waited for Hanks to find his conscience.

If the man had a conscience.

"We pause now for breaking news about the Hawthorne Bridge disaster." The radio announcer's voice shook Bret from his musings. He tensed. How had they discovered the news about the explosion so quickly? Surely the FBI was keeping it under wraps as long as possible until they had answers to offer the public. Had someone leaked the information? An early announcement might set off a panic that would get in the way of the investigation.

"Thirty minutes ago Navy Seals recovered one more body from the Willamette River, an as yet unidentified man. That makes four victims recovered today, two men and two women, bringing the death toll to a tragic thirty people in all. The other victims found today include Cynthia McFadden and Marcia Pablos, who both leave behind spouses and teenage children. The first male victim found earlier this evening was identified as Dennis Reid. His fiancée told reporters they had planned to marry this fall. We will announce more information about this new victim as soon as it becomes available.

"According to authorities, today's discoveries leave only one person still missing. His or her identity has also not been released to the public. Our hearts go out to the families and to all the victims of this tragedy. As we've said before, a fund has been set up here for donations to help the victims' families, especially for children who've lost one or both parents. You can donate by phone, in person, or on our website. Thank you, Portland, for the generosity you have shown thus far.

"We'll be taking music requests for the next hour, so if you have a special song you want played for that special person . . ."

Bret quit listening. Another victim. Possibly Autumn's father. He turned the car around and headed back to the river, the scene of the devastation. If it was Winter Rain, he had to find out now so that Autumn wouldn't have to hear it from a complete stranger.

*T*awnia stretched, her neck feeling sore from her second night on a couch—first hers and now Autumn's. Oh, she'd thought about using Autumn's bed, but she'd been worried about not being able to hear her in the night. As it was, she'd listened at Winter's closed door for a long time but hadn't heard anything. She'd hoped that meant Autumn was sleeping, but she could just as well have been sitting on the bed staring into emptiness.

How would she feel if her own father was missing? She wouldn't like it, of course, and the idea of her mother being alone was more than a little terrifying. Her mother would hate being alone. She'd likely move to wherever Tawnia was, for the company.

Tawnia dialed home on her cell as she made her way to the kitchen to find breakfast. It was a small narrow room, smaller even than the kitchen at her bungalow. Room enough for a round table next to the fridge, across from which stood the range, a sink, and two feet of counter space. There was, of course, no microwave. The few cupboards were painted white, though she suspected they were solid wood. Tacky, her mother would say.

The loaf of bread on the counter was hard, and there was nothing edible in the fridge, though there was a great collection of mold growing in a pan of rice casserole and a head of green leaf lettuce that was decidedly brown. The milk showed promise, though, as did the bag of organic granola someone had left on the counter.

"Hello?" Her mother's voice came over the line, sounding as if she'd been awake for hours, which she had because it was two hours earlier in Kansas.

"Hi, it's Tawnia."

"Honey, how good to hear from you. Is everything okay?"

"Fine. How about you and Dad?"

"Everything is wonderful. I'm going out to lunch with Madge today. We're playing bridge afterwards."

Bridge. Tawnia had never learned to play. "That's great." The tension in her frame relaxed. Her parents were safe. "Hey, Mom."

"Hay is for horses."

Tawnia chuckled, though she knew it wasn't really a joke. Not with her mother. "I've been wondering. Well . . . I . . . you see, there's this girl . . ."

"A girl? What are you talking about?" Confusion laced the words.

Tawnia shut her eyes and rushed on. "I met this girl here who looks like me—a lot like me. It makes me wonder if, well, do you have any information about my adoption? I think we might be related."

Her mother was silent so long Tawnia wondered if her phone had lost connection. Then finally, "You're thinking about finding your birth mother, aren't you? Do you know what that does to me? Do you know how much I sacrificed raising you? I didn't do all that to lose you now."

"Mom, it's not that. Really. It's not about finding my birth mother. I haven't cared about that since I was seventeen. But even if I did, it wouldn't mean I didn't love you and Dad."

There was a loud sniff in her ear. "I'm sure I have the name of the adoption agency somewhere, but that's all. It was a closed adoption, and unless the birth mother wants the records opened, there's nothing more you can find out. Why is this suddenly so important?"

"I told you, it's this girl I met. You know about the bridge collapse. Well, she was on the bridge. Her dad's still missing. Bret met her and introduced us."

"Bret? He's there?" There was sudden animation in her mother's voice. She'd met Bret once, briefly, and liked him. He was the sort of man that fit her criteria for Tawnia: young, hardworking, stable, from a good family, and no baggage. Not like Orion, who not only worked a dangerous job but had been married before and might have questionable designs on her virtue.

"Yes, he came because of the bridge. Anyway, she looks a lot like me, and now she has no one. She was adopted too, and her birth mother is dead. But we thought maybe her mother was a sister to my birth mother, maybe even twins. If we're related, I thought it would help her to know that she still has family."

"Impossible. You're making this all up. Do you think I'm stupid? Do you want to hurt me? Look, if you want to find your *real* mother, just do it. I don't want to hear about it." The line went dead.

"That went well," Tawnia said with a sigh, dropping her

phone onto the table. Actually, the conversation had gone on much longer than she'd expected.

She put granola into a bowl and sniffed the milk before pouring, her nose wrinkling at the sour smell. She dumped it down the drain and rinsed out the sink.

"There's always eggs." Autumn was in the kitchen doorway, still wearing Tawnia's jeans from yesterday. The red top half of her hair stood on end, but her face looked rested. How long had she been standing there? Not that Tawnia could complain—it wasn't her apartment.

"I looked for eggs. There's none in the fridge."

"I don't keep them in the fridge. There's no need if you don't wash them and if you eat them within a couple weeks. These are fresh from a friend's farm. Well, fresh at the end of last week. They're from free-range chickens, which, if you know anything about chicken farming, is a lot healthier for us and more humane for the chickens. Winter sells the eggs in his store." Her voice went softer at the end of the sentence, but besides that she showed no reaction to the reference to her father. She stood on tiptoe, opened the cupboard above the sink with her left hand, and brought down a cardboard carton of eggs.

Brown eggs. Tawnia had never seen brown eggs before, though she knew they existed. Something about a different kind of hen. Maybe.

"Here, let me." She took the egg away from Autumn, who was trying awkwardly to crack it into a bowl with her good hand. "Have a seat, and I'll fix you breakfast. We have to hurry, though. I have to go to work."

Autumn went to the table without protest. "I heard you talking to your mother. What happened?"

"She doesn't believe you exist. She thinks I want to find my birth mother and replace her."

"And do you?"

Tawnia turned from the bowl of raw eggs. "Growing up with my parents wasn't exactly easy. They expected a lot from me, but I know I had a better life than a lot of children. I know they care about what happens to me. I never went hungry, I always had clothes, and I had a great education. Looking back, I think there were things I could have done to make life easier for all of us. I . . ." She shrugged. "I don't know. This morning I woke up worried about them. That's never happened before. I never thought much about them not being there."

Autumn nodded. "Death does put things in perspective."

"You have any margarine to cook these in?"

Autumn blanched. "Hydrogenated oil that has been bleached and colored? No way. I do have butter, though."

"That'll do." She accepted the butter Autumn retrieved from the refrigerator. "You look better this morning. Rested."

"I feel better." Autumn's smile faltered. "At least until I start to think about everything. I mean, the idea that I'll never see Winter again. That he'll never walk through that door . . ." She looked to the kitchen door, as though waiting for him to do just that.

"So, what was it like growing up with hippies?" Tawnia flushed as she asked the question.

Autumn laughed. "You mean as opposed to stuffy, rich people like your parents?"

"Something like that."

Autumn considered for a moment. "I think it was the best life a child could have, despite Summer dying. I mean, I suppose I could have gotten some terrible disease because I never had immunizations, and they never cared about my grades at school or if I wore the same clothes for a week. I never had to wear shoes. As a teenager, my hair changed colors more times than I washed my jeans. None of that was important. I suppose some kids could have gone wild, but Winter—and Summer when she was alive—lived in a way that was well, wholesome, I guess. If someone was a danger to me, a friend on drugs, or something, Winter loved them and was in their face so much they either changed or left me alone. As for me, I never needed anything more than him and our close friends."

"Sounds wonderful."

"It was. She gave me a great life."

"Your birth mother?"

"Yes. You want to see her picture?"

Tawnia brought the cooked eggs to the table. A bagel would have made this breakfast more filling but it would have to do. "I'd love to."

Autumn was gone for only a minute, coming back into the kitchen with a family album. Turning to a page near the beginning, she pointed to a photo of a woman and a young girl, who couldn't have been more than sixteen. The girl looked a lot like Autumn, though the eyes were both blue and her short hair was a lot lighter, nearly blond. But the shape of the face and her build were very similar.

This girl might be related to me. Tawnia wanted to feel moved as she looked at the picture, but she only experienced an odd lump in the back of her throat that she recognized as pity. "She's very young."

"I know. When I was her age, I used to wonder how she must have felt having a child. I'm glad she felt she could trust Summer and Winter with me."

"If she'd lived, you'd have probably seen her again."

"Probably. That's how Winter and Summer are—were. They might even have adopted her as well. We've had a lot of people living with us over the years." Autumn left the photo album open and began eating her eggs.

Tawnia's attention went to Summer. Obviously older than Autumn's birth mother but still young. She wore her brown hair very long, with the bangs braided down one side, as though to prevent them from going into her serious gray eyes. She was pretty in an earth-mother sort of way. The kind of woman who would be comfortable wearing holey jeans and no makeup. A woman who would look at home playing a guitar around a fire. She would worry about dolphins and global warming and preservatives. She would have loved to have a dozen children, but given only one, she would have made the best of it because nature had spoken.

Tawnia ate in silence, deep in thought, her appetite matched only by Autumn's. "I should have made more."

"I'll go shopping later. We'll have a big dinner tonight to make up for it."

"Here?"

"Why not? Just the two of us. Maybe I can get ahold of that doctor who placed me while I'm at work today. I found the box of old papers. He's probably moved, though, after all these years." Autumn's voice faltered as the doorbell rang, her face going pale. "I wonder who that is?"

"I'll get it," Tawnia said through a mouthful of eggs. "I'll tell any neighbors you aren't ready for company," She jumped to her feet and hurried into the hall before Autumn could object. Truthfully, she was more worried about the police than the neighbors. After all, who'd go to someone's house at seven in the morning if they weren't bearing bad news? What if they'd found Winter?

She swallowed her mouthful and looked through the peep hole, her breath catching in her throat. Bret. Great, and she was still wearing her oldest set of pajamas, which made her look distinctly like a scrawny bag lady dressed in something she'd found in the bargain bin at a large-sized clothing store.

She opened the door a few inches, but Bret took that as an invitation and pushed his way inside. "I have news," he said. "But again, it's confidential. Well, some of it."

"Winter?" she whispered.

His voice lowered to match hers. "They did find another victim last night. Not Winter."

Tawnia nodded. "What else?"

"Is Autumn around? She should hear this." He hefted a set of folded papers in his hands.

Tawnia stifled the desire to grab them from him. "In the kitchen."

Bret's eyes wandered up and down her body, taking in her attire. "Don't you have to get ready for work?"

She folded her arms across her chest. "Yes, so get talking already." She pointed at the doorway leading to the kitchen.

Autumn was still sitting at the table when they entered. Her face brightened at seeing Bret, and for a moment Tawnia felt horribly jealous. But Bret wasn't hers. Not now, not ever.

He unfolded the papers, all of which seemed to be copies of the same drawing. "Have either of you seen this girl before? Her name's Sheree."

She was the type of girl Tawnia's mother would have prevented her from befriending, perhaps rightly so. A girl who cared only about her own satisfaction. Or was that her mother talking? Would Winter have loved the girl into finding her best self? It was hard to say, and Tawnia bet if she herself ever had children, she wouldn't take the risk.

"Never," Autumn said with surety.

"Really? Never down at the river?"

"Nope."

"She doesn't look the slightest bit familiar," Tawnia agreed.

Bret frowned. "That's what everyone has said so far. But someone has to have seen her."

"Why?" Autumn looked again at the drawing. "What does she have to do with the bridge?"

He shook his head. "I can't tell you the details. For your protection, really. But this girl might somehow have been involved with the collapse."

"Tell me!" barked Autumn, her hand fisted at her side. There was a hardness in her face that Tawnia hadn't seen before.

"You could get in trouble if you knew," Bret said.

Tawnia snorted. "Oh, come on. You act as if you're with the FBI or something."

"Well, actually, I have been working with them all night."

"You haven't been back to your hotel?" His clothes did seem rumpled.

"No. I've been helping determine what kind of explosives and how much was used."

"Who's the girl?" demanded Autumn.

"Yeah." Tawnia lifted her chin. "Don't change the subject. You told us about the bombs, and we haven't told anyone, so you can tell us about this."

Bret sighed and sank into an empty chair at the table, his gaze going from one to the other. "The girl allegedly enticed the bridge operator out of the control cabin shortly before the boat hit the bridge. But someone was in there because the lift went up."

His slight hesitation told Tawnia he was omitting at least some details, but given the increasing color of Autumn's face, she let it go for the moment.

Autumn exploded. "You mean thirty-one people died or

are missing partly because some bridge operator was flirting with this girl instead of doing his job?"

Bret lifted a hand to ward off the tumble of words. "Wait a minute. We don't know for sure how this connects to the explosives. At this point we know only what the bridge operator is claiming. It could all be a lie." He pointed to the bottom of the drawing near the girl's left arm where there was an unreadable flourish of a signature. "Alec Hanks," Bret said. "That's the bridge operator. He drew this. Know him?" Both Tawnia and Autumn shook their heads.

"What does the FBI say?" Autumn asked.

Again the slight hesitation that signaled omission of details. "They'll do their own investigation, of course. I'm just asking around because I've been close to many of the employees lately."

"Then you think it might be an inside job?" Tawnia sat down on the chair beside him.

Autumn cast her an admiring glance. "It has to be."

"Nothing is for sure," Bret said. "We don't know anything."

"Except that the bridge was blown up." Tawnia sighed. "And you're still hiding something from us. About this picture."

"Okay, I am. The fact is that the FBI actually aren't investigating anything to do with this girl yet. Alec Hanks is the son of the Bridge Section manager Clyde Hanks, and they haven't reported his absence from the cabin to the police or given them a copy of this drawing."

Tawnia stared at him. "But they have to."

"I told them that. I think they will, but meanwhile, I'm doing some checking around about the girl." Bret folded the papers together again. "There is some good news. A couple of hours ago in the rubble we found a charge that didn't go off. Wires weren't connected right or something. Saves us a lot of time figuring out how they did it. Turns out they used a kind of blasting gelatin. It's called high velocity, and it's the most powerful of all commercial explosives. Since it's waterproof, it can sit in water for days without degrading. It can even be used in really deep water without misfiring, though I believe the regular grade would have worked very well in this case. The billows of clouds everyone saw were not only from the collapse itself but from the fumes of the explosives. The noise of the explosion was muted because of the water, but many people remember hearing some sort of rumbling or explosion."

"Like a boom," Autumn said softly. "I think I remember that now. But the grating noise was there almost from the beginning too. I thought they were part of the same thing. Or maybe that was the boat hitting the bridge."

Bret nodded. "I think everyone assumed that."

"Are you saying the boat and the lift had nothing at all to do with the collapse?" Tawnia asked. "That it was a coincidence the boat just happened to be passing by?"

Bret shrugged. "The boat could have simply been another innocent victim, I suppose. Or . . ." He trailed off.

"Or what?" Tawnia pressed.

"It might have everything to do with it. That boat could have been used to plant the explosives."

"And then they set it off before they could get away?" Autumn shook her head. "They ran into the bridge, remember?"

"I know." Bret rubbed a hand over the stubble on his chin. "It doesn't make sense that they'd use the boat and then not let it get free."

"You said yourself the explosives were waterproof," Tawnia said. "They could have been set days before, and the boat used for a distraction. Or cover-up, more likely."

"That does make more sense. But I just keep thinking of those fins on the boat."

"The ones we found." Autumn rose and began pacing.

"Yeah, I keep asking myself what happened to the rest of the suit. I thought when I first saw them that the authorities had confiscated the rest of the equipment to test for explosives or something, but I asked the FBI, and they didn't know anything about it."

Autumn ripped off a bit of nail from her thumb with her teeth. "Maybe there never was a suit. Maybe the owner sometimes goes swimming in the river in his underwear."

"I suppose. It still bugs me, though. I don't know many men who go swimming in their underwear with fins."

Tawnia had to smile. This was the Bret she knew—careful down to the tips of his fingers. A lot like she was. Maybe that was the real reason they hadn't been able to make it work.

"I know a lot of people who swim without anything on," Autumn put in. "I grew up with hippies. I don't think the fins mean anything."

"Maybe not."

Tawnia looked at the apple clock on the wall. "Well, you two go ahead and play detective. I have fifteen minutes to get out of here if I want to make it to work on time." At least she wouldn't get lost since Autumn lived so close to the agency. She hurried from the room, giving Bret a last glance as she left. His eyes met hers, and she looked away.

Fourteen minutes later she found Bret and Autumn sitting at the kitchen table, their heads close together as they peered over Autumn's picture album. Tawnia felt a familiar surge of emotion she was beginning to associate with jealousy. She didn't want Bret looking so happy without her. Or Autumn so content. Shaking her head in disgust, she started to leave without speaking, but Bret jumped up from the table.

"Wait." He quickly covered the space between them. "Take

a copy of the drawing. Pass it around. You never know who might have seen her. Someone in this town has to know who she is."

As Tawnia accepted the paper, his fingers brushed hers. She glanced up at him quickly, but he was already walking away.

"What did you do?" Dustin Bronson challenged Tawnia as she approached her office.

She stared at him blankly. "What are you talking about?"

"First you land the billboard account, and now my biggest account suddenly calls up and cancels everything? Something stinks."

Tawnia took a moment to let that sink in. "Are you talking about Multnomah County?"

"Of course I'm talking about Multnomah. But then you already know that, don't you? I thought it was suspicious when I talked to that engineer yesterday. He's from Nevada, and I bet you know him, don't you? What did you say to him?" He looked like an angry blond-haired rooster, with his spiked hair and arrogant expression.

"I really don't know what you're talking about."

But suddenly she did. Now that the cause of the collapse had been traced to explosives, the county was no longer accountable. They couldn't have prevented this mess, and no lawsuit could win against them. In fact, the threat of terrorism might bring all of Portland together far more effectively than any publicity campaign. Naturally, Multnomah would opt out of paying so much money for publicity they no longer needed.

Of course, she couldn't tell Dustin any of this until the authorities went public with the news, but it gave her no small satisfaction that the man was crashing and burning because of his own dishonesty. If she'd won that account, she'd be the one holding the bag, but now the higher echelons would wonder what Dustin had done to cause the county to cancel.

"Did they give you a reason?" she asked lightly.

"They said they'd changed their minds." Dustin's sneer told her what he thought of that excuse.

She tilted her head to the side and studied him. "Then maybe that's what actually happened."

Turning on her heel, she stepped through the open door to her team's room. Already there was life in the cubicles, as Canda's blond head could be seen in Sean's space, moving as she talked animatedly.

Dustin's hand closed over Tawnia's arm, stopping her flight. She stared at his hand silently until he drew it away. "Look, I can't say I'm sorry, Dustin, because I still think you're a snake, but I had nothing to do with it. Even if I had the connections, that's not who I am."

He nodded, looking slightly appeased.

Tawnia remembered the drawing and took it from her purse. "That reminds me. Have you seen this girl?" Dustin's connection with his college co-eds might be useful.

He studied the drawing. "There are dozens like her in my classes, but no, I don't know her in particular. Why do you ask?"

Tawnia hadn't thought of an explanation. "A friend is looking for her. Apparently, she left a memory of her face but not her phone number."

"I see." Dustin's eyes flicked to the drawing again briefly and back to her face. "Well, later. Maybe we can do lunch."

Not on your life, Tawnia thought, but she did feel a sliver of pity for the man. "If I were you, I'd call that Multnomah guy and try to sell him something else. A scaled-down something. You never know."

"Thanks. I'll give him a call. He's a jerk, though, so I doubt he'll go for it."

As she watched Dustin leave him, a new thought came to her. Was it only a coincidence that Alec Hanks was the bridge operator the day of the collapse? Had the girl known he'd be there or had she been prepared to seduce any man away from his task? If Alec had been chosen specifically, was it because he had a known weakness for women, or because someone wanted to get back at his father? If so, that might narrow down the list of suspects. Terrorists might not be involved at all.

She wished she could talk to Bret about it, but he was probably still with Autumn.

How long would it take them to fall in love? It had taken her only a few weeks to fall for him.

I can't think about this now. Plastering a smile on her face, she lifted a hand in greeting to her team members before going into her office.

CHAPTER 14

"Well, look at you, girl!" Jake beamed at Autumn as she walked into the store. He was more handsome than the last time she'd seen him, though the dreadlocks would have been a little startling if she wasn't accustomed to them. Today he was again wearing immaculate off-white cargo-style pants, this time with a snug blue T-shirt that showed his muscles to good advantage.

"You look fabulous," he continued. "Well, your hair's a little interesting, but besides that, fab. Just fab."

"You try to wash and style your hair with one hand," she retorted, feeling more defensive than the comment merited. She lifted the long cotton sleeve she'd worn to hide the splint on her broken arm.

"That would never work for me." He clicked his tongue in pity.

Autumn knew. Some thought people with dreadlocks never washed or took care of their hair, but the truth was Jake carefully

washed his four-inch locks every two or three days with a resi-
due-free shampoo, and he maintained the style by rolling in
loose hairs and by using special products to make sure the tips
had good knots. The maintenance time involved wasn't as great
now as when he had first started the dreads a few years ago,
but the style was a lot more to take care of than the buzz he'd
previously worn.

To go with the dreads, he sported a smattering of facial
hair along the line of his jaw and his upper lip, which he always
trimmed short every few days. He was a hit with all the ladies,
from the older ones who enjoyed his nice smile and stared
in fascination at his hair to the younger ones who noted his
muscles and blushed whenever he glanced their way.

Jake had already opened both the Herb Shoppe and
Autumn's Antiques, and several customers drifted between
the stores by way of the double connecting doors. Because
customers could ring up at either desk, recordkeeping had at
first been tedious as they struggled to figure out which profits
went to which business, but Jake had a friend who'd written a
program for their computers, and now Autumn hardly gave it a
thought. Not that it mattered much even in the old days, except
to determine inventory and purchases, because she and Winter
had shared everything. Of course, now both stores were hers.

"Did I say something wrong?" Jake's face showed concern.
His strong arm was around her instantly.

"No, I'm fine," Autumn made herself say. "Really. It's just
weird being here . . . without . . ."

Jake gave a sympathetic shake of his head. "You sure you
want to be here? I can call my little sister. She's glad to help out
after school."

"No. I have to do this." Besides, he'd been here too much

alone as it was, and he'd probably had to endure several rushes with impatient customers.

"Okay. But let me know if you need to leave." The arm around her tightened. "Don't look now, but here comes the blue lady. You know, the one who has the thing for Winter."

Autumn looked and saw Thera Brinker bearing down on them from the Herb Shoppe, her white hair swooped up elegantly on her head. She wore all blue, as she always did, because it was a calming color and she'd had "too much excitement with that first no-good husband of hers." Today she wore a huge multi-strand blue bead necklace that made her look slightly ridiculous, but she was a kind woman who was fun to be around. Autumn had begun to suspect of late that Winter might think the same.

"Oh, Autumn, I just heard. I can't believe it! What you must be feeling!" Tears punctuated her words. "I'm so sorry!" Thera swept Autumn into her arms, crushing her to the bosom that would have been soft had it not been for the bulky beads.

This was the part Autumn had dreaded. The running into people who had been close to her and Winter or who had somehow been a part of their lives. She didn't want the pity, the questions, the agony they would bring when she was forced to talk about him.

"You don't have to say a word, sweetie, unless you want to. Your father was a wonderful man, and we all know it. We're going to miss him—and we're certainly going to take care of you."

Autumn let herself be rocked in Thera's arms, finding a comfort she hadn't expected. Maybe she'd been wrong to hide out by the river, avoiding all her friends.

She did have friends. They came in all day as word spread

that she was back. Regular customers, people who lived in her apartment building, and owners of other stores on the block. Though she'd thought she had no more tears left, she cried repeatedly, but these tears were cleansing, without the lonely bitterness of before.

Between talking with her friends and taking care of the few strangers who came through the door, Autumn was in the back room on her phone searching for the man who'd delivered her and brought her to Winter and Summer to raise. She had no memory of the doctor, except what Summer had told her, but he was supposed to have visited quite often in her first few years of life. Why had he stopped? A move, probably.

So far, every number she'd called from the box of papers or from the phone book belonged to someone else. Jake appeared over her shoulder. She'd told him about Tawnia, and he seemed as excited as she was about contacting the doctor.

"Maybe he's dead. Did you think of that? It's been a lot of years since you were born. I mean, he could have been old even then."

"You're not helping!"

"Well, I'm just saying. It's a possibility."

Autumn sighed. "If he's dead, I might never find out if we're related."

"You could find out on the Internet, I bet. If he's still alive, I mean." A bell sounded, signaling that someone had entered one of their shops. "I'll take care of that."

After one last futile call to a clinic in Portland, Autumn grabbed the small box of her parents' records and headed for the computer that she also used as a register. Clumsily, with only the fingers of her left hand, she typed in "Oregon death records," followed a link, and ended up on Ancestry.com.

"Floyd Blaine Loveridge," she murmured, typing in the doctor's name. A few names came up, and one of them matched exactly. The year of death was twenty-seven years earlier. She tried clicking on the link, and up came a menu offering a free trial membership, so she signed up, but she didn't learn any more. Dr. Loveridge was dead. Surely there couldn't be another man with that exact name who had lived in Portland. Apparently, her search had been over even before Summer had died. No wonder she didn't remember him.

Autumn let her head drop to her left hand. Now what? Then she remembered the note. She dug in the box for the age-yellowed paper and re-read it:

> *"BervaDee and I can't make it to Autumn's 1st birthday party, but you can be sure we will stop by and see her later in the week. We are happy things are working out so well. Thanks for all you continue to do to help the girls from our mothering classes."*
>
> *Floyd Loveridge*

BervaDee was probably his wife, though Autumn didn't remember her being listed on the records. If she was his wife, she might still be alive. Maybe she never remarried. It was possible. Many widows decided one man was enough for a lifetime. Even if the woman had remarried, the name BervaDee was pretty rare. There might not be another in all of the United States, much less Oregon.

The bell at the door jingled again, but the customer was entering the Herb Shoppe and not her store. Autumn settled down to work, looking up the name on the Internet. There was no BervaDee Loveridge, and she had to try several more White Page links before she found one she could type in just a letter for the last name. She tried different letters of the alphabet, but nothing came up.

"Useless," she muttered, exiting the browser. "Waste of time." BervaDee, whoever she was, seemed to have dropped off the face of the earth.

"Look who's here." Jake came from the linking doors, his kid sister, Randa, in tow. "Just got out of school. Stopped by to see if we needed help." Randa was tall and beautiful, if a tad too slender. The top and sides of her hair were braided in thick cornrows, ending with a ponytail in the back where the rest of her long hair splayed down her back in tight ringlets.

Autumn smiled at them. "Hi, Randa. Thanks for all your help this past week. I really appreciate it."

"It's been so slow today," Jake said. "Well, besides all your friends dropping by, and I got to thinking. Randa here is a whiz with hair. She could, uh, you know, help you out. Since your arm's broken and all."

Autumn wouldn't put it past Jake to have called his sister for that reason alone. Even if she didn't care, hair was important to him, and so was her well-being. She started to shake her head, but then an idea that had been percolating since the day before resurfaced. "Can you do color?"

Randa shrugged. "Depends on what you want."

It didn't really matter if it turned out perfectly. Autumn only wanted to see what difference hair would make in her similarity with Tawnia. "I want to get rid of the red. Go all brown, like my natural color."

"Easy."

"Can you do it here? There's a sink in the bathroom."

"Well, I'll have to get some stuff, but I can do it."

"Okay, then."

"Should I wait till closing time?"

"No. It's pretty dead now."

Dead. The word hung in the air, too late to call it back. Jake busied himself rearranging a display of vases, while Randa backed to the door. "I'll be back then. In a bit."

"Wait! Here's some money." Autumn punched in the code to her till and scooped out a couple of twenties. "That enough?"

"Plenty."

Autumn watched her leave before looking at Jake. "I hope I know what I'm doing."

"It'll be fine," he said. "Randa's a smart kid. And besides, you can always fix it later."

Autumn looked in the bathroom mirror, turning her head this way and that. The color was better than she expected, though she looked rather too plain now, and the style Randa had chosen was a little more youthful than she wanted. But at least she no longer looked like she'd barely dragged herself from her bed.

"Thanks, Randa. It's perfect. Here, let me pay you."

"No. It's something I wanna do. It's just . . . I'm real sorry about Winter." Randa's eyes met hers briefly before careening away to focus on a section of white wall.

"Thanks," Autumn said quietly.

"I'll meet you at your house later, then. To help with your friend."

"Great." Autumn watched her leave the back room, hoping Tawnia would go along with the plan she and Randa had hatched over the past hour.

Seconds later, Jake stuck his head in the door. "See?" he said. "Much better. Look, that guy's out there for you. That firefighter."

Orion. Autumn tossed her head, smiling. Now was the time to try out her new look and see if she could get Tawnia a date with a certain handsome older man.

CHAPTER

15

Bret's day was grueling. He spent hours being asked his opinion on the explosives used on the bridge and about Multnomah County's employees. After the first fifteen minutes, he had nothing more to tell them about either, but the FBI agents in charge seemed to think the more they talked, the more information they'd extract.

The only interesting thing that happened was when he told the FBI interviewer about visiting the boat and the fins he and Autumn had found. This time the authorities were interested and immediately sent someone to retrieve them. So far no one on board the boat, captain or crew, had admitted to owning the equipment.

"It could be that our suspect took a complete set of scuba equipment on board and then decided he didn't need the fins or left them behind accidentally," the FBI man said. He was a small man with piercing dark eyes that seemed to accuse Bret of lying even when he wasn't. His blond hair was cut so short he was almost bald.

"But why right then?" countered Bret, who himself kept going back and forth on whether or not the two events were related. "He could have set the charges three days earlier, for all we know. Why risk your life by diving from that boat and blowing up the bridge so quickly? Given the time it would take to set the charges, I don't see how it was possible."

"The captain says there was a delay. He'd been trying to radio the bridge operator for some time without success."

Because Hanks junior was flirting with some chick. And probably a lot longer than fifteen minutes.

"But long enough to be able to set the charges and get far enough away?" Bret asked.

"If he was experienced and had a device that propelled him through the water."

Ah, now he understood where they were going. "Which was why he wouldn't need fins."

"Well, our man should have used them anyway. Easier to navigate."

"Or she." The extra copies of the drawing Hanks had given him weighed heavily in Bret's pocket.

The agent cracked a smile. "Maybe. Anyway, there may have been reasons we aren't aware of: he was interrupted, he thought he'd need to hold onto the supports with his legs while setting the charges, his feet were too large. Or maybe it has nothing to do with anything."

"I see." This was getting old. They still didn't know much more than they had learned when they discovered the explosives.

Bret wondered when Hanks would come forward, and thinking that only made him feel guilty for not reporting what he knew. "What about the governor?" Bret asked. "Has any connection been made? Has he received any threats?"

"No threats, and we can't find the slightest connection to him. And since no one has claimed responsibility, we can't trace any backward connection that might exist."

That no one had claimed responsibility didn't make sense to Bret. The collapse of the bridge should be seen as a huge success for whoever was responsible. He sighed. "Well, if you're finished with me . . ." He glanced at the door.

"You can go. You've been really helpful. Let me know if you think of anything else." Rising to his feet, the agent offered Bret his hand.

Bret shook quickly before turning away from that keen stare.

He wasn't the only one given special attention. Multnomah's employees, particularly anyone connected with bridge maintenance, were also interviewed extensively. Robert Glen. Bret's former shadow, emerged from another room at the same time Bret did—his third interview, if Bret had counted correctly. His face was as dark as his red hair.

"Bozos," he muttered. "Stinkin' waste of time."

Bret smiled. "Yeah, I know what you mean."

"Wish they'd let me get back to my job."

"I'm afraid that's going to take a while. A lot of people died."

"I know, but they act like it's our fault. We did everything we could to make the bridges safe—everything management would let us. If there's a problem, that's where they should look."

Knowing about Alec Hanks, Bret had to agree. "Yeah, but this is terrorism. Once word of that gets out, there's going to be panic for sure. It'll hit a lot of people at home. The FBI needs to find out as much information as possible so when people demand answers, they can give them something."

"I'm still not convinced someone planted explosives at all." Robert took a step, lifting his face closer to Bret's, his voice low. "I think they're barking up the wrong tree."

"But you saw the damage. That couldn't possibly have been caused by a stress collapse."

"You might be wrong." A tiny trickle of sweat slid down Robert's left temple, and damp circles stood out under his arm. "I think it was an accident, plain and simple. No one wanted this collapse."

Bret was surprised at his vehemence. He took a step back. "Look, I know how you feel—"

"You don't! They're treating us like criminals—at least those of us who really work here. There's even talk of a lie detector test." He snorted, shaking his head. "You give thirteen years of your life to a company that turns its back on you. I should have known. Government is famous for tricks like this."

"Well, they have good reason this time."

"Do they? Or are they trying to shift the blame? It was an accident. Period."

Bret looked at him without understanding. "Why do you keep going back to that? Even if you don't believe the damage is evidence, they have proof in the failed charge we found."

Robert blinked at him. "What?"

"The charge, the one that didn't go off." When Robert showed no reaction, Bret went on. "You haven't heard? The divers found it early this morning, and it proves absolutely that this was terrorism. Everyone's talking about it—well, everyone in the know, that is." As the engineer manager, Robert should have been privy to everything.

"I got here late." Robert squeezed his eyes shut, thick brownish red lashes standing out against the paler color of his lids. "And this morning, they've kept me busy with all these stupid questions." He opened his eyes and met Bret's gaze. "Only I guess they're not stupid, are they? What did they use?"

"Blasting gelatin. High velocity."

"The most powerful thing they could get their hands on."

"It could have been planted days in advance, though the FBI seems to think otherwise."

"We still have nothing to do with this! No one here would have done something like that. We may groan about management and protest policies, but you'd have to be crazy to use explosives on any bridge."

"Exactly." Bret fell silent as an employee walked past them in the corridor. He didn't recognize the man, but Robert nodded to him.

"This can't be happening." Robert stepped back, resting against the wall, as though it was the only thing keeping him standing.

"You knew this was a possibility all along. You told me yourself, the collapse shouldn't have happened. You were right."

Robert nodded, the angry flush on his face seeping away. "I knew my bridge was stronger than that. If they'd listened to me and fixed certain things, it might even have withstood this attack."

"I don't think so. Someone went to an awful lot of trouble and expense to make it go down. But maybe there's more to this than we think. I want to show you something." Bret pulled out a copy of the girl's face. "Ever seen her before? Name's Sheree."

Robert briefly glanced at the drawing. "Nope. Pretty little thing, though." He pushed off the wall. "Well, I guess I'd better get going."

"Don't you want to know why I'm asking about the girl?"

He hesitated. "I'm sorry. It's just all this questioning. What has she got to do with this? You looking for a date?"

Bret snorted. "Hardly. Anyway, I can't tell you how she's connected to the mess. But she's someone of interest."

That got his attention. "The FBI is looking for her?" The furrow between Robert's eyes deepened.

"Not yet. But it's only a matter of time."

"Let me have the drawing. I'll ask around for you. I know more people here than you do."

Bret felt relief. Robert would do a better job of it, and Bret wouldn't have to worry about accidentally showing it to an FBI agent. "Thanks. I appreciate it."

"It's nothing."

"Call me any time if you get a lead." Bret paused. "Hanks has already seen it, so you don't need to show him."

"Fine. Hey, I just remembered. I tracked down your tools this morning. Between interviews. Sorry it took me this long."

"Really? That's great!" Bret had almost given them up for lost.

"Yeah. I locked them in with the others that night, but someone else sent them up to the regular maintenance office. It was only discovered when the janitor couldn't figure out what it was. The box is still locked and all, so everything should be fine. I left it at the front desk for you."

"Great. I won't need them any more here, but I'm relieved to have them back."

"I knew you would be. Well, back to the grind—until they haul me in for questioning again. But I tell you, I'll refuse to submit to a lie detector, if that's what it comes down to. That's plain degrading." Lifting a hand in Bret's direction, Robert strode down the hall, his shorter, bulky form oddly graceful.

Bret stared in the direction Robert had gone. The loan of the county's tools had been adequate, but how interesting that his tools would show up now that his investigation had been cut short by the discovery of the explosives. Was there a connection?

Why would anyone have purposely taken them? Robert was the only one who'd known they were his or even what the box contained, and he wouldn't need them with the county's equipment at his disposal. Or would he? The idea of Robert having some nefarious purpose was ludicrous. He was as simple and down-to-earth as they came.

"I'm just getting paranoid," Bret muttered in disgust. "Completely paranoid."

CHAPTER

16

"**Y**ou don't look like cousins," Randa announced in Autumn's apartment after cutting and styling Tawnia's hair exactly like Autumn's. "You look like twins. Here, let me have your phone. I'll take a picture of you together."

Tawnia handed her phone over willingly. She preferred long hair, but she'd been as eager for this experiment as Autumn. They leaned in close as Randa snapped away.

Sure enough, their faces in the photograph were nearly indistinguishable. Tawnia's slightly fuller cheeks and Autumn's tanner skin were the only notable differences, and you had to look closely to see that much.

Autumn glanced briefly at the picture, but didn't say anything as she walked Randa to the door.

"It's not possible." Tawnia continued to stare at the picture, her hand going to her new short locks. If she didn't know better, she'd have thought the image was actually two separate pictures of the same person copied and pasted together.

Autumn returned to the kitchen where Tawnia was standing by the sink. The curling iron Randa had used was still plugged into the outlet. "Maybe this wasn't such a good idea," Autumn said. "I mean, if it bothers you that much."

Tawnia turned off her phone. "It's only a haircut. My hair grows fast—it'll be long again in no time."

They both sat at the table. Autumn had put some kind of free-range chicken and brown rice casserole in the oven earlier, but Tawnia didn't know if she'd be able to eat. Her mother hadn't been any help, and now they'd learned that the doctor who'd delivered Autumn was dead, and not newly so, but for almost their entire lives. If he knew the secret of their family, it had gone to the grave with him. The mysterious woman, BervaDee, might hold the answer, but she was nowhere to be found.

Autumn scooted her chair closer to Tawnia's. "Maybe our birth mothers were twins," she said into the silence, "and they married twin brothers. I saw that once in a movie. And then what if they both had babies?"

"At the same time? That's not likely."

"They could have planned it that way. And the babies would have been genetic twins."

"Don't you mean siblings?"

Autumn thought for a moment. "Yeah, that's right, genetic siblings. Not identical twins."

"Which brings us back to where we started. Why would they place their babies for adoption if they were married? Your parents never said anything about your mother being married, did they? Or involved with a man?"

Autumn shook her head. "She was a teenager, too young for marriage. Or to have a baby for that matter." They both fell silent.

"Twins married to twins," Tawnia muttered after a while.

Autumn nodded solemnly, but a corner of her mouth twitched. Tawnia saw it, and to her surprise, she let out a chuckle followed by a snort.

Autumn giggled. "It's really ridiculous, isn't it?"

"Insane."

They were both laughing full steam now, and Tawnia's melancholy seeped away as though it had never existed.

"It doesn't really matter," Autumn said, grabbing her hand suddenly. "I don't care how it happened. We're here, and that's all that's important."

Tawnia returned the grip, grateful that Autumn also felt the connection between them, strong and solid. But in one thing they differed: Tawnia still craved to know the truth. She wanted to examine it from every side, force it open to see what lay inside.

Autumn went to check on the casserole. "Oh, I almost forgot," she said, bending over the open oven door with a hot pad. "You have a date tomorrow night. He's going to pick you up here."

"What are you talking about?"

"Orion. He came by the store."

Warmth flooded Tawnia. "Really? But he asked you, right? Not me."

Autumn straightened, the steaming casserole balanced precariously in one hand. "No, he asked me pretending to be you pretending to be me." Autumn's brow wrinkled. "Or something like that. Look, it doesn't matter. You like him, and I don't. So I made the date for you. I'm not going, so if you don't go, it'll look like we—you—stood him up."

Tawnia sighed in defeat, but inside she was excited. "So

where am I going on this date?" She grabbed a pair of hot pads and rescued the casserole.

"I don't know where exactly, but he said to dress up."

Tawnia was already mentally going through her wardrobe. "Would black be all right?" Her mother had always said you couldn't go wrong with a little black dress.

"Red would be better. Men can't take their eyes off you if you wear red. If you don't have a red dress, I have just the thing. It needs matching heels, though. I don't have any."

Tawnia set the casserole pan in the middle of the table on two more hot pads. "I have red pumps. Several pairs, in fact."

"Come on. This needs to cool a bit before we can eat it, anyway. I'll show you the dress."

The capped-sleeve dress was a bright red that followed Tawnia's curves perfectly. Simple, yet elegant. "I have jewelry to go with this," she told Autumn. "My parents gave a set to me when I was sixteen—a gold necklace with rubies. And matching earrings and bracelet."

"Perfect." Autumn was staring at her, and Tawnia couldn't help but return the stare.

"So I take it this date with Orion is the real reason you wanted to cut my hair?" Tawnia asked. "So he won't be able to tell us apart?"

"No. I'd decided to ask you before he showed up, though you have to admit the timing was great. He'd already seen you earlier and probably noticed my hair was different."

Tawnia laughed. "I've gone a week or more before the men I worked with noticed I changed my hair."

"Yeah, well." Shrugging, Autumn started for the bedroom door but hesitated before reaching it. "When you were a kid, did you ever imagine what it would be like to have a twin?"

When Tawnia didn't immediately reply, she rushed on. "Well, I did. And it didn't even have to be a twin. I told you before that I wanted a sister but not how much. I wanted it a lot. I pestered Summer about it constantly, and I didn't understand why my begging made her so sad. How could I have known how hard it was to get a baby if you couldn't have your own? Especially when you don't have any money." She was quiet for a moment before adding. "I'd planned to name her Spring."

Winter, Summer, Autumn, and Spring. It made perfect sense, if you lived in the Rain family. Tawnia wanted to laugh at the ridiculousness, but she couldn't because a part of her wished she could be that Spring.

"There were twins at my school," Tawnia said into the growing silence. "They looked exactly alike, except one had a tiny mole on her face. She was the tomboy. She loved to play ball with the boys, and she was good at it too. The other girl would play jacks or hopscotch with the girls. So at recess we could tell them apart, but in class it was impossible, unless you looked for the mole."

She had dreamed then about being a twin, but she couldn't say it aloud. Not now. Not the way Autumn was looking at her—with her own face. It was just too impossible.

"People do look alike without being related at all," Autumn said softly. "Celebrities are always running into look-alikes."

Not this similar, Tawnia wanted to say.

Autumn was smiling at her now, with her head slightly tilted. It was disconcerting to see, as though Tawnia were looking at a life-sized video of herself.

"Get changed and we'll eat," Autumn said. "I'll set out the rest of the food. I have organic salad, yummy cucumber dressing, lots of things to drink, and bread to die for. And for dessert, well, I know you're not into health food, but I have this carob pie that is out of this world."

Tawnia turned around. "Okay, but unzip me first."

A few minutes later they were feasting with enough food to feed a half dozen hungry women, and between the two of them they managed to make most of it disappear. Tawnia enjoyed everything except the carob pie, which was too bitter for her taste.

Give me plain old unhealthy pie every time, she thought.

Autumn appeared to enjoy the taste. "I grew up on this stuff."

Tawnia tried to remember what she had eaten while living with her parents. There had been many interesting-sounding dishes, particularly at her mother's parties, but none that she remembered enjoying. Wait, there had been chestnuts at Christmastime. Her mother would buy them, and they would roast them together on Christmas Eve. Even her father would be home for once. A smile came unbidden to her face.

"Chestnuts," she said. "That's what I'm remembering. Have you ever eaten them?"

"A few times. I think it's an acquired taste. They're kind of expensive."

Expensive. Yes, her mother hadn't needed to worry about things like that.

"Are you okay?" Autumn licked a bit of pie off her finger.

"I was thinking about my mother and our conversation on the phone this morning. She's really threatened by all this. That's why she doesn't want to believe what I told her about you and me looking alike."

"I'm sorry."

"Even if I happened to find my birth mother, it's not going

to change who I am or what I do. I am who I am now. And I think she probably made the best decision she could at the time. I bet it wasn't easy."

"Summer said in the beginning my mother went back and forth daily about whether she would go through with the adoption. Maybe in the end she did it only because she knew I'd be with Summer and Winter."

"I should call my mom."

Autumn chewed on her bottom lip. "Hmm, maybe not."

"Why not?"

"You could send her that picture Randa took of us. Just text it to her and see what happens. She has to believe her own eyes."

"I don't even believe it." But Tawnia was already reaching for her purse. She dug out her phone and began entering a message to send with the picture:

> *Me with the girl I told you about. Don't want to hurt you, but I need to know why she looks like me. Love T*

"Winter refused to have a mobile phone," Autumn said. "He worried about cancer." She looked down, hiding the tears Tawnia had glimpsed in her eyes. "I'm sorry. I shouldn't have brought that up."

"You bring him up whenever you want." Tawnia put an arm around her. "I don't mind."

Autumn lifted her eyes, her tearful gaze holding Tawnia with an almost physical power. "It's been nearly a week. Why haven't they found him?"

"They will."

"Some part of me hopes they won't. Maybe he got out of the river, and he's wandering around with amnesia or something."

"Is that what you really think?"

"No. I think he's dead." She leaned into Tawnia. "I'm so glad you're here."

"Me too."

Tawnia had time to rub Autumn's back in a few small circles before the doorbell destroyed the moment.

Autumn drew her fingers under her eyes and went to answer the door. "Probably more neighbors. I hope they bring food. Now that I'll be here to eat it."

Tawnia smiled and followed her to the door, just in case.

"Bret!" Autumn opened the door wide.

Bret's gaze swept between them. "What did you guys do? You look incredible! Wait, don't tell me. I can figure out who's who."

Tawnia had forgotten her new haircut. She stood rooted to the spot as he examined them. What if he couldn't tell them apart? What would that mean? She couldn't see the differences very well, not in the picture, so why should he?

He made a display of walking around them, looking them up and down until Tawnia felt herself going red at his attention. Finally, he pointed at her. "You're Tawnia. I like the short cut." He turned to Autumn. "But I think you should have kept the red."

Autumn laughed. "Wow, I'm impressed. Don't worry, I'll get the red back, but for now I want it like this."

Could he really tell which of them was which? Or had he based his decision on their clothing? After all, Tawnia was still wearing the tan slacks and pink ruffle shirt she'd worn to work, while Autumn was wearing jeans and a long-sleeved cotton shirt she'd picked out to hide her splint. Or perhaps he'd noticed the swell of the splint under Autumn's sleeve. He could also have remembered that Autumn had lost a bit too much weight, even if her shirt did a good job of hiding it.

Stop it, she told herself. What did it matter?

"We sent a picture to my mother," Tawnia said to Bret, more for something to say than for anything else.

Bret groaned. "You know she's not going to get any sleep now, don't you?" He looked at Autumn. "Tawnia's mother is a sweet lady, but she's one of the biggest worrywarts I've ever met." His voice rose to a falsetto. "Are you sure you're wearing your coat, dear? And did you get that mechanic to check out your tires? You know there's nothing worse than getting a flat on your way to work."

"You only met her once!" Tawnia protested.

"Well, she made an impression." He grinned. "I made one on her too, if I remember correctly."

"She would have been picking out china for us and a house, if I'd let her." Tawnia regretted the words the minute they escaped. There had been a time she would have liked that herself.

Bret put a casual arm around her. "Hey, what about tomorrow night? We could get that dinner I was talking about the other day."

"I'd like that." An entire evening alone with him. Yes, she was willing to take the risk.

"You can't!" Autumn elbowed her as though they'd known each other for years. "You have a date, remember?"

"Oh, that's right!" Tawnia fought down her disappointment. "I'm going to dinner with a friend."

"A tall, dark, handsome, older friend," Autumn put in. To Bret, she added, "Tawnia really likes him."

Tawnia was beginning to see the disadvantage of having a sister. She turned her face away from Bret and mouthed at Autumn, "Would you shut up?"

Not seeing Tawnia's glare, Autumn hooked her undamaged

arm through Bret's, pulling him in the direction of the couch. "Don't worry, we can make a night of it ourselves, if you want. I know a great restaurant."

"Sounds fun." Bret didn't even glance at Tawnia.

Tawnia could see them together now. Bret, the perfect gentleman, would pay for the dinner, and he would be charming all evening. He was careful to be attentive to the woman he was with, not like some men she'd dated. Autumn would be beautiful and fragile with her newly styled hair and her recent tragedy. Tawnia told herself she should be happy for them.

"Honestly, Bret," Autumn's face grew grave as she settled on the couch, "I'm glad you'll be here. It's been good having Tawnia with me. I don't know if I'm ready to be alone again. I think I had enough of that at the river."

Tawnia immediately felt repentant. Of course Autumn shouldn't be alone. What if her father was found? No one should be alone for news like that. She walked around the couch where Bret was now seated with Autumn. There was space next to him, but it would be odd for her to choose that space, crowding them. Instead, she settled on the easy chair near Autumn. "Actually, I have to go back to my place tonight," she said. "I don't have clothes for tomorrow. I could get them and come back."

Autumn hesitated only a minute. "No, you go ahead. I'll have to face this sometime. Probably better from the first."

Still partially irritated, Tawnia was tempted to let her, but the memory of how Autumn acted when they entered the apartment the day before pricked her conscience. "Why don't you come back with me for one night?" she said. "I'll even let you have the bed. I'll drop you at your store in the morning, and tomorrow night we'll stay here again."

Autumn's smile made her beautiful. "Okay. Thanks."

Tawnia glanced at Bret to see if he would be tagging along to her bungalow, but his attention was riveted on Autumn. "How's your arm, anyway?"

"Since they immobilized it, there's almost no pain. Well, except at night, but that's all."

"Good."

Autumn's eyes grew wide. "That reminds me. Tawnia, we'll have to do something about your arm for your date tomorrow."

"My arm?" Oh, yeah. Orion would expect it to be wrapped.

"I have a cloth brace, I think. At the Herb Shoppe. We can get it tomorrow."

"What are you guys talking about?" Bret was staring at them both now, in turn, as he had when he'd first entered.

"Never mind!" Tawnia said before Autumn could speak. The last thing she needed was to have Bret know that she was stealing Autumn's date.

"Her date thinks she's me," Autumn told him, her grin wide. "It's a long story."

Tawnia squirmed as Bret's eyes came to rest on her. "I have plenty of time," he said. "I'd like to hear the story. It sounds interesting."

Throwing up her hands, Tawnia went to pack her things, leaving the blabbermouth Autumn to explain.

*T*awnia's mother rang Friday at noon, though Tawnia had been expecting the call much earlier. She was sitting at her desk with a homemade sandwich as she reviewed the accounts for her meetings that afternoon.

"Hi, it's me," her mother said. "This picture isn't a joke, is it? I know you can do a lot of things with your computer."

The truth was that Tawnia could have easily created such a picture, using two images of herself. More easily than her mother could guess. If she knew how easily, she wouldn't believe in the picture for a moment. Fortunately, her mother knew little about the world of computer design.

"It's real. I tried to tell you." Then because she was still so disturbed by the image herself, she pushed away her sandwich and asked, "Can you tell which is me?"

"One face is thinner," her mother ventured, a note of disapproval entering her voice. "Too thin."

"That's Autumn. Her father died in the bridge collapse.

He's the one they haven't found yet, if you've been following the story. She's taking it hard, but she seems to be eating again."

Usually, her mother would be quick to offer sympathy. Women were supposed to offer sympathy, and Ellen McKnight always did what she was supposed to do. That she didn't now told Tawnia she was more shaken than she wanted to admit.

"This is too unreal," her mother said.

"I know. That's why I wanted to find out about my adoption. I mean, I know people can look alike, but this is too close."

Tawnia realized she'd gone to her mother in the hopes that she could fix her life. Hadn't she always done just that? The right clothes, the right schools, the right words. Tawnia had rebelled against it all by leaving, but now what she craved more than anything else was for her mother to put things back to normal. Not to give her a hug, or love, but to make things normal. Make them into something Tawnia could count on.

"A woman brought you here," her mother said quietly. "Mrs. Mendenhall—I still remember her name after all this time. She worked with the adoption agency. She was about my height but more sturdy in an athletic sort of way, with long hair that was beginning to show a bit of gray. She was a nice-looking woman and seemed well educated, but she wore a cheap suit that didn't fit well—I suppose social work doesn't pay very well. You looked so tiny in her arms. You were barely over five pounds but healthy and strong. You grabbed my finger when I took you in my arms. We signed some papers, and then she left. Afterwards, your dad dropped her at the airport." Her voice had become a whisper. "The agency was located in Portland."

Tawnia caught her breath. This was more than she'd learned in all her growing-up years. During her teens, when she had romanticized her birth parents, she had pestered her mother as much as she'd dared for information, though never in the presence of her father. Her mother had told her a woman had brought her to them but hadn't mentioned any of the rest. Not about Portland or the woman's name. Portland meant she and Autumn had a greater chance at being related.

And now she knew why her mother had cried over her latest move.

Yet what stood out most in her mind was the reverent hush in her mother's voice as she talked about how her new baby had held onto her finger.

She swallowed hard. "What was the agency called?"

"I looked it up this morning in the adoption papers. It was Children's Hope, and the birth certificate we have for you lists a clinic in Portland."

Tawnia grabbed a pen and started writing. "Thank you."

"I don't know anything else. I didn't want to know." Her mother hesitated. "I guess I almost convinced myself you weren't adopted at all."

Tawnia blinked at the tears threatening to spill over. "I have to find out what's going on here, but that's not going to change anything for us. I just have to know."

Could her mother detect the insincerity in her voice? Because things had already changed; Tawnia could no more leave Autumn now than she could quit breathing. Since arriving at work, she'd called Autumn twice at the antiques shop to make sure she was all right. The last time Autumn had laughed and said, "I promise to call you if anything happens. And no, I haven't found BervaDee yet."

"I understand," her mother said. "I wish I could be there for you."

"You do?" Why did this surprise her so much?

"I've always wanted what's best for you."

Well, Tawnia had known her mother wanted what was best for the family, but that wasn't necessarily the same thing as wanting what was best for her.

"Thank you, Mom. Look, I have to go back to work now. My art director needs to talk with me." Tawnia could see Kacey Murphy in one of her dark suits, waving at her from the narrow window by her doorway. She motioned for the older woman to come in.

"By all means, go. I don't want you to get fired."

Tawnia gave a mental sigh. As the creative director, she was over Kacey, but of course her mother didn't understand the company pyramid. "Goodbye. I'll call you later." It was a white lie, but no doubt they'd talk soon because her mother would call her instead.

"Hi, Kacey," she called. "What's up?"

"Mr. Lantis is here early for his meeting. I've got the preliminary billboard designs we've worked up. They're looking good. Canda outdid herself on the writing. But I have a few visual changes I wanted to run by you." Kacey was pulling up a chair as she spoke. "I told Canda to entertain Mr. Lantis for a minute in the conference room. She has donuts."

Tawnia's ears perked up at that because she was still hungry, though for once her half-eaten sandwich had little appeal. Autumn had insisted on using some kind of whole-grain bread that morning, and the bread was heavier than a thick notebook and had about the same taste. "Eat it eleven times," Autumn had said, "and you'll start to like it. Everything takes getting used to. Your body will thank you, and soon you'll love it, like I do." Tawnia sincerely doubted that.

She opened the folder Kacey had plunked down beside the sandwich and began flipping through the advertisements. "Beautiful. I like the model for this one. Good, good, great.

Uh, this one needs something. I can barely read the words. I thought we were going with a dark blue."

"It made too much of a contrast with the baby. I have that in here as well to show you, but what if we put in a slash of darker blue here through the middle and print the words in white there instead of black? It'll make the other blues stand out as well."

"Perfect. Can we work it up while he's still here?"

"I've got Sean on it now, though he's a little grumpy."

"Why?"

"Canda."

"What?"

"He's got a thing for her, and he thinks she's in there flirting with Mr. Lantis."

This was news to Tawnia. "What does he care? Sean's always flirting with me."

"That's different." Kacey rolled her eyes. "That's like a dog worshiping his master. Canda is attainable."

"She is?" With her porcelain skin, fabulous figure, and overt confidence, she could have her pick of men. Tawnia doubted that the awkward Sean would be anywhere near the top of her list.

Kacey grinned. "Canda likes him, make no mistake. In fact, I think we'll have a wedding before another year."

"You've got to be kidding." Tawnia still couldn't see the two of them together.

"Canda is a smart girl. She's looking forward to what Sean will become, not the boy you and I see now. And she's right. You learn these things after raising four children." Kacey's dark eyes went back to the folder. "These next three are the other designs I thought could use a little something more, but I'm about out of ideas. Twenty-five billboards in just a few days has run us dry."

"Better than the whole fifty-five." Tawnia tapped her finger on a design for a children's clothing store. "This one needs a cardboard cutout or a dummy of some sort waving his arms. It'll give dimension and soak up this empty space here in the middle."

"Good idea. Moms can't help but look at a kid waving his hands. We might actually be able to make the arms move. I've seen something like that before. I'll ask the others. Probably best to use a little boy."

They went through the remaining problem billboards, and in a matter of minutes Kacey had a small pile of designs she would rework before the meeting with Mr. Lantis ended.

"Thanks, Kacey. This is great stuff."

Kacey smiled, but she didn't leave. "Uh, Tawnia, I don't mean to pry, but is there something different about your eyes today?"

Tawnia had forgotten she wasn't wearing her contact. Doing so had actually been Autumn's idea, a challenge to see if anyone would notice. Though she'd talked in length with at least half a dozen people, no one had except now.

"Nothing wrong." She faked a nonchalance that she didn't feel. "I was born with different colored eyes, that's all."

"That's unusual." Kacey grew thoughtful. "I wonder if we could use it in a billboard somewhere?"

They laughed, and Tawnia found herself wondering why she'd ever been so uptight about anyone knowing. It wasn't as though having heterochromia was some deep dark secret that could destroy her life.

Tawnia gathered the folder of completed designs and started for the door. "Well, I'd better get to the conference room before Mr. Lantis asks Canda out and Sean quits on us."

"Yeah, hurry. We're already stretching ourselves as thin as we dare."

It was true, but Tawnia could tell Kacey was happy. So was Tawnia. The harder she worked, the less time she had to worry about the mystery of her birth or her date that evening with Orion. Or about Bret. Had she imagined it last night, or had he seemed a little bit jealous when Autumn was ratting her out?

It doesn't matter.

As she entered the conference room and greeted Mr. Lantis, Tawnia made a mental note to look up the adoption agency as soon as she had a free moment.

By the time she finally managed to call, the agency was closed for the day.

The fitted dress made Tawnia feel romantic and beautiful while not exposing too much cleavage. "You don't want to look like a tramp," Autumn said, agreeing that it was perfect. "Men who are serious about a relationship don't like loose women. Those shoes are nice."

"As if you'd wear them." Tawnia felt wobbly in the extra high heels. "Good thing Orion's tall."

"Well, better you than me. My feet would pinch all night, and my back would be thrown out of joint for weeks." Autumn drew up her bare feet on the bed to sit Indian-style. She was wearing a sleeveless dress with large blue flowers that reminded Tawnia of a dress she'd owned as a child. Tawnia might wear such a thing to the beach, if she were going to one, but never out to dinner. She wondered where Autumn and Bret were planning on eating tonight, but she forced herself not to ask. Later that night, she and Autumn would surely tell each other everything, since she planned to come back here after her date. The anticipation of sharing that with Autumn was almost as compelling as the date itself.

"Do you think the adoption agency will be open tomorrow?" Tawnia asked.

"Possibly. They might have a minimal staff on Saturday morning. But I don't know if they'll be able to tell you anything. Adoptions were so secret back then."

Tawnia studied herself in the full-length mirror on the back of Autumn's bedroom door. "Maybe my birth mother is looking too, and has signed forms to let her name be released."

"That could happen."

Tawnia frowned at herself in the mirror. She didn't think it would, not really, and at the moment she cared more about the mystery of Autumn than about finding her birth mother.

"Oh, I almost forgot!" Autumn jumped off the bed and dug into the huge shoulder bag that served as her new purse. "Voilá!" She pulled out a black brace. "Sorry, I didn't have it in red."

Tawnia had been feeling all right about the deception until she saw the brace. She sank to the bed. "I don't know if I can do this. It makes it seem like so much more of a lie. Maybe we should tell him the truth."

"Maybe. Well, definitely. But not tonight. First let's see if he's even an option. I mean, he may pick his teeth with his fork and kiss like a snake." Autumn made obnoxious hissing sounds that made Tawnia helpless with laughter. "Besides," Autumn added, "if you don't like him, maybe I'll take a stab at it."

"Does that mean you think you like him?"

Autumn whacked her leg with the brace. "Stop it already. If I had designs on him, I wouldn't have set up this date for you. But sometimes any date is better than none."

Was she talking about Bret? No. Impossible.

"Okay, okay. Gimme that stupid thing." Tawnia fit it over her wrist, arm, and elbow, securing the velcro straps, which Autumn awkwardly cut to size with her left hand.

"Since when did they stop putting casts on broken bones anyway?" Tawnia asked, rubbing her hand over the brace.

"What I gather from talking to people in the store is that casts are mostly for little kids and really bad breaks. You should be glad they stopped using them, or there's no way we could pull this off." She tilted her head. "Well, actually, I do know this homeopathic doctor who sets bones, and he might have . . ." She waved the words away. "Anyway, they said something about needing to move my elbow after Wednesday, and I'll be able to use only the sling after that, if I need it." Autumn frowned at her arm. "It'd sure be nice to be able to do my hair. I mean, ordinarily I wouldn't care so much, but I don't want to look odd around Bret."

"I'll help you. There's time."

"Do it like yours, okay? I like that look. It's better than how Randa did it."

Instead of blow-drying her hair and ratting the top, Tawnia had crunched it so the slight natural curl was enhanced, scattering becomingly over her head. Autumn had lent her a sparkly faux diamond hair pin that, along with the rubies from her parents, made Tawnia feel as if she were attending a fancy ball.

Tawnia's styling Autumn's hair meant that they looked more alike than ever, except for their clothes and the jewelry, but that was the least of Tawnia's worries. How would she feel if Bret and Autumn fell in love? How could she make it through a whole night pretending to be Autumn? She wasn't about to go around without shoes and eat tofu anytime soon. That would be over the top. She wouldn't do that for any man.

At least, as Autumn had suggested, she'd know after tonight if there was any magic with Orion, and if there was even a small possibility of magic, it would be worth the risk. She told herself she would make things up to Orion in the end. He'd have to understand that she had never done anything so crazy in her life.

The doorbell rang, and Tawnia's stomach felt an annoying flutter that reminded her how she'd felt on her first date back in high school. She'd been popular then and had dated a lot since, but she'd never had a serious boyfriend—until Bret. Given how that had gone, she couldn't exactly count him. Maybe Bret was right. Maybe if Christian had lived everything would be different. But different how? She would never know.

"Go on, answer it," Autumn whispered. "Hurry!"

Smoothing her already smooth dress, Tawnia made her way past the living room to the door. She caught a glimpse of herself in the gilt-edged mirror above the gas fireplace. She looked like someone she didn't know.

She looked like Autumn.

She opened the door, and for a moment Orion said nothing. He stared at her as the fluttering in her stomach grew to outlandish proportions. He was dressed in a dark tuxedo, complete with a white shirt and bow tie. His hair had been combed back neatly, the sprinkling of white making him more distinguished, and the faint scent of cologne drifted toward her. His brown eyes looked black in the dim light of the hallway, staring at her as if he could see her soul.

"Hi," she said uncomfortably. But it was the delicious discomfort of being with someone new, someone who might possibly become important in her life. She lowered her gaze to the bouquet of red and white roses in his hands. "Are these for me?"

"You look stunning." He handed her the flowers.

"Thank you. These are beautiful. I'll put them in some water." She walked into the kitchen as steadily as her high heels would allow. Where did Autumn keep the vases? Well, the pitcher in the first cupboard would do. She had the jar three-fourths full of water and had begun to settle the flowers inside when Orion appeared behind her. She turned the handle toward the back where he couldn't see it. "Ready," she said.

He smiled, his cheek dimpling, and he looked so handsome that something inside her chest hurt. When he proffered his arm, she had to hold it tightly to steady her emotions. Under her fingers, his muscles were apparent, despite the intervening fabric, and she felt a little thrill. Something a week ago she would have been disgusted at anyone else for mentioning. Of course he'd be in shape. He was a fireman, after all.

They rode down the elevator to the first floor. Outside, a limousine waited. "Orion, you shouldn't have."

He smiled easily. "The company owed me a favor."

They sat close on the seat and had drinks, while the driver weaved through traffic. "Where are we going?" she asked.

"You'll see." He gave her a mysterious smile.

Ten minutes later they arrived at a sprawling building she didn't recognize. Not exactly a restaurant. Orion took her hand and helped her out of the limo, and that's when she noticed the helicopter on a landing pad some distance away. With a wave to the limo driver, Orion offered his arm to Tawnia.

"We're going in that?" She eyed the helicopter, whose twin blades began to rotate as they approached.

"Scared?" He looked amused, but his voice held a challenge.

"Of course not." But she'd expected him, a civil servant, to be a more conservative. After all, they hardly knew each other, and such an elaborate date wasn't practical. It wasn't as if he'd be proposing tonight.

At least she hoped not.

Orion helped her inside and then gave the pilot a thumbs-up. He leaned over and said in her ear, "On the way back, when it's completely dark, the lights will be even more fabulous."

She was stunned by what she was seeing now. Portland from the air was incredible. The buildings, the cars, the maze of roads. The Willamette River curving through the city, its impressive bridges spanning the dark water. Her eyes fell on the Hawthorne Bridge, or at least the part that remained. There was activity on both banks where debris was still being carted away. Her smile faded, and for the moment she was Autumn, thinking about Winter trapped somewhere beneath the water.

Orion's warm arm went around her shoulders, and he pulled her closer, away from the window till the remains of the bridge were out of sight. "I would do anything to give your father back to you. I know I can't, but if I could, I would."

The thought was comforting, at least to Tawnia, though she couldn't begin to guess how Autumn would feel. Purposely, she looked in another direction, determined to enjoy the sights that Orion had gone to so much trouble to show her.

After a circle around the city, the helicopter landed on top of one of the high-rises. Tawnia, being new to the city, had no idea where they were, but she didn't ask, afraid that Autumn would know such things.

Some distance away from where they landed, a length of carpet had been spread on the cement, and on top of it sat two chairs and a table with two full place settings. A waiter stood nearby, his hand resting on a trolley filled with dishes. Lights spaced at intervals along the rooftop illuminated the slowly darkening night.

Tawnia laughed. "I can't believe this."

"I'm glad you're surprised." Orion jumped from the helicopter and reached back for her hand to help her step down. They hadn't arrived at the table before the helicopter rose again into the air.

"He'll be back later," Orion said.

"How did you manage all this?" Now that the helicopter was gone, she could hear romantic music coming from a boombox on the bottom rack of the trolley.

"Favors. I've been a firefighter a long time."

"I see."

The waiter served soup, followed by a plate containing salmon, rice, and steamed vegetables. Then he left them alone, disappearing through the door at the far end of the roof.

Tawnia loved salmon, but she'd been around Autumn enough to know that she would ask if it had been tested for mercury. Pushing down the thought, she studied her companion. They hadn't talked much, so far, and she was beginning to feel a bit awkward.

"So," she said, still trying to get the hang of eating left-handed, "you've been a firefighter how long?"

"Twenty-two years. But I went into kind of a semiretirement when my daughter died. I only work a day or two a week now."

"That's got to be hard financially." The words slipped out before she could stop them. "I'm sorry. I shouldn't have said that. I don't mean to pry."

"It's all right."

He looked away from her and for a moment she thought the subject closed, but he turned back and said, "I've made some good investments over the years. My parents left me a trust fund, and I was always a saver, so retiring really hasn't been that challenging. The way I look at it, I have a chance to start a second career, something perhaps that I've always wanted to do."

Now they were getting somewhere. She knew about dreams, if not exactly how to attain them. "Like what?"

He gave a short laugh. "That's just it. I haven't thought of anything I like better than fighting fires. There's something about the danger, I guess. It's a bit of a rush."

"I'd be scared to death."

"You'd be surprised what you can do when you have to." He smiled wistfully, and Tawnia wondered if he was thinking of his wife and daughter.

"How old are you anyway?" She fluffed her rice with her fork so she wouldn't have to look at his pain. Better to wait until he wanted to share it.

"How old do you think?" His voice was teasing now, so she looked up.

"Mid-forties, I'd guess."

"I'll be forty-seven later this year."

That meant nearly fifteen years separated them. Was that important? Maybe not.

"This is really great salmon," she said, to show the age difference didn't matter to her. "I haven't had such great salmon for years."

"There's a restaurant here in town that does it right. I'll take you there one day."

"I'd like that." But her thoughts went back to his age. Obviously he didn't care about the age difference or he wouldn't have asked her out. Yet what about a family? Would he even consider starting over? Having children was one of her dreams.

She bit her bottom lip. That wasn't something she needed

to worry about now, was it? Then again, she'd had a coworker once who'd married a man who didn't want children. Though she loved her husband madly, not having a child was the biggest heartache of the woman's life.

For no reason at all, Bret popped into Tawnia's mind. She'd thought once that he would be a part of her dream. A spurt of anger came from nowhere, engulfing her and sending her emotions into a spiral. She hadn't realized there was so much resentment left inside.

"Autumn? Are you okay?"

Two seconds passed before Tawnia remembered that tonight she was Autumn. "I'm fine. Thanks. I was just thinking."

"I do that too. It's normal when you've lost someone. The trick is to let it pass and go on."

She could do that. She hadn't even lost someone, not really. Neither Bret nor Christian had been hers. And she'd never known her birth mother.

"Do you have a picture of your daughter?" she asked.

He reached in a pocket of his tux for his wallet, passing it to her. There was a portrait of a younger Orion with a pretty woman and a teenager at that awkward stage everyone seemed to pass through. The next photo showed that same girl as an older, attractive teen, now in full bloom.

"Arleen was eighteen in that one. It's the last picture I have of her."

The girl had blond hair like her mother, though a bit darker, but her eyes were Orion's brown. Her heart-shaped face held a fragileness that didn't belong to either of her parents. Had the fragility been what had led her to jump from the bridge?

Next to the photo was a drawing of the girl, the strokes lovingly outlining each curve. Tawnia felt she had seen the drawing before. But where? She looked again at the photograph. No, she'd never seen the girl before, so why did the drawing look familiar?

Then she had it. Bret's drawing, the one of the girl, Sheree. The girls depicted were different, but the style of the drawings themselves were familiar. "Who drew this?" she asked.

Orion leaned forward. "Oh, that. It was done by one of Arleen's friends. I don't know which one. It was about a year after my wife's death, and I still wasn't coping very well. But Arleen loved it. She had it in a frame by her bed. I still have it. I made this copy to carry with me. I love how happy she looks."

More than happy, like a woman in love. But Tawnia didn't say that aloud. It wouldn't be a good thing, because the boyfriend's desertion was apparently the last push she'd needed to end her life. Poor thing, Tawnia thought.

Orion had survived, though. Orion, who was looking at her with an emotion in his eyes that she could not classify. Tawnia swallowed hard. She wasn't sure if she wanted to scream with joy or run for the hills.

"How about a little dessert? If you're finished." Orion arose and went to the trolley. "We have chocolate mousse."

"Mmmm," Tawnia said, all the while thinking that Autumn might ask if the cream had come from a grass-fed cow, and, if the recipe contained eggs, if the chickens were free-range or fed slop in crowded pens.

She took a bite without mentioning any of it. "Wow. This is excellent." The richest kind of chocolate with a hint of rum flavoring.

After they'd enjoyed the mousse, Orion took her hand, lifting her from the chair. "How about a dance?"

Tawnia hadn't been dancing since that time with Bret here

in Portland. The lights had been low and the music slow, and she'd thought all her dreams were coming true.

Orion drew her close and they did the sort of tight waltz that most people reverted to when dancing for the first time alone. Her arms rested on his shoulders. Because of the angle of her brace, they had to be quite close. She could smell his cologne mixed with the heat of his breath.

He kissed her after the second song, a slow kiss that tested the waters. She felt an answering passion in her response—and a tremor of fear as well. If this was the beginning of a relationship, she couldn't let him keep believing she was Autumn.

She stepped away, trying not to see the disappointment in his eyes.

"Something wrong?" he asked.

"My feet. These heels are killing me." It was true. At the moment she envied Autumn her bare feet.

He led her to the chair and crouched in front of her. "Let's take them off." His hands were strong and gentle, sending warm shivers up her back. "There. Is that better?" He was massaging her foot now, and it did feel delicious. There seemed to be nothing more natural in the world than being on a secluded rooftop with this strong, handsome man rubbing her foot.

Maybe she liked Autumn's life.

"Look, Orion. There's something I want to tell you."

"What?" He glanced over his shoulder where the helicopter had reappeared, as though out of nowhere, the engine and the whirring sound of its blades growing louder as it approached.

"It's just, well, you don't really know me." She raised her voice. "I mean, we've just met, and there's a lot you don't know."

Like the huge fact that I'm not Autumn.

He released her foot and took her hands, pulling her face

close to his. "There's a lot you don't know about me, either, but does it really matter? I know what I feel here and now."

That wasn't good enough for her. She didn't want here and now, she wanted forever. "I'm not looking for a fling."

He didn't hear. The helicopter was landing behind her, and he stood, pulling her to her feet.

They rode back to the limousine in awed silence. The lights were breathtaking, and Tawnia felt as though the whole city had dressed up just for her. Somewhere down below, Bret and Autumn were in a restaurant together. Were they enjoying themselves as much as she had? Because whether or not Orion was her future, this had been the most magical, romantic night of her life.

At the limousine, Orion paused before opening the door. He took her in his arms. "I'm not looking for a fling, either," he whispered.

Then he kissed her again. Long and slow and deep.

*A*utumn was a mess. The minute Tawnia walked out the door and she was alone, the apartment seemed to squeeze in on her. Everywhere she looked were memories of Winter: the colorful afghan Summer had made for him, his favorite spot on the couch, the round stain on the antique coffee table from the herbal tea he'd taken each evening before bed, the pictures of them together on the end tables.

She sat on the couch and drew her bare feet under her. Feeling cold, she pulled the afghan up to her neck. The yarn was fuzzy from years of washing, but the stitches were close enough to keep her warm on even a cold night.

At what point would they give up looking for Winter? She'd called the county several times, but they had only assured her they would find him. They hadn't yet given his identity to the media, but it was only a matter of time until word got out. People talked, and even the best intentions went awry. Then she would have hordes of strangers asking her what it was like to have her father missing.

How long had she been staring at the wall, reliving the moment the car had plunged into the water? If only she'd understood that it would be the last time she'd see him. If only she'd held his hand.

Her body was shaking, her breath coming fast. She pulled the afghan over her head and tried to breathe slowly. Her right arm began to ache as it did sometimes in the night, a dull, persistent ache that drove her insane. During the day she barely noticed.

The medication. Tossing off the blanket, she went to the kitchen and began rummaging through the cupboards. Where had she left it? That's right. In Winter's room. The nightstand near the bed. She ran to the room, fumbled with the package. Only one pill left. She gulped it down without water and sank to the bed, calculating the moments before it would take effect. Tears spilled down her cheeks. Her limbs felt leaden.

"Autumn? Autumn?" a voice penetrated her thoughts, but she didn't move from the spot. She could still smell Winter here. How long until his smell faded?

"Autumn!" Bret appeared in the doorway to Winter's room. "I've been ringing and ringing. I finally just came in. Did you know your door's unlocked?"

What a silly question. Who cared about locking doors? Summer had never bothered when she was alive. Maybe Autumn would never lock her door again. What did she care if someone stole her antiques? The most important thing was already missing.

"Autumn, what's wrong?"

She looked in his direction, though her tears blurred his

face. "I miss him," she whispered. "I miss him so much. And I keep thinking of him under the water. I keep thinking of him somewhere else missing me. Or maybe he's with Summer and doesn't care that I'm not there at all." Grief felt heavy over her entire body. She couldn't move. Maybe she would sit here forever in this exact spot.

"They'll find him, and of course he's missing you—wherever he is." He walked over to the bed and sat down next to her. The silence grew loud enough to penetrate her grief.

"I'm sorry," she muttered. "Sorry that you have to see me like this."

"Actually, you were like this the first time I met you." His words were matter-of-fact, not meant to wound.

"You gave me Tawnia." She didn't look at him when she spoke the words. "I know this is really stupid and strange, but when I'm with her I don't feel so awful. It's like we're a part of each other. Just like Winter and I are. When she left tonight, I suddenly felt . . . alone." Alone didn't begin to touch what she felt, but it was the best word she could find.

"That's not stupid; it's called distraction. You don't feel alone at work, do you? When you're busy or talking, there's no time to think of the grief."

He was wrong. Several times at work, even when she'd been helping a customer, the blinding, horrible loss had hit her so hard it was all she could do to continue whatever she was doing. Sometimes customers had bought things and left without her even remembering what they had bought or how much they had paid.

"He's always been the most important part of my life."

"I know what you mean. I think my brother was that for me. I admired him more than I ever told him, even though he was totally irresponsible about so many things. But he was happy, and he enjoyed life to the fullest. I wanted to be just like him."

"He was an artist?"

"When he had time. He worked in advertising, like Tawnia. That's how they met."

"She met your brother first?"

"She was on a date with him when he died." Now it was Bret's turn to look away. "It wasn't her fault. He climbed a tree to take a picture. He was reckless."

"And you wanted to be just like him?"

He looked at his fingers in his lap. "Everyone loved my brother."

"Even Tawnia?"

"I don't know."

Silence fell, but the medication was taking effect. The pain in her arm was subsiding, and suddenly Autumn thought how funny the poster of John Lennon looked on the wall. She grinned. "A grown man with a John Lennon poster. Winter loved John Lennon."

"Christian had one of Julia Roberts," Bret said.

That made Autumn laugh. She flopped herself back on the bed, giggling, her legs still dangling over the side. "I bet that went over well with his girlfriends."

"They usually weren't around long enough to give an opinion."

"Usually?"

"I think Tawnia might have been the exception—if he'd lived."

"Might?" She sat up. "I was under the impression you two had dated."

"For a while. It got too hard."

"Why?"

"I guess I kept wondering how Christian would feel about me dating his girl."

"His girl? But he was . . ." Dead. Autumn stopped herself from saying the last word just in time. Even in her present disoriented state, she knew that would hurt him. But the thought of his not dating Tawnia because his brother had liked her made the giggles bubble up inside her. It was so ridiculous.

One giggle escaped. "I'm sorry," she gulped. "That wasn't for you. I don't know what's happening. It's that stupid medication."

Bret stood. "Come on. Let's get you out on the couch."

"Aren't we going to dinner?"

He paused, standing so close she started thinking he might kiss her. Or was it in case she fell? "I think maybe we should stay in." He rubbed a thumb over her cheek, wiping off the drying tears. "I could order pizza, and we could get a movie. How does that sound?"

"I love pizza. I know a place that does organic."

He grinned. "I assume that means it costs twice as much as a regular pizza."

"It's cheaper than eating out."

"Good point. So what video do you want to see?"

A video meant his going to the rental store, and because she couldn't face going there, that meant waiting in the apartment alone. She didn't want to be alone. "I have cable," she said. "There should be something on."

He took her arm as they walked to the living room. She tripped on the carpet and laughed hard as Bret caught her. He laughed with her.

Once again Autumn had gone from crying to silly to morose as the medication took its course. It was getting late, but Bret was loath to leave her alone. They sat together on the couch, staring at an old black-and-white film. Something about a couple who bought an old house and sank into debt because of all the problems related to it. He disliked these kinds of films because how could anyone be so stupid? Everyone with sense knew it was easier to be happy without huge debt than with it.

Autumn laid her head on his shoulder, a tear sliding down her cheek. "See?" she said. "It doesn't matter about how much the house cost or the trouble they're in. They have each other and the children. They'll make it work."

He felt a rush of emotion for her then because she was right. Family was what mattered. He'd learned that a little too late, at least where Christian was concerned. He could never make up the time he should have spent with his brother, but he could learn for the future.

Autumn wiped her face with the ridiculously bright afghan that she'd draped over them, though he wasn't cold, and then snuggled closer to him. His arm went comfortingly around her narrow shoulders. Her face lifted to his. They'd been close all evening, and it would be natural to share a kiss, and he'd be crazy not to take the opportunity because he did like her, but he kept thinking of how she'd been crying about her father when he'd arrived. Wouldn't he be taking advantage of her?

"I should go," he said. "It's late."

Her mismatched eyes studied him. "Don't you want to kiss me?" Her tone was curious.

"Actually, I do. More than anything." His voice was gruff. "But you're . . . grieving."

"So? It'll take my mind off things."

She said that now, but what if in the morning she changed

her mind? What if she hated him for taking advantage of her vulnerability?

What if Tawnia came home?

"Is Tawnia coming back here?" he asked.

Autumn's eyes flew to the large clock on a corner table. "She's supposed to." She drew away from him slowly, her face thoughtful. "I hope everything's going well with her date. She was pretty nervous when they left. I think she really likes him. You should have seen how wonderful she looked."

Bret swallowed hard. He could imagine. Autumn herself was looking incredibly attractive, her hair tousled and her eyes heavy-lidded with sleep. She was rising now, and he wished he could turn back the clock to the moment when she'd asked to be kissed. Why did he have to be so chivalrous? Christian wouldn't have hesitated.

"I should go," he repeated. "But you shouldn't be alone."

She smiled at him. "You could always sleep on my couch."

That was when they heard noise outside the door. Autumn froze, but then her sleepiness vanished. "Hurry," she hissed. "They're here. We can't let him see us. We've got to hide!" She ran toward Winter's room, pulling him along. They hid behind the door, which Autumn left open a crack.

"You don't lock your door?" came a male voice.

"Must have forgotten." There was a healthy dose of nervousness in Tawnia's voice. "Well, I had a wonderful time tonight. Thanks for everything. It was beautiful."

"Like you."

There was a long moment of silence, and Bret's fists tightened at his side. What was going on? He wished he could see into the living room, but the opening Autumn had left was too small and at the wrong angle.

They started talking again, but quietly, so this time Bret

couldn't hear the words. "Should I go out there?" he mouthed to Autumn, hoping she could see him well enough in the darkened room. Maybe Tawnia was having trouble getting rid of the guy.

Maybe she didn't want to get rid of him.

Autumn shook her head violently. "He can't see you," she mouthed back.

Bret guessed it wouldn't be too good for Tawnia's chances with the fireman if there was a man waiting for her in her apartment.

More silence. Interminable silence. And then, finally, the door closing.

"Autumn, are you here?"

Autumn burst from the room and practically threw herself at Tawnia. Bret held back, emerging more slowly.

"Well?" Autumn demanded. "How'd it go? Tell me everything. *Everything.*"

"Oh, it was exactly like a movie," Tawnia gushed. Her back was toward Bret and he was sure she hadn't seen him. "First we went in a limo, and then a helicopter—such beautiful scenery! We had dinner on a rooftop. I have no idea where, but it was the most incredibly romantic date I've ever been on. I mean, honestly, it was so impractical. Silly, really. A waste of money this early in a relationship, almost like he was trying to make something up to me."

"You nut—he was trying to impress you."

Tawnia laughed, "Well, I was impressed and surprised."

Autumn pulled Tawnia toward the couch. "So did he kiss you? How was it? Tell me!"

"It was amazing. I thought—" Tawnia must have sensed Bret's motion because she fell silent, her eyes flying to his in surprise.

She's not wearing her contact, he thought. *That meant . . . what?* He didn't know.

"Bret," Tawnia said weakly. "You're here." She looked past him to Winter's darkened room.

"We stayed in," Autumn told her. "My arm was hurting so I took the pain medication, and I got sort of silly."

"She giggled an awful lot," Bret confirmed.

Tawnia grinned. "You did that the first night I met you."

"Well, that was the last pill. I'm taking something else from now on—if I need to." Autumn rolled her eyes. "As it is, you two are probably never going to let me live this down."

Bret noticed Autumn said nothing about her tears for Winter. He'd have to tell Tawnia later so she wouldn't leave her alone too long.

"So," he said, approaching the women, "you were going to tell us about the firefighter's kiss?" His stomach tightened at the thought, though he knew she had every right to kiss anyone she pleased.

"It was nothing." Tawnia avoided his gaze.

He arched a brow. "Actually, I think you said amazing."

"The date was amazing. Or at least flying in the helicopter. I never imagined how beautiful the lights over the city were at night. The only bad part was seeing the bri—never mind."

"What about the kiss!" Autumn said in apparent agony. "Tell me about that."

Tawnia glanced at Bret. "What kiss?"

Autumn groaned. "The one you were doing just a minute ago in this apartment. Don't tell me you didn't! I heard the silence. The *long* silence. It was all I could do not to peek! Must have been some kiss."

Tawnia said nothing. Instead, she studied the antique figurines on the coffee table.

Sighing, Autumn turned to Bret. "She's not going to tell me anything with you here. You know she's not." She came around the couch and started pushing him toward the door with her good arm. "Thanks for staying with me tonight. I really appreciate it. Next time I'll take *you* out, okay? It's the least I can do."

"Wait a minute." Bret wanted to hear about the kiss too. Had Tawnia fallen for this guy? What was so great about him anyway? He was old, for crying out loud. Just because he was a firefighter with a build to match and obviously knew how to impress a girl didn't mean he was a good person. It didn't mean his kisses were amazing.

They had reached the door, and somehow he already had his suit jacket over his arm. Autumn was looking at him expectantly, waiting for him to leave. Tawnia gazed at them from the other side of the couch, biting her bottom lip. She was beautiful. Her hair was slightly windblown, her face flushed, and that red dress did fabulous things for her figure. It was all he could do not to march around the couch and kiss her himself.

He'd show her amazing.

"Goodbye, Bret," she called.

Hot fury came over him for no reason he could determine. He fought it down. Why was he being so stupid? He turned toward the door.

"Oh, wait!" Tawnia walked around the couch to where they stood. "I don't know if it means anything, but I thought I should mention it. Orion"—she reddened at his name—"had a drawing in his wallet of his daughter that looked like that other drawing you had."

Bret blinked. "His daughter is Sheree?"

"I thought Orion's daughter died," added Autumn.

"No, the girl isn't the same. The drawing was similar.

Maybe the same artist or someone who works in the same style. I couldn't see a signature."

Bret fought down his disappointment. "Well, I suppose that doesn't make a lot of difference if it's not the same girl. Hanks could have drawn pictures of a lot of people."

"I take it you've had no luck identifying the girl?" Tawnia asked.

"No luck at all. But I gave a copy to a guy who works for the county, and I'm hoping he finds someone who knows something."

Autumn frowned. "I showed all my customers today. I forgot to give Jake a copy, though. He could be showing it too."

Bret reached into his jacket pocket where he had folded the last two copies. "Here, take one of these. But I wonder if we've hit a dead end with her. Might not find anything unless the police and FBI are brought in."

"Hanks hasn't said anything yet?"

"No. But he'll have to soon. Rumor is they're bringing in a lie detector."

Tawnia whistled.

Autumn's expression was intense. "Good. I hope they find the jerk responsible and lock him up forever."

Bret gazed at Tawnia and Autumn, noting again their similarity. But he could tell them apart immediately, and not only from the flushed and dreamy look on Tawnia's face.

Amazing. He could do amazing.

Tawnia bent to pick up the red high heels by the door and started back to the couch.

"Well, I'll see you tomorrow," Bret said to Autumn. Then he did what he should have done earlier. He put his arms around her and gave her a long, hard kiss.

An amazing kiss.

Maybe.

Autumn had to catch her breath when the kiss was finished. She smiled. "I'll see you tomorrow, then."

Bret sauntered from the room, but as he closed the door, he looked over his shoulder and saw Tawnia staring at him with a blank look on her face. Completely emotionless. He'd seen the look before when he'd told her he couldn't stop thinking about Christian. On the day he'd called it quits between them. She had looked exactly this way, and the expression had haunted him because it so contrasted with the vibrantly alive woman he had come to care about. He'd told himself it was because she hadn't really cared or because she knew he was right.

Now he wasn't so sure.

CHAPTER

19

*T*awnia stretched in Autumn's bed, looking around the room with leisure since it was a Saturday and she didn't have work. The room was an odd mixture of child and adult. Autumn must have saved every favorite toy she'd ever owned—dolls, stuffed animals, and boxes of games. The most interesting display was a doll with a pink watch that sat on a shelf in the middle of a train set. The adult Autumn seemed to enjoy pottery with odd colors or pottery with faces. One clay coffee cup had a frog sitting in the bottom. A huge, beaded macramé wall hanging decorated the wall behind the bed. The room was full, vibrant, and alive. Almost too smothering for Tawnia. So different from the uncluttered way she ran her life.

A tap on the door came, followed by Autumn's voice. "Tawnia? Can I come in?"

Tawnia sat up. Now would come the talk. Last night after Bret left, Tawnia had felt too tired to share the evening with

Autumn. Something inside her had wanted only to curl up in the bed and stop thinking.

"Come in," she called, but Autumn was already pushing the door open. She was dressed in army pants and a brown shirt made of stretchy material.

"All you're missing is army boots," Tawnia said, pushing herself to a seated position. "You going somewhere?"

"The store. It's not closed on Saturday." Autumn grimaced. "That's one drawback of working for yourself." She sat on the end of the bed, drawing her bare feet under her as she always did. Tawnia felt a little self-conscious in her pale pink nightie. As far as she knew, Autumn either wore her clothes or her underwear to bed. She immediately repented of the thought. After all, Autumn had been through a lot in the past week, and sleepwear wouldn't be high on her list of priorities.

"How's the arm?" she asked.

"Fine. Only seems to hurt at night." There were deep circles under Autumn's eyes, as though she hadn't slept.

"You should have woken me if you needed something."

Autumn shook her head. "It wasn't that. Not really." She fell silent, as though thinking. Her eyes lifted to Tawnia's. "I saw your face when Bret kissed me. You still have feelings for him, don't you?"

Tawnia felt her face coloring as she answered slowly. "I don't think it really matters. Bret told me in no uncertain terms that he couldn't have a relationship with me because of his brother."

"You were with him when he died."

"It was our first date."

"Was he cute?"

Tawnia smiled despite her growing urge to cry. "Adorable. All the women at work wanted to go out with him, and he went out with a lot of them. Never lasted. I don't know why. He wasn't a lot like me . . . or Bret. He was a lot like, well, the wind or something. He drifted a lot. But he was happy." She snorted. "Most of this I learned afterwards, from Bret. The truth is I didn't know Christian that well, but Bret seems to think I would have been the lucky girl to marry him. For Bret, even being with me was betraying his brother."

"And what do you think?"

"I think Christian would have introduced me to Bret and that would have been that."

"Christian would have stepped aside?"

"I don't know. I could be totally wrong. Christian did have a way of making life seem wonderful. I felt free when I was with him—and that was actually a little scary at times. But in the end, it really doesn't matter. He's dead. It was a horrible accident, but I can't make choices for the rest of my life based on what might have been."

Autumn sighed. "You should have told me you liked Bret. I wouldn't have let him kiss me."

"Like I told you, it doesn't matter."

"You're wrong. Bret may have looked like he was kissing me last night, but it was you he wanted."

"That's not true!"

"Then why was he so mad at you for kissing Orion? And for saying it was amazing?"

"He wasn't mad."

Autumn sighed again, this time more loudly. "We can talk about this later. I have to get to work."

"I could go with you." Facing the day in this overstuffed apartment wasn't appealing to Tawnia. "I'd be interested to see how you spend your days."

Autumn grinned. "I'd love to have you. Saturday is usually my biggest day. Of course, it may shock my regular customers when two of us show up."

Tawnia pulled her feet from the blanket and swung them to the carpet. "That reminds me. I was going to call the adoption agency, if they're open."

"We won't be *that* busy. You'll have time."

"So does this mean I finally get to meet Jake?"

"Yep, dreadlocks and all. Just don't get any ideas romantically," Autumn added. "Two men seem to be more than you can handle."

"One man, you mean. And for now Orion is just a nice guy—an impractical nice guy."

Autumn bounced from the bed. "Girl, I should have gone on that date. It's right up my alley. I would have relished every minute and not given a thought to how much it cost or what Orion planned for the future."

Tawnia was tempted to say Autumn could have the next date, but she wasn't ready to give up on Orion yet. There was something about him that appealed to her—and not just the way he kissed.

"I think," she said, as she picked up the bag with her toiletries to take to the bathroom, "that Orion is looking for something permanent."

"Well, he is the marrying type. After all, he did marry once before."

Was she implying Bret wasn't the marrying type? Well, it didn't matter, because as Tawnia had told herself a hundred times before, Bret didn't want her.

Jake was a young black man who was far better looking than

Autumn had let on. Tawnia had thought dreadlocks would make him look like a gangster, but the small, chin-length locks were close to his head and very neat. His dark, handsome face was enough to make a woman's heart beat faster. That is, if she didn't already have more man trouble than she could handle at the moment.

Jake's face lit up as he spied Autumn, and he did a double take as he saw Tawnia behind her. "My sister told me you two looked alike, but this is crazy." He walked around them, eyeing them up and down until Autumn punched him with her good arm.

"Stop that! You have a customer. Didn't you hear the bell?"

Jake glanced toward the door that joined the two shops. "They can wait. It's not every day I get to see two women as beautiful as you."

Autumn rolled her eyes. "That reminds me. I forgot to show you this the other day." She pulled out a copy of the drawing from her bag. "Ever seen this woman before?"

Jake glanced at it, his face becoming serious. "I know her. I mean I've seen her quite a few times down at one of the clubs I go to. Danced with her once. Her hair's something else, but she's definitely not the sort of woman I like. Too much makeup and way too fresh. You know the kind. You might have seen her there yourself—it's that club you went with me to last month."

"I guess I don't notice the women much."

"You're too busy dancing, that's what. But what's this girl got to do with anything, anyway?" Jake adjusted his position to get a better view of the customer in the herb store.

"I can't tell you, except that it's related to the bridge bombing."

Jake stared at Autumn, his customer forgotten. "Did you just say bombing?"

Autumn glanced at Tawnia helplessly. Tawnia shrugged. "That's what she said, but it's a secret. At least so far. We know an engineer who's working with the FBI on the case. You can't tell anyone."

"Please don't ask me any more," Autumn added. "I'm going to be in trouble for saying that much."

Jake studied her for a long moment before speaking. "Okay, babe, have it your way, but I'm here to talk if you need me. If you want to find that woman, you should go to the club tonight. Saturdays are big. She'll probably be there." He walked to the adjoining door with a lazy grace that fascinated Tawnia, pausing at the double doors. "That reminds me," he added, "there was some reporter here just before you arrived. Said he was trying to find the woman whose father was still missing. Told him I'd call the police if I saw him here again, but you know reporters. Let me know if you need me to run someone off. You'll have to be careful now at your place."

"Looks like you should stay with me for a few days," Tawnia said as Jake disappeared.

"Think your landlady will go for it?"

"If we explain the circumstances. Mrs. Gerbert likes you. You know, Jake is really . . . well, hot. Seems nice, too."

"Yeah, I guess." Autumn walked over to the counter where the computer sat.

"You and he ever go out?"

"Go out with Jake?" Autumn looked so shocked that Tawnia laughed.

"Well, he's got to be near our age. And he mentioned going dancing with you."

"That was a group of us."

"Well, why not go out with him?" Tawnia knew if she had been considering dating Jake, her mother wouldn't approve because of their racial difference, but Autumn's parents would have welcomed him with open arms.

Autumn shook her head. "We're friends. Good friends. I don't want to ruin that. And he's been there for me since Winter . . ." She blew out a shaky breath. "Is it crazy for me to think Winter might still be alive?"

Tawnia didn't mind the change of subject. That's how grief was for Autumn, she'd learned. Completely rational one minute and obsessing the next. She'd learned not to take either too seriously. "Not crazy, just improbable—as you pointed out yourself. In your place, though, I think I'd feel the same way. It's normal."

Autumn picked up a few papers on the counter and moved them to new random spots. "I don't feel normal. I feel lost."

Tawnia covered Autumn's hand with hers. "You have friends. Don't forget that."

Autumn smiled. "What's your father like?"

"I don't know." Tawnia shook her head, feeling the load of wasted years. "He worked hard, expected a lot of me. Too much, I always thought. But lately I've been thinking maybe I'm as successful as I am today because he taught me how to work."

"He wasn't very loving, was he?"

"Not in the way I think Winter was. But if I needed something, he was there. Even today, he and my mother would be on the next plane here if that's what it took." Tawnia blinked back the tears. It was hard to admit that many of the youthful conflicts with her parents had probably been her fault. "I'm so sorry, Autumn. Sorry about Winter. I wish I'd known him."

Autumn sniffed. "Thank you. Now you'd better go call that adoption place right away. My phone book's in the back. I'm going to tape this drawing to the back of my computer so everyone can see it, and then I'll call Bret to let him know we're going dancing tonight." She gave Tawnia a mischievous look. "Too bad we can't invite Orion and make it a double."

"Like that's going to happen any time soon." Tawnia almost volunteered to call Bret herself, but the memory of his kissing Autumn was too fresh in her mind. How would she feel if they became serious? What if they ended up getting married? In these few days she'd grown as close to Autumn as a sister. She didn't want to give that up, but seeing Bret every day at arm's length would be torture.

Biting her lip at the thought, Tawnia practically sprinted to the back room.

Taking her cell from her purse, she dialed the number of the adoption agency. After three rings, someone picked up. "Children's Hope. How may I help you?"

"This isn't the answering service, is it?" Tawnia asked.

"No, this is Lynn Fairchild. I'm a receptionist here at Children's Hope."

"Then you're open today." Tawnia felt stupid as soon as the question left her lips. Why else would they be answering?

"Yes, we're open every Saturday morning. How can I help you? Are you a prospective parent or a birth mother?"

Tawnia sank into the ratty easy chair by the fridge. "Actually, I'm an adopted child."

"I see. And what can I do for you?"

"Well, I was wondering if you can give me any details about my adoption."

"Name please. And date of birth."

Tawnia gave her the information, trying not to hope too much. Autumn peeked in on her, and she shook her head to tell her she hadn't come up with anything yet.

"I'm sorry, but those records are closed," the woman said.

"I really wish I could help you. I can put a note in your file, though, in case the other party comes in."

"What if she's dead?"

"I wouldn't have that information."

Tawnia fought down her frustration. "Look, does a Mrs. Mendenhall work there? I'd like to talk to her. If she's still working there, I mean."

"Do you mean Deirdra? Because if you mean BervaDee, she's retired."

Tawnia felt goose bumps ripple down her spine and spread out over her entire body. BervaDee! Autumn had been looking for a BervaDee, a woman she thought had been married to Dr. Loveridge.

"Do you know which of them took me to my adoptive parents?"

"Sorry, I can't give out that information. There is, however, an online adoption registry you might try. They have matched up many adopted children and birth mothers."

"It has to be BervaDee." Irritation was beginning to replace Tawnia's frustration. "Her name has come up before. Can't I at least talk to her?"

"She wouldn't be able to give you any additional information."

"She knows about my first day of life. She flew all the way to Kansas with me." Tawnia knew she was begging, but it was either that or start yelling at the unemotional woman.

"I'm sorry, but as I said before BervaDee Mendenhall retired. I don't have any information I'm permitted to give you regarding her whereabouts." A pause. "You might, however, check the phone book."

"Thank you." Tawnia hung up as Autumn peeked into the room again.

"That bad?" she asked, coming all the way through the door.

"They have no idea what it's like." Tawnia stood, trying to smile, but she was sure it looked more like a grimace. "I did at least find out the first name of the woman who placed me. Or maybe her name. You won't believe who it is."

"Who?"

"BervaDee."

Autumn gave a swift intake of breath. "Then her last name isn't Loveridge."

"Not then at least."

"I thought she was Dr. Loveridge's wife. No wonder I couldn't find her anywhere."

Tawnia let a few heartbeats go by before saying, "You know what this means, don't you?"

Autumn nodded solemnly. "There's a connection. Somehow, somewhere, we're connected. I knew it!" Autumn hugged her, and Tawnia hugged her back, tears pricking her eyes.

"We have to find her," Tawnia said as they pulled away. "She might not be willing to talk to me over the phone, but if she agreed to see me and—"

"We both show up." Autumn snapped her fingers. "Give her a shock, and she might let something slip."

"Exactly. If she's still alive, that is, and if we can find her." Tawnia wasn't altogether unhappy to hear the bell at the door, signaling a customer.

"I'll get that," Autumn said. "Come on. You can start looking up Mendenhall on my computer. There's a good white pages site that I—" She'd reached the door to the back room but stopped walking so suddenly Tawnia ran into her. Autumn turned and practically tackled her onto the worktable.

"What—" Tawnia began.

"Orion!" hissed Autumn. "He can't see us together. Not now."

Tawnia groaned. "Gotcha. Now can you let me up? You're pretty strong for such a tiny little thing with one arm."

Autumn lifted her weight from Tawnia. "I'm not tiny."

"Are too."

"I just got good genes."

Genes that I might have too. Tawnia felt like laughing. The threat of Orion finding out her secret was nothing next to that. "Maybe we should tell him," she whispered. "I almost did last night."

"Better wait and see how you feel about him. I'm not too proud to take leftovers, if it includes romantic dinners and helicopter rides. He's older, but he is a babe, after all." Autumn winked to show she wasn't serious, but Tawnia didn't know her well enough to figure out her meaning. Was she subtly referring to Bret as well.

No, she decided, *Autumn isn't as cynical as I am.*

"You go see what he wants," Tawnia said. "But remember, I can't go on a date with him tonight. We're going to that club."

Autumn lifted a brow. "You can go out there and talk to him instead. I'm perfectly fine hiding back here."

"What if he asks me something about an antique? Or what if a customer comes? Besides, I don't have the brace for my arm."

"Okay, okay. But you aren't embarrassed because of last night, are you?"

Tawnia grimaced. "Maybe just a little. What if he decides he doesn't like me?"

Autumn snorted. "His loss. But remember, he's not Bret. Not all men are that stupid. And Bret is stupid—even if he is a good kisser."

"Autumn!"

"Okay. I'm gone."

Tawnia watched her go and then tiptoed as close to the door as she could without being seen. The bell at the door was ringing again, and Tawnia hoped that meant more customers so Orion couldn't bring up anything too personal. What if he mentioned something from last night and Autumn didn't respond correctly? Had Tawnia even told her what they'd had to eat?

"There you are." Orion was at the counter, close enough for Tawnia to hear.

"Hi, Orion. Good to see you."

"I had a fabulous time last night." His voice was a caress.

"Me too." There was a laugh in Autumn's tone, and Tawnia knew it was directed toward her. Orion was apparently not changing his mind.

"You look wonderful. Not many women look good in army pants."

"It's one of my many talents." Autumn twirled around like a runway model. "Like eating tofu and walking across hot coals. I did that once at one of my father's herb seminars. Crazy, but fun."

He laughed. "Every time I see you, you're different."

"That's a bad thing?"

"It's refreshing. New. I enjoy being with you. In fact, that's why I stopped by, to see if you're busy tonight."

"Oh, I am." Autumn managed to sound disappointed. "I have plans with a couple of friends. It's kind of important to them, and I can't let them down. But I'd like to see you soon."

"I'll call you, then." His voice had changed, becoming odd and tight.

"Have you seen her before?" Autumn asked.

Tawnia realized he must have discovered the drawing Autumn had taped to the back of her computer. Was that the reason for the change in his voice? Or was it because he thought Autumn was making excuses?

"No—no. I haven't seen her."

"Oh, it's because of the drawing in your wallet, isn't it? I thought it was a lot like that one when I first saw yours, but the girl is obviously not your daughter. I'm so sorry. I didn't mean to shock you like that."

"It's okay. They aren't really much alike."

"But you're sure you've never seen this woman before?" Autumn pressed. "Look closely."

Tawnia risked a peek around the door and saw Orion leaning forward to study the drawing.

"Nope, never seen her before. Why is this important? What has she done?" His voice had returned to normal.

"I'm not sure, really. Bret, that engineer the county brought in, gave it to me. Apparently, she's someone of interest. The bridge operator for the bridge drew the picture."

Thankfully this time Autumn didn't slip and say something about explosives. Neither of them wanted to get Bret in trouble. The sooner the authorities went public with the announcement, the more comfortable Tawnia would feel. Then again, with no suspects apprehended, the panic after such an announcement might be horrific. And how could it be otherwise? What if another bridge *was* blown up? Tawnia laid her head against the wall and let out a long, slow sigh. At this rate, she might take to avoiding all bridges.

Autumn and Orion were still talking but only casually because they'd been joined by a customer. "I'll call you tomorrow," Orion said as Autumn was totaling the customer's purchase.

Tawnia peeked again through the door and watched him leave the store. She waited a few more minutes for good measure.

When she walked into the store, the customer gazed at her and smiled. "All these years I've been coming here," he said to Autumn, "and I didn't know you were a twin."

Autumn and Tawnia grinned at each other. "We surprise a lot of people." Autumn gave him back his change.

"Who would have figured?" The man tipped his balding head toward them. "Oh, and I'm so sorry about your father. I just heard on the news that he's missing. He helped me through several health challenges—a good man. I don't even know what to say. I'm really sorry."

Autumn nodded calmly, though her smile had vanished, and Tawnia could see a sheen of tears in her eyes. "Thank you."

They were silent as the man left. "So I guess the reporter went public with your name." Tawnia went around the desk, checking the street for signs of reporters. "It's only a matter of time until more people come snooping. Let's look up the social worker's phone number and get out of here. Maybe Jake's sister can come in for a few hours to watch the store."

Autumn lifted her chin. "I'm not leaving, and if any reporter sets foot in my store, I'll kick him out. Or sic Jake on him."

"Atta girl." But Tawnia worried about Autumn if such a confrontation were to take place. Autumn's emotions were far too visible in her face.

Tawnia sat in front of the computer. "What was that white pages site you were talking about?"

In a couple of clicks, Tawnia had the names of two hundred people with the last name of Mendenhall. There were no BervaDees, but six initial Bs.

"Better than two hundred," Tawnia muttered, pulling out her cell to begin the calls.

At the same time the store phone rang, and Autumn picked it up. "Good morning. Autumn's Antiques." She listened a moment, her face paling. "No comment," she said tightly. "And if you have any respect for me, you won't call again." She set the phone gently down on the counter. "Reporter."

"I'll answer the next time."

Autumn nodded.

The first three phone numbers for B Mendenhall didn't turn up a BervaDee, but the fourth woman hesitated a moment before saying, "I'm BervaDee Mendenhall." Her voice was soft and husky, as if it belonged to a woman of mature years.

Tawnia gave a thumbs-up to Autumn, who came rushing over from a nearby display of cast iron toys to hear what she could of the conversation.

"My name is Tawnia McKnight. Thirty-two years ago you were working for Children's Hope Adoption Agency, and I think you took a baby—me—to Kansas on a plane. I know you probably placed a lot of babies, but I was hoping you could give me some information."

"I'm not allowed to talk about the adoptions. Things were closed in those days. Even if I remembered the details, I—"

"Please," Tawnia interjected, "I just want to meet with you. There's something I have to show you. It's something I found recently, and I don't know what to make of it. Please, it means a lot to me."

The woman didn't immediately respond, and Tawnia held her breath. Autumn was leaning close to the phone, biting her lip in a way that was strangely familiar to Tawnia. *A stranger's face,* she thought. *A stranger's face that is my own.*

"I remember you," BervaDee said suddenly. "I did place a lot of babies, including a few in Kansas, but I remember you. I didn't personally do the case work on your parents, but I did work with your birth mother, and I took you to Kansas. Yes, I remember."

There was a lot she wasn't saying, that much was clear. Yet something had obviously made Tawnia's adoption stand out from all the others BervaDee had participated in over the years. Could that somehow be related to Autumn?

"My mother said I was a small baby," Tawnia babbled. "She said I grabbed onto her finger."

"She was radiant. Your father too. He was a hard worker. I thought he'd take care of you. Did he? Did you have a good life?"

Memories rushed at Tawnia, good ones, instead of the bad ones her brain normally dredged up: birthday parties, her grandparents until they died, her mother taking her shopping for a prom dress, the nice used car her father had given her at graduation.

"Yes. I had a good life. It wasn't perfect, but it was really good. Better than I knew at the time."

"Your father was a little severe. I could see that then. But he was a good man. Better than many in that day and age."

Tawnia swallowed. "So, will you see me?"

Again a pause, longer this time. Tawnia squirmed in her seat.

"Yes. You can come," BervaDee said finally. "You can come to show me what you've found, but you'll come also because I have something to tell you. Rules or no rules, there's something you should know about your mother before you try to find her." The woman's voice was shaking but determined.

"When?" Tawnia barely got out the word.

"Tomorrow, dear. After my church. If that's okay."

"Perfect. What time? Noon? One?"

"One o'clock. Do you have my address?"

Tawnia had the listing, but she wrote it down to be sure. She hung up the phone and stared at Autumn. The goose bumps were back, but now they were at her temples the way they were when she was frightened. What was BervaDee Mendenhall going to tell her about her mother? What was so important that a lifetime employee of the adoption agency would go against the rules?

"How am I ever going to wait clear until tomorrow?" she whispered.

Autumn put an arm around her. "You've waited thirty-two years. You can wait another day. Besides, we have important plans tonight."

Tawnia looked past her to the window where she spied a news van pulling up. A man with a camera emerged from the passenger door. She made a noise of dismay in her throat.

Autumn followed her gaze. "Oh, no."

"It's your turn to go to into the back room." Tawnia put her cell phone in her purse under the counter. "This customer is for me."

"You sure?"

"Yes. It'll make me feel better. Just watch. They won't make it past the door." Putting on her poker face, Tawnia sauntered to the door, head held high. This was for Autumn.

CHAPTER

20

Bret drove to the antiques shop after spending most of the day with the county officials and the FBI. Autumn had closed the antiques shop, but she and Tawnia were inside waiting for him. Autumn wore a close-fitting hat, a brown T-shirt, and baggy green army pants that nearly hid her bare feet. She appeared younger than her thirty-two years. Tawnia was looking great in a pair of black culottes and red shirt with a v-shaped neckline. She had on red pumps, again, though this time without the three-inch heels. With their differing attire, especially Autumn's hat, they wouldn't be causing double-takes all evening, though the lines of their faces were nearly exact.

He realized he was still wearing his suit, not exactly his favorite club wear, but if he lost the jacket and rolled up the shirtsleeves, it would do in a pinch. "You two look ready for a night of dancing," he said lightly.

"Actually, I look more like the beach." Autumn gazed down

at her army pants with resignation. "But we didn't want to risk going back to my apartment."

"Why?"

"Because the media found out about her father," Tawnia said. She didn't quite meet his gaze, but he'd expected that after his display last night. Had he really kissed Autumn? Oddly enough, it was Tawnia's immobile face he remembered most.

"They came here too," Autumn said, draping her arm around Tawnia. "You should have seen Tawnia. She pretended to be me when they came. They were rude, despicable, exploiting idiots who had nothing more in mind than bringing ratings to their stations. Never mind my feelings. They came right into my store, shoving that camera in her face, saying things to make her react. She stared them all down and asked them to leave. When they refused, she dialed the police. They got out as fast as they could after that. I was giggling so hard I thought they'd hear me." Autumn sighed. "It was beautiful."

"I'll bet."

Tawnia shrugged. "You do what you have to do." Her eyes traveled the length of his body. "Are you wearing that suit to the club? Won't it be uncomfortable?"

That was practical Tawnia. "I'll roll up the sleeves," he said. "Shall we?" He opened the door to the store with a flourish. "My chariot awaits."

"Why are we taking your car?" Tawnia asked.

Autumn turned her key in the lock of the antiques shop. "Because it doesn't make that weird noise like yours does."

"It doesn't make a weird noise. Well, not too weird. I guess they messed something up when they fixed the air conditioner."

Bret grinned. "Besides, we don't want to get lost on the way."

"He has a point," Autumn said. "I've only been there a couple of times myself with Jake, and I'm not too sure where it is. Jake printed directions from the Internet. He wanted to go, but his cousin was having a bar mitzvah. Good thing because he's hard to tell no." Fishing a wrinkled paper from her bag, Autumn shoved it at Bret.

Bret opened the back door of his car, and Autumn slipped past Tawnia into the seat. "I'll sit back here." She put on her safety belt but sat with her feet tucked under her.

"Will they even let you in without shoes?" Bret asked. "I thought that was illegal." He was about to open the passenger door for Tawnia, but she beat him to it. He noticed her longing gaze toward the back seat. Was it so terrible to sit next to him?

"I've never been kicked out of any place for not wearing shoes. Though there was a manager at one restaurant who objected to me standing on my head at the table." Autumn grinned. "That was during my yoga phase."

"That's some yoga." Tawnia glanced at the sheet of directions lying between the front seats. "Bret, don't you think we should consider calling the police? They could look for this girl."

He shook his head. "They haven't even seen the drawing, remember? As far as I know, Hanks hasn't come forward with it yet. I'll probably have to force his hand." Bret tossed his suit jacket into the backseat next to Autumn before pulling away from the curb.

"Which reminds me—two things happened at the county building today." When he saw he had their attention, he continued. "They questioned people again today, but one of the guys didn't show up—name's Robert Glen. Now at first that didn't bother me because it is, after all, a Saturday, and

Robert has been a bit defensive about the whole questioning thing from the beginning."

"You think he's guilty?" Tawnia asked.

"Not at all. I mean, he's just an ordinary guy. And standing up the agents a time or two wouldn't likely hamper the investigation too much. I didn't think he could possibly have any information of value."

Autumn was leaning forward, her arms on the seat. "So what do you care that he didn't show?"

"Well, he was the guy I gave a copy of the drawing to. He was supposed to pass it around. He knows everyone, and they trust him. Yet not one person has seen the drawing or him. That gets me worried."

"He's hiding something," Autumn said.

"Maybe."

"Do you know where he lives?" Tawnia asked. "It's still early. We could stop by."

Surprise waved through Bret. "That's a good idea. I know where he lives. Well, I have the address, at least. It's a bit out of our way. Autumn, will you get my phone from my jacket there? And look up Robert Glen in my addresses."

"Let's see." Autumn went down the names. "Glen, Glen. There it is. Oh, I know where that address is, or at least the general area. I go to yard sales there. Lot of good stuff for cheap. I can get you near it, I think."

On the drive to Robert's, Bret's eyes occasionally drifted from the road to Tawnia. Her face wore a faint smile, and she was staring out the front window with a distracted, faraway look. Was she thinking of that firefighter?

"So what else did you guys do today?" he asked casually.

"Tawnia talked to the woman who took her to Kansas as a

baby," Autumn said, placing her hands on the front seat again. "We're going to see her tomorrow. She says she has information that Tawnia needs to know about her mother—probably not exactly what we're looking for, but we're hoping to shock her into telling us more."

"What if she's a convict or something?" Tawnia said, turning toward them. "Or what if she left me a letter saying she never wanted me to contact her?"

"Well, you didn't start this search because of her, did you?" Bret asked.

Tawnia's mouth curved into a sad half smile. "You're right. Somehow Autumn and I are connected, and that's what's most important. Yet . . ." She trailed off.

"It would be nice to know." Autumn exchanged looks with Tawnia, a look that completely excluded him. That didn't bother Bret as much as it once might have. When he was gone, it would be good for them to have each other.

The thought was so depressing he didn't say another word. The girls chatted quietly, and he let their voices roll over him, soothing the something in him that ached.

"Uh, I think we're lost," he said after a while.

"That's okay." Autumn put a hand on the door. "Stop here, and I'll ask that guy over there for directions. And don't give me any macho attitude about finding it on your own. I like meeting new people."

Robert's house turned out to be located in an older area, much like the neighborhood where Tawnia was renting, except it wasn't quite as well kept. Several houses badly needed paint, and the yards were overgrown. Not so with Robert's house. His lawn was freshly mown, with the edging finished, and the house was attractive, though Bret didn't think much of the blue door, standing in stark contrast to the white boards on the house.

"There's a woman." Autumn gestured toward the single garage, where a woman in gardening gloves was holding a shovel.

"It's probably better for me to go alone. I'll only be a minute." Bret left them in the car and hurried up the walk.

"Hi," he called out after only a few steps. "I'm looking for Robert Glen. I'm Bret Winn. From Nevada. I've been working with him this week. Does he live here?"

The woman wore shorts and a tank top that showed aging skin on her arms and legs. Her shoulder-length red hair was streaked with white and pulled back into a ponytail. She was older than Bret, probably older than Robert too. But determining age had never been his forte.

"He's not home," she said.

"You must be his sister." Bret wracked his mind for her name. Nora? No, Noreen. He hoped. "Are you Noreen?"

She smiled. "Yeah, I am."

"I can see that now. You and Robert have the same smile. I'm leaving town soon. I hoped I could see him."

"Sorry. I'll tell him you stopped by."

"When do you expect him back?"

She shrugged. "I don't know. He does what he wants. He's a grown man. Sometimes he stays a few days with friends."

"I see."

She looked at her shovel, obviously expecting him to leave.

"I missed him at the county building today," Bret said. "Like a movie, all those agents. He was pretty upset yesterday. That's why I'm here. I'm worried about him."

"Wasted his whole day, that's what. But then the county is good at wasting other people's time. When I worked for them, there was hardly a day that went by that they weren't taking something from the workers. Seemed like, anyway."

"You worked for them?"

"For fifteen years."

"Not anymore?"

Her hand gripped her shovel more tightly, and Bret had the urge to step back out of range. "I'll tell you what happened. The boss's son needed a job—my job—so they fired me and gave it to him. Oh, they didn't say so in so many words, of course. They said it was because I was late to work too many times and that I was drinking on the job. Bridge operators can't drink, you know. But I never took a drop while on duty, and I wasn't late more than the boss." She glared at Bret as if everything were his fault.

"That stinks," he commiserated. "The boy who took your place, he wasn't Hanks, was he?"

She nodded. "Yep. And since then I haven't had steady work. I got depression. If I didn't have Robert, I would have starved. Robert's a good brother."

"He is a good man." Bret tried to smile, but his mind was reeling with the knowledge that Alec Hanks had replaced Noreen. Was it possible Robert had wanted to seek revenge? "Look," he said, "I really need to talk to Robert. He should have my number already, but if he doesn't, it's on this card. Ask him to call me, okay? It's important."

"He didn't do anything wrong." Noreen's voice was firm. "No matter what you might think."

How had she jumped to that conclusion? "I didn't say he did. Is there something you're not telling me?"

"You should go."

"Wait a minute. I have something to show you." Bret sprinted to the car for a copy of the drawing and then back again. "Have you ever seen this woman?"

"No, I haven't." She was either telling the truth or she

was the best liar he'd ever seen. Bret hoped she was being truthful. For Robert's sake. "Robert showed me that already, you know. Said you gave it to him." At least this proved Robert was showing the drawing to someone. Maybe the man simply hadn't run into the people Bret had met today.

He thanked Noreen and took his leave. As he walked to the car, he drew out his cell and dialed Clay Hanks.

"Hello?"

"Hanks, it's Bret Winn. Look, I know this is coming out of nowhere, but what do you remember about a Noreen Glen working for you possibly a year or two ago? At least I think her name was Glen. She was a bridge operator."

"I remember her. Robert's sister. We had to fire her for drinking."

"Really?"

"It's too dangerous letting someone who drinks operate the lift."

"I understand that. But I've been looking for Robert and ran into Noreen. She's saying she was fired so your son could have a job."

Hanks barked a laugh. "The woman's a mental case, a pathological liar. She was fired for incompetence. Nothing more. The fact that my son was given her job later doesn't mean anything."

Bret had reached the car, but he didn't open the door. Autumn rolled down the window, obviously not ashamed to eavesdrop.

"What it means," Bret said, "is motive for revenge. Someone used your son, and like it or not, he's in the middle of it. I know I said I'd wait, but you have to go to the FBI with the drawing—or I will. I think I know where to find the girl, but we'll need them to pick her up."

"I don't want my son involved."

"He's already involved! Tell me what's worse, having a drink on the job or leaving your post for an hour of flirting? I don't know, because both could have the same result."

Hanks cursed. "I should never have trusted you. Well, get this: you're fired. You aren't needed here anymore. I'll clear it with the FBI, and if you go without a word, I won't send a poor review to your boss."

"Threaten me all you want, but keep in mind that if you aren't the one to go to the authorities, you probably won't have your job by the time the dust settles." Without waiting for a reply, Bret hung up.

Autumn stared at him flatly. "Care to explain?"

As they drove to the dance club, he told them about Noreen and his conversation with Hanks. "It doesn't look good for Robert, but I'm having a hard time imagining him doing something like this. Killing all those people. It's not like him."

"How well do you really know him?" Autumn asked.

"I'm beginning to think that's a good question."

Tawnia's face was thoughtful. "So are you going to leave? I mean, if they've taken you off the job."

He shrugged. "I was finished anyway. They don't need me."

Yet he didn't want to go. In fact, he'd been thinking of asking for a few vacation days, if his employer in Nevada could spare him further. Provided, of course, that he even had a job waiting for him after the fiasco with Hanks.

A hand on his arm drew him from his thoughts. "I'm proud of you for standing up to Hanks," Tawnia said. "You did the right thing."

He smiled. "Thanks."

CHAPTER
21

*A*s she predicted, Autumn had no problem getting into the club without shoes. Neither the cashier nor the bouncer so much as looked at their feet, though a man without a shirt was refused entry. "I told you so." Autumn winked at Bret, and not for the first time he wondered what she'd thought about his exit last night. At the first chance, he should probably talk to her.

Probably. He was nervous about it, though, because he didn't know how he felt about her. She was attractive and fun, and he didn't mind her kookiness in the least, even if it might be hard to take her skiing. Did she wear shoes in the winter? Of course, the added bonus to a relationship with Autumn was that Christian didn't stand between them.

"Let's spread out," Autumn suggested.

Bret drifted through the aromas of body odor and perfume that wasn't altogether unpleasant. It seemed to come in waves, with one fragrance being stronger than the other for brief instances. People gyrated on the dance floor to the music, while others lined the walls, standing or sitting at tables with cups in their hands. The men ignored him as intently as the women seemed to watch him, their smiles inviting.

He quickly lost sight of Tawnia and Autumn, but after checking out the two largest rooms, he spotted Tawnia talking to a man on the far side. She was shaking her head and showing him the drawing. She walked away from the man, whose gaze followed her until she left the room.

Bret went back to work. He searched each face he passed, without success. Either the mysterious Sheree hadn't arrived yet, or she looked far different from the drawing. Tawnia had disappeared entirely, but he came across Autumn at the bar showing the drawing. She motioned for him to approach.

"That bartender there says she comes in every weekend, sometimes twice, but he didn't work last night and doesn't know if she was here." She'd barely finished the words when her left arm shot out and grabbed his. "Don't turn around! Tawnia's over there, and she just signaled me. She must have seen the girl. Let's drift apart and see if we can find her."

Bret spied Tawnia, who was moving slowly toward the door. He followed her at a distance. In the first room, he saw the girl in the drawing standing by a female friend. Her blond hair reached halfway down her back, thick and long enough for three women her size. It was her only true beauty because her face was plain under the heavy makeup, and her short figure was sturdy and straight, as though she could hardly be bothered with a waist. The plunging neckline of her blouse did little to enhance her lack of curves. Bret nodded at Tawnia to signal that he'd seen her.

Tawnia moved toward him. "Ask her to dance," she whispered as she passed. "Then find out where she lives. Maybe ask her for a date tomorrow."

Right. Easy for her to say. Why didn't women realize how hard it was to ask a woman to dance, much less out on a date? Then again, maybe it was only difficult for him. Christian had never had a problem with it.

Christian bumped his shoulder. "Which one do you want to ask?"

"That girl with the dark hair. She's really pretty."

"Then go talk to her. Go on."

"What if she says no?" Truth was, Bret had been far too busy with his college studies to visit any clubs in the past years. In fact, he hadn't been to a dance since high school. He'd only come tonight because Christian had teased him into it.

"So what?" Christian said. "Then ask another one. There are millions of women in the world. That's what makes it so much fun."

Bret blew out his breath as he approached. Up close he could see the girl was wearing a lot of makeup, looking more like a child who had rummaged through her mother's things than a woman in her own right. Like half the women at the club, her jeans were so low and form-fitting that her stomach puckered out over the waistband.

She glanced at him, and he began looking for the signs. If she walked away or turned her head, that meant they would have to come up with another plan. But she stared at him boldly, taking in his slacks and rolled-up sleeves with a whisper to her friend. She didn't turn away.

"Want to dance?" He doubted she could hear him over the music, but she smiled and nodded.

The friend, a lovely dark-skinned girl with straightened hair, gave them a smile and flounced away, her hips weaving a path through the growing crowd.

Only when they reached the dance floor, did he realize how out of practice he was. The girl was shaking and moving all over the place like the young thing she was, and suddenly he felt every one of his thirty-six years. She couldn't be more than twenty, if that. There was a whole lifetime separating them. She didn't seem to mind, and neither did any of the other mismatched couples who were also dancing, but he was uncomfortable. What was this music, anyway? Something a bunch of gangsters threw together in their basement? There didn't seem to be any words he could understand.

He caught sight of Tawnia and Autumn at the edge of the dancers. Autumn was dancing alone with fluid motions and seemed to be enjoying herself. Tawnia's head bobbed in time to the beat, but she was pointing to her mouth, obviously wanting him to talk to the girl. How could he do that? He couldn't even hear his own voice.

As he leaned toward her, a lock of her hair whipped over his mouth. The taste was awful. Probably hair spray or whatever women used these days. She stopped moving and swayed closer to him, her limbs brushing against his body.

"So, what's your name?" he yelled. "I'm, uh, Christian." If she somehow did know Robert, she might have heard his real name before.

"Sheree." She looked at him with lowered lashes, a provocative look, he assumed, but it only made him uneasy.

"Where you from?"

"Portland." She didn't ask where he was from, which was just as well because he'd have to make something up.

"Whereabouts?" He hesitated a second before adding, "I mean, I'd like to call you. Or maybe we could go out. I could come over tomorrow." Would she see right through him? In his world this approach was far too fast. Maybe she'd slap him or walk away.

She laughed and put her arms up around his neck, still

moving back and forth to the beat. He smiled. Her hand pulled his head down to her mouth. "What's wrong with tonight?" she breathed into his ear.

Bret looked toward Tawnia and Autumn, who were laughing aloud. Then he stiffened as he saw who was behind them, searching the dance floor with frantic sweeps of her head.

Noreen. Robert's sister.

He guided Sheree behind some other dancers. "I have to go somewhere later," he said. "In fact, I was thinking about leaving when I saw you." He found his phone in the pocket of his pants where he'd shoved it before leaving the car. "Well? Where do you live?" He hoped she wouldn't give him just her number, which was really the sane thing to do. What if he was a serial rapist or something?

Sheree looked at the phone and laughed. "You must be okay. I've never seen anyone here with a phone that ancient before." She opened her mouth to say more, but Noreen appeared out of nowhere. She grabbed Sheree, screaming something in her ear. Sheree's eyes widened a second before the two women ran.

Bret followed, hoping Tawnia and Autumn had seen what happened. He weaved through the dancers, occasionally losing sight of the women, but always finding them again. They were heading to the exit, running full speed now, ignoring the cursing that followed them as they plowed into people. Sheree and Noreen ran past the surprised cashier and bouncer, and Bret followed more sedately, trying to hurry without appearing to do so. Once in the open, he was sure he could overtake them. Or at least follow them to their destination.

By the time he was outside, they had separated, and only Noreen was in sight. Bret veered off toward her, ducking behind cars to hide. Where had Sheree gone?

Noreen kept looking behind her, but she was moving

slower now, obviously not aware of his continuing pursuit. She went to the street, going down the line of parked cars that had overflowed from the club's lot. She found her keys and pressed the switch.

Bret jumped out from behind the cars. "Wait, Noreen. Please!"

She lunged for her door, dragging it open.

"Wait," he called again. "I just want to know where Robert is. Please. Maybe I can help!"

She hesitated. "He didn't do it! I swear!"

"You knew the woman in the drawing. I bet you both did." Bret approached her car, slowly, but keeping it between them so she would feel safe enough to talk.

"He doesn't know anything about the explosives. Nothing! We just wanted to teach Hanks a lesson. We didn't—" She broke off, her face marked with misery. "It wasn't supposed to turn out this way."

"Then let me help you! Don't you see that Robert's disappearing is making him look guilty? The police are going to catch up with your friend eventually—you saw the drawing— and when they do, they'll get to the bottom of what happened. People died, Noreen. A lot of people. If Robert's not responsible, he has to come forward with what he knows before anything like this happens again."

"He didn't mean for anyone to get hurt." Her voice was a plea.

"I can help, Noreen. Where is he?"

"He's at a hotel. We didn't know where else he could go."

"Take me to him. I don't believe for a minute he meant to hurt anyone, but he needs to tell me what happened."

"Okay."

"I just need to get my car, all right?" Bret didn't dare leave Noreen in fear that she'd make a run for it, but driving with her didn't seem like such a good idea either. He still didn't know how much he could trust her. "Come with me to get my car. Okay? I'm not too far from here, and then I'll drive you back and follow you over."

"All right."

He took out his phone as they began walking, as far apart from each other as was possible on the sidewalk. "I'll call the friends I came with and tell them I'm leaving. That I'll be back to pick them up. Is that okay?"

When Noreen agreed, Brett dialed Tawnia's number.

"Hello?" the word could barely be heard over the music.

"I'm with Noreen," he said.

"Good, because we found Sheree again. She came back inside after you left. She's sitting at a table now. Looking around a bit but apparently not too concerned."

That was surprising. "Okay, you keep an eye on her, but don't do anything that might be dangerous. We still don't know how she's connected to all this."

"What about you?"

"I'm going to see Robert. Noreen said she'll take me to the hotel where he's staying."

"Are you sure you should go? That doesn't sound safe."

"I've worked with the guy all week. He might have a grudge against Hanks, but I'd lay bets he isn't a murderer." Bret glanced at Noreen and saw she was listening. He hoped he was right, but there was always the possibility that he was horribly wrong. Noreen had turned out to be a pretty good liar after all.

"He could be working with someone," Tawnia said. "Besides his sister, I mean."

"That's what I'm going to find out."

"If I don't hear from you in an hour, I'm calling the police."

Bret smiled. "So you do care."

And, probably to show him just how much she did, Tawnia promptly hung up.

*T*awnia looked at her phone for a minute before tucking it in the pocket of her culottes. Now Bret was chasing after bad guys. What had happened to the conservative engineer she'd known in Nevada? He was acting more like Christian than himself.

"He find her?" Autumn asked.

Tawnia nodded. "He's going to talk to Robert. What if that's a stupid thing to do?"

"Noreen doesn't seem like a criminal to me."

"What about Robert?"

"Well, I only met him once, and I didn't like him. But I had a broken arm at the time, and I was really hungry."

"Maybe they've been sucked into a terrorist organization."

Autumn laughed. "You've really been watching too much TV."

"Maybe you're right."

Autumn lifted her chin. "Looks like our bird is getting

a call." They watched Sheree chat on her phone. Every time the girl glanced in their direction, they carefully averted their gazes.

"Doesn't seem too stressed," Tawnia commented.

"She's shifty-eyed."

"No law against that. It's called bad genes. A lot of women would kill for all that hair."

Autumn shrugged. "So what's the plan? Hey, those guys are going to her table. Think she'll dance? No, she's shaking her head."

"Looks like she's arguing with her friend." They watched the friend walk with one of the men in the direction of the dance floor. Sheree glanced at her phone and then toward the exit.

A man in baggy pants and a silver necklace asked Autumn to dance. "Sure," she said. In Tawnia's ear she added, "Might as well have some fun while we wait. I'll stay where I can see her."

Smiling, Tawnia watched her go, and only because she was beginning to know Autumn better did she see that she was struggling for normalcy, to forget Winter for a few moments. She'd probably rather tell the guy to get lost, but she would at least try to make it through the evening in one piece.

Eyes drifting again toward Sheree's table, Tawnia let her thoughts wander back to last night when she'd danced with Orion, comparing his grace and confidence to the time she'd danced with Bret. Bret had been awkward at first—she had been as well—but once he loosened up, they'd had a lot of fun. Dreams had seemed possible.

"Would you like to dance?"

She lifted her gaze to see a nice-looking man, with trim facial hair and a T-shirt that said, I lost my phone number— can I have yours? He looked young, but not too young, and if she hadn't been playing detective, she would have enjoyed dancing with him.

"I'm sorry, but I'm waiting for someone."

"You sure?"

"Yeah, but thanks for asking."

"That's okay. The good ones are always taken."

She laughed. "That's sweet."

"Have a good night. If you change your mind, I'll be around." He winked at her and was gone.

Sheree was staring at her phone, apparently reading a text message. She looked around carefully before standing.

She's leaving.

Tawnia waited five heartbeats and then followed her outside. She exited in time to see a squarish automobile pealing out of the parking lot. Since there was no roof on the vehicle, Tawnia could see that Sheree's companion was male, but it was too dark to note any identifying characteristics. There wasn't time to see more than a blurry license plate.

Autumn arrived behind her, slightly out of breath. "Where'd she go?"

"Someone picked her up. I didn't see who. They must have texted her when they pulled up."

Autumn sighed. "Did you get a good look at the car?"

"Just that it didn't have a top. Tires were big—looked like they'd be good in the mountains. Sorry, it was too dark, and they were too far away."

"Oh." Autumn rubbed a hand over her splint. "Well, it seems we have some time to kill. What do you say we go dance? I need to apologize to that guy for running out."

Tawnia grinned. "Okay, but we still need to remember to call Bret in a while. He might have learned something."

The hotel where Robert was hiding was a tiny rundown operation near the edge of town, whose only benefit seemed to be that it accepted cash, no questions asked. Noreen rapped on the door with a pattern, presumably to let her brother know it was her. Under the harsh glow of the overhead streetlight, the fine wrinkles on her face were more pronounced.

Robert opened the door, his eyes widening when he saw Bret. He tried to close the door, but Noreen blocked him. "It's okay, Robert. He's here as a friend." She stared flatly at Bret, as though daring him to challenge the statement.

"That's right," Bret said. "I'm here to help, but you have to tell me what's going on."

Robert fell back and let them into the small room whose main focus was a queen-sized bed and a low dresser holding a blaring television. A miniature round table and two chairs had been squeezed into a corner by the bed. Robert headed there, while Noreen took a seat on the bed itself.

Robert's red hair was oily, and he looked exhausted, as though he hadn't slept in weeks. For all Bret could tell, he seemed to be wearing the clothes of the day before.

"I didn't kill anyone," Robert blurted.

"I'm not saying you did." Bret sat by Robert, placing his hands apart on the table, trying to seem open and relaxed. He'd read somewhere that many people responded to body language better than verbal communication. "Tell me what happened."

"Noreen was fired from her job a year or so ago. They trumped up charges about her being late and drinking, but they weren't true."

"She was never late?"

"Not often. And Noreen rarely drinks. On holidays, maybe."

He glanced at Noreen, who nodded. She had her hands folded and her arms crossed. Her lips were pinched shut.

"And then they gave the job to Alec Hanks," prompted Bret.

"Exactly. That no-good son of our noble manager. The kid couldn't even make it in college. He's always been trouble, and that's why his dad sent him away in the first place. Got some young girl in trouble, or at least that was the rumor at the time."

"Just a rumor?"

"Well, I never heard anything more. Might be that Hanks was worried something might happen to destroy his son's life. He was barely out of high school."

"So his dad sent him away to college and then brought him back."

"After two years. He didn't even finish. Couldn't finish, or he'd have been hired by management."

"Probably will still be promoted," Noreen grumbled.

Robert nodded. "They harp and harp at us about working hard, but we're the ones who do everything."

"So you had a grudge."

Robert blinked. "Well, not a grudge exactly. Okay, a little one. I thought we could teach him a lesson."

"Was that when you came up with the plan to have Sheree distract Alec?" Bret should have known something was wrong when he'd first shown the drawing to Robert. He hadn't even been curious about the girl. He'd understood immediately what the drawing was about.

"I knew Alec couldn't resist her. It was easy enough to make sure the feed from the surveillance cameras was interrupted so there wouldn't be a valid record. Just a blip in service."

"That maybe Alec would be blamed for later," guessed Bret.

"But the boat wouldn't have started under the lift unless it was going up. You must have had someone sneak in."

"I did that." Noreen unfolded her arms and clenched her hands together. "We knew a guy on board the boat. He didn't know about our plan, but he told us when the boat was coming. It was easy enough to get in the control cabin—I know my way around, and I still have friends who work there. Anyway, I punched in the commands and got out of there as fast as I could so I wouldn't get caught. After I left the cabin, I passed the Hanks boy as he ran to see what was happening. I was wearing a disguise; he didn't even notice me."

Robert leaned forward. "No one was supposed to get hurt. No one. I figured the boat would stop short of touching the lift, and there would only be a write-up on Alec. Or even if it hit the lift, I knew my bridge, and I knew it would hold."

"Only it didn't."

"I didn't plant the explosives!" Robert's eyes were wild. "None at all. I swear to you. I wanted revenge, but I'm not a monster."

"Then who did it?"

"I don't know, but those fins you yacked about to the FBI—they're mine. Just yesterday I noticed they were missing from my gear at the house. When the FBI searches my house, I'm as good as dead. They'll think I was on that boat and planted the charges."

Robert had done a lot wrong, but Bret believed him. "I still don't see how the charges could have been laid so quickly, but they probably will think that—unless you help them find the real person responsible. Think. Have you seen or heard anything that might tie anyone else to the explosives?"

"No," Robert agonized. "There's no one. It must have been pure coincidence."

Bret rubbed a hand over his jaw. "I think someone found out about your plan and decided to make their plan coincide with yours."

"But only we knew about it." Robert motioned to his sister. "We didn't tell anyone else, even if we used them for information."

"Except Sheree."

Noreen shook her head violently. "She wouldn't tell anyone!"

"How do you know that?"

"She stayed with me all through high school after her parents kicked her out. I practically raised her. She was furious when I lost my job. She volunteered to help us."

"But if what you two claim is true, and you didn't tell anyone, then it had to be Sheree. She's young. She probably didn't think telling a friend or two would make a difference. Look, the only way we're going to get to the bottom of this is if you turn yourselves in."

The background droning of the television sounded suddenly loud in the silence that followed.

Noreen stood and began pacing. "Sheree doesn't have anyone to tell. She doesn't talk to her family—we're her family now. She doesn't even have a boyfriend. Well, she was dating this guy for a while, but that was over weeks ago."

"Who else had a reason to hurt Multnomah County?" Bret asked.

Robert looked at him blankly.

"You wanted revenge. Maybe someone else acted for the same reason."

"Revenge against Hanks?" Robert snorted. "You wouldn't have to go far to find people who dislike him. Half the crew wouldn't attend his funeral if he died."

Bret digested the information. As much as he didn't like Hanks, he couldn't be sure he was the cause. "It could just as well have been someone with a grudge against the county or the city itself. Or even the state. Or against someone who commutes on the bridge each day. It could be almost anyone."

"You're right." Robert looked at Bret steadily. "I mean about telling the police. It's the only way."

Noreen's face was wet with tears, but she nodded. "Just so they know it's not Sheree's fault. We put her up to it."

"I have some friends who are watching Sheree now. We can call and have the police pick her up." Bret drew out his phone and began dialing.

"Hello?" It was Tawnia, sounding out of breath.

"What's going on?"

"We're dancing."

"What about Sheree?"

"She left in a car. I'm sorry. We couldn't stop her."

"That's fine. Robert's going to turn himself in. I need to call around and hook him up with the FBI, but I'll be by to pick you up in a while."

"No need. Jake's here."

"Who?"

"The guy who works for Autumn. They're dancing now, but he already offered us a ride home." Laughter came through the phone. Sounded like the women were having fun without him.

"Okay then. But be careful, okay?"

"You're the one who needs to be careful."

"I will. Bye." Bret sighed as he hung up the phone. "Sheree already left, so I hope you know where she's living." At Noreen's nod, he stood. "Come on, Robert, let's go."

Robert followed him to his car, but Bret paused as he opened the door. "So I'm curious. What really happened to my tools? Did you take them?"

Robert looked down at the blacktop. "I wanted you to use the county tools so I could calibrate the readings to make sure that we engineers weren't blamed for the collapse. It couldn't have been our fault, but I knew I'd get blamed. That was before I knew about the explosives."

"I always recalibrate every device before I use it, whether or not it's mine." Bret held the door open for him. "I double-check every readout. Your maintenance was not the problem, Robert. I never thought it was."

*A*utumn watched as Tawnia went into the bathroom at her bungalow for the fourth time that morning. Shaking her head, Autumn followed. She found Tawnia holding a brush as she leaned forward, studying her eyes in the mirror.

"You're going to brush your hair right out of your head," Autumn said from the doorway.

Tawnia met her gaze in the mirror, a faint smile touching her lips. "You know, for the first time in my life, I'm seeing my eyes as exotic and not as a birth defect."

"Well, no wonder with parents who bought you a contact lens to hide it."

Tawnia shook her head. "For years I've thought they were responsible for my feelings, but maybe they did it because it bothered me. I remember being upset about my eyes. I thought no one would want to be my friend if I was different."

"Who buys their ten-year-old a contact? They should have taught you to love your eyes."

Tawnia sighed. "That's just not who they are. They see a problem and fix it. I'm not saying they didn't want a perfect child—they did. But looking back now, I think they wanted it for me every bit as much as for them." She paused, thinking about everything else she'd blamed on her parents over the years. "How could my memories be so skewed?"

"Maybe because most kids don't think about their parents as real people trying to do their best."

"They're ungrateful, you mean."

"Speak for yourself." Autumn took the towel from the rack by the door and threw it at her. "I was grateful every day. Grateful not to have to eat my green beans, grateful I could wear my favorite holey jeans, and grateful I didn't have to wear shoes."

Tawnia laughed and tossed back the towel. "Yeah, right." Her face sobered. "The knots in my stomach are getting bigger every second. What time is it anyway?"

"We still have an hour before we need to leave for BervaDee's."

"What if she tells me my mother was a prostitute? Or in a hospital dying of AIDS?"

"I don't think she'd have you come for that."

Tawnia nodded. "For all I know, my mother's happily married with five other children."

"I don't know what's worse," Autumn said softly, "knowing someone is dead and never coming back or not knowing for sure."

Tawnia hugged her. "I'm sorry."

"Don't be." Autumn gave her a last squeeze and pulled away. "But with how we look—I've started wondering if maybe the girl Summer told me was my mother wasn't my birth mother at all."

The idea had occurred to Tawnia as well. "I know. Look, I think I'll lie down for a few minutes," Tawnia said. "We got back so late last night, and I didn't sleep much after that."

"I'll wake you when it's time."

Autumn went out onto the porch of the bungalow. Jake had taken them back to her apartment last night to gather some clothes and then dropped them off at the store to get Tawnia's car. So far they hadn't been tracked by the media.

She sat in the lounge chair. The neighbor couple was walking by, arm in arm, dressed in Sunday clothes. They waved and Autumn waved back. This was a nice, friendly neighborhood. Tawnia had called the landlady that morning, and she had been gracious about Autumn's staying for as long as she needed.

How long would that be? Autumn's life had changed and would never, ever be the same. She took a deep breath to stop the panic. She hadn't told Tawnia, but she was as eager and nervous as Tawnia was about the appointment with BervaDee Mendenhall. She and Tawnia had talked big about staying close no matter what, but Autumn was frightened. Over the years many friends had come and gone, but only family remained. Even if the family was not related by blood, like Summer and Winter, they stayed. A connection of family would tie Tawnia to her forever.

She closed her eyes and lay back. The warmth of the sun penetrated the coldness in her broken arm and for the moment she was content.

Bret arrived minutes later, sprinting up to the house with an energy Autumn envied. "Hey," he called. "You look comfortable."

She smiled up at him lazily. "Have a seat."

"I think I will." He settled in the rocker. He didn't ask who

she was, so either he knew or had assumed she was Tawnia.
Maybe she'd wait and see.

"So what's up?"

"The FBI thinks they have an open and shut case. They
suspect that Robert and Noreen set the charges, though both
deny doing so. Robert worked for the marines a long time ago,
and they think he must have learned about explosives there.
Apparently when they found the fins on the boat, they also
found some of the explosives—that stuff you thought was clay."

Well, at least that told her who he was talking to. Autumn
swallowed with difficulty. The memory of that day on the boat
was hazy because of her fever, but she did remember the clay,
disguised in a box of children's art supplies. She'd actually held
it in her hand.

"So, basically," Bret continued, "they think Robert
concocted the whole boat thing to cover up the real cause of
the collapse."

"Hoping the authorities would never figure out that explosives had been used."

"Exactly."

"Well, he did look dishonest when I met him."

"You were in pain that day."

"So? I didn't think you were untrustworthy."

He blew out a frustrated breath. "You might be right. Still,
for one person to be responsible for all this, it'd take a lot of
money, and I don't know where Robert would get it."

Autumn thought a moment. "Then there's someone else
responsible. A group. Maybe working with him."

"But if Robert's working with terrorists, why on earth would
they want to damage this bridge when there are so many better
targets? Targets that could do serious damage to the economy?
I mean, one part of the city is a mess, that's true, but we can

always go down to the next bridge to cross the river, so it's not like everything in the city will stop."

"So that's why they think it's Robert." Autumn sighed. "He probably is guilty. What about Sheree? Did they find her? What's she saying?"

"She's vanished completely. The FBI went to her apartment, but she hasn't been there all night. Nothing's missing. Her friends and family haven't heard anything. No one has seen her since we did last night."

"She's hiding."

"Maybe. Or maybe the guy who really did this got to her first."

A shiver rolled down Autumn's spine. Bret had a point. Someone who would collapse a bridge that killed dozens of people wouldn't hesitate to get rid of one more.

"Look, Autumn, about last night. I mean, Friday night."

She sat up, swinging her legs to the ground. "You mean when you kissed me."

"Yeah." He scooted forward until his feet touched hers. "I've been thinking hard about it all night, and I really, really like you, Autumn. I'm glad we met. I think . . . well, I think we might have something here. Maybe we should date and see what happens."

He leaned down from the taller rocking chair to kiss her and for a moment, Autumn was tempted. Bret was an attractive man and dating him for however long it took for one of them to come to their senses wasn't altogether an unpleasant idea. But yesterday morning Autumn had glimpsed the extent of Tawnia's feelings for Bret, and she wasn't about to betray those.

Autumn drew back, shaking her head. "You know what I think? I think you've talked yourself into liking me because you hope I'll be Tawnia without the baggage related to your brother. But I'm not Tawnia, and I never could be. The truth is, I'm weird. I eat strange food, I often dress funny, and I wouldn't wear shoes for my own wedding."

He grinned and reached for her hand. "That's okay. It's who you are, and I like that."

"You might think so now, but you won't always. Believe me, I know. I've had lots of boyfriends, and it never works with guys like you." He opened his mouth to protest, but she hurried on. "You'd never go to a store barefooted with me, and I don't think you're ready to give up microwaves or refined sugar. You have no idea how bad preservatives are for you, and you probably haven't taken an herb in your entire life. You might think you see me when you look at me, but deep down, I know it's Tawnia you really want. If you were anyone else, I'd ride this train to see where it goes—because you really are kind of cute—but I won't hurt Tawnia this way. She means too much to me, especially now that Winter—" She broke off, knowing she simply couldn't explain the connection she felt with Tawnia.

"Tawnia and I aren't dating."

"Because of a dead man?" she retorted. "Because she dared to like your brother?" Now it was Autumn's turn to lean forward and look deeply into his eyes. She saw the shock there, but she didn't care. He needed to understand. "Get this—it didn't mean she was going to marry him, and even if it had, you can't hold it against her. You think your brother would sit around worrying about dating someone you liked if you'd been the one to die? No, he'd get on with his life. We all have to." Autumn felt the tears in her eyes. "I know what it's like to lose people you love. But losing them doesn't mean you stop living. It can't."

Gently, she pulled her hands from his and added, "Tawnia

cares about you—or at least she did. You know where you should be, but if you're too dumb to get there, I can't help you."

Bret looked angry, but he held his tongue—the sign of a good man in Autumn's book. The shock in his blue eyes gradually faded. "You might be right," he admitted. "My pride doesn't want you to be, but I"—he stared down at his hands—"I did miss her a lot after she left, and if I was honest, she's one of the main reasons I agreed to come out and look at the bridges. I wanted to see her again."

"That should have been a clue. You should at least try again. It should be her you're asking out. And let's not pretend it was me you wanted to kiss on Friday night. We both know you were putting on a show for Tawnia."

He lifted his head. "Even if you're right, it might not matter. She seems pretty gone on that firefighter."

"Maybe that's because she doesn't think there's another choice." Without another word or a backward glance, Autumn stood and went inside.

She walked quietly to the bedroom where the door was slightly ajar. Tawnia was on the bed, lying on top of the blankets, breathing evenly. Asleep at last.

Had she done the right thing? Tawnia might have already given up on Bret for good, and maybe someone like Orion would be better at taking care of her.

Autumn just didn't know.

T he house was a nice one, older, with a double garage, two tall stories, and an attic window. The yard was immaculate, with sweeping flowerbeds and attractive shrubbery. The wide porch ran the width of the house, wrapping around the corner. Large hanging baskets of mixed flowers and vines hung from the porch at regular intervals. The furniture on the porch was obviously of the best quality. The feeling of the house, if not the design, reminded Tawnia of her parents' house in Kansas. A homesickness she hadn't felt since the first year of college curled in her belly.

"Nice place." Autumn was wearing a flowered blue summer dress that nearly hid her bare feet, and she looked as though she fit in with the house and yard. She squatted down by one of the beds. "Rosemary, thyme, sweet basil, chives."

"What are those, herbs?" Tawnia asked.

"Yes, mostly for cooking. There's a lot here, more than most people know what to do with."

"Like the pots in your window at the apartment."

"Exactly. It's best to grow them yourself if you want organic."

Tawnia nodded, not really hearing what Autumn was saying. Her stomach was doing strange things, and it was all she could do to appear calm. Questions still came to her mind about what BervaDee Mendenhall had to tell her, from the possibility that her mother was in prison for attempted infanticide to the more remote possibility that her mother had been a foreign princess who was visiting the United States when she became pregnant and had to give up the baby in order to keep her crown.

I feel like a teenager again, Tawnia thought at the seesaw of emotions. She ran her moistening palms over the green skirt of her suit. She shouldn't have worn the jacket; the heat of the day was stifling.

They went up the steps, and Autumn held back to let Tawnia ring the bell. Footsteps came almost immediately, not slow or brisk, but steady and purposeful. A woman opened the door, her slightly full figure erect in a blue dress and high heels. She was taller than Tawnia, with short silver hair that perfectly framed the classic lines of her face. *A beauty in her day,* Tawnia thought. Now the beauty had become a sort of regal handsomeness.

"Are you Tawnia?" Her voice was the same as on the telephone, huskier than most women, but pleasant and inviting.

"Yes. I'm Tawnia McKnight. You're Mrs. Mendenhall, aren't you?"

"Please, call me BervaDee. I still think of Mrs. Mendenhall as my mother-in-law."

"Thank you for seeing me." Tawnia stepped sideways and turned slightly, allowing Autumn to come into full view. "This is Autumn Rain. I think you knew her parents."

They had planned this moment to the letter. Though their clothing was different, they'd taken care that their hair and makeup was exact—even if that meant Autumn had to wear her hair flatter on top, and Tawnia had to compromise with more eyeliner. Tawnia wasn't wearing her contact, and in the sun, their identical mismatched eyes were obvious. Autumn was still noticeably thinner in the face, and the scar near her left eye could be seen, but their similarities overwhelmed those small differences.

BervaDee's brown eyes widened in surprise. "Autumn Rain. I knew you as a child, but how—" Here she broke off as she looked back at Tawnia, disbelief etched on her face. But was it disbelief at their similarity or surprise that they had found each other?

"Now you see why I had to come," Tawnia said. "She's what I found."

BervaDee nodded. "Please, come in."

She led them through a surprisingly narrow entryway, given the size of the house, and into a sitting room where a jar of lemonade and a plate of treats awaited. BervaDee indicated the leather sofa. "Please, have a seat." She herself chose a plush chair opposite them, sitting delicately on the edge. Her eyes went from Tawnia to Autumn and then back again. But when she spoke, it wasn't about their appearance.

"I heard about your father on the news," she said to Autumn. "I am so sorry. He was a good man."

"Thank you." Autumn looked down at her hands, and Tawnia could tell she was fighting tears.

"We found a note," Tawnia said, "in a box of records at Autumn's house. It was from Dr. Loveridge, and it mentioned your name."

"We thought BervaDee must be his wife," Autumn added.

"It was only after we talked to Tawnia's mother and the adoption agency that we made the connection to your real last name."

"It proved we were somehow connected." Tawnia fell silent, watching the woman. How much did she know?

BervaDee poured them each a glass of lemonade, her sturdy hands the tiniest bit unsteady. At last she looked up and met Tawnia's stare. "I had planned to tell you today that your mother was dead. I didn't want you to waste years searching for her." She glanced at Autumn. "But this . . . I never expected this. Both of you with those eyes. It's unmistakable. I swear to you, I didn't know. I mean, I was as happy as Dr. Loveridge that he found Summer and Winter a baby when he did, but if I had known where he found her, I wouldn't have let him do it. It wasn't right."

"What wasn't right?" Tawnia could barely choke out the words.

"Separating twins." BervaDee nodded at their shocked silence. "There is no other explanation. Tawnia, your mother died after childbirth. It was a long, hard delivery, and she wasn't quite sixteen. I was responsible for taking you to the parents she chose. The McKnights in Kansas."

"And Autumn?" Tawnia asked.

BervaDee's shoulders lifted in a delicate shrug. The fine wrinkles around her eyes standing out in the bright light streaming through the sheer blinds. "While I was gone to Kansas, Dr. Loveridge found a baby for Summer and Winter, but seeing you two, I realize there were two babies born to Tawnia's mother that night, not one."

"No! That's not how it happened!" Autumn set down her glass on the tray, slopping juice over the edge. "My mother was Kendall. She stayed with Winter and Summer and saw they would be good parents, and that's why she decided to let them raise me."

"That is also true." BervaDee leaned forward. "Don't you see, dear? Kendall was Tawnia's mother too. We didn't have the access to ultrasound machines in those days that we do now, and Kendall was a poor girl who had to depend on free care. She had maybe two doctor visits in her whole life—once at a few months along and then not until seven months, shortly before you were born. When she measured so large, we thought she was further along. I should have realized something was up when Tawnia was so small. My guess is you were born early, together, and Dr. Loveridge hid it from me."

Tawnia was stunned. It would explain everything, of course, but hearing it was a shock. She saw a tear sliding down Autumn's face, and she reached out and took her hand. Twins. If what this woman was saying was true, they were sisters. A surge of joy shot through her, as painful as it was delicious.

"Kendall loved Summer and wanted her to have a baby," BervaDee went on, smiling at their joined hands. "In the week before the birth, she asked Dr. Loveridge if she could change her mind, and of course he called me to let me know there might be a problem. At that point it would have been a terrible mess to take the baby away from the McKnights, but Dr. Loveridge was always adamant that the mother should have the final choice. We talked for hours about it but came to no conclusion because Kendall herself seemed to waver. She really liked the McKnights as well. They sent her beautiful letters with pictures of the room they'd made for the baby. She wanted her baby to have all the opportunities life could offer."

BervaDee sighed and folded her hands in her lap. "The baby came early, or so I thought, but twins nearly always come early. My best guess is that when Dr. Loveridge realized Kendall was having twins, he tried to fulfill both of her wishes. She may even have agreed to it before she died. We'll never know. But I do know that you are both her daughters. You look very much like her."

"How could he separate twins?" Tawnia asked. Images of what it might have been like to grow up with a sister assaulted her mind, and an intense hatred of the man who had stolen that from her came out of nowhere.

"I'm sure he did what he thought was best," BervaDee folded her hands primly in her lap. "Giving each of the families a child would make a lot of people happy, and the babies couldn't long for what they didn't know they lost, could they?"

"Yes, they could." Tawnia was crying now. "My entire life I've been so restless, moving around from state to state. All this time I think I was looking for Autumn. My sister."

Autumn squeezed her hand. "We ended up in a lot of the same cities. Maybe we were looking for each other."

"Dr. Loveridge felt guilty for years after Kendall died," BervaDee said. "He blamed himself for her death. That's why he kept such close tabs on you, Autumn. Until he died."

I hate him! Tawnia thought. Look what he stole from me!

"Didn't you ask where he got the baby for Summer?" Autumn asked.

"He said it was a private adoption through another agency, and I had no reason to doubt him." BervaDee frowned. "We had barely begun to date back then, and I didn't know him as well as I came to later. We had both lost our spouses, you see. We would have married if he hadn't died. He even left me this house." A tender sadness had entered her voice.

"All these years we could have been together," Tawnia said.

BervaDee looked at her steadily. "Would you give up your parents, then? Or wish that Autumn had given up hers?" She waited a moment, and when neither answered, she continued. "I know you missed out on a lot, not growing up together, but you gained a lot too. Your birth mother sacrificed to give you a good life, and from what I can see, you've both had that. Now, shouldn't you start thinking about all the future you still have together rather than wasting time regretting the past?"

Tears fell down Tawnia's cheek. She looked at Autumn, whose face was also a river of wet. Tawnia leaned her head toward her sister's, their cheeks touching, their tears mingling.

"This is the happiest day of my life," Autumn whispered. "How would you feel about changing your name to Spring?"

Tawnia choked out a laugh, her anger at Dr. Loveridge seeping away. "You can call me anything you want." Their linked hands tightened.

BervaDee watched them for several long seconds before she dropped another bomb. "Kendall wrote a letter for her baby to read when she was of age." Her voice was calm, but her eyes were intense, showing clearly that she knew what this would mean to them. "Not every agency encouraged that in those days, but I did. Unfortunately, she went into labor early and I never got the letter to pass on to Tawnia's parents."

"What happened to it?" Tawnia asked eagerly. "What did it say?" Surely the older woman wouldn't bring it up if she didn't at least know the contents.

BervaDee smiled serenely as she stood and walked to the bookcase against the far wall. There, she picked up a rectangular pewter box, the lid raised in an intricate flower and leaf design. She brought it over to the girls. "I found the letter in here after Dr. Loveridge died."

Tawnia's hand trembled as she took the outstretched box. It was heavier than she expected, and the inside was lined with black velvet. A single thick blue envelope lay on the black velvet, the outside decorated with stickers and hearts drawn with multicolored markers, now faded with age.

Emotions swelled inside Tawnia, each demanding expression: anger, betrayal, excitement, hope. A letter from her mother. Her eyes met Autumn's, whose face mirrored her own feelings. No, a letter from *their* mother.

Tawnia lifted her head toward BervaDee. "Why would he keep this from us? Why would you?"

BervaDee's eyes glistened with tears. "After I read it, I decided not to send it to your parents. Probably for the same reason Dr. Loveridge didn't. But now that I know you are twins, I realize the decision for him was not as simple as I'd thought. Whether I agree with him or not, I believe he did what he felt was best for all of you."

Tawnia lifted the letter and took out the many pages of tiny, neat handwriting. Had their mother always written so beautifully, or had she rewritten the letter several times to get it just right? Unfolding the pages, she moved it over so Autumn could also drink in the words. BervaDee sat again in her chair, watching them with a smile on her lips.

To My Daughter,

I'm writing so you will know a little of what happened in my past and how you came to be where you are today. I have put off writing this letter, though Mrs. Mendenhall has been after me for weeks. She says it's best before the baby comes.

I want to start at the beginning, or almost, because as bad as some of it has been, everything that happened has also led to much good. And even if I hope I'll be able to tell you about it someday, I might not remember every-thing the way it really was, so I've decided to write it all down in this letter.

I left my mother's house when I was fifteen. I was happy to leave. I would never have to see her or her drunken boyfriends again. I wouldn't have to run from my bed in the middle of the night. I found a job as a waitress in a little café. A dump, really, but the tips were good because a lot of truckers came in. They flirted with me, but Russ, my boss kept them away if they got too friendly. He and his wife, Suzy, let me sleep in the kitchen for two weeks until I'd earned enough to pay for a tiny apartment. I tried not to think about my mother.

Sometimes after the lunch rush, I went behind the café and spread a blanket under a tree and sat there and read books I got from the bookmobile. In school I hated reading. They make you read the wrong books, so it's amazing anyone likes reading at all. I hope you love to read. The books I like best are the romances where the girls are firefighters or pilots or doctors. The girls take care of themselves, even though there's a cute guy in their life. The romance books show it better than in real life. Safer. Cleaner. Less painful. Way less painful. I would like to have that kind of romance someday. But not until I'm older.

Russ and Suzy became my friends, and I felt guilty for lying to them about my age. Sometimes I'd wonder if my mom ever thought of me, if she noticed I left the bear she gave me for my fifteenth birthday. After what happened to me that night, I wanted her to know I was too old for stuffed animals.

After a few weeks I got sick. At first it was just a few hours, and then all the time. I thought I was allergic to the grease or that I had a disease or something. I tried to hide it, but Suzy found me throwing up in the bathroom and said I must be pregnant. She made me take a test, and it was positive! I've never been so scared in my life. Well, except two other times back at home.

I didn't know what to do, so I went home and told my mother. The house was messier than before, and her boyfriend was gone. She didn't look good, and when I told her about you, she laughed at me and said it served me right, that I should have known better.

I lost it big time. I yelled and told her it was her fault. She'd left me alone with him. I HATED that he came into my room and did those things to me. She slapped my face and said it was my fault he'd left her and I should be ashamed to cause her so much pain. If I was going to have a brat that was my business, but she didn't want any part of it. That it would be better to have an abortion. I think she was telling me she wished she'd aborted me. At the time I wished she had too.

I did go to the abortion clinic, but I knew right away I couldn't hurt you. None of this was your fault. I prayed every night for something good to happen. Then I realized that a baby is good and that I could make a life for you. I could love you, and you would love me. As long as we had each other, what more did we need?

Suzy took me to see a doctor in Portland—Dr. Loveridge. I was really nervous, but he didn't touch me anywhere that made me feel scared, and Suzy was there the entire time. He talked to me about adoption, but there was no way I was going to do that! I could take care of my own child. I did agree to go to his mothering classes, even though I had to take a bus to get there. I wanted to be a good mother. Some of the girls at the mothering classes were planning to have their babies adopted, but I hurt even to think about it.

Pretty soon I wasn't so sick anymore, but I started to get really fat. I didn't have money, so I left my pants unzipped and strung a rubber band through the buttonhole to make them fit. I was afraid to ask for government help because they might make me go back to my mother.

I didn't go to doctor appointments, though they told me I could get them free. I'd heard they talked a lot about adoption at the appointments, and I didn't want to think about that. I did take vitamins from the health food store near the mothering classes. The owner, Summer Rain, gave all the girls from the mothering classes half price.

Then I had a visit from my mother, who tracked me down at the café. It was busy and there was a lot of noise, but she marched up and said she needed to talk to me. Out behind the café, she told me she was sorry for everything and that she was getting help. I felt stunned! I hadn't heard her talk like that since I was a kid. She said I could come home, if I wanted, and she would help me do whatever I decided for my future. The only condition was I had to give you up for adoption. She said, "I know you want to keep the baby because you're probably thinking it will give you everything you need, but you don't know anything about raising a child or how hard it is." That made me wonder. Is it even remotely possible she once felt I would give her everything she needed?

Before she left she said something that cut me deeply.
"Kendall, I love you. I always have, but I should have
given you up for adoption, because then you might have
had a good life, not the lousy one I gave you. There's still
time to choose a better life for your child."

I screamed at her to leave, saying she was crazy and
I liked her better drunk. She didn't yell back. Didn't try
to slap me. That showed me more than anything how
serious she was about getting her life together. But I
hated her that day. She was wrong. I loved you, and I
believed I was the only one who could really take care of
you because I knew what it was like not to be loved.

Pretty soon my life became hard. People in my apart-
ment building made rude comments about me being
unmarried. I don't know why it hurt so much, but I still
wonder how they would have acted if they had known I
was raped by some guy who was probably too drunk to
know what he was doing.

My feet swelled. I couldn't walk without pain. I
couldn't miss work because I wouldn't have enough
money for food. My tiny apartment felt like a refriger-
ator. The wind seeped through all the windows until I
began to think I'd be warmer outside. At night I wore
my coat and three pairs of socks, and I'd still shiver under
my blankets. I tortured myself with wondering how I
could take care of a baby when I couldn't even take care
of myself. Was it fair to the baby?

I finally knew why Dr. Loveridge kept saying that
a girl who chooses adoption isn't giving her baby up but
giving the baby a chance to have what every child should
have—a mom and a dad and a life without worries
about where the next meal is coming from. A safe life.

Thinking that made me want to die. If I couldn't keep you, I couldn't see the point of living at all. And yet I still had some dreams for my future. I wanted to finish school and go to college and eventually get a good job. I could become one of those smart girls in the romance books! But I couldn't do any of that and raise a child alone.

I knew what I had to do. When I told Dr. Loveridge, he said he would set everything up for me, including a place to live. I cried for the next two days straight. I didn't go to work. I cried for me, for you, and for my mother. I hated her, but I wanted her too. I wanted her to tell me things would be all right.

Most of all, I kept thinking that I didn't want you ever to feel so lonely.

I said goodbye to Russ and Suzy at the café. Leaving work was hard because they'd been so nice, but Dr. Loveridge said the café was too far away for me to commute to every day, even if I had been feeling well enough to work.

I went to live with Summer Rain from the herb store, and it was the beginning of something wonderful. Her husband is Winter, and at first I thought they were strange. People call them hippies, but they are so kind to me that sometimes I cry with happiness. If Summer sees me crying, she puts her arms around me and holds me for as long as I need. Being with them is such a relief! All the stress and worry about not having enough money is suddenly gone, and I can focus on eating right for my baby. For you.

I'm the third girl from the mothering classes they've had live with them. Both of the others also placed their babies for adoption. I don't have to work anymore, but

I do help out at the herb store for fun. Summer gives me stuff to help the swelling in my legs, so that's a bit better too. She says I'll have to start going to the doctor regularly after the Christmas holidays, and I said I would if she went with me.

Two days before Christmas, I was with Mrs. Mendenhall at the adoption agency, and I picked out a family for you. I thought it would be hard, but they stood out to me right away. He's an economist for a big company and makes very good money. She stays at home. They've been married eight years. They are good-looking people. Elegant, just like their names, Sherman and Ellen McKnight. They both have parents who are alive and successful as well, so I figured there was no chance you wouldn't have everything you need. Except you wouldn't have me, of course. But I don't matter here. I must do what's best for my girl. (Now it's true I don't know for sure you're a girl, but somehow I feel you are.")

Anyway, after they heard about my choice, the McKnights wrote me a letter about how happy they were to adopt you. They want a baby more than anything, and that day I really felt the McKnight family would be perfect for you.

At times, though, I wonder if I'll actually be able to make myself go through with the adoption. But I'm not even sixteen, and I have a lot to learn before I can be the mother any baby deserves. I hope and pray that maybe someday you will understand why I'm doing this.

Christmas was wonderful, mostly because Summer and Winter are so good to me. But I started feeling sad for them because I know Summer well enough now to know how heartbroken she is that they haven't been able to have a child of their own. It's funny how I no longer think they're strange. So what if they don't use those new microwave ovens (which I think are really cool) or believe in cars or go around with bare feet half the time? What's important is that they are fantastic people. They are kind to everyone—even to rude customers and to people who make fun of them or try to cheat them. They just smile and go on with their lives. I wish I could be more like that. How different my life would have been if I'd had a mother like Summer. And I can't imagine a better father than Winter. They really care about me.

For instance, a week or two ago Summer started thinking that I might be farther along than seven months because I'm so big. She called over a midwife friend of hers who delivers babies at home, even though I was going to the doctor the next week. She said it was better to be safe than sorry. The midwife said I was definitely measuring further along. I suppose it's possible. Those last months at my mother's are very unclear to me. I try NOT to think about them.

Anyway, the midwife let me hear your heartbeat. It was so strong and steady. I could have listened forever! You're a fighter, and I know you'll be all right without me. I only hope I can be all right without you.

That's about the time I had my great idea. What if Summer and Winter adopted you instead of the McKnights? I know after I leave here in March, I'll still be friends with them and that I'd get to see you. But that's not the real reason. The real reason is because I know they'd always love you no matter what you did. They'd be absolutely the best parents ever.

I talked to Dr. Loveridge on the phone about making

Summer and Winter your parents. He said it was my choice, though it would be difficult because I'd already taken money from the McKnights and I can't pay them back, or pay the hospital bills, either. I understand why I shouldn't change my mind, but I got so angry that I refused to go in for my doctor's appointment with him. I know it was childish of me, but because of the midwife I knew you were healthy. Besides, you're always kicking me and moving around inside. Everything is perfectly fine.

After talking to Dr. Loveridge, I decided I'd have to go through with my promise to the McKnights. They seemed so nice, and I didn't want to hurt them. I told Summer I was sorry I couldn't give her my baby, and I could tell she was surprised I was even thinking that way. She said not to worry about it. She wants the best for you and for me too.

Summer eventually talked me into going to see Dr. Loveridge a few days ago. He was really worried about how big I have become in the last month. Apparently being too big can mean a lot of problems or even sicknesses. He told me about this new machine they've been using the past few years that shows a picture of the baby inside the mother. A sonogram, I think he called it. He wants to use it on me, but he doesn't have one of the machines at his clinic. I guess they cost a lot. I explained that I might be further along, like the midwife told me, and he said she was probably right—which means nothing is wrong. Still, he wants to do the test, and I'm going to let him because I'd like to see you. We'll do it next week, he says.

That's my story, but not quite all, because as I write

this I can see how important Summer and Winter are in my life. Take today, for instance. I'm not feeling well, so Summer stayed home with me and phoned the doctor just in case. Winter has already called us three times from the store to check up on me. Could they be more wonderful?

No. They couldn't. So I've decided for absolutely sure that I'm going to tell Dr. Loveridge and Mrs. Mendenhall that Winter and Summer will be adopting you after all. Even if I have to work for years to pay the McKnights back, I want you to be raised by parents I'm positive will always love you no matter what. Making it possible for Summer and Winter to have a baby is the second-best thing I have done so far with my life.

I do hope that in the years to come I'll get to visit you every now and then. I know Winter and Summer will tell you how very, very, very much I love you. Soon I will experience the greatest joy a mother can know by giving birth to a baby and also the greatest sorrow in saying goodbye. But my sweet, dear baby, you deserve a good life, and I can give you one. That will be the first best thing I have ever done.

With all my love,
Kendall (your birth mother)

So short a letter to span all the lost years, yet so much more of the story than either of them had known before. Tawnia rested her finger on the last words, her eyes filled with tears. *That will be the first best thing I have ever done.* She felt sorrow and pride for the woman who had given them life and then died. Kendall had been little more than a child herself, but she'd had the courage to want something better for her baby. Babies.

"You see," BervaDee said gently. "Clearly, Kendall had decided to give her child to the Rains, so I didn't know what to do with the letter. I didn't think it would be helpful for Tawnia to know that Dr. Loveridge had betrayed Kendall's wishes, though now I see maybe I was wrong. If I had given it to you, you might have discovered the truth more quickly."

Autumn shook her head. "You did the best you could. You couldn't have known what Dr. Loveridge did."

Part of Tawnia kept imagining BervaDee at least copying part of the letter and sending it to Kansas, but she was filled with light at Autumn's easy forgiveness. Her sister had surely learned that from her adoptive parents, and Kendall wouldn't want any less for Tawnia.

Tawnia lifted her eyes to BervaDee's. "Thank you so much for giving us this letter."

Not until BervaDee relaxed in her chair did Tawnia notice how tense the woman had been as she awaited their reactions. "I knew Kendall fairly well," BervaDee said, "and now that you've found each other, I think the only thing she would want is that you stay close to each other and be happy."

They talked for a while longer, asking questions and sipping lemonade. Then, after promising to visit again, Tawnia and Autumn took their leave. BervaDee stood in the doorway, holding the screen open as they walked to the car.

Tawnia drove a block before pulling over to the curb. She looked at Autumn. "I don't know how to take this all in. I mean, there are so many things we don't know about Kendall, her life, who our father is. How Dr. Loveridge came to such a decision. What happened to Kendall's mother . . ." She swallowed hard.

"Being your twin is the best thing that ever happened to me, but the questions—I'm afraid they'll eat me alive."

"Everything doesn't have to be put in a little labeled box," Autumn said, rubbing her thumb over the back of Tawnia's hand. "Life isn't like that. So what if we don't know what happened? Life isn't going to stop. I feel so incredibly blessed because I've been given a second chance at a family—and my first was great to begin with. Let the questions go. Please. Let's just enjoy being sisters." She held out her arms for a hug, and Tawnia squeezed her tightly.

"Okay," Tawnia whispered. She would do everything in her power to fulfill Autumn's wish. "There's just one thing I have to do," she added, pulling away. "I need to call my mom."

"Go ahead. I can wait."

Tawnia punched in the number. "Hello?" came the voice at the other end.

"Mom?"

"Tawnia? Are you okay? Do you need something?"

"No, I'm fine." Her words belied the tears on her cheeks and in her voice.

"Something's wrong. Are you crying? Sweetie, tell me!"

"Everything's perfect, Mom. I just wanted to call and tell you I'm so glad you're my mom. And Dad too. I know I haven't always told you, and sometimes I've acted like a spoiled brat, but I love you so much. You gave me a wonderful life. I love you for everything you are and everything you've given me. For everything you've helped me become."

Her mother started crying too, but that was okay, because it was happy crying.

When she hung up at last, having told her mother what she'd learned from BervaDee, Tawnia felt cleansed. She grinned at Autumn. "They'll be coming soon to meet you. And she invited us both for Christmas."

Autumn smiled. "I hope they like me."

"It's the tofu they won't like. But you'll get by. We have lots of health food stores in Kansas."

They were nearly to the bungalow when Tawnia's cell phone began ringing. She looked at the caller ID and tossed it to Autumn. "It's Bret. You tell him. I still need to get us home."

"Hello?" Autumn said. "No, it's Autumn." A long pause and then a gasp.

Tawnia glanced over and saw that Autumn looked visibly ill. Her hand shot out for the phone. "This is Tawnia. What is it?"

"It's Winter," he said. "They've found him."

CHAPTER 25

*T*awnia tried to follow Bret's directions to the medical examiner's office so Autumn could make an identification, but she ended up having to stop four times to ask people how to find the place. Autumn was little help, having withdrawn into her grief. She'd wanted to go to the river to see Winter, but Bret had convinced Tawnia to talk her out of that.

"I'm down here now, and he looks pretty bad," he told Tawnia. "He's bloated, missing some flesh, and the smell . . . well, let's just say Autumn shouldn't be in the same room with him until someone works some magic. They can barely touch him without hair and skin falling off. Most of his fingernails are gone." He gave an audible shudder. "I hope she'll be okay after this. It's not going to be easy for her."

"She'll be all right. She has me." Tawnia didn't tell him about their discovery. There would be time for that later.

Autumn gripped her hand tightly as they walked up to

the doors of the building, where Bret was waiting outside. "I'll show you where to go." In silence they made their way through the halls, one of them on each side of Autumn.

They hadn't gone far when they were stopped by a man. "Hello, I'm Dr. Brady. We're not quite ready. If you'll wait here." He indicated some chairs in the hallway. Bret and Tawnia sat, but Autumn, pale and silent, began to pace. Tawnia watched her, searching for signs that Autumn needed her.

"So, how'd it go?" Bret asked.

Tawnia didn't look at him. "How'd what go?"

"At the adoption worker's house."

"Oh." She tore her eyes from Autumn and met his gaze. "You won't believe it. We *are* sisters. Twins."

"Incredible." His eyes roamed her face. "Or maybe not so incredible, given your resemblance. I'm glad for you. But how did you get separated?"

"The doctor who delivered us made the decision. He didn't think it would hurt anyone."

"I'm sorry."

Tawnia shook her head. "Nothing to be sorry for. This is the best day of my life." As she repeated the words Autumn had said earlier, it occurred to her that today both she and Autumn had lost a parent and gained a sister. She wished Autumn's loss didn't have to be so fresh. Her eyes went back to her sister.

Sister.

Silence fell, and the minutes seemed to tick by slowly. Bret's leg was touching hers, and at one time that would have driven Tawnia to distraction, but now she only worried about Autumn.

"Look," Bret said. "There's something I'd like to talk to you about."

"Yes?"

Bret leaned forward, moving partially in front of her face to get her attention. She looked into his blue eyes, feeling at last that little tingle his presence had always brought to her heart. With a nod, she indicated that she was listening, not trusting her voice to speak.

"About before, what happened between us in Las Vegas." He paused, and she felt her heart sinking. This was when he told her he was in love with Autumn and asked if she could live with that. Well, she'd have to, wouldn't she? She wouldn't give up her sister for any man or any amount of pain.

"What I'm trying to say is that I've been an idiot."

Her eyes widened, and she wasn't sure if her heart was still beating. Was he saying what she hoped he was saying? And was she still naive enough to hope for such a thing?

The door next to them opened. "We're ready."

Tawnia jumped to her feet. "I'll get Autumn."

"It's time."

Autumn whirled around to see Tawnia behind her. Funny how she hadn't heard her step. Tawnia put an arm around her as they walked back to Bret and Dr. Brady.

"Which one of you is the daughter?" Dr. Brady asked, his eyes behind his glasses going from one to the other in apparent surprise.

"I am." Autumn stepped away from Tawnia's arm.

"But I'm her sister, and we're going in together," Tawnia added.

Autumn felt a rush of love for her. They'd known each other for less than a week, but acting like sisters of a lifetime seemed to come naturally.

"You can all go in. That's fine." If the doctor thought it odd that two sisters who looked so much alike didn't share the same father, he didn't comment. Nor did he comment on Autumn's bare feet, though he studied them briefly.

Autumn had expected to be in the same room with her father, but instead there was a window between her and the sheet-covered figure lying on the metal cart.

"You have to understand," Dr. Brady said. "He's been in the water a long time. Because of the debris covering him and the coolness of the water, there's less damage than there might have been, but water has its own challenges." He hesitated, as though unwilling to say more, and Autumn nodded to signal she was ready.

A woman on the other side of the glass pulled down the sheet to reveal the face. Despite her mental preparation, Autumn jerked at the sight. His face was a mottled blue, the skin bloated and torn away in spots. Bunches of the white hair on his head and in his beard were missing. But it was Winter, no doubt about that, and for all the horror of his appearance, there was a peace in his closed eyes and in the stillness of his face.

This body is only a shell, Autumn thought. *Somewhere out there he's with Summer, and they're happy.*

She put her hand against the cold glass. Winter, she told him, I found my sister. I'm not alone. Don't worry about me.

The doctor cleared his throat, and Autumn nodded. "It's him. It's my father, Winter Rain." Tears rolled down her face, unbidden, but welcome for the release they gave her aching heart.

Tawnia's arms went around her. "I'm so sorry."

Autumn clung to her as they left the room, the doctor saying something to Bret about funeral arrangements. Would they let her have a home funeral as they had with Summer or had state laws been changed to forbid it? Well, now wasn't the time to worry about the funeral. Autumn would face that battle in a few days. For now, she had to concentrate on not being swallowed by her grief.

At least she knew for sure what had happened to Winter. Despite what she had told Tawnia earlier about not dwelling on the unknown in their past, this was one box she needed closed.

They were leaving the building, when Bret groaned. "Don't look now, but we've got company."

"Orion!" Tawnia gasped. They stopped, frozen on the sidewalk as he approached.

His eyes went first to Tawnia and then to Autumn, whose face was streaked with tears. "I heard on the news," he said. "I came to see if I could help, but it's obvious I'm not needed." He uttered a muffled curse. "Can anyone here tell me what's going on?" He looked at Autumn, gesturing to the splint on her arm. "I assume you're Autumn, but who are you?" His stare challenged Tawnia.

"I—I meant to tell you," Tawnia stuttered. "I started to tell you Friday night."

"*You* were my date Friday?" When she nodded, he looked at Autumn. "But it's you I've been talking to in the store and at the river."

"Mostly," Autumn admitted.

He shook his head in disgust. "I can see I'm the brunt of this joke." He turned on his heel and started walking away.

"No!" Tawnia took several quick steps toward him. "It's not a joke! Please, Orion, let me explain."

Orion paused. "Okay, talk." He glanced at Bret and Autumn. "Better yet, let's go somewhere without an audience."

"Good idea," Autumn said. "Honestly, Tawnia, I'll be okay.

Bret will stay with me." When Tawnia looked torn, she added, "We owe Orion that much. Bret and I will go back to your place. We'll meet you there. I'm okay, really. I promise." She did feel much steadier now that the shock was fading. She'd known for over a week that Winter was gone; today had only confirmed that knowledge.

"I'm not sure this is a good idea now." Bret clenched his fists at his sides. If the day hadn't turned so grim, Autumn would have been tempted to laugh.

Autumn arched her brow at Bret. "You mean you can't stay with me?"

"Sure, but—"

"Go ahead," Autumn told Tawnia. "I'm going to take a nap, and by the time I wake up you'll be home."

"All right. I'll see you in an hour. But here, take my phone in case I need to call you."

Accepting the phone, Autumn turned to Orion, who had been watching the scene silently. "Orion, much of this is my fault," she said. "Tawnia wanted to tell you right away, but I made her wait."

Orion didn't respond. He turned on his heel and started walking briskly toward the parking lot.

"See you in a few." Tawnia hurried after him.

Bret watched them go, an unreadable expression on his face.

Autumn bumped him with her good arm. "Please," she said, "let's get out of here."

"I'm sorry. Yes. Come on." But as he opened his car door for her, she saw that he was still looking in the direction Tawnia had gone.

"She'll be back," Autumn said confidently.

"I hope so."

She knew what he meant. If Tawnia's heart was lost to Orion, part of her would never return to Bret.

They drove to Tawnia's in silence. There, Bret turned on the television and then paced back and forth between the kitchen and the living room. Autumn sat on the couch, her legs curled up under her. She was trying to think of nothing at all and certainly not the figure under the sheet. She began to feel sleepy.

"You hungry?" Bret asked.

"No." It might be days before she got her appetite back.

"Shouldn't she be here by now?"

"It's only been half an hour."

The phone in Bret's pocket rang. "Hello? This is he." For long moments he listened to the person on the other end. "What? You're kidding!" He sank to the couch, the color seeping from his face. "Who? Oh, no. That can't be. My friend's with him now. If this is true, she could be in danger." Another pause. "Okay, thanks."

"What is it?" Autumn felt frightened at the way he pulled on his hair and how close he looked to tears.

"They've found evidence linking Orion to the bridge bombing."

Autumn gasped. "What link?"

"He bought a ticket to Mexico in Sheree's name. But it wasn't used. They think she's dead. They also found some communication with a company in Mexico that sells explosives."

Autumn shut her eyes in agony. And she'd practically made Tawnia go with Orion. This was her fault. "We can't call her. I've got her phone."

"Come on." Bret started texting. "I'll pull some strings to get his address. I'm going there. Now. The police should be there too, but I have to make sure . . ." He didn't finish.

Autumn knew exactly how he felt. "I'm going too."

CHAPTER

26

*T*awnia hated leaving Autumn. They should be together on a day like this one, a day with so much joy and tragedy. The logical part of her knew they had the rest of their lives to share and that an hour of explaining things to Orion wouldn't damage their sisterhood, but the emotional part of her refused to be comforted at leaving her sister.

Sister. Again, the surge of wonder and joy.

Orion had reached his vehicle and was opening the shiny black door with his key. A Jeep, she saw, reading the make. Not new but obviously well taken care of. On the seat was a bouquet of flowers and take-out from Smokey's.

Tawnia's heart sank. Not only had he come to see her, but he'd come bearing gifts he knew she'd like—that both she and Autumn would like.

He rolled down his window. "Would have had the top off, but it's not very private that way." He gave a dry chuckle. "Besides, I didn't want the flowers stolen."

"Orion, I'm really sorry." Something about his words bothered her, but she wasn't sure why. Now that they were away from the others, he was being awfully nice about her deception.

"So who did I ask out?" he asked, putting the Jeep into gear.

"Well, you asked Autumn out, but it was Autumn pretending to be me. You see, I met you at the river the time they found that body, and something . . . well, when you took me for Autumn, I didn't know what to do. We were getting along so well, and then later, since she knew I liked you—" She broke off with a sigh. "There's no excuse. I shouldn't have done it. I was just afraid you wouldn't understand and would call it quits before we had a chance."

He didn't look at her, but was she imagining the softening of his jaw? "I wasn't aware Autumn had a sister." His voice was still stiff.

"She didn't know—we didn't know—until recently. We met through Bret by accident. He called me when she was sick because he didn't know what to do and because we looked so much alike. We're both adopted, and somehow we ended up being given to different adoptive families."

"I didn't think they did that, even thirty years ago."

"Not in the open." Tawnia studied the side of his face. "With Winter gone, I'm all she has left."

"Not all." His jaw worked. "She has her store. And I thought she had me. But now I find the woman I was falling in love with is actually two people."

I've blown it, Tawnia thought. *He's a nice man, and I blew it.*

Aloud, she said. "I'm really sorry, Orion. I know it wasn't a nice thing to do, but for what it's worth, I loved our date. Being with you was . . . magical."

He smiled at that, making the dimple in his cheek noticeable.

"I'm glad, Tawnia. It is Tawnia, isn't it? I thought I heard Autumn call you that."

"Yes. Tawnia McKnight."

"So who are you exactly, Tawnia McKnight?"

The question embarrassed her, but she answered anyway. "Well, just me. I guess. I work as a creative director at an advertising firm. I like art."

"Well, you are creative, I'll give you that." Again the softening in his jaw. "No antiques or herbs?"

She shook her head. "And I hate tofu."

"I take it that means Autumn loves it."

"Yes. And anything organic."

He snorted. "What does that mean? Everything we eat is organic."

"Well, yeah, I guess. But she means as close to a natural state as possible. It's supposed to be more healthy. I'm sure she's right, but it's too much effort for me to think about at the moment."

He nodded in agreement.

They had arrived at an apartment building with an underground parking facility. "Where are we?" she asked.

"My place."

He gathered the food and the flowers, and Tawnia wondered if she should offer to carry something, but if she did, he might think she was presumptuous. He wouldn't likely be inclined to give her the flowers after her deceit. They went up several floors in the elevator in an awkward silence before arriving at his apartment.

Inside was a modern designer's dream—a white carpet with black-and-white throw pillows, white couches, black tables, black and white vases, and black-and-white abstract art hangings. Only the occasional flash of red broke through the black and white decor, making what could have been a tedious display into a work of art.

"Nice," she said.

"I had someone redo it last year." Orion's black T-shirt and the gray sprinkling in his black hair blended well with the room's motif. She was glad to see the tenseness in his face had eased. He strode past the couches to the adjoining kitchen, setting the food bags and the flowers on the black granite countertop.

She walked slowly around the room, wondering what she should say, and decided to start at the beginning—at the feeling of belonging she'd experienced during her first trip to Portland with Bret. Talk. It was what she did when she was nervous. Babbling, Bret called it.

Orion had stopped fiddling with the food bags and listened as she walked around his living room, pausing before the displays as she talked. For all the modern beauty of the room, she'd expected something different in his living quarters, something warmer, perhaps. Where were all the pictures? Maybe he kept them in his room.

"Would you like to see the rest of the apartment?" he asked, as though reading something of her feelings in her expression. "Then we could eat."

"Sure." She came to meet him in the kitchen, where he smiled and took her hand. At that moment she knew everything was going to be all right. He was still upset, and had every right to be, but he wasn't going to throw everything they felt out the window.

Yet where did that leave her with Bret? What had he been hinting at in the coroner's office? Her chest felt heavy, which didn't bode well for her relationship with Orion. Maybe her parents were right. Maybe she was afraid of commitment.

That was when she saw it—a squarish black garbage bin

under the small, built-in desk in the kitchen. Sticking out of it a few inches was a framed drawing, like the drawing she'd seen in Orion's wallet. A shiver ran through her. She pulled her hand from his. She took one step and then another, her eyes locked onto the drawing. It was Orion's daughter, all right.

"Why did you throw this away?" She bent down, retrieving the frame. There was a spider web of cracks over the surface of the glass, and the bottom part of the frame had been completely torn away. Not only had someone thrown it there, but they had first tried to destroy it. She looked toward him, waiting for a reply.

"Yesterday in the antiques shop," he began. "Was it you or Autumn?"

She wasn't sure what that had to do with her question. "Autumn. But I was there. In the back. I heard you talking."

"She showed me the drawing of Sheree. I saw the signature and knew it was done by the same person who had made this drawing. Sure enough, when I ripped the frame apart it was his signature." He paused before adding tightly, "This drawing was made by the boy who killed my daughter."

Tawnia understood how he'd connected the two drawings. Hadn't she done the same? But accusing Alec Hanks of murder seemed farfetched. "I thought your daughter was alone on the bridge."

"My daughter killed herself because of Alec Hanks and his father. End of story." Pain and fury tinged his voice, and the lines on his face were more pronounced.

"I'm so sorry." The connection was beginning to fall into place. Alec Hanks had been the boyfriend who'd gone away to college, leading a fragile Arleen Harris to her desperate act.

Tears glistened in Orion's eyes. "I tried to tell her it would be okay, but she didn't understand. She couldn't believe she would ever get over him. I tried to talk to Hanks, to see if he would allow at least some contact. I didn't like the kid, but I couldn't stand to see my daughter in so much pain. Hanks wouldn't even hear me out. He didn't care what happened to Arleen."

Bitterness made the words ugly, and sudden fear leapt to Tawnia's heart. Orion had reason to hate both Alec Hanks and his father. He also knew Sheree's name, and Tawnia hadn't heard Autumn tell him that yesterday. And the dark automobile that had sped away from the club last night was similar to Orion's Jeep without the top.

No, there couldn't be a connection. Her crazy imagination was simply working overtime again. Even so, her heart thumped heavily in her chest, warning her . . . of what? Would Orion, with his training in firefighting, have the knowledge to set explosives?

Probably. Or he could have learned in the three years since his daughter's death.

The police should look into Orion, she thought. *I need to tell Bret that his daughter was dating Alec Hanks.*

"You know what?" she said. "I feel really sad about your daughter, and I appreciate you confiding in me. But would it be all right if we do this another time? I'm feeling anxious about getting back to Autumn. Her father—you should have seen him. Nine days in the water. It was awful." She placed the broken frame on the counter and backed away.

"What about the food? I know how much you like Smokey's." Then he sighed. "Or was that Autumn?"

"We both love it. But I really shouldn't have left my sister." She turned and started walking to the door. Orion was probably innocent of any wrongdoing related to the bridge, but now she'd never feel comfortable with him until Bret had him checked out.

In several paces Orion beat her to the door, stepping in front of it with a graceful movement. The expression in his dark eyes had changed. His face looked as hard as the black granite of his countertops.

"You know, don't you?" he asked. "What tipped you off?"

"Orion, what are you doing?" Panic threatened to choke her. "I'm sorry about everything. It's just bad timing. Please let me leave."

"I didn't mean to collapse the bridge." He spoke the words wearily, as though he was too tired to care that they came out. "I only wanted to cripple it, to see both Hanks and his son lose their jobs. But I don't know much about engineering, and it was difficult to calculate how many to use.

"How could you?" She was crying now, almost too terrified to get the words out.

His expression turned pleading. "Hanks had to pay, one way or another. I knew Robert Glen was angry at Hanks— news gets around. I'd been planning my revenge for three years, and I thought about getting Glen to help me. I made sure to talk to those closest to him, including Sheree, to find out how he might react. I realized right away that he'd never go for the explosives, but I kept watching for an opportunity. Sheree liked me, so we kept in touch. We had dinner a few times. When she let slip what he was planning, to have her entice the boy away, I knew I had my chance to take my revenge and walk away a free man."

How was Tawnia going to get past him? Maybe if she could keep him talking, she could figure something out. "You set Glen up," she said.

His mouth twisted into a smile that held no mirth. "I got Sheree to give me Glen's fins, and I put them on the boat with a bit of the explosive I used on the bridge disguised as a child's toy. That way if they did find signs of my charges, they'd trace it back to him. But I was hoping they'd think the boat was responsible. It was easy enough to have a guy on the inside to make sure the boat actually hit the bridge. That almost failed because the captain saw they weren't going to make it and tried to stop the boat. My man on board had to knock him out."

Tawnia's anger momentarily overcame her fear. "You killed Autumn's father! You killed children!"

He nodded. "And I will live with the guilt for the rest of my life."

"Please let me leave."

"I'm sorry." Orion pulled on her arm. "Come over to the couch. It's more comfortable."

Tawnia glanced at the door longingly, a mere two feet away. She'd never make it, not with him grabbing her arm. "What are you going to do now?" She tried to make the words calm, but her voice rose at the end.

He gazed at her in surprise. "I meant it when I said I wished I could change things. I didn't want your father to die. I mean, Autumn's father." He shook his head. "I wanted to make it up to her. I planned to take care of her."

The sorrow in his eyes was unbearable, and Tawnia had to look away. "I know." On Friday night she'd felt he was trying to make something up to her. Or to Autumn, rather. "So it seems I'm not the only one hiding something," she said. "The sad thing is I really thought there might be more between us."

"There was. Between us, anyway. Not the times with Autumn."

So there had been a difference for him as well, though he hadn't known what it was.

With his hand still gripping her arm, she walked to the

white couch and sat, her heart rate beginning to slow. Orion remained standing. Was it possible she could walk away from this? That she could see her sister and Bret and her parents again?

"Do you honestly think," he asked, "that we could go on from here? Because if I thought for a minute that was possible, I would buy two tickets to Mexico and we could disappear."

Should she lie? Even if she could leave Autumn, the sight of him sickened her now.

"You have to turn yourself in," she said gently. "I'll go with you. You'll serve time, but if you work with them, it'll be a lot less."

"I killed thirty-one people. I'll get the death penalty."

"You've also saved a lot of people over the years." She noticed in his count he'd only included people who'd died in the bridge collapse. The FBI hadn't found Sheree, and Bret had wondered aloud to both her and Autumn if the woman might have met foul play. But if Orion hadn't hurt Sheree to shut her up, maybe he would let Tawnia go as well.

"I can't live like this." Orion walked to a black wall table under a mirror near the door. Opening the drawer, he took out a gun. A shiny black, it looked like it belonged in the room.

Tawnia's breath caught in her throat. He'd lulled her into thinking he might let her go free, but all along he'd had the gun there, waiting to use.

"No," she whispered.

He turned to her, the slightest curve of a smile on his handsome face. The gun was coming up. "I'm really sorry it has to end this way. I was beginning to think there could be another way, but I was wrong, and when it all comes down to it, I have nothing left to lose."

She had a brief and vibrant image of her red blood spreading over the white couch. Would he buy another one or try to have it cleaned?

"I'm sorry, Tawnia." Orion turned the gun on himself, the barrel next to his heart.

"No!" she cried. "There's already been enough death. Please don't make this one more image I'm going to have to live with for the rest of my life."

He hesitated.

"Please," she said again.

Orion stared at her sadly. His hand moved downward to his side. He took one step toward her, and then another.

There was a soft explosion, the sound of something moving through the air at high velocity. Orion jerked, eyes opening wide in surprise, his free hand going to his opposite shoulder. Blood seeped from under the fingers. His eyes lifted, not to Tawnia but to the figure that had appeared from the hallway leading to the rest of his apartment.

Tawnia whipped her head around to see Sheree. The girl was dressed in jeans and a tight shirt, her thick hair gathered in a braid down her back, leaving her face unremarkable. She looked about sixteen. In her hand she held a gun.

"Stupid girl," Sheree muttered. "You should have let him kill himself."

"Sheree." Orion lurched a step in her direction, his face a mask of pain.

"Surprised to see me?" She walked swiftly toward him, her gun pointed at his heart. Tawnia could see the gun had a silencer and that no one would be alerted to her presence here no matter how many shots she took. "Thought I was in Mexico spending all your beautiful dollars? Oh, I'm going to, make no mistake about that, but first I have one more job to do." Reaching him, she took away his own gun from his loosened grip.

Sheree sneered at him. "You think all of this happened because you wanted it? No. It happened because *I* wanted it. I controlled everything. I was the one who gave Robert the idea of getting back at his boss, and I was the one who made you think because of Robert's plan you could get away with your revenge. I sent the contacts your way and arranged for you to get such powerful explosives for next to nothing. Of course they destroyed most of the bridge. That's what we planned."

"We?" Orion's face was utterly devoid of color. Blood dripped down his arm, the crimson beads falling onto the white carpet.

"This is so much larger than your petty revenge."

"Why?" The words were ripped from Tawnia's throat. "Why would you do such a thing? Who are you working for?"

Sheree's head turned in Tawnia's direction. Her eyes seemed surprised, as though during her confrontation with Orion, she'd forgotten Tawnia's existence. She brought up Orion's gun, pointing it at Tawnia. "Real Americans. People who are sick of the way this country is run. My friends and I aren't going to sit back and watch crazies ruin our way of life."

"So you blow up the bridge? How does that preserve your way of life?"

Sheree's eyes narrowed. "It wasn't the bridge. It was who was on the bridge. Or supposed to be."

"The governor," Tawnia said, making the connection. "You wanted to kill the governor. But you made a mistake about the timing."

Sheree smiled. "He left early. But he won't be a problem after tonight, and Orion here will be blamed for all of it. But by then, he'll be beyond caring." She glanced at Orion. "I have a car waiting. Don't try anything, or I'll shoot you just like I'm going to shoot her. It's unfortunate you got in the way, but we can't let anyone warn the governor."

Casually, Sheree switched her silencer to Orion's gun, as though she had planned this all along and had chosen her own weapon to be compatible with his. She raised the gun, pointing it at Tawnia.

Her finger tightened on the trigger.

Orion lunged at Sheree, and a bullet dug into the couch beside Tawnia. "I won't be responsible for her death!" he growled.

The two of them struggled. Sheree put a bullet from his own gun into Orion's hip. He screamed.

"Get out of here!" He yelled at Tawnia. His face dripped sweat.

Tawnia leapt from the couch, her feet propelling her forward. A shot whizzed past her head.

She made her decision almost without thinking. She grabbed at the large black vase standing by the couch, the long-stemmed black grasses it had held showering to the carpet. With effort, she flung it at Sheree. It smashed into the small woman, knocking both her and Orion to the ground.

Sheree twisted. She'd lost Orion's gun, but she held hers to his temple. "Stop! Now." Her voice was deadly, and her eyes icy hard.

Tawnia froze. Orion's brown eyes reproached her for not leaving. But what kind of person would she be if she had escaped and left him to die?

Sheree eased herself into a sitting position, still holding the gun at Orion. His eyes lost focus for a moment, and Tawnia wondered if he was going to faint. How quickly everything had spiraled out of control.

A banging came at the door, followed by an anxious voice. "Tawnia? Are you there?"

Bret! He'd come. But would his presence only mean another fatality?

More banging.

"Tawnia!" Autumn's voice now. Tawnia didn't know whether to feel more hope or more despair.

"You'd better not hurt her, Orion!" Bret yelled through the door. "The police are on their way!"

The words distracted Sheree for the tiniest second. Orion slammed his elbow into Sheree's head, throwing her back. She recovered quickly, and let off another shot, this one unsilenced, that crashed into the coffee table.

Tawnia threw herself onto the floor, grabbing Sheree's wrist as she tried to aim the weapon at Orion's head. The door burst open. Tawnia caught sight of Bret and Autumn with a man holding a set of keys who must be the building manager. Bret immediately jumped into the fray and wrested the gun from Sheree.

Sobbing with relief, Tawnia crawled to Orion, pressing her hand over his wounded shoulder to stop the flow of blood. He lay still on the white carpet, now marbled with red. His eyes slowly closed.

"He needs an ambulance," Tawnia cried. "And we have to stop the bleeding." There was too much blood from both his hip and shoulder.

Autumn raced to the kitchen for towels. Bret drew out his phone.

Sheree, seeing their preoccupation, jumped to her feet and ran toward the door. Bret shouted at her to stop and waved the gun, but Tawnia knew he could no more shoot the woman than she could have in his position. The man with the keys grabbed Sheree. She fought him off and vanished.

Tawnia felt bitter that Sheree would get away, but as Autumn knelt beside her with the towels, there was more scuffling in the hallway. Sheree began screaming and cursing.

Uniformed men appeared in the doorway, one dragging a struggling Sheree. "It doesn't matter what you do," she screamed at them. "There are more of us."

A man wearing a jacket with an FBI logo took over for Tawnia, tying bandages over Orion's wounds. She breathed a sigh of relief. She was shaking so badly, she couldn't respond to the questions another man fired at her. Autumn's hand tightened on Tawnia's, anchoring her in the sea of confusion.

Orion opened his eyes and met Tawnia's gaze. *I'm sorry,* he mouthed. She knew what he meant. He wished he'd kept her out of it. He wished he hadn't brought her here today or threatened violence in front of her. He wished he hadn't set off the explosives or let himself be used by Sheree.

Tawnia nodded, and his eyes slowly closed. The FBI agent continued working over him, but finally he looked at Tawnia and said, "I'm sorry."

Orion was gone. There would be no more pain for him. No missing his daughter. No hatred. No death sentence. He'd done so much bad, but in the end he'd saved her life. And he'd pulled Autumn from the river. Tawnia would be forever grateful for that.

Autumn threw her arms around Tawnia. "I'm sorry," she whispered. "I'm so, so sorry. I should never have made you go with him."

"It's not your fault. It's me who's sorry." Sobs shook Tawnia. "How come I can't tell the bad guys from the good guys?" But

Tawnia knew it wasn't as simple as that. Autumn hugged her harder, their tears mingling together.

"How did you know to come?" Tawnia added.

"The FBI found out Orion bought a ticket to Mexico for Sheree that she never used. That led them to finding some connections to an explosives company in Mexico. The FBI knew Bret had talked to Orion and wanted to see if he knew anything. They also wanted to make sure Bret stayed away from him."

"Orion wanted revenge. But he didn't mean to kill all those people."

"But he did kill them."

Tawnia nodded, tears dripping down her face. She thought of Winter's still form under that sheet at the medical examiner's office.

"I'll take her in," said the agent holding Sheree.

"Wait. Sheree said something about killing the governor," Tawnia remembered. "Tonight."

Sheree shot her a venomous look, but one of the agents took out his phone. "We'll contact the governor. Don't worry. We'll find out everything we need to know from Miss Activist here. They always break when they're faced with the real-life consequences of their actions."

Sheree spat at him, but he stepped casually aside to avoid her saliva, a hard smile on his face.

Sheree was taken away, and an ambulance came for Orion's corpse. After what seemed like a million questions, Tawnia was at last permitted to leave that place of horror. She rode down the elevator to the lobby with Bret and Autumn. Jake was waiting for them there, his worried expression relaxing as he spied them.

"I came right after you called me for directions," he said to Autumn, barely acknowledging the other two. "I was worried."

Autumn smiled wearily. "We're okay. I'm glad you came."

"Come on," Jake said. "There are some benches outside. The police and the FBI have this entire area roped off from the crowd. Apparently someone tipped off the media."

Tawnia followed the group blindly to the benches, sinking onto one with relief. The air was warm and the sky a brilliant blue that seemed to wash away the vestiges of terror from her heart. She took a deep breath and let it out slowly.

Autumn didn't sit beside her. She looked at Bret, his hands thrust deep in his pockets. "Your turn," Autumn told him. "Don't blow it again." Squeezing Tawnia's shoulder, she walked with Jake to the other bench. Jake put an arm around her, and they began talking quietly, heads close together.

They make a great couple, Tawnia thought.

Bret sat beside her, his eyes scanning the roped area beyond which a crowd had gathered. Tawnia saw a news van, and she turned her face away.

"The county offered me a job today," Bret said. "Clay Hanks's job. I told them yes."

He wasn't leaving! Tawnia managed a smile.

Bret scooted closer, lowering his mouth to her ear. "I've never been so scared in my entire life. Not even when I heard about Christian. I couldn't believe I might lose you forever."

Tawnia considered the many possible reactions. She could make light of the seriousness of his tone, pretending she really didn't care. Or say something to imply he was just a friend. Either of these would prevent any future pain where he was concerned. Yet her dishonesty with both Bret and Orion hadn't helped any of them so far.

The other choice was to lay her feelings on the line—whatever the consequences. And she'd known almost from the first how she felt about him. That had never been the problem.

"If you're asking for another chance," she whispered, "the answer's yes."

His arms were around her in an instant, and Tawnia melted into him. His lips touched her cheek, sliding along her skin until his mouth found hers. It was every bit as wonderful as she remembered, the taste of him, the way he made her feel. As if she stood on a tall precipice at the top of the world, her breath stolen away by his touch.

"I love you, Tawnia McKnight," he whispered. "I know I have a lot to make up for, but I plan to spend the rest of my life doing that."

Before she could tell him she loved him too, he was kissing her again, and she was back on that tall cliff. *It's you,* she thought. *Even when I tried to forget, it's always been you.*

When he let her breathe again, Tawnia smiled. "Now that," she said softly, "is what I call amazing. And I love you too."

Bret grinned. "I think we should try again. I'm betting we can do better than amazing."

Autumn appeared beside them. "Hey, stop that." She pointed to the television cameras. "You're on national TV. Tawnia's mother will think I'm a bad influence."

"So what?" Bret said. "Her mother likes me."

Laughing, Tawnia kissed him again.

RACHEL BRANTON has worked in publishing for over twenty years. She loves writing women's fiction and traveling, and she hopes to write and travel a lot more. As a mother of seven, it's not easy to find time to write, but the semi-ordered chaos gives her a constant source of writing material. She's been known to wear pajamas all day when working on a deadline, and is often distracted enough to burn dinner. (Okay, pretty much 90% of the time.) A sign on her office door reads: Danger. Enter at Your Own Risk. Writer at Work.

Under the name Rachel Branton, she writes romance, romantic suspense, and women's fiction. Rachel also writes urban fantasy, paranormal romance, and science fiction under the name Teyla Branton. For more information or to sign up to hear about new releases, please visit www.RachelBranton.com.